HUMAN AFTER ALL

A BECKER GRAY NOVEL BY

CHRIS WENDEL

Chrissanne — I'm So Happy To See You. Thanks —

HP

Holden Publishing, Inc.

First Edition: © 2012 Chris Wendel | Holden Publishing, Inc.
Second Edition: © 2017 Chris Wendel | Holden Publishing, Inc.

ISBN: 978-0-615-67284-7

Holden Publishing, Inc.
5304 S Florida Ave, Ste 404
Lakeland, FL 33813

DEDICATION

To David and Joyce Wendel
and
Holden Wendel

And In Loving Memory of
Sue Deaton

ACKNOWLEDGMENTS

Lucky isn't the right word, but it fits. I've been lucky to have the love and support of so many family and friends that I know I'll leave some out as I write this. On behalf of my failing memory, I apologize to anyone left off this list. It in no way is a measure of how appreciative I was and continue to be of everyone who supported me in the writing of this novel – the first edition and this re-issue.

Thanks to Michi Bonnin for being quite simply the best supporter I've ever had.

To my whole family: David, Joyce, Al, Mary, John, Peggy, Bill, Bryan, Michelle, Carli, John Lamar, Anne Marie, Erica and David Balcom, Donna Torres, Blake Hendricks, and all those extended loved ones.

But, especially to Holden for allowing me time all through your life to write and for being such a great inspiration. This book is about being a father, and being a good one is the only real goal I have.

And my friends – John Wentworth, Jason and Melanie Macklin, Karen Hudson, Andrea Wiggins, Keith and Stephanie Sanford, Mitch and Rachel Lyons, Brad Betenson, Andrea Polito, Chris Gutierrez, Bart and Bridget Ross, Holly Geddie, Sharon Burress, Mary Fuller, Stephanie and Tony Colon, Jimmy and Shannon Waller, David and Karen Grisham, Andrea Hormuth, Benton and

Debbie Eisenbach, Leonard Clayton, Amy and Bill Turpin, Pat and Terry Lewis, Chuck and Claudia Chritton, Holly Lopez, Linda Malzone, Imar Dacuhna, James Laflame, Mimi Osiason, Holly Cain, Connie Porter, and Nikki Barnes.

Plus, a ton of other friends, like Lana Swartzwelder, Mike Sweeney, Dory Rodriguez Joseph, Cristina Criser, Katie Worthington, Nikki Puterbaugh, Melissa Kinsey, Brandi McLaughlin, Lee Ann Leonard, Chrissanne Long, Linda Foster, and Kylie Dunbar.

Special thanks to Robert Tate, who reached out in support when he had no reason to do so. To Derek Stross for tremendous business assistance. Brian Hall at Dual Brain for your friendship and web expertise.

And finally to Jean Gonzalez — my editor; my might-as-well-be co-writer; my friend. I set out to write the best story I could in the moment of time I was writing it, and you made it oh so much better. You made me an oh so much better writer. Thanks.

PROLOGUE

August 7 – 4:57 p.m. – 10 Years Ago

Home finally came into view. Valerie Hardy remembered thinking that an hour before she had crested the top of the steep hill just outside her family's property line. The sun set in the remote sky, and she could recognize her father's silhouette as he rode a tractor in the foreground. Between the two, she saw rolling hills, the sporadic forested areas surrounding the farm, cows grazing in the near field, and acre after acre of potato crops. She had pulled her Nikon camera with its 35mm lens from her army-green backpack and snapped a quick shot. A canvas of complete rural perfection highlighted with the varying shades of purple, red, and orange in an Idaho sunset laid out before her.

She remembered squealing with excitement running down the hill, thinking the photograph had been the best one she'd taken all day. Mountain bluebirds scared off their perches flew out of the branches of nearby western white pine trees and fluttered all around her. She had felt exhilarated, alive, and free.

But that was a faraway thought now. The envelope had changed everything. Plain, white, and ordinary in every way. But it wasn't.

Once at home, Valerie had bathed in a hot shower. The heat made her fair skin redden and the steam made her feel extra clean. She could feel her father's heavy footsteps moving throughout the house, a raised structure with crawl space beneath which ensured loud, hollow vibrations any time Jack Hardy walked around in his work boots. He was a large man. She had heard the farm workers describe him as thick. Most of the time he had a day's growth of facial hair on his tough face, which gave him a ruggedness she'd only seen in movies. He was the biggest, strongest man she'd ever known, but he had a gentleness that allowed her to crawl into his lap to kiss him goodnight or hear a story about his day. Most importantly, though, she could tell him about the great pictures she always took.

That was her plan that night after dressing – climbing into his big lap and telling him about the rabbit she'd seen inching out of its den that morning. Even more so, she couldn't wait to get his help developing the pictures. Valerie often went on what her mother called walkabouts that sometimes lasted all day and often after sunset. A fine photographer in development, Valerie took pictures of anything she thought would be beautiful on film. That desire spawned from when she was five years old and her father would flip through *Yosemite and the Range of Light* with her before naptime.

But now her father didn't have time to read to her.

After the shower, Valerie had pulled on her pajamas and rushed into the hallway from the bathroom. "Dad," she had called, "I've got a bunch of pictures for us to develop."

Her father replied, but whatever he said was muffled as it traveled from the other side of the house. She skipped back into her cluttered bedroom and retrieved the rolls of film from her backpack. Each in a capped black tube. That was when she had noticed it – the plain, white, ordinary envelope.

The envelope rested on her desk among dirty clothes, school notebooks, a used cup and plate, stacks of photographs she had taken, and a Hello Kitty lamp her mother, Marie, had given her for her fourth birthday. She recalled questioning who would be writing her. Valerie seized a shirt off the chair, wrapped it around her long, wet brown hair and squeezed, forcing the shirt to absorb water. She dropped it to the floor when she finished, concentrating fully on the envelope.

Her name and address on the envelope were written aslant with sloppy handwriting and her name was misspelled. That didn't stop her from tearing into the envelope and yanking out the piece of loose leaf paper.

Jack Hardy stepped into his daughter's bedroom entrance. "I thought I asked you to clean up your room." He didn't even look up from the electric bill to speak. "We'll do the pictures after dinner, okay?"

When he didn't get an answer, he raised his gaze and found Valerie frozen with what looked to be fear. Her shaky hands rattled the letter. "What's wrong, Val?" he asked.

Valerie held out the letter to her father. Tears welled in her eyes, but Valerie fought them back and swallowed hard, trying to be strong like her father. She cleared her throat, trying to keep her voice from cracking, and then said as evenly as possible, "A really bad joke, I think."

Her father took the letter and read it quietly to himself. As he did, his face changed.

Sum men axe me to let them taist your tong. I SAY NO!!! 1 wonts to shaiv your skin & raip you wif a nife. NO AGEN! Cut you open like a dear & draink your blud. NO! this i protect you from Valary not your father ME & I alwaiz will becuse men wont to hurt you & to saiv you we will hafta be to gether 1 dai & i cain't wait to taik you awai from your parents 4eva. Your father dont desurv you no wai. i do. i do i do & you do.

As Jack's eyes rose from the paper, Valerie saw the same terror and confusion she had felt, and right then she knew the letter was no joke.

Her body felt instantly weak, and the tubes of film slipped from her hand, bouncing on the hardwood flooring and rolling to a stop under her dresser, left there in the shadowed darkness. All attention paid to the envelope and the letter. Always now the envelope and its contents. Never to the photographs, the dreams they held, or the excitement for the future. *Always that fucking envelope and letter.*

PART I

CHAPTER 1

July 28 – 11:30 p.m.

Detective Becker Gray arrived at the scene after processing had begun. Portable lights had been set up at the perimeter and directed in, casting a brilliant light across the work area. The scene appeared relatively cut and dry – a solitary car hit a tree some distance from the street. The car's driver side door remained open with the window smashed out, the light inside dimly working.

So why am I here? the detective wondered.

When he saw his partner emerge from the scene activity, Gray approached him. "What the hell?"

"Don't know yet." At six and a half feet tall, 280 pounds, Jeffrey Parker towered over Gray, who ended his growing at six feet. Parker referred to his notepad. Out of habit. He didn't have any real information yet. "The driver's in the wind, and Boudreaux's got his shit in a twist. I haven't even gotten to look at the car yet." He slapped the notepad against his palm.

Gray scanned a thick wooded area to the scene's right. Flashlights danced and dogs barked. "They're out there checking for a body?"

"Looks that way. They're in the lake, too." Parker motioned toward the lake where several divers were bobbing up and down in the shallow lake water.

Gray saw Boudreaux heading their way. "I guess we're about to find out."

Chief Reginald Boudreaux still had an athletic walk, even if his build didn't match. Since he'd been promoted to Chief of the Lakeland Police Department four years ago, he had slowly lost that street edge he'd once had. His face used to be chiseled. In the last four years, it had rounded. Yet, like his walk, he still had the same charisma, that same authoritative presence which helped earn him that position. He interrupted their conversation. "You caught up, Gray?"

"Except for what's going on."

"Let's walk." Boudreaux led them further into the police activity. "You guys read the paper? Have you seen the articles about Valerie Hardy?"

Parker crinkled his brow. "I haven't."

Gray didn't tell them he'd read the day's article. He figured it was better to just let Boudreaux tell them what they needed to know.

"Ten years ago, a still-unidentified subject threatened the lives of five girls," Boudreaux explained. "Each of the girls subsequently went into hiding."

"What do you mean threatened?" Gray asked. The article he had read didn't detail any threats.

"The man synchronized delivery of letters to these girls, who all lived in different states. He threatens to kidnap and kill one of the five girls in – what I'm told – a rather heinous way. Then he said in three days he'd write the parents to let them know where the body is."

Parker asked skeptically, "I remember something about this. Didn't they call the guy the Pen Pal?"

"One of the girls has secretly been living here in Lakeland, hasn't she?" Gray added, trying to hurry along the story.

Boudreaux nodded and got to the point. "The father called an hour ago and said his daughter ran out after an argument. She hadn't come back."

"Is that her car?" Gray asked.

"The make, model, and plate of her car," Boudreaux said, not letting Gray spoil his tale, "match this one." Boudreaux pointed at the red Cavalier in the field. "So, I need you two to figure out what happened here. I need you to find her. Fast."

CHAPTER 2

The morning of July 28 – 6:50 a.m.

Metal clanked against glass to produce a dense, low knocking sound. Again and again the noise echoed inside Becker Gray's head. *Time to get up.* His version of an alarm clock had gone off.

Gray shifted in the driver seat of his Honda Accord. Blinding morning sunlight blasted his eyes, making it difficult to make out the figure standing outside his car. But he knew who was there. *Clank. Clank. Clank.* Mike Todd unrelentingly banged the butt of his Mag-Lite against the car window. Gray waved him off then rolled down the car window, allowing the traffic noise on Florida's Interstate 4 to attack the quiet, inner sanctum of the car, bringing with it a gust of warm, humid air.

"Mornin'," Mike said. "I'm glad you pulled over here last night." The Florida Highway Patrol trooper motioned to the deserted, fenced-in remnants of a rest area just east of Exit 33. "The traffic's bad this morning. Worse than most mornings, really. If you had stopped on the shoulder like you normally do, those sons-a-bitches would've ran you right off the damn road." He shook his head. "I'm even afraid to get out there in it, the crazy bastards. You want a cup of coffee?"

"I'd love one."

Gray opened the car door, which gave a metal-on-metal squeal.

"You ever getting that fixed?" Mike yelled over the traffic.

Gray closed the car door behind him. Another squeal. "Probably not."

They had this conversation every day. Gray mouthed Mike's next statement.

"All it would take is some WD-40."

Gray's backache showed up like an old friend who visits every morning, reminding him that he used to be an athletic man and now was a little out of shape. An all-American basketball player in high school, he had scholarship offers from universities all over the country, but he ended up never accepting any. Life had other plans.

"Did you fall asleep on your way out or coming back in?" Mike asked, handing Gray a small white cup of coffee.

Gray couldn't recall when he stopped sleeping in his bed, but it had been a long time. And neither man could remember when Mike began waking Gray, but it had become their daily ritual.

"Little of both." The coffee smelled great. Gray noticed the vehicles continued to speed even though the trooper's cruiser was on display on the side of the interstate. Gray pointed with his head, "They don't even pretend to slow down when they see you, do they?

"Blatant disregard for authority."

"Speaking of blatant disregard," Gray said. "No donuts today?"

"You should be thankful just for the coffee."

"I am. Thank you." He held up the coffee mug as if to toast Mike Todd.

Gray's phone interrupted their ten-minute morning visit, so Gray took a refill and left Mike to fend for himself on the interstate. As Gray closed his squeaky car door again, he pulled up the text message from his partner, Jeffrey Parker. It read: *It's turning into a big day. The chief wants you here. Now. Where you at?*

CHAPTER 3

The Accord came to a halt in an uncharacteristic traffic jam just before reaching downtown Lakeland, Florida. Railroad tracks ran east and west through downtown and periodically a train would stop and block traffic, but Gray didn't recall that ever happening at this time of morning.

He navigated the Accord left, so he could look out of the car window. Seeing up ahead a few blocks outside the police station, the northbound lanes of traffic had been cordoned off and, thus, congested the whole three-way intersection at North Massachusetts Avenue and Pine Street.

Gray turned the steering wheel as hard as he could to the left and then mashed the gas, barely missing the car in front of him. After a quick drive down Bay Street, the Accord's scrape guard connected with the concrete as Gray steered the car into the staff entrance of the police department parking lot. He braked hard.

Despite the sign indicating the entrance was for staff and deliveries only, two news vans were parked in the small entrance area, and a dozen or more reporters, cameramen, and photographers were crowded around the security gate. Gray's temper festered. *Reporters* ...

He ignored a volley of questions shouted at him through his open window as he fed the electronic scanner his security card, which parted the gate. In their questioning, the reporters shouted a name Gray couldn't ignore – Malcolm Turner. *What did all this have to do with Malcolm?*

Gray's normal parking space was taken, which made his already irritated mental state grow more so. After he found a spot, Gray noticed that reporters had converged on staff door. They must've gotten through the gate.

Four journalists saw him exit his car and immediately headed his way. Gray avoided them by moving through the fence gate at the building's side and then went on toward the front entrance out on Massachusetts, where he found a larger group of media personnel. *Oh, come on.*

He stopped briefly, weighing his odds. No matter what entrance he used he'd have to deal with the media. He reluctantly continued up the wheelchair accessible ramp leading to the building's front entrance. More questions shouted at him. Malcolm Turner's name again.

Gray pushed his way through the crowd, but it grew denser the closer Gray advanced toward the glass double-door entrance. He turned and yelled at the crowd to move away so he could enter the building. Instead the crowd shifted forward. Someone grabbed Gray's arm. He turned, fist cocked, ready to fire.

"You want in or not?" Jeffrey Parker protested his partner's reaction.

"I don't want to stay out here with them." Gray let Parker pull him inside. Two uniformed officers at the front door helped Parker close the doors again.

"Someone took my parking space," Gray said.

CHAPTER 4

The lobby of the police department had been prepared for an occasion. Chairs had been set up, a podium identified the front of the room, and two long tables held trays of pastries and cartons of orange juice.

Parker waited for Gray at the top of the stairs. He leaned on the railing and looked down at the lobby, which buzzed with activity. Two uniformed officers approached and forced Gray and Parker out of way. One carried another tray of muffins and the other officer wielded a ten-gallon metal coffee maker.

"Didn't you wear that yesterday?" Parker teased.

Although he knew his partner was offering a friendly jab, Gray still rolled his eyes. "Seriously, what the hell's going on?"

"Remember Malcolm Turner?"

Turner was the No. 2 man in a gang called Creep Show. Its insignia — the word CREEPY enclosed by a circle — marked its territory; dumpsters, abandoned houses, out-of-business gas stations, alleys, bathroom stalls, and sometimes on people's garage doors, business buildings, and even churches. And the territory had grown to stretch across Florida, up into Alachua and Leon counties, and south into Palm Beach and Broward too. Creep Show had graduated past local gang status.

They'd also graduated past small-time criminal activity. Creep Show was now involved in loan sharking, gun brokering, fencing stolen property, credit card fraud, managing several large prostitution rings, and even murder. The gang was known as the top producer and distributor of methamphetamine for Polk County, Florida, a place it strategically exploited for its personality. Although a largely rural area that is generally known for its sleepy, small towns and devoid of a large metropolis, its central location in Florida made it a perfect distribution point.

But recently the Creep Show's organizational cracks were turning into crevasses. They'd had five leaders in the last two years due to various internal power struggles. Most of those leaders had been found dead or had disappeared. Yet, somehow Malcolm Turner remained the No. 2 guy through all that turmoil.

"Yeah. So?" Gray asked.

"From what I heard, the chief goes to the same church as Turner's mother. Or aunt. Something like that." Parker shrugged his shoulders. "The details are sketchy at this point."

"You're a hell of a detective, Jeff."

Parker smirked. "One way or the other, the church thing led to the chief working out some deal with Malcolm's mother. Results? He's on his way in. He's going to turn himself in."

"Then what the hell's all that?" Gray pointed to the lobby.

"Only thing is Malcolm wants it to be some big deal. The chief gave in, and this is it."

"We're throwing him a reception?"

"Kind of, I guess. Going away party, is more like it." Parker laughed at his own joke. "He's supposed to pull up out front, where he'll be detained and escorted through the reporters and then taken back to booking. That," Parker gestured toward the lobby, "is for the chief's press conference."

"Of course, it is," Gray said.

"Word is the kid can close more than 20 open cases."

"Boudreaux panders too much to those damned reporters."

"Jesus, Gray, enough with the reporters," Parker said with a hint of frustration. "What the hell? Did you hear what I just said? Twenty cases."

"Yes, I heard you. Any of them ours?"

"One."

"Which one?"

The conversation cut off. Chief Reginald Boudreaux rounded the corner from his office, entourage in tow.

"Important day, gentlemen," he said in his signature deep voice while passing.

As he began his descent of the stairs, the lobby doors parted and his beloved reporters entered clamoring for prime seating positions. Pleased with the situation, Boudreaux smiled brightly, stationing himself behind the small podium. Lights gleamed off the chief's face as video cameras began recording. He waited patiently for everyone to settle, and they did so quickly. In fact, it looked to Gray as if all the reporters were waiting with bated breath for Boudreaux to speak.

"Today marks the end of a multi-agency campaign to curb the infiltration of our communities by one of the largest gangs in Florida's history. Today Malcolm Turner will surrender himself. Turner is one of the known leaders of the Creep Show criminal group, whose illegal activities are responsible for corroding our state, our communities, our children's school, and our homes."

The speech included impressive statistics, like man-hours and cost to the various cities involved, meant to boost the various communities' admiration for their respective departments. Gray thought spreading the credit was commendable, rather than taking all the credit for himself, as he had thought Boudreaux would do.

The chief finished his speech by announcing Turner's arrival. The media turned away from Boudreaux and focused on the lobby doors, but the doors didn't part and Malcolm Turner didn't enter. The excitement in the room dipped, took a darker turn. At least, that's how Gray took the shift in mood.

As he watched worry settle over Boudreaux, a smirk spread across Gray's face. The detective found pleasure in things going wrong with this media circus. Turner's no-show would serve Boudreaux right for allowing Turner to dictate this kind of publicity. However, just as Gray's pleasure settled in, it disappeared. A murmur made its way through the crowd of reporting professionals. Turner's black 2003 Cadillac Escalade was in sight. Gray watched Boudreaux let out a sigh of relief.

Boudreaux and three uniformed officers followed the crowd of reporters out the front doors. Parker nudged Gray to trail behind. When Gray and Parker came out the lobby doors, they could see reporters clamoring for the best photo positions. The pair walked over and stood near Boudreaux, where they could observe the surrender from behind the crowd. Meanwhile, two uniformed officers made their way through the crowd of reporters to the curb to wait to process Turner's surrender.

The freshly waxed black Escalade with flashy rims and mirror-tinted windows approached. Once it came to a stop, the reflection of dozens of camera flashes sparkled across the shiny vehicle. But the doors didn't open. The vehicle just sat there with its motor running. One of the uniformed officers looked back to Boudreaux. Gray saw worry return to Boudreaux's face. He still wasn't out of the woods with this whole stunt. Boudreaux nodded, giving his approval for the officer to advance toward the vehicle. The officer knocked on the passenger window of the Escalade, only to receive no reply. The vehicle shook a little, like someone was moving around inside.

Gray scanned the street. Northbound traffic had begun to flow again, so cars drove by the police station on Massachusetts Avenue in both directions. The traffic light on Massachusetts turned red and the cars stopped. Pine Street's light changed to green, and a light blue 1970s Chevy Impala pulled alongside the Escalade.

Gray froze.

Something bad was about to happen.

Then gunshots rattled off.

CHAPTER 5

July 28 – 8:10 a.m.

"Marie." An echo bounced back at Jack Hardy, who slammed the front door behind him. Anger pulsed through his veins and heated his blood to what felt like a boiling point. *I can't believe what she's done!* He headed down the hall toward Valerie's bedroom where he found her door closed. He figured she was still sleeping, which wasn't uncommon for his daughter at eight ten in the morning.

"Valerie." He threw open his daughter's bedroom door but found the room empty. He looked at the newspaper in his hand, slammed it against the doorframe. "Marie," he called out again.

Hundreds of images and mixed emotions made his mind spin. *Boom. Boom. Boom.* The pounding in his chest moved to his head.

PART TWO OF FOUR, the newspaper had read. Did Valerie have any idea what she had done?

The sliding glass door leading to the outside lanai grinded inside the door's frame, and the noise drew the Hardy family together in the living room. The Hardy women had just finished their breakfast of eggs, bacon, cheese grits spread across freshly baked ciabatta bread, and fruit, and they were coming inside to clean their mess. It was just a typical morning in the

Hardy house – that is, except for Jack's intimidating posture and the infuriated look upon his face. Actually, Jack's posture and look weren't so unfamiliar. Over the last few years he and Valerie fought every time one of them crossed the invisible line they'd drawn in the figurative sand.

"Oh, honey," Marie Hardy noticed her husband. "You're up! I'll make you a plate, if you want breakfast." Then she saw his facial expression, more intense than usual, and knew something was wrong. "What is it?"

Valerie was naïvely curious about her father's mood until she saw the newspaper grasped inside his tight fist. "I can explain," was what came out of her mouth. It wasn't what she'd rehearsed saying.

"Is that all you can say?" Jack smacked the paper against his free hand's palm. "Is that supposed to make what you did all right?"

Marie didn't have any idea what the conflict between Jack and Valerie could be today. She usually didn't. "Stop it. What's going on?"

"What's going on?!" He sounded appalled she would question him. "Have you seen the paper?" Fury made his voice gravelly.

"No. It hasn't been delivered the last few days."

"Or someone's been stealing it." Jack watched Valerie avert his eyes. He then handed the newspaper to Marie. "Take a look."

"Mom, don't read it. Let me explain first."

Valerie had to act quickly. Of her two parents, her mother was more likely to become an ally in this than her father. She had to get the paper before her mother read too much of its content. Valerie made a stabbing move to snatch the paper from her mother, but Marie moved quickly out of Valerie's reach.

"Let me explain."

But it was too late. Marie's eyes were already moving back and forth across the front-page article which wrapped around a photograph of her daughter's smiling face.

Letting out a deep, uncertain breath, Marie lowered the newspaper. "I think we all need to calm down a bit." She knew this could – and would probably – turn into a full nuclear war between Jack and Valerie.

"Calm down? You want me to calm down?" Jack blasted back at his wife and threw his hands up in the air. "Do you understand the danger Valerie has put us in?"

Valerie waited for her moment to step into the conversation and explain herself – this time, the way she had rehearsed it.

Jack ignored Marie's hands, extended in the air, signaling him to stop talking. "I'd say we need to pull up and move, but seems as though the media's taken an interest in this story, but, you know what?" He paused before continuing, mostly to catch his breath. "I'm glad they are, because if it wasn't for the reporter out in our front lawn, I might never have known about this."

"What?" Valerie and Marie responded in unison.

Valerie darted into the Santa Fe-styled sitting room that the front door opened into, and she pulled back the curtains. As Marie made her way to the sitting room, she placed her small hand inside Jack's rough-skinned hand. Holding his hand tightly, she peered over Valerie's back and saw the slender, handsome reporter from the regional all-news channel standing just off their property line. He waited patiently, his arms folded across his chest, microphone in hand, cameraman nearby.

This is perfect, Valerie thought to herself.

"This is horrible, Valerie. How could you have done this?" Marie's voice trembled.

"The story's going to make it all over the nation." Jack pulled his hand from Marie's and left the sitting room in favor of the living room.

All over the nation ... the words echoed in her mind's ear. He had said it like it was a bad thing.

"You know what'll happen next?" Jack continued from the living room, pacing. "We'll have damn reporters everywhere. Nowhere to hide and no way to protect ourselves. To protect her!"

As Marie and Valerie filtered back into the living room, the telephone rang, like his statement had been an omen. Fifteen times later, the ringing ceased.

Once the ringing stopped, Valerie spoke quietly but stern, "I'm not hiding anymore."

The audacity of his daughter. "And, how do you expect to protect yourself?" Jack asked.

"I don't know."

"You don't know? That's right! That's because you've never had to protect yourself. I always took care of that, so you wouldn't have to worry about it." He paused as another thought pounded its way from his brain to his mouth. "And you know what? You may have really done it this time, Val. You may have made it so I can't protect us anymore, but I guess I won't worry about it anymore since you're so smart. You want to be in charge? Take over. Go ahead. You tell me what we are going to do? Go ahead."

The story was a calculated move, one that could force the police to take an interest in the case again. With a lot of media coverage and using science nonexistent ten years ago, the cold case could heat up. There could be DNA on the envelopes that could crack the case wide open.

Since the letters had arrived, the Pen Pal hadn't come after Valerie or any of the girls. To Valerie, it was a safe bet he was in jail for another crime or he was dead. These stories were her last chance to save her own life. *I dare that bastard to come for me, but he better be ready because I'm not going without a fight.*

Brave words and a big gamble.

While Valerie had been lost in her own thoughts, Marie had been lecturing her. She was saying something about how they had to assume the Pen Pal still wanted to kill Valerie, but Valerie didn't care. As far as she was concerned, the simple fact of the matter was that she had been apart from the human race far too long.

Come for her or not, she would reclaim her spot in the free world.

CHAPTER 6

Year after year Valerie had begged her parents to let her have a life, and each plea ended without a word of acknowledgement. Resentment had grown exponentially through each year, and Valerie just couldn't control the internal explosion.

"We handed all control over to this guy," she finally yelled a response. Almost hysterical and cutting off her mother's lecture, "And he wasn't even anywhere near us. That's all he wanted. He wanted to control us. Don't you guys get it?"

"I don't want to listen to this psychological bullshit again," Jack said. "Just tell me what we're supposed to do. We can't hide anymore."

"I couldn't have said it better, Dad."

"What are we supposed to do?"

Marie, quietly, calmly, put forth her best effort to control the outcome of the argument by utilizing the only weapon a mother at times has at her disposal – guilt. "Valerie, you put the other girls in danger, too."

A contrived look of shock converged on Valerie's face. She had to maintain the lie. Valerie didn't want her parents to know she knew all about the other girls. Had for a while. And, because of what she knew about them, she had to prove the Pen Pal was gone. They were part of why she had to reclaim her life.

"How confident about his whereabouts are you now?" Marie's voice was amazingly calm and measured. "I know. I've done some research, too. Chances are he is gone. What if he's not? Those reporters are going to be trying to find the other girls, and that's just going to jeopardize whatever safety zone they've set up for themselves."

Valerie's face registered surprise, like Marie had said something Valerie hadn't thought of. Truth be told, Valerie knew he wouldn't be going after any of the other four girls. There wasn't much left there to find. Instead of telling them the truth, Valerie decided to give them the same old response. "If he's out there, this might draw him out. He'll come for me, not them. He'll be mad at me. Besides it'll take the reporters forever to find the other girls. If he's out there waiting, he won't be able to wait that long. He'll need to do something now. They'll be safe. And he won't come after me as long as all the media's around. I mean," she raised her voice for emphasis and in frustration, "none of that matters because he's gone."

"I see you rationalizing this," Marie replied, "but all I hear is guesswork, so just stop. I know you thought it through. You're just like your father. It's part of who you are, but if you left a hole like this in your plan, imagine the other holes that we haven't found yet."

Valerie couldn't endure the pointless arguing anymore. She hadn't left any holes. She'd been planning this for years. She knew more than she could possibly even tell her parents.

"Why don't you ever look at this from my point of view?!" she yelled. "I was the one who lost all my friends. I was the one who lost her life. And now I want it back. I want one. I'm 18 now. I'm not a little girl anymore."

"Then stop acting like one," Jack fired back.

"It's done, and I don't care what you think." Valerie's eyes watered.

"You're living in my house."

"This had to be done." Valerie stomped her way toward the front door. She grabbed the car keys off the coffee table.

"Where are you going?" Jack yelled.

"Away from you." She marched out the front door and slammed it behind her.

CHAPTER 7

Anyone could have found her, thanks to local media outlets.

The all-news channel covering Florida's Tampa Bay area was the first to plant a van and a reporter on the Hardy's home in the hope of nabbing an exclusive interview with Valerie or her parents. The family didn't even know he was there until that morning, and when the father came out of the house, he had refused to be interviewed.

With the camera rolling, the reporter showed Jack Hardy that day's edition of the local newspaper. Jack became enraged and stormed back into the house.

It was those reports that led the owner of a dark blue 1969 Chevy Nova to the Hardy house. A five a.m. news update gave all the information needed. The camera work showed the vehicles parked in the driveway, the decorations on the front door, and the house details. And on the reports coming in during the six to seven a.m. hours gave the proximity. The top right hand corner of the screen showed Lakeland's McIntosh power plant in the distance, its operational lights dotting the background and the aircraft warning light flashing like a beacon.

From there, all it took was some fast exploration before finding the Hardy home halfway down a dead end street near Lake Parker, Lakeland's largest of 38 named lakes. He recognized the cars and the house. The news vans out front helped too. Now three news vans marked the spot.

He had parked his Nova on the side of the residential street. A vacant lot, seven houses down from the Hardy home, had overgrown grass. It looked like the last available lot on the street. Inside the car, the driver smiled, delighted with his own genius in finding her. His plan was coming together better than he'd hoped. And faster, too. Valerie wasn't his original desired target. Not until he saw the articles. They were what convinced him that she was the one. He would have her, own her even. Forever. He just had to wait for the right opportunity.

After 45 minutes of waiting and watching three more news vans arrive, he saw movement at the Hardy home. Valerie, wearing baggy black jeans and a black T-shirt displaying a large red star, sprinted from her front door to the red Cavalier in the driveway. The waiting reporters jumped to action and dashed toward her and the car. Then a man – her father, Jack Hardy, he guessed, exited the house after her. *Chasing her?* he wondered. The cluster of reporters split. Half to Valerie, half to her father. Valerie backed the car out of the driveway, avoiding the frenzied reporters and blaring her horn. And Jack – the reporters blasting questions in his face and cutting off his path toward the moving vehicle – was caught in the crowd of circling reporters. *Why didn't he just push them out of the way?* The way too polite father still looked determined to catch up to his daughter, trying to sidestep the journalists, but he didn't ultimately reach the car before it drove off.

This is it! The Nova's powerful engine turned over. He felt the rumble in his seat, which ignited his sexual impulses. He bit his bottom lip, hoping to draw blood.

The driver followed Valerie's Cavalier, keeping an eye out for any reporters who might be jumping into their own vans to pursue. But, he saw in his rearview mirror, they were too preoccupied by Jack Hardy's presence to pursue her. Almost gleefully, he was alone, tailing Valerie. She made her way through Lakeland, Polk County's biggest city. Early on, its economy was built on citrus and phosphate, but was now it was sustained by a few of multibillion dollar companies, snowbirds, and because of its proximity to Orlando by tourism. Lakeland was the typical picture of suburbia, a city that thinks it's bigger than it is.

Valerie stopped the Cavalier outside the large building that housed the local newspaper. The front of the building, with mirrored glass across the rounded anterior, gave the building a modern aesthetic. At the back of the building, visible from where Valerie had parked her vehicle, several medium-sized cargo trucks were backed up against the building, supplies being loaded into or out of. Valerie couldn't tell. Nor did she care. About that or the immaculately manicured grounds she traipsed across on her way to the front doors.

The Nova's driver parked his car under the huge oak tree a row back and a few spaces down from where Valerie had parked her car. There, he watched Valerie push open the building's front doors.

He wondered what his and Valerie's next move might be. He'd been so genius finding Valerie, he wanted an idea equally as genius for taking her. To initiate that idea, he decided he needed to gather more intelligence. Juices flowed, excitement raged inside him. He was so ready for all this! So sure of himself. He didn't even think walking across this parking lot and checking out the contents of her car was a risk. He had this under control.

As the sun bore down on him, sweat broke out on his upper lip. He licked it off, pretending it was Valerie's own sweaty skin. He'd been waiting a long time for this move that he could barely contain his eagerness.

Lost in that fantasy, he didn't wonder about her being here. Why she would rush out of her parents' home during the swelling media frenzy. Why she would go to the newspaper. None of that mattered, just so long as she came back out to him.

Gunshots in the distance drew his attention, broke his fantasy. What seemed like a lot of them, all at once, then numerous single shots rang out before another band of shots sounded. Quiet quickly returned and then maintained. He began wondering if the far off sounds would soon draw reporters from the newspaper building, heading out to wherever the uncommon sounds originated. He quickened up his cocksure pace.

At her car door, he jammed his hands into his pocket to avoid the temptation of touching the car while he looked inside. *Smart of me.* The interior of the car looked clean, as if it was recently vacuumed and polished. A coin purse sat in a drink holder between the two front seats. A cell phone was plugged into the cigarette lighter. He didn't see anything else in her car that he needed to know about. The phone was the most worrisome item, but he planned on taking her so quickly that she wouldn't have time to use it. *No worries.* He checked the lobby doors again. No reporters were rushing out of the building, but he hurried back to his Nova anyway.

Behind the wheel of his car, he continued strategizing. When would he make his move? Surprising her, that was best. But when? How? He set his genius in motion, but he was distracted by his excitement. He calmed himself, trying to breathe slower. He reminded himself that he had nothing to worry about, that his smarts would take care of it.

CHAPTER 8

Mayhem and panic reigned. Reporters screamed. Brakes screeched. Horns blared. Glass shattered. And bullets ripped through whatever was in their path.

While Parker covered Boudreaux and forced him to the ground, Gray's instinct had him pulling his Glock and running toward the Escalade. As he leaned against the big vehicle, the shooting stopped. Gray edged around the front of the vehicle in time to see the Impala pull away from the scene, the shooter still hanging out the window waving an automatic rifle. Gray nearly fired off multiple rounds, but stopped himself. Civilians were in their cars, hiding from the shooting. Others had jumped from their vehicles and were running for cover. If he fired at the shooter and missed . . .

Gray lowered his weapon, reluctantly. He knew he could hit the shooter, but he knew it better to not fire on a busy street. Another collection of bullets sprayed erratically from the Impala, as the shooter slipped back inside the car. Gray almost ignored his reservations about shooting, but he saw two police cruisers, with flashing lights and screaming sirens, emerge from Bay Street to give chase. The Impala's driver saw them too. He ignited the engine and sped off, disappearing within seconds and taking the cruisers with it. Gray holstered his weapon and turned around.

Some bewildered journalists sat on the ground and collected their thoughts, others were crawling for safety, still fearing for their lives, and yet more wandered through the scene, recording images of the chaos with their cell phones, and making notes on their pads of paper. None seemed hurt. They all seemed worried about themselves and weren't helping one another. Gray counted two television news cameramen recording the carnage.

A horde of police officers emerged from the lobby, barreling their way out the front door. Some tended to the reporters while others, including Parker and Boudreaux, hurried toward Gray. That was when Gray looked down to his right and saw an officer on the ground. Blood soaked through the front of his dark uniform and spilled onto the cement.

Parker yanked open the officer's shirt. The blood seemed to be everywhere. Another officer helped Parker pull undone the bulletproof vest. Having missed the vest, the bullet had entered through the officer's shoulder. No exit wound. Parker applied as much pressure as he could until someone arrived with a medical kit. Within seconds, gauze and towels were everywhere around the officer's body. Minutes passed like hours until the paramedics arrived. The paramedics pushed their way through the hovering police and took over for Parker.

It was then Gray saw the officer's face. It was Clarke, the man who'd knocked on the Escalade's window when it pulled up to the curb. Gray couldn't recall the officer's first name, but he knew Clarke had a wife and family and he liked to tell jokes. Gray noticed the cameramen again. This time they were recording the work being performed on the wounded officer, and that made Gray lose control.

"Hey, stop recording!" Gray shouted, rushing toward the cameramen. He pulled one of them away from the camera positioned on a tripod-type device. The guy fell to the ground, protesting the assault, which

Gray ignored by kicking the camera stand over. The next cameraman stopped recording and tried to get out of Gray's way, but Gray grabbed him and pushed him aside anyway. More officers rushed over to diffuse the situation. They grabbed hold of Gray and ushered the other cameramen away.

"He's a human being!" Gray yelled. Then he jerked his arms free of the officers holding him back. "Get outta here!"

He turned away from the reporters and saw that citizens were still parked in the street. Officers were in the process of shutting down all the roads near the police station, as other officers were spreading throughout the halted traffic to search for possible victims of stray bullets. Amidst honking horns and screaming motorists, officers tried to get statements from those who witnessed the event.

Boudreaux stopped an officer running by. He pointed to the marks in the building's walls where stray bullets hit. "Get someone inside to make sure everyone's all right."

From his peripheral vision, Gray spotted the back passenger door of the Escalade opening. Pulling his Glock again, Gray hurried to the vehicle, not sure who or what to expect next.

A very dazed Malcolm Turner emerged. Covered in blood.

CHAPTER 9

After quickly escorting Malcolm Turner through the station, Gray and Parker set him down into a cold metal folding chair behind a small square table. Small, gray, and set in the back corner of the Criminal Investigations office, the interrogation room was the perfect hiding place away from the bedlam outside the police building.

All three men were out of breath and overwhelmed. Gray sat down next to Turner and rested his head in his hands, while Parker leaned against the wall. Neither detective knew where to begin yet. So much had happened so fast.

Boudreaux, enraged about the situation, was the last one to enter the room, and he slammed the door closed behind him. Unlike Gray and Parker, Boudreaux knew where to begin.

"What the hell happened out there?" Boudreaux shoved Turner's shoulder. "I'm talking to you!"

"I don't know, man," Turner said, wrought with his own boiling emotions. "Fuckin' G and Driver, man. All those years together." He choked up, his voice softened, and his volume faded as he continued talking. "I was just telling them goodbye ... and thanks, you know? They always watched my back. Always."

His softening burst into a tantrum. His arms flailed and his body bounced in the metal chair. "If I got out of the car when we stopped, they'd still be alive!" He looked directly at Boudreaux, his eyes raging with an emotional fire. "If I never made this deal with you, they'd still be alive!"

Boudreaux snapped back at him, "That's not where all three of you went wrong."

"Who set you up?" Gray demanded to know.

Turner's tone turned steely and cold after Boudreaux's response. "I don't know, but soon as I find out, I'll have their heads delivered right to you."

"That's not happening, Malcolm," Boudreaux chimed in.

"Give me a name," Gray said.

"I fuckin' told you, I don't know, and that don't matter anyway. You can arrest who you want, but they still coming for me. Why don't you just worry about fixing me up some special protection, and I'll worry about fixing them bitches who tried to kill me."

Boudreaux already had someone working on Turner's protection while inside jail, but he didn't want to tell him that. Instead he slapped him across the face. "Don't you tell me what I should be worrying about, kid." He called him a kid to make sure Turner knew that he wasn't in charge. He slapped him because he wanted to. "Who can give you protection, Malcolm? Who?"

Turner held the palm of his hand against his face, trying to soothe the stinging from Boudreaux's strike. "In here or out there."

Boudreaux leaned on the table. "Everywhere, kiddo. People trying to kill you out there and they'll be trying to kill you in jail, right?"

Turner's response was silence.

"Who, Malcolm, is the only person who can protect you from everything everywhere?" Boudreaux wanted Turner to know who was in charge, who had all the power.

"You," he grunted, hating the answer, hating his loss of power.

"Who tried to kill you out there?" Gray asked.

"I don't know," Turner responded, maintaining eye contact with Boudreaux.

Boudreaux believed him. "I want you to tell these two guys everything they want to know. Your life is literally depending on it." Boudreaux backed away from the table and stood in the corner, crossing his arms in front of him, staring menacingly at Turner.

"About what?"

"About Timothy McDonough," Parker added.

Hearing his partner speak that name shocked Gray. Over a year ago, Timothy McDonough had been found inside his car at the school parking lot with three friends – Aaron Johnson, Mario Beasley, and Paul Scarborough. According to all three of Timothy's friends, Timothy was playing with a gun he'd found when it went off, shooting him in the head. The case and the family weaved their way into Gray's head deeper than most, and hearing the name brought him right back to them.

Turner looked back to Boudreaux. "You want me to get into that right now? Somebody just tried to kill me. I can't be dealing with that dumb bullshit right now!"

"I do," Boudreaux said. "Then I'm bringing in another set of detectives who will ask you more questions. Then another and another. And the first time I think you're lying or stalling, I'll release you and make a public statement thanking you for providing us with specific, strategic information about Creep Show and its connected gang affiliates."

He waited like he was considering his options. Finally, he shook his head, knowing he had no choice but to talk. "Fine." Turner shrugged his shoulder. "Whatcha wanna know?"

"What you know," Gray barked, barely restraining his irritation with Turner now that the information he had pertained to the McDonough case.

"You talking about T-bone." Turner laughed at the ridiculous name Timothy McDonough used in order to sound tough. "Not one damn other person called him T-Bone. Stupid ass. He was a punk, you know?"

"Don't talk about him like that," Gray said.

"Was he some kind of friend of yours?" Malcolm chuckled and shook his head.

Gray ground his teeth. He knew he couldn't suppress his annoyance much longer.

"Timmy is what they really called him. A boy. Him and his friends weren't no angels, man. There was four of them, I think. They was stupid-ass, wanna-be gangstas, but they couldn't hang with none of my boys." He seemed proud of that statement. "Still … they weren't no good." Turner shrugged his shoulders. "Live and let die, right? Here's whatcha wanna know. You ready?" His eyebrows rose and his mouth smiled wide, arrogantly believing he was building anticipation. "One of them boys T-Bone hanged out with … shot little T-Bone right in the fuckin' head." Turner leaned forward and crowed, "That gun didn't accidentally go off. You stupid coppers got it wrong. My boy, Cheech, rented them a gun he'd used to have."

The reports of the case flowed through Gray's head like a whitewater river. Deep down, Gray hadn't totally believed the boys' story about what happened to Timothy, but there hadn't been anything else that suggested otherwise. Trajectory of the bullet was believable. Gunshot residue was on Timothy's hand and the boy who was in the front seat with him. Paul Scarborough was his name. And even that made sense according to the boys' story. McDonough was going to hand the gun to Scarborough when it went off. Scarborough was reaching for it.

"Timothy McDonough was murdered?" Parker asked, thinking out loud.

"This is what I'm saying!" Turner turned to Boudreaux and asked sarcastically, "This is one of your best detectives?" Turner shrugged his shoulders. He realized none of the policemen were listening anymore. Each had wondered off inside their own thoughts. "Hey!" he yelled, catching their attention. "This is story time with Malcolm! You listening to me or not?"

Gray lost control of himself. He snatched Turner's thumb and twisted it back. Turner grunted, and his body arched with pain. Gray held his grip for another few seconds. He wanted to twist the thumb right off Turner's hand, shove down his disrespectful throat.

Turner finally yanked his hand free from Gray's grip. He smiled, brimming with arrogance. "Anytime you do business with me it's a show. Period. You got your Chief McMuffin over there with his press conference, the reporters and TV people, my Escalade. Fuck, even my attempted murder was a damn show!"

Boudreaux leaned on the table across from Turner. "Finish telling them about Timothy McDonough and his friends."

"I think I'm done here," Turner said, holding his throbbing thumb.

Boudreaux slapped Turner across the face.

Turner's face showed defiance.

Boudreaux slapped him again.

Turner growled, so Boudreaux slapped him one more time, which brought Turner out of his chair. Boudreaux didn't flinch though. Gray and

Parker, however, jumped into action and grabbed hold of Turner, setting him hard back into his metal chair.

"This is my show, Malcolm," Boudreaux growled back.

It took another couple minutes for Turner to calm himself enough to talk. "The four of them ... they thought they was bad asses." He spoke through gritted teeth. "Been mugging people. I think they carjacked an old lady. They even got so ... what's the word you cops use? Brazen?"

Gray interrupted, "We don't use it. The newspapers do."

"What-the-fuck-ever, man! They got so ... *brazen*," he eyed Gray, "that they even robbed a couple jack-and-run stores in Plant City and Mulberry. Shot some dogs, too, I think. Stupid shit like that."

"When?" Gray folded his arms.

"I don't know when, bitch. Check your fucking records." Turner shifted in his chair. "I heard T-Bone was a pussy. He felt bad for what they was doing and was about to step off and leave their little gang. I guess them other boys decided he ain't going nowhere."

Parker stood. "This better check out, Malcolm."

Turner rolled his eyes. "If it don't check out, it means you ain't doing enough of your detective shit."

"Who can back up your story? Where can we find Cheech?" Parker asked.

"That dumb ass is dead. Got in a scrape with the wrong crackhead. Got stabbed 12 times."

Gray leaned on the table. "You said one of the kids rented the gun from Cheech." Gray's voice was even. "Which one rented it?"

"It wasn't one of them kids. It was some other dude. A piss head called Billy McGee."

Boudreaux replied, "He wasn't one of the friends in the car with the McDonough, was he, Gray?"

A twinge of nerves shot through Gray's body. The name stung. "No, he wasn't." Billy McGee was Timothy McDonough's cousin.

"How are you so sure Billy McGee got the gun?" Parker asked.

"He gets high with my friend, Lil P. I seen Billy a few times, and he done told me about that shit. Even thanked me for the gun one time."

CHAPTER 10

July 28 – 8:30 a.m.

A hint of vibration spread across the lobby floor of the local newspaper. The huge press beyond the lobby walls would run for a few minutes, stop, then start again. Valerie wasn't sure if the shaking inside her was from the machine or from her own adrenalized heartbeat and anger-fueled nerves. She paced the lobby, waiting on the receptionist to grant her access to Michael Edwards. *The reporter who ruined my story,* Valerie fumed.

Originally Valerie had wanted to approve the articles before they went to press, but Edwards said that wasn't possible and it was non-negotiable. Just like he had to trust that her story was truthful, she would have to trust him to do his job. Like in all negotiations, it's important for both parties to feel like they won, so Valerie dismissed that demand in favor of just getting the articles published. And now she was kicking herself. *The articles are pieces of crap!*

She had been very clear. The stories must convey the range of emotions she had experienced for the last decade. From the hate and anger she felt after receiving that first letter August 7, 2004, to the numbness and frustration of her day-to-day imprisonment by her well-meaning parents. The desperation, isolation, and loneliness of her life. It needed to paint a dark picture of her existence, so people would understand what the letter writer had done to her. All that, while also showing her strength, bravery, and determination. Edwards had agreed to that, suggesting a four-part series. He promised her he would abide by her wishes, including her idea for the final article where Valerie had sculpted the perfect dare for the Pen Pal to come after her.

But, in the end, Edwards had lied, and he wrote the stories differently than they'd agreed. The first two articles that were published were the biggest fluff stories Valerie had ever read. It victimized her, made her look weak and simple. What pissed her off most was that the second article made her look afraid, and she just couldn't have that. *I'm not afraid.* Valerie had given that up years ago. She worried most about how the fourth article had been changed. Did her perfectly crafted dare still exist? Would it be effective? Would it have the impact she desired and needed?

I should have demanded to see the articles, Valerie thought to herself as she marched across the lobby. *Non-negotiable my ass, you son of a bitch.*

The front desk receptionist dialed Michael Edwards for the third time since Valerie arrived and began pacing the lobby floor. Edwards answered this time. They spoke out of Valerie's earshot. She rushed over, trying to listen in on the conversation.

"She looks angry," Valerie heard the woman relay

"Is he coming downstairs?" Valerie asked, not waiting for the end of the conversation to find out.

"He said it would be a few minutes." The reception returned the phone to its cradle.

"A few minutes?!" Valerie stepped back from the reception desk. "A few minutes?!" She nodded her head, looked up at the loft above the lobby and yelled, "Edwards get down here, you asshole!"

The security guard who had been positioned at the entrance approached Valerie to stop her, but she continued yelling, garnering more attention from people filtering in and out of the lobby. "You're butchering my life! Come down here, you hack!"

"All right. Time to go." The guard ushered Valerie toward the front doors.

"Don't touch me." Valerie pulled her arm away from the guard. "Edwards, get down here! Come and face me."

Edwards emerged from the staircase that led to the press room. When he heard Valerie's yelling, he picked up his pace and stopped the guard from escorting Valerie out the front door.

"Let her go. Let her go. It's okay."

"She was causing a commotion." The guard attempted to explain himself.

"I know. I heard." The white bearded, slightly bookish looking man grabbed Valerie's arm where the guard had been holding it, but Edwards didn't grip it as tightly as the guard had.

"Nice fucking articles!" Valerie stated without lowering her voice.

"Let's go outside." It sounded like a suggestion, but it was a command. He looked over his shoulder at the guard and the other newspaper employees who were gathering as the commotion escalated.

"I don't want to go outside," Valerie protested.

Edwards led her through the glass doors, and when they closed behind them, he said, "What are you thinking? You can't just come —"

"Don't tell me what I can and can't do." She pulled her arm free from his grip. "I'm the only one in our little group here that's kept her end of the bargain."

"What are you talking about? I got your articles published." He crossed his arms in front of his chest.

Valerie did the same and then shot Edwards a dirty look. "And I look like a total loser."

He sarcastically shot back at her, "You're certainly making up for that right now." Edwards looked back into the lobby. The crowd had more than doubled. "You don't look like a crazy wacko at all."

"I needed the articles to be a certain way. They needed to be about the Pen Pal."

"I know who they were for, Valerie. I submitted the articles the way we talked about, but my editor tore them apart. I got them published how my editor would allow them to be published. Isn't that better than nothing?" He paused for the logic to sink in, but when Valerie didn't answer, he went on. "I mean, that's what I said I'd do, get your story in print again."

"You're throwing a damn loophole at me?" She threw her arms into the air in exasperation.

"No." Edwards grabbed her shoulder to steady her focus and looked her right in the eye. "I'm just trying to make you see that I'm still on your side. Look what happened. AP picked up the articles, and they're popping up in papers across the country. In New York City, even in Albuquerque, New Mexico of all places. And now that the television stations are interested, everyone will hear the story."

Her eyes were beginning to regain their girlish glint he'd noticed the first time they'd met four months ago. He continued, seeing his argument was hitting home with her. "This is what you wanted. Take it how you can get it. You can still do everything you said you wanted to do with it."

She sighed and her shoulders slumped, emotionally depleted. "I've just been thinking about it so much. This is my last chance. I envisioned it a certain way."

"It'll work out fine."

Edwards hugged her. After a few seconds, she hugged him back. He was one of the few people in the last ten years, aside from her parents, who had embraced her. Every time it happened it felt weird. But she liked it. *Kind of.*

Too soon, Edwards let her go and looked in her eyes. "Just know I'll be here for you, if you need anything."

She ignored his support. "If I don't get what I want from these articles and I get trapped at home with my parents again, I'm going to kill myself."

Edwards was shaken by her words, saw the truth in her eyes, and the blame. "Don't do that without calling me first."

She nodded in agreement, but his gut told him he'd never hear from her again. Edwards wondered if he should tell someone what she'd just said? While watching her walk through the parking lot, another question came to mind – how should the front-page headline marking her suicide be written? Sure, Edwards wasn't proud of the thought, but it was the natural, most logical question he, as a journalist, should ask.

CHAPTER 11

July 28 - Early Evening

Valerie thought she had it all figured out, every aspect covered, but even after talking to Edwards she felt these alternate articles had ruined her plan. And she'd been so overwhelmed, she'd forgotten to ask Edwards about the fourth article. *How could I be so stupid?*

With no desire to go home anytime soon, Valerie spent the day on her own. Sometimes berating herself, other times churning the plan over repeatedly in her head, and yet at times calm and content to be alone. However, the fear of the Pen Pal never left her. Truth was, she was afraid.

Near sunset, Valerie found herself at a chain bookstore, where she ordered a coffee and browsed the aisles. Being somewhere she considered a safe place eased her mood. Her foggy mind cleared and allowed her to think things through.

Not having been exposed to much televised news, she hadn't fully factored that outlet into her plan. Her parents didn't allow a television in the house. That began after the letters arrived. They didn't want her to see coverage, thinking it would add anxiety and fear to the situation. Later, they thought having one would stunt her education. That's why she reached out to Edwards. The newspaper was delivered to her house every day, so she figured that's how most people stayed up to date on news items. But, i f Edwards was right and news on television would be interested in her and her story ...

How can I use that to my advantage, even without knowing the content of the fourth article?

If the fourth article didn't draw out the Pen Pal, then she could use the news crews outside her house as the first step in her TV coverage. *Would they be willing to allow me to say what I want to say on TV? Wouldn't the public be thrilled to watch an angry woman spew vengeful words at a man who'd terrorized her for so long?*

Valerie wouldn't have to stop with local shows either. She could contact the big networks. *Or Oprah!* With Oprah on her side, she bet the Pen Pal would just give up straightaway. *If he's still out there ... which he's not.*

When she came out of her thoughts, Valerie noticed a man staring at her. He immediately looked away. He was an older man, close to her father's age, and wore a wedding ring. His hair was both greying and receding. He looked at her again before looking away, attempting a nonchalant posture. But there was nothing nonchalant about the situation. Fear consumed Valerie instantly.

The articles had first been published yesterday, Sunday, and the Associated Press had picked them up immediately. *Oh, shit.* She realized there was every reason to believe the Pen Pal could have traveled to Florida from anywhere in the country in a day's time. In fact, the man who'd just been staring at her could be the Pen Pal.

Valerie shifted her brain back to the original psychological profile she had created of the Pen Pal – white male, not athletic, mid-thirties to mid-forties. This man in the bookstore fit that description. The wedding ring didn't work for the profile though. The Pen Pal couldn't handle that type of relationship. Then another man rounded the corner of a display and caught Valerie's attention. He looked at her for an instant before looking away. He also matched her profile of the Pen Pal. With her heart suddenly racing and her body heat rising, she stood and took a quick survey of the store. There were almost ten men that matched her Pen Pal profile. *Any one of these men could be the Pen Pal.*

No! The voice in her head screamed. She needed to snap back into reality. None of those men could be the Pen Pal because he wasn't around anymore. He was dead or in jail. *Right?*

Valerie swallowed hard. Despite her desperate attempts to assuage her fears, doubts about her plan and about her future emerged.

Valerie barreled out of the bookstore through two sets of double-doors into the humid Florida evening. She practically ran to her car, checking over her shoulder the whole way. She fumbled with the keys when unlocking the door, but she still was able to quickly lock herself inside the car. Checking again over her shoulder, she saw one of the men from the store exit. Her fear felt lodged in her throat and strangled her. She had no other choice.

Valerie lurched across the passenger seat and popped the glovebox. She snatched the Smith and Wesson 317 revolver from the compartment and waited, using her mirrors to watch the man who'd come outside right after she had. But the man didn't come outside to follow Valerie. He lit a cigarette and paced the sidewalk running across the front of the store.

Now self-disappointment flooded her senses. Instead of listening to her own voice of reason, she became crippled with fear and emotion, and she was ready to shoot that man. *An innocent man.* Her disappointment led to doubt. Again. And there was no stopping the tearful fit that culminated after the emotional day.

Yet, even in her despair, she continued to convince herself she was right all along. *He's dead or in jail.* She thought to herself. *Dead or in jail. Dead or in jail.*

CHAPTER 12

July 28 – 9:15 p.m.

Valerie thought the side streets her father made her travel seemed darker than usual. She wondered if she'd just never noticed the darkness before tonight. Still amped up from her experience at the bookstore, Valerie was speeding home. The speed limit on the road was 25 miles per hour, but she zipped along at twice that. To her left Lake Parker. Her headlights on the brightest setting allowed her to see the edge of the lake just feet away from the road's edge. She thought about not going home. The only thing waiting for her there was her mother and father. And their questions. And their not understanding. And their prison. But fear was still in control – of the Pen Pal, of her parents, of nothing changing.

What exactly was she going to tell her parents? Where had she been all day? Why was she out after dark? Why hadn't she called them to let them know where she was? Why hadn't she picked up her cell phone when they had called her? Whatever their questions, Valerie knew her answers wouldn't suffice.

The thoughts of her parents vanished when a loud bang exploded outside her car window. She startled. Her heart forced adrenaline through her body so fast she could hardly feel her hands. *What the hell?*

Red lights, seemingly floating in the darkness, cut hard in front of her car. Taillights. Out of nowhere. Valerie's headlights showed the impression of a car. It immediately skidded to a stop right in the middle of the road. Right in front of Valerie. Without warning. Valerie's foot pressed hard onto the brake pedal, but her reaction was too late.

The seatbelt locked and the airbag deployed when the Cavalier slammed to a stop against the right rear quarter panel of the stopped car. Her mind spun, doing a mental bodily inventory. She thought of her cell phone. *Dad.* Then fear. *The articles. The men at the store. The Pen Pal.*

The phone had flown from the passenger seat to the floorboard at impact. She reached, but the seatbelt restrained her. *No.* Then she heard the clicking of her car's door handle. Three times in a rapid succession. *What the hell?*

The next few seconds passed in slow motion. Valerie turned toward the door and saw a man pulling his body back like a batter about to slam a homerun. His face was intent on getting inside the car; his eyes concentrated on the window not Valerie. The guy was tall and thin. Even in the darkness of night, she saw the paleness of his skin. His face gaunt. Eye sockets sunken, deep, and dark.

The gun! Before Valerie could make any effort to reach the glove box latch, the man outside the car swung, and the window shattered all over Valerie and her car interior. She lunged for the glove box, but the locked seatbelt continued to hold her back. She heard the man groan but not a groan of struggle – one of pain. She turned back toward him and saw that the window had cut his arm when he reached through to unlock her car door. Blood trickled down his left arm to his rubber-gloved hand which pulled open the door. He grabbed at her, pulled and tugged at her.

As she kicked and squirmed in a wild flurry of rage, Valerie clicked the release button on her seatbelt, which gave her freedom to move. She used her right leg to push off the side of the floorboard and propel her toward the glovebox. But her attacker pushed aside her flailing legs and jumped into the car on top of her. *His breath smells.*

Valerie managed to turn her body from underneath him and reach for the glove box, but he grabbed her hair and hit her as hard as he could in the back of the head. Valerie's dazed mind and body fell limp for an instant then something wet and acrid slapped against her face. Over her mouth and nose. She started kicking her legs into the man's back. Valerie fought him off with her left hand as her right hand reached out for the glove box latch.

I have to get to the gun.

But her sight soon blurred and her fight faded, then she fell limp into blackness.

The fight over, the Nova's driver caught his breath before pulling Valerie from the car. Picking her up in his arms stressed his weak back muscles. His arms shook from strain. He lumbered over to the Nova and put Valerie in the passenger seat. He placed a blanket over her to hide her. Heading back to the driver's side, he rubbed his stinging back muscles then slid behind the wheel. He jammed the Nova into gear and drove into the night with his prize, Valerie Hardy.

CHAPTER 13

Gray raised his arms high into the thick evening air and stretched his back. It had been a long day. With the familiar squeak of metal on metal, he slammed the car door closed, not bothering to lock it. He would be right back.

The day had dragged on after a fast, violent start. Officer Clarke who'd been shot during the Malcolm Turner assassination attempt, had made it out of surgery successfully. After Gray and Parker had their time with Turner, they'd spent the rest of the day combing through the McDonough case files, reacquainting themselves with the case specifics and trying to track down significant persons mentioned in the files. They hadn't made much progress, though, even with the extra information Turner had provided.

Step after heavy step, Gray carried his duffle bag to the third floor of his apartment building. He unlocked his apartment door and entered the empty abode. In all the years Gray had lived there, he had never bought furniture. A lawn chair acted as the living room sofa and three old milk crates as an entertainment center. No dining table. In Gray's bedroom, there sat only a frameless box spring and mattress on the floor. No dresser, no mirror, no nightstand. He found no need for those pieces of furniture anymore.

The duffle bag opened easily and the worn clothes inside joined a pile by the bathroom entrance. He pulled out a pair of shoes, something rattled around inside one of them. Gray put two fingers inside the left shoe and retrieved a 6-ounce, unopened bottle of whiskey. He twirled it between his thumb and forefinger, saw the others spread about the bottom of the bag. *I should throw these away.* He dropped the small bottle back into his duffle bag.

His closet doors were open, exposing clothes haphazardly organized. Gray sifted through them until he found the next day's attire. He turned on his iron and set up his ironing board. While the iron heated up, Gray caught sight of himself in the bathroom mirror. He hesitated at the reflection, but he grabbed a fresh razor off the counter then shut off the light before he thought about what he saw there.

Ten minutes later, he was back inside his Accord, which smelled as it always did – lived in. Fast food restaurant bags laid crumpled on his floorboard. The air freshener hanging from his rearview mirror had dried up. "Time for a new one," he said, tossing it to the floor with the bags. He started the car and sped away from his apartment.

He first stopped at a convenience store, where he parked near a garbage can. By emptying his car of all the old food bags, the old air freshener, empty coffee cups, junk mail and other clutter, Gray hoped his car might smell better. To aid that effort, Gray went inside to buy a new air freshener, but the day's newspaper caught his attention. It wasn't so much the actual newspaper as it was the photograph of a young woman on the front page. Her smile drew him in, but her intense green eyes held his gaze.

He read the caption below the picture to get her name – *Valerie Hardy.* The headline read, GROWING UP AFRAID FOR HER LIFE with CHOOSING FREEDOM PART TWO OF FOUR in small letters under the heading.

"Hey, you paying for that?" the attendant asked.

Gray paid for the newspaper and a pine air freshener then hurried back to his car. He opened the air freshener and hung it from his rearview mirror, the scent overwhelming out of the bag. It smelled better than the car though. Gray rifled through the newspaper, pitching the unwanted sections on his passenger seat. All he wanted were the Valerie Hardy articles.

According to the articles, she had spent her teen years home-schooled by her mother, squandering her free time by wishing she could play with other children, and go to a regular high school, attend prom, and the like. She wanted a best friend and a boyfriend, but she only had her mother and father. The article alluded to a terrorizing event occurring in her childhood, which would be covered in Part Three.

Making a mental note to pick up a newspaper tomorrow, Gray headed toward Tampa on Interstate 4. Traffic was light, and he drove the speed limit. After all, he was in no hurry.

Less than two hours later he arrived at Clearwater Beach. To lull him toward sleep, Gray counted billboard signs along the way, like other people count sheep, but it didn't work tonight. He stopped for water and a snack, and checked his watch: 9:30 p.m.

Only 9:30, he thought.

Back on the interstate, he traveled east, back toward Lakeland. He tried to get tired, but his counting routine failed again. As usual, the day's developments churned through his mind. This time it wasn't case specifics, per the norm. It was about Timothy McDonough's family and what they'd been through since Timothy's death. Mainly Frank McDonough, Timothy's father. *To be honest, I'd prefer to think about the case.*

McDonough had performed his son's eulogy. He had stayed behind at the burial site and insisted on helping fill Timothy's grave with dirt. Gray recalled watching from his cruiser, shaken by the activity. Later McDonough had struggled with depression, lost his job, and he and his wife almost divorced. It was only when McDonough began volunteering at the police department, helping with the victim's assistance program, that he pieced his life back together. His employer accepted him back. He and his wife's relationship seemed stronger than ever. To Gray's amazement, for a long time McDonough helped other families cope with their own loss by repeatedly reliving his own. Gray couldn't fathom why or how McDonough had done that. What really vexed Gray's thoughts was, with the development in the case, now McDonough was going to go through it all again, only with a twist, which would make it a brand new hurt.

Still not sleepy, Gray exited I-4 at Highway 98 in Lakeland for a bite to eat. The waitress at the 24-hour eatery recognized him from previous late night meals and a few minutes later brought him his usual – an omelet with ham, cheese, peppers, onions, bacon, and salsa. As he lifted to his mouth a fork full of omelet, his cell phone rang.

CHAPTER 14

July 28 – 11:50 p.m.

Scuffmarks covered the wall around the gas and brake pedals. The driver side floor mat was pushed up high behind the pedals, even folded and crumpled in front of the pedals. The driver's side car window was busted out. Blood smeared along both the inside and the outside of the car door. And a cell phone laid on the floorboard in front of the passenger seat.

Gray and Parker made their own notes on what they saw, so they could discuss later. The crime scene techs were still processing the vehicle and were in the detectives' way, so Gray and Parker headed to the roadway.

Rubber marks on the asphalt left by brakes locking up and the car coming to a screeching, sudden halt. A crowbar. A damp rag. A shower of exploded glass. Small pieces of bent, dark colored metal. Large pieces of a broken headlight.

"That crowbar changes things, huh?" Parker asked.

"It looks bad for her."

"I'm crossing off the possibility that she got in a car accident and wandered off with a head injury."

Gray noticed activity down by the lake. "What's your girlfriend over there doing?"

"Who?"

"You know who," Gray said. "That shit'll get you in trouble one day."

"Being friendly to a co-worker isn't an HR issue."

"I'm not talking about work trouble," Gray said and stepped away from Parker.

Parker met Gray at one of the three sets of tire tracks in the grass. Crime scene technician Maddy James laid out the tools she'd need to create a cast of one of the tracks. She paused when Gray and Parker approached, watched Parker in particular.

"Maddy, it's been a long time," Parker placed his notebook in his pocket.

"You know you don't have to wait on shit like this to happen to say hello, right?" She smiled brightly up at Parker from her squatted position. Her teeth were as white as paper, and her hair, even pulled back in a pony-tail, was thick, curly, and very becoming.

"How have you been?" Parker politely smiled back, but he didn't want to mean it as much as she did.

"Lonely." She smiled playfully.

Gray jumped in. "Can we move on, you two?"

Maddy, ignoring Gray's rudeness, lowered her head and returned to her casting liquid.

Parker mouthed to Gray, "Thank you."

Gray rolled his eyes at Parker.

"Best chances for a mold are here," Maddy stated. "I looked at the other two places, but that heavy rain we had yesterday left that side of the road soaked. If this turns out all right, we should be able to run it through the database. Maybe get the tire brand. Maybe track it to a particular make and model vehicle."

"At the very least," Parker asked, "if we find a car, you can match the mold to the tire, right?"

"Absolutely." Another perky smile for Parker.

"All right. Let us know."

"Jeff," Maddy called to Parker.

"Try to stay focused," Gray said, as he continued walking away.

Maddy smiled brightly again. "I'll bring you the results as soon as I get them."

"Great," Parker replied. "Thank you."

"Is he always a dick?" she asked, motioning toward Gray.

"Who? Gray?" Parker watched his friend study the contents of the street again. He smiled. "He pulls it out now and again."

"Detectives." A voice called from the vehicle.

Gray waited for his partner to join him on the roadway before heading back to the Cavalier.

"Don't say it," Parker said.

"Wasn't going to."

When Gray and Parker arrived at the car, the technician said, "I thought you'd want to see this."

They both leaned into the car and saw a revolver inside Valerie's glove box.

"What was she doing with that?" Parker asked.

"Let's go ask mom and dad."

CHAPTER 15

As soon as Gray and Parker pulled onto the Hardy's residential street, they knew which house was the Hardy's home. A handful of media trucks camped out in front. Media staff loitered around the trucks, tripods, lights, and cameras ready for action.

"Great," Gray said.

As Parker cut the engine, those lights and cameras came to life and showed the detectives their attention. Gray and Parker climbed from the car and were greeted by a barrage of questions, which they ignored. Uniformed officers left their post at the front door and aided in holding back the media so Gray and Parker could go inside.

From the house entryway, Gray saw Marie Hardy keeping herself busy cleaning the kitchen counter. Jack Hardy emerged from the living room. His face a mixture of shock, guilt, and worry.

"Now who are you two?" Jack asked.

Parker led the way. He was better at the small talk. "We're the detectives assigned to find Valerie."

"You find her?"

"No, sir," Parker said.

"Then come on in and ask your questions, so you can get back out there." He turned and went back to the living room. "Marie," he called to the kitchen.

Marie appeared again with a tray of cups filled with coffee and containers of cream and sugar.

"I made it when…" her voice trailed off as she looked at the uniformed officer standing guard over them.

Gray motioned for the officer to give them some privacy, so the patrolman stepped outside the house.

As quickly as Marie had set the coffee down on the table in front of the couch, she picked up a stack of clutter. Magazines, books, and the last couple days' of newspapers.

"No, leave those," Jack commanded. "The papers."

After leaving the newspapers in Jack's lap, Marie rushed off with the magazines and books. She returned before the detectives had finished doctoring their drinks. She sat on the edge of one of two recliner chairs facing the couch, where Gray and Parker had sat. Her foot tapped on the floor, and she wrung her hands.

"Ma'am, we hadn't introduced ourselves before, but I'm Detective Parker, and this is Detective Gray. We will be leading the investigation. We're here to hopefully answer some of the questions you have and perhaps you'll be able to do the same for us."

"She'll be dead within three days. You know that, right?" The torment in her voice was tangible.

"We've heard about the letters, ma'am," Parker replied. "We understand the time constraints."

While she hated voicing that, Marie felt a glimmer of relief knowing that fact was out in the open. She moved over to the love seat and sat next to Jack. She slipped her hand into Jack's and squeezed it lovingly. She leaned on him.

"I don't have any questions for you two," Jack said. "I don't want to slow you guys down with my need to know what's going on. If you're going to find Valerie, then you need to be out looking, not talking to us. Your chief gave me his direct line. I'll get information from him. You guys just take what you need, do what you have to. We won't get in your way at all."

Parker shot them an appreciative, comforting smile. "Then we need to know everything." Parker attempted to pull Marie into the conversation, "Mrs. Hardy, we're going to ask you a lot of questions, and we may have to ask them over and over until we understand things the way we need to understand them."

"We've been through this before, detective." Jack said, "Ask what you need."

"I noticed the four locks on the front door and the security system."

"Yes," she said, nodding her head frantically.

"Little good that did," Jack said.

"The article in the newspaper discussed a certain imprisonment here at home."

Jack Hardy's temper flared and made him react loudly. "Those damn articles." He tossed the papers from his lap onto the coffee table. "She in no way was imprisoned here. Although it doesn't surprise me she thinks that."

Marie clarified. "She's been a bear to live with for the last six years. She's become so angry. Just ... a dark person. She fought us on everything, no matter how unimportant whatever it was may have been."

Jack calmed as quickly as he flared. "We love our daughter. Marie gave her schooling every day. We took her to the movies. To church. Every other weekend we went to a theme park in Tampa or Orlando. We took trips. How many 18-year old girls have been to the Bahamas, Brazil, Mexico, and seven different states?" He paused, replaying the statement in his mind. "I don't know. Maybe a lot." He shook his head. "I'm talking nonsense."

"Did Valerie have any friends?" Gray asked.

"Are you insinuating she *was* held prisoner?" Jack flared again.

"No," Marie said. "I don't think she did."

"They're just questions, Mr. Hardy," Parker said.

"Did she usually travel alone?" Gray asked.

"No."

"Why was she out today by herself?"

"We had a fight this morning," Marie said.

Jack continued, "She did those articles and never said a damn word to us about them."

Parker stopped writing in his notepad. "You didn't know?"

"Hell no!" His temper took over again. "She told that son of a bitch where we live. She showed him what she looked like. And, she..." He fought to control his hatred, but he couldn't hide it. "The Pen Pal." It came out through gritted teeth. "I hate that fucking name. Stupid reporters." He breathed heavy, like his lungs were constricted. "He did this."

Gray asked, trying to keep the family on track, "What time did Valerie leave the house today?"

"It was before nine, I think," Marie replied.

"Did Valerie check in with you after she left?" Gray asked

"No," Jack said. "And we tried to call her, but she didn't answer her cell phone."

"Is there a place Valerie likes to go when you take her out, a place she might go if she was in trouble?" Parker asked.

"Church maybe," Marie said, melancholy and a lack of confidence in her voice.

"Home was her true safe place."

"What was she wearing?" Gray asked Marie.

"Baggy black jeans. A black shirt with a big red star on the front of it. Red sneakers."

Parker turned to Jack. "Had she ever done anything like this before, running off in a heated huff and not returning for many hours?"

"Never."

"She was a young woman, Mr. Hardy," Parker nudged. "She never snuck out?"

"Yeah," Jack conceded. "Okay. Sure. We'd caught Valerie sneaking out in the past, but it was to go take pictures. She hasn't done that in a long time."

"She had always wanted to be a photographer," Marie added.

"Did she take her camera with her today?"

"No. It's in her room," Marie said. "You're welcome to search there."

"That takes time. Time we don't have," Jack said.

"It could help, even with the timeline we're up against," Parker said. "Did Valerie have any other hobbies or interests?"

"No," Jack said.

The answer didn't satisfy Parker, who turned to the mother. "What do you think, Mrs. Hardy? Any interests at all?"

"Psychology," she said. "Lately she'd been reading up on it. But other than her usual — watching TV, listening to music, playing video games — there wasn't much else."

"What about money?" Gray asked. "Did Valerie have her own supply of cash?"

"We thought it was very important to allow Valerie to buy her own things, like clothes. She did chores around the house to earn an allowance, since getting a job seemed unsafe."

"And she purchased items with a credit card?"

"We have her statements," Jack added. "I'm guessing you want copies."

"Yes," Gray answered. "And we'd like to look into phone records for both the home phone and her cell phone, if that's all right?" Gray asked, as he wrote notes.

"That's fine," Jack said.

"You mentioned video games," Gray continued. "Did Valerie have her own computer or PlayStation? Something like that?"

"A computer. You'll see it when you go into her room," Marie said.

"Her own e-mail account?"

"Yes."

"We'll want to go through it — the computer, any information, e-mails, documents, search history," Parker said, receiving a nod from both parents. "Okay, let's talk about Valerie's behavior lately. You said she had been difficult these past few years. What about in the last month or so?"

"In the last two or three weeks, she'd actually calmed down a bit," Marie said. "I suppose in hindsight that could have been because she was working on those articles. Maybe talking about it with someone else besides us calmed her."

"Look where that got her," Jack countered. "I'd rather her home arguing than ..." He couldn't finish voicing his thought.

Parker felt for the man and didn't want to push him too hard, but he and Gray needed more information. "Those articles ... why do you think Valerie did it? What did she think she was going to get out of them?"

Both parents were silent for a moment. While Jack's stared off in the distance, Marie met Parker's eyes. "Freedom. She thinks the Pen Pal is dead, since he hasn't come after any of the girls yet."

"She doesn't know that," Jack said in a low, distant voice.

"She felt like she did," Marie said. "Valerie's a logical young woman. She'd never heard anything on the news about any of the other girls getting kidnapped. She never found anything about it on the Internet either. So she thought it was logical that this ... monster ... was dead."

"Naïve more than logical," Jack quipped.

Marie struggled with her husband's negativity. She defended Valerie and her intentions, saying, "If she could show us there was no danger, I think she thought she'd be able to ... I don't know, live on her own."

"Mr. Hardy, I know you said before you think this is the Pen Pal, but is it possible it could be someone in your immediate circle?" Parker asked. "Friends? Coworkers? Acquaintances?"

"No. It's the Pen Pal," Jack said confidently.

"You automatically assume the only person who can hurt Valerie is the Pen Pal?" Gray shot back.

Jack Hardy didn't answer Gray's question, which led Parker to asked another. "Nevertheless, could we have a list of your friends?"

"Just take the address book. Contact whomever," Jack said, as he got up. "I'll take you to Valerie's room so you can look in there and get back out there to find her."

Although Parker stayed seated, Gray stood and asked one more question: "Did you know Valerie owned a revolver?"

"What?" Marie said. "That's not possible," Marie said.

"Detective, no matter what we've been through we're just not gun people."

Gray said, "Valerie apparently was."

CHAPTER 16

Gray slipped on rubber gloves standing outside Valerie Hardy's bedroom, a jungle of clutter, clothes, books, and audio electronics. In the background, he heard Parker speak in the living room. Then Valerie's parents replied in a murmur of words. Gray was glad he had left the room. Parker was better at handling people.

Walking through the hallway to Valerie's room, Gray noticed approximately 30 framed photographs on the walls. Valerie and her family in various stages of vacationing while at theme parks, at the beach, at Mount Rushmore, at the Lincoln Memorial in Washington, D.C., at the Grand Canyon, and at the Atlantis hotel in the Bahamas. Gray noticed that Valerie looked much different in these pictures than in her newspaper photograph. In these pictures, she wore black. Black lipstick, black nail polish, black hair, black eyeliner. Everything. Yet the photograph in the paper was so vibrant, colorful, and innocent. A marketing ploy? Sell the girl next door image?

While the room looked ordinary, Gray knew it was anything but that. This house was her whole world. This room, her private place. Her only place.

Valerie's bed wasn't made. Gray checked between her mattress and box spring, under her pillow and sheets and comforter. He found nothing.

Books scattered across the floor offered a window into Valerie's thoughts. "The Anatomy of Motive," "Criminal Profiling: An Introduction to Behavioral Evidence Analysis," "Forensic Psychiatry," "Handbook of Psychology," "Crime Classification Manual," "Obsession," and the "Handbook of Forensic Psychology." Heavy reading for an interest. The newspaper articles about Valerie touched on the fact that she wanted to reclaim her life. Her parents said she was after freedom. *How did these books play into that?* Gray wondered.

He thumbed through the books, finding pages earmarked and highlighted. Valerie had been studying the sections and chapters on stalkers. Had Valerie been taking a proactive approach to her "imprisonment"?

As Gray sat at Valerie's desk, he noticed the only link to her childhood in the room was a Hello Kitty lamp, situated next to the computer monitor. He wondered why it remained when everything else about Valerie's room looked so much less alive. He searched the drawers, hoping to find a journal. Maybe she wrote about what she had found in the books, and what that information had meant to her.

But he found nothing.

He pressed the power button to Valerie's personal computer and explored her electronic files. There weren't many. He found a list of goals and accomplishments with a "Last Modified" date of three years ago — clothes shopping without her mother, enrolling in college classes, learning to play the guitar, and talking to her parents about adding an apartment onto the back part of the house.

What happened to Valerie in the last three years that put her on a collision course with this possible abduction? You don't go from wanting to learn the guitar to laying your life on the line. Maybe she just grew up. Her innocence lost with the natural maturation of a child to a woman.

But what he found even more interesting is how her list of goals and accomplishments didn't mention anything about cameras or taking pictures. Valerie's parents said she'd wanted to be a photographer. Gray scanned her room, noticing numerous photo albums. He picked one up. It held exquisite shots of bugs, animals, flowers, sunsets, sunrises, houses, people, buildings, statues, cars, among other things. To Gray's untrained eye, the photographs were quite good. He took her camera off the desk to flip through the digital inventory, but the memory card was blank. *Did she give up on her dream of becoming a photographer?*

He set down the camera and thought about hiding places. There had to be something hidden. A hard drive. Memory card. Notebook. Something. *This kid hid the fact she had a gun,* Gray thought. *She had to be good at hiding other stuff too.*

Valerie's closet was dark, even with a light on. It was jammed full of clothes and accessories. Mostly black garments. Under the clothes, inside an old hat box, Gray found three composition notebooks filled with Valerie's handwriting. *Finally.*

He lifted the cover, and with the bend of a stiff spine, he had found a way into Valerie's mind.

CHAPTER 17

July 29 – 1:58 a.m.

Something smelled. Like urine. Valerie felt wetness stretching from her stomach down both her legs. Her jeans felt adhered to her legs as she adjusted herself. Her mouth was stuck open and throbbed. Something gripped her whole head tightly, her whole body actually. She realized she couldn't move her legs or arms. *Am I paralyzed?* she wondered.

Valerie slowly became conscious of her surroundings. Her first thoughts were a diluted awareness, as if she was having a dream. She opened her eyes to a hazy vision and gathered that something covered her head and had been pulled down over her face. *What the hell?*

Wherever she was, darkness mainly surrounded her. Little light seeped in from somewhere and allowed her to see she was in an unfamiliar place. The result of that realization led to her almost hyperventilating. It hadn't been a dream. It was worse. She knew what had happened.

Her plan worked.

She had drawn the Pen Pal from a decade-long hiding. She baited him to attack her. And he had.

Calming herself and easing her breathing, she tried to remain focused on the facts, not feelings. She wasn't paralyzed; she could clearly feel the pain of her hands and feet having been hog-tied behind her back. Whenever she moved her legs, her shoulders ached from the strain. When she pulled her arms up, her hamstrings, knees, and hips throbbed with pain. Her mouth was filled with something hard and round, and she could feel straps holding it securely inside her mouth.

The light that trickled into the room came from behind two sets of curtains. Valerie could also see light outlining a doorframe. Neither light source was enough to illuminate the room clearly, but she could make out a wall to her right, where one set of curtains hung, a window probably behind it, and what looked like a tall dresser next to the curtain.

Valerie rocked in place and guessed the soft, bouncy surface below her was a mattress. She rocked to build momentum and roll over, despite the pain of her movements. However, her body wasn't centered on the bed, and when she rolled, she slipped off the edge. Valerie landed face down on the floor. The ball gag banged against her teeth, shooting pain across her skull. The landing knocked the air out of her lungs. Her chest burned, eyes watered, and her mind raced with panic.

No! she thought to herself. *This is no time to panic!*

As she sucked in needed oxygen, the frantic rate of intake made her nose whistle. Something about that sound made her laugh. But soon her emotions took over again and her laugh morphed to tears. As her lungs cooled and her heartbeat normalized, her mind raced with thoughts of regret and doubt.

Why didn't I listen to my father? I should have given him a chance, told him what I was planning. How is this happening? How could this really be the Pen Pal? There's no way he could still be out there! How could he have found her this fast? Or, has he been in Lakeland the whole time? Watching me? Wanting me? God dammit!

The tears continued as she allowed self-pity to set in. Only for a minute, though. Because that wasn't who she was. She left that part of her, along with depression and hopelessness, behind three years ago when she began this mission to escape her prison. Now all she had was hope and fight. And knowledge. She knew everything about the Pen Pal. And the first thing she thought of was his timeline. *Three days and I'll be dead.* She needed to act.

She forced her mind toward her plan, her goal, her future, but her emotions weren't ready to relent yet. Then her anger erupted into a tantrum. Valerie floundered about on the floor as hard as she could. If she could just get one hand or leg loose, she'd feel safer, like she had a chance to fight back. *The binds must give way.*

Valerie pulled her arms up at the same time as she pushed her legs out, cutting off blood flow to her hands and feet. Her efforts didn't result in what she wanted, the binds didn't loosen at all. She rested a moment, drained of energy, then took in a full breath before she pulled and pushed again, sending pain shooting in all directions.

The door must have opened because the room filled with the light from the hallway. Valerie suspended her struggling, her analytical mind kicking in. She quickly scanned the room. A bathroom in the corner. A dresser. A nightstand next to the bed. Photographs or drawings framed on the walls. *Is this someone's home?*

A shadow cast then footsteps grew close. Valerie turned. The Pen Pal's dark, ghoulish eyes met hers.

"Are you all right?"

CHAPTER 18

Boxes strapped in with seatbelts occupied the backseat of the police cruiser. One on each side of the car. They held the contents Gray pulled from Valerie Hardy's bedroom – photo albums, composition notebooks, and various media storage he found in her desk. Wedged between the two, Valerie's computer tower rested on its side.

The detectives were on their way to police headquarters to set up a static command center for this case in one of the conference rooms near their office, but Gray had another idea.

"We need to make one more stop," he said.

"What? Where?" Parker said.

"Pull in to the next gas station."

"All right. There's one up ahead. What are we doing? "

"Valerie's parents acted like they were with her twenty-four hours a day, but they didn't know anything about those newspaper articles. How could that be?"

"You know as well as I do parents don't know everything about their kids," Parker replied as he steered the car into the gas station lot.

Although Parker's comments were directed about the Hardy family, Gray couldn't help but also think of what Malcolm Turner had said about Timothy. That information would tear the McDonough family apart, re-open painful wounds, and probably create new ones. But despite his mind pushing in that direction, Gray didn't want to think about it.

"Be right back," Gray said as he exited the vehicle.

Parker quickly put down his window. "Hey! Wait." He tried to hide his smirk.

Gray walked back toward the car. "What's the matter?"

"You didn't ask if I needed anything."

"What?"

"It's just polite," Parker said. "You're going into the store. You should ask if I need anything. Chips. A soda. Slim Jim."

"Do you?"

"Do I what?"

"Want anything?"

"No, I was just saying." Parker lost control of his smirk, which spread across his face.

"Asshole."

Parker shook his head and laughed as he put up his window and watched his partner enter the store. A few moments later, Gray returned to the car with one item, which he showed to his partner.

"This guy probably has some answers," Gray said, pointing to the byline on the front page of that day's *The Ledger* newspaper. "I say we wake up the reporter who wrote these articles and get us some answers."

Parker read the name and then made a call to dispatch. After identifying himself, he made a request for an address for the reporter.

≈   ≈   ≈   ≈

Parker navigated the desolate late night streets through Lakeland to Michael Edwards' home. Someone – *surely Edwards wasn't getting his hands dirty,* Gray thought – kept the yard well-tended. Shrubs lined the front of the house and the sidewalk leading to the front door. A massive oak tree supported a tire swing in the front yard. Not far from the swing a Venetian-style, metal bench took residence inside a mulched circle, outlined with a combination of purple, yellow, and red flowers.

Parker rang the doorbell. Gray was happy to inconvenience a reporter by waking him in the middle of the night, so he reached across Parker and repeatedly pressed the button, sending a seemingly endless set of chimes throughout the house. Soon, a house robe and slippers-clad Michael Edwards opened the front door.

"The first bell woke me," Edwards said, as the door chimes continued to play from the incessant button pushing.

"Detectives Gray and Parker. We need to talk about Valerie Hardy."

"And it couldn't wait until morning?"

After just ten seconds, Gray disliked the guy. Truth be told, the reporter didn't even have to open his mouth before Gray disliked him. Gray didn't like any reporters. He'd dealt with them too much in his lifetime, and he didn't recall ever having a positive experience with any of them. Edwards' question only intensified Gray's loathing and allowed him to solely focus his disdain for all reporters on Edwards.

"How many times have the police come to your door at two a.m.?" Gray growled.

"Never."

"Then what makes you think we could wait till morning?"

Edwards demeanor changed to one of nervous and uncomfortable posture. "Did something happen to Valerie?"

"May we come in?" Parker asked, recognizing the lack of Gray's patience in his tone and abrupt attitude.

After opening his house to them, Edwards sat at his dining table before Gray and Parker. The table was bare of ornamental pieces between them. The waxy polish looked more worn where Edwards sat than at the rest of the table's seats.

"You live alone?" Gray asked.

"Divorced. Kids every other weekend."

"Girlfriend?" Gray asked.

"What's that have to do with anything?" Edwards shot back.

"So ... no?" Gray asked.

"How did you know we were here about Valerie?" Parker asked.

"She came to see me this morning. I just figured ... "

"What time?" Gray jumped at the unexpected information.

"Ten or so."

"Where?" Gray continued.

"At the office."

"What'd she want?" Parker hoped to take over the conversation. Gray's attitude was going to make Edwards defensive, and they didn't need him to shut down.

"I didn't have anything to do with it, if something happened to her," Edwards confessed.

"That's quite a statement of innocence from someone we're not accusing of any wrongdoing," Gray said.

"I know how this works. You come in here, asking if I live alone and have a girlfriend. Valerie's a beautiful young woman and I worked closely with her. Now something clearly has happened to her. And you're here to insinuate that I had something to do with it." He looked at the detectives emphatically. "And I didn't."

"So you did think was beautiful? You do live alone? And, you did work closely with her?" Gray pushed.

"What did she want when she came to see you?" Parker repeated his question, trying to keep the conversation from derailing.

"She was upset at the way her story was published."

"What was it about the articles that upset Valerie?" Parker continued.

"She didn't like them. They weren't what she wanted."

"And what did she want?" Gray barked at Edwards reply not being an actual answer to the question.

"Freedom." Edwards continued, "She figured if she could prove to her parents the threat was gone, then she could get on with her life."

"The articles were a vehicle for Valerie to come out from hiding?" Parker asked.

"Yes. That was her official story. But every now and then she'd get to talking. I don't think she had anyone she could really talk to. She told me she wanted to draw the Pen Pal out of hiding by making him angry, by disrespecting him, by acting like she wasn't afraid of him. And, less the reason, she thought the police may re-open her case."

"You told her you'd write the articles the way she wanted, but you didn't?" Gray asked – accused.

"I'm a journalist. I write the story as I see fit." Edwards defended himself and his profession. "I did write them the way she wanted. Although, my editor didn't like the attacking tone of the articles. Valerie's strong. Driven. To the point. Probably even abrasive. Ultimately, he made me change the verbiage and portray her differently. He wanted her to inspire public sympathy. Frankly, it's hard to inspire sympathy when someone seems like a cold, hard bitch. He wanted her to appear more wholesome."

"Because wholesome sells more papers?" Gray asked, jabbing, not wanting a reply.

"Because bad things that happen to good people get attention," Edwards replied.

Parker asked, "And Valerie didn't like her softer portrayal?"

Edwards shook his head. "No, she didn't. I don't think she felt it would get the response from the Pen Pal she wanted. She didn't care if the public bought into the story. She wanted the Pen Pal's interest. That was really it."

"This girl contacts you," Gray said, "and tells you she deliberately wants to put herself in harm's way, and you were fine with it?"

"She didn't tell me that, and I don't know if I was *fine* with it."

"You don't know if you were fine with it? How do you not know?"

"She needed her story told. And she asked me to tell it. I'm a reporter, so that's what I did."

"Meanwhile not giving a damn about the actual person behind the story," Gray said.

"That's enough," Parker said.

"You weren't there to help her, were you? You get your story and you move on." Gray, brimming with agitation, continued attacking Edwards. "Nothing changes with you reporters."

"I don't know what you're taking about, but I suggest you bring it down, detective," Edwards said. His nervous uncomfortable posture had finally morphed into a defensive stiffness. "You don't get to come into my home and attack my character."

"You mean lack of character."

"Becker, stop," Parker said.

"All right, you guys are done here." Edwards stood to escort them out. "I need you both to leave."

Parker stayed put. "Mr. Edwards, was that all she said about the articles."

"Yes," he answered even though he didn't want to.

"How did your relationship with her start?" Parker asked, feeling Gray's brooding presence behind him.

"I don't want to discuss this any longer, detective."

"She's gone," Gray said. "There's an exclusive for you, Mikey."

"What do you mean *gone*?" Edwards did sit back down.

"Abducted it looks like, and your articles put her in danger."

"How'd you two start communicating?" Parker asked.

"By the Pen Pal?" Edwards appeared genuinely shocked.

"I need you to focus," Parker said. "How did you two communicate with each other?"

Edwards tried to push aside his feelings. "She contacted me by e-mail at first. Then we met a few times as I wrote the articles."

"Her parents didn't know all this was going on, so how'd you two meet up?"

"She'd sneak out. Sometimes she drove here, and sometimes I'd pick her up. She said she snuck out all the time."

"We're going to need dates and times. Did you record your meetings with her? Or just keep notes? We'll need copies."

Edwards ignored Parker and said, his mind still reeling a bit, "There's something else you need to know."

"What is it?" Parker asked. He felt Gray step closer.

"When I saw her today," Edwards said, "she said she might kill herself if things don't go her way with these articles."

Parker protested before Gray could. "And you waited until now to tell us? Why didn't you alert us earlier in the day?"

"She wasn't serious," Edwards said.

"Are you sure about that?" Parker barked.

Gray pointed his finger at Edwards. "I swear if there's an article in tomorrow's paper about Valerie being suicidal ... "

"Don't threaten me, detective."

"It's not a threat."

CHAPTER 19

Parker received a telephone call from his wife at 4:30 a.m. then went home. For Gray, there was no point in leaving. He wasn't going to sleep anyway. He asked someone to grab him a to-go breakfast and a copy of the day's newspaper. Then Gray locked himself inside the conference room designated as the command center for this investigation.

He set out Valerie's belongings on the table before him: composition notebooks, textbooks, and photo album after photo album. Gray grabbed one of the notebooks and thumbed through it. Luckily, Valerie had dated her entries, so Gray arranged them in chronological order before reading through them. The oldest notebook's cover crinkled and creaked as he opened it. He flattened the cover and examined the page. Having been through a handwriting analysis class a few years earlier, he noted Valerie's cursive writing slanted far left.

Not much different than mine. He hadn't thought about it in a long time.

A slant to the left indicated a withdrawn state of mind. Her writing was large though, so she had a decent ego. But the loops in her upper zone letters, like L and B, were narrow, which Gray took to mean she was holding back, reserved. Maybe his memory of the class was great or maybe knowing what he already knew about Valerie led him to conclude she suffered from times of low self-esteem and had a strong sense of insecurity.

As he read the text, he saw that Edwards was right. Valerie was to the point, to say the least. She hated the Pen Pal, but she hated her captivity more. Death by his hand or by her own hand would be freedom for her. She'd read numerous books about criminal profiling, as well as psychology textbooks. She was a huge fan of real crime books by Ann Rule and John Douglas. It seemed to Gray that Valerie was obsessed with understanding the man who'd kept her captive for so long.

Valerie's notebooks seemed like Valerie's only friend. She didn't limit the topics she discussed in them to the Pen Pal. She talked about her parents, her father mostly, how he was never around, and when he was around, he was always so strict. Valerie wrote that it was like the Pen Pal took away his ability to love her, to allow Valerie to feel alive. Every time she'd try to break through her father's hard exterior, they'd end up fighting. He'd always end the argument with something about how he was protecting her. She was beginning to think he lost grasp of what that meant, that maybe he was surviving by hiding, too.

She spent much of her time pouring out her feelings into the notebooks. The feelings ranged from loneliness to anger, rage to despair, and betrayal to hopelessness, seemingly jumping from one to another in a small amount of time.

His breakfast and paper finally arrived. As he ate cold eggs, he skimmed the paper, mostly interested in Part Three of the Valerie Hardy series of articles. But he was also checking to verify Edwards hadn't snuck in an article about Valerie being suicidal. However, he couldn't find either of those articles. There was, although, an article about the abduction, detailing what was known as of press time, which wasn't much. In that article, he found an editor's note about Edwards' series on Valerie. Out of respect for Valerie's family and the current circumstances, the paper decided to not run the remainder of the articles. At least for now. *Damn it.* He tossed the paper aside then finished his breakfast.

Out the window, he saw the darkness over the city was lifting, and he decided he should finally be tired. Gray grabbed another cup of coffee and left the conference room with an armful of Valerie's belongings to keep him company if he couldn't sleep. *Which was entirely likely.*

At his apartment, Gray left the belongings on the kitchen counter with his keys, phone, wallet, badge, and weapon, while he took a short nap before cleaning up and dressing. Within 90 minutes, he was ready to head back to the police headquarters. As he collected his things off the counter, he noticed one of Valerie's items that he'd brought along was a photo album. He peeled back the cover and found childhood pictures of Valerie. The photos ranged from her birth to toddler years. *Just close it and leave it,* he told himself. But, he didn't. In one of the pictures, Valerie and Jack Hardy were coloring on the floor. Both of them were lying on their stomachs, right next to each other.

Gray's stomach twisted and tears built in his eyes. *I told you to close the damn book.*

He tried to focus on the case, but that wasn't going to happen. Instead the photos and the handwriting analysis turned his mind inward, where he least liked it.

Fuck. He finally closed the album, grabbed the items, and left his apartment.

The drive back to the police station was slow. He rode in morning traffic and seemed to get stopped at every red light. The various baby and toddler pictures kept appearing inside Gray's brain – a birthday party, bubbly bath time, playing with animals, dressed up for Halloween as a giant pumpkin, and countless other images of a toddler's life. Weariness overcame him. He wondered if was he tired or if the images had taken even more life out of him?

His cell came to life from his passenger seat. Parker was calling.

"We got a line on Billy McGee."

CHAPTER 20

After aggressively cutting through congested morning traffic, Gray slammed on the brakes in front of the police headquarters. People honked their horns at him as they narrowly passed him on Massachusetts Avenue. Parker rushed out of the lobby and jumped into the car with Gray.

"Where?" Gray barked.

"Tampa. Go!"

Gray accelerated, sending his Honda Accord's engine racing. *Billy McGee.* Gray's mind and heart rate accelerated just the same, thinking of putting a final nail in the McDonough case.

"My friend at Tampa PD said they have a guy that matches McGee's description inside a crack house. They haven't moved in on him yet. They've got it under surveillance, but I told him we'd like to be there," Parker told Gray and pointed at a car slowing down in front of them. Gray avoided the slowing car and about a hundred more on the way west to Tampa.

"What did you find in the girl's notebooks?"

"I haven't finished them." Gray knew his partner was asking for information that had been inside the notebooks. Perhaps clues, but it was Valerie that struck Gray the most. He said, "A lot of loneliness. Sometimes she seems desperate. Other times she seems amazingly intelligent. Then like a little girl."

"She's all over the place," Parker noted.

Gray nodded, staring at the road ahead, his tiredness fading as adrenaline kicked in.

Parker continued, "Boudreaux did tell me the old case files should be here by noon."

Almost ignoring Parker's statement, Gray said, "I'm surprised he's letting us do this. I thought he'd want us solely on Valerie's case."

Parker found Gray's wording odd. *Valerie's case?* That wasn't how Gray typically referred to cases he worked.

"He wants this McDonough case taken care of."

"No," Gray said, finally looking away from the road. "He wants a fast return on his deal with Malcolm Turner."

Once they made it to the interstate, the ride only took 20 minutes. Gray flew, did almost 100 mph the whole way. They got off the interstate at 50th and Columbus. The ride, mostly through residential areas, to the crack house took almost as long as the interstate drive. There were a lot of red lights and neighborhood people out and about, slowing them down.

Parker remembered something else Boudreaux told him. "I almost forgot. This should make your day. Boudreaux's alerted the FBI."

"Perfect." *Not perfect.*

Parker went on, "Also, the BOLO hasn't brought in anything good yet on Valerie."

"Why'd he bring in the FBI?"

"I think just for profiling."

Parker pointed to a side street, and Gray obeyed, and turned the car. Most of the houses in the neighborhood were decaying. The yards were either dirt or weeds, no grass. They stopped next to an unmarked police cruiser.

Parker greeted his friend. "Hey, Mackey. Damn, you look like hell."

"Haven't slept in a couple nights."

Parker looked at Gray and then back at Mackey before sarcastically responding, "I'm used to that look on a person."

Mackey didn't know what Parker meant by that remark, so he filled them in on the situation. The Tampa PD, DEA, and FDLE had been cracking down on a local drug ring, and they were down to the last few places they were going to hit. One of the girls they arrested said something about Billy McGee. She told them he was at this particular house and was armed pretty heavily. He was going crazy, kind of paranoid, like he'd been high for a week straight and was freaking out.

"I know you cats brought your guns. You ready for this?" Mackey said, obviously liking the excitement.

"Yeah," Parker replied. "Got a couple extra vests?"

The windows of the crack house were either boarded or covered with aluminum foil. The door, with shiny, brand new locks looked like the only thing on the house that had been replaced in the last 50 years.

In a coordinated effort, the law enforcement team surrounded the house, and, on mark, battering rams busted open the doors. First inside the house went the smoke canisters, which exploded with disorienting blasts. Then the team moved into action.

Gray and Parker kept to one another. Gray thought that this whole production was unlike Billy McGee. This was not who he was. McGee was a coward, a thief, and a junkie. Although, he'd seen better people than McGee fall further down the evolution scale because of drugs.

Shouts of "Police" came from every direction, and the smoke made it nearly impossible to see anything.

"Upstairs!"

Shots fired. Three. Four. Then ten.

Gray and Parker darted for the stairs quickly and cautiously. Another two shots. Gray arrived in time to see a police officer on the stairs writhing in pain. Mackey was with him, applying pressure to a bloody wound.

"Keep going," he barked at Gray. "Jeff, help me."

Gray pushed up the stairs, stepping around Mackey. He edged close to the top of the stairs and poked his head above the flooring, trying to see between the officers' boots and legs. He took another step and saw a man holed up inside a bedroom while holding what looked like an automatic rifle. He'd fired at the police. They'd fired back.

"Where is he?" Gray asked the officer closest to him.

The officer's Glock and eyes stayed trained on the doorway when he replied. "I think we shot him about six or seven times, but the guy's high as hell."

"He didn't go down?"

"He's dead. His body just don't know it yet."

The man in the bedroom popped out from hiding and swung the rifle at police again. One of the officers shot and hit him, which dislodged the rifle from his grip. He pulled out a revolver, shouting something unintelligible.

"Gun. Gun. Gun." Officers shouted across the front line.

Each of the front-line team members fired again at the man, hitting him repeatedly. Gray watch from the stairs, while covering Parker, Mackey, and the cop who'd been shot. Gray watched as the man charged at the line of cops, who unloaded their weapons at the man, who was firing his revolver wildly. The bullets to the knees finally had an impact, and the man went down. His body shook involuntarily. One officer hurried over and kicked the revolver away, though it was probably out of ammunition, the way the man was firing it. Two other officers zip tied the man's hands. Then stillness finally set in.

Some of the team verified the guy was dead, while others came down the stairs and helped carry their wounded teammate outside to paramedics, who were pulling up outside the house as they emerged.

Mackey led Gray and Parker into the room.

Mackey said, "We wanted him alive for you. Sorry. Parker told me how important this case is, but this cat didn't leave us any other option."

Gray nodded, understanding the situation. Mackey stepped aside and Gray could finally see the man's face. He squinted to see beyond the blood and bullet hole in the man's left cheek.

"He's not our Billy McGee."

CHAPTER 21

July 29 – 11:22 a.m.

The smell of bacon permeated the house and made its way to Valerie's nose. Lingering between asleep and awake, a vision of her mother fired across her mind's eye. The combination of bacon and her mother brought a slight smile to Valerie's face – *home* – but it disappeared the instant she fully woke.

She wasn't at home.

Her mother wasn't making the breakfast she smelled.

And her father was no longer protecting her.

She was on her own.

Despair set in. She'd set this whole thing in motion with the assumption she'd be able to control it. But she couldn't control other people, no more than her parents had ever been able to control her. Why has she been so stupid? So naïve?

The bedroom door cracked open and a tired, scratchy voice called to her, "Are you wearing the hose?"

"Yes." Why did he keep putting panty hose over her head? It didn't make sense.

The Pen Pal came into the room, in his hand a plate loaded with breakfast. Valerie squinted to see the contents but couldn't until he placed the plate next to her bound body. Steaming eggs, hot toast topped with melting butter, and bacon called out to her, made her mouth water. She looked up at him and saw his face blurred by the pantyhose.

The man stepped back from the bed, maybe two feet. "Are you hungry?"

"Yes, I'm hungry." *He backed up. Is he afraid of me? Or just unsure around women?*

"Would you like me to untie your hands, so you can eat?"

The night before, when she saw him without the panty hose covering her face, he flipped out. He screamed at her, turned out all the lights, and attacked her. She fought as much as she could, but the hog tie was too tight. He moved Valerie from the floor to the bed again. He removed the ball gag, so she could tell him she was not hurt. He walked over to the bathroom, retrieved something from beneath the sink and returned to Valerie. He forced another wet cloth over her mouth. The next thing she knew, she smelled bacon.

"Let me go." Not the answer he was looking for, she was sure.

Probably subconsciously, he took another step back, which pleased Valerie, but then he surprised her.

"I think I'll just feed you myself then."

He approached the bed. Bent and reached for Valerie's face. She pulled away, but there was nowhere for her to go. She eventually complied, and the Pen Pal rolled the hose from her neck over her chin and rested it on the bridge of Valerie's nose. This created a gap she could see through, if she looked down her nose. The roll blocked sight in all other directions though. He stepped away from the bed again to where Valerie could hear him moving but not see what he was doing.

"I hope you don't mind," he said, approaching the bed again.

Valerie looked down her nose. Saw his bare legs, white with black hair. *What the hell's he doing?* As he got closer, Valerie saw his penis, testicles, and lower abdomen.

"Why are you naked?"

She asked the question even though she knew the answer – he was taking control away from her again.

"You can see, can't you?" he asked. "Yes," he answered for her, a tone of pleasure in his voice. He bit down on his lip, the pain accompanying the pleasure. Genius struck again. He smiled, tasting blood from his lip, so pleased with his brilliant instantaneous ideas.

As he grabbed her face and straddled her, Valerie pulled on her arms and kicked with her legs, but the binding held tight. Her thrashing about was having no impact on his advance. *Please, God, no.* As visions of rape and assault entered her consciousness, Valerie tightened her whole body in an effort to refrain from crying in front of this monster.

He shushed her in an attempt to calm her, but she continued to struggle, most of which was contained by the ties. He rose slightly and stuck his hand under his testicles. He hauled them up, sat down on her chest, and gently laid them on her sternum. She could smell human musk, which bolstered her fight.

"I'm just going to feed you," he assured her. The Pen Pal lifted the plate of food. "Some bacon?" Out of her eye sight, he licked the sliver of bacon then wafted the piece in front of Valerie's nose. She was finished playing games. Lost her appetite at the sensation of his testicles on her chest. She refused the food, whipping her head from right to left to avoid the meat.

"Fine."

He rose again off her body and moved backward over her stomach.

Valerie wished she could raise her knees in a violent thrust. She'd kick him, slam her legs right into his back. Give him whiplash so bad, he'd break his neck.

The Pen Pal scooped up the scrambled eggs and rubbed them all over his genitals, his penis hardening. Some stuck to his body and pubic hair, but most of the eggs fell onto the bed and Valerie's stomach.

"Still hungry?" He scooped the eggs into his hands.

"No. No. No." Valerie fought harder, knowing what he'd done with the food. She saw pubic hair in the eggs as he brought them toward her mouth. "No," she screamed. She clinched her lips and her eyes, locked her jaw.

He cupped the eggs in one of his hands and clasped her nostrils with his other hand. Soon she opened her mouth to breathe. When she did, he jammed the eggs inside then clasped her jaw closed to keep her mouth closed.

"Swallow."

He strained from above and pushed on her face. She twisted and arched from below. Neither was winning, but Valerie was definitely losing. Suddenly she froze and became rigid.

"Eat it!"

As her mouth filled with a warm liquid, her eyelids popped open and her eyes revealed the panic that accompanies the act of vomiting. Liquid exploded from her mouth and riddled his naked body. She heaved again and more vomit covered her clothes and the bed.

He jumped off Valerie. "What have you done?" Then he started laughing. "You've made such a mess."

He unbound Valerie and yanked her off the bed. She hit the floor with a thud and a sudden aching detonated in her left shoulder. She grabbed at the shoulder to hold it. Then she rolled, instinctively ready to defend herself, and when she did, she immediately saw his erect penis. Then his gruesome smile. Then his posture. He was going to pounce on her, like he was an animal.

He tore at her, slapping away her arms. He punched her in her hurt shoulder, ceasing the majority of her fight. He clawed at her pants, yanked and ripped and thrashed until they'd pulled over her ankles and came free. She kicked at him, but he swatted them away and jumped on top of her again, ready to tear at her shirt and bra next.

Valerie fought for her life, but he punched her shoulder again and overpowered her. She screamed out at him. Kicked with all her might. But she knew he was going to rape her. He laid on her and she expected his cruel and forceful insertion, but he just moved around on top of her. He reached for her, pushed and shoved. Searched. He dug his head into her shoulder, arching his back. Trying. But then he screamed in frustration. Got up on all fours over her. Punched her shoulder again for good measure before standing above her. His once erect penis had fallen flaccid.

He pulled the bedspread and sheets from the bed and wrapped them around his body before running out of the room.

Valerie sobbed into the carpet, holding her throbbing shoulder, wanting to vomit again. "Why?" she whimpered. She hadn't expected the Pen Pal's sexual aggression toward her. Intimidation, control, sexual degradation, this type of violence ... She was wrong about him. And she was sure she couldn't keep up the fight against this man, which meant she may never go home again. She cried for as long as the tears would come.

CHAPTER 22

The house felt empty. Empty of everyday noise. Empty of warmth. Empty of hope. Jack and Marie lied on their bed, neither asleep and neither making contact with the other. The frustration from that emptiness surged and abruptly forced Jack from the bed and out of the bedroom.

As he stomped his way to the kitchen, he noticed the pictures on the hallway wall. Valerie's life, framed, always in a box. Again he saw photographs he didn't recall. Where had they been in them? What had they been doing? Why was Valerie smiling so widely? How could he be in the pictures and not recall anything about them?

For the past ten years he worked to protect his family. But he felt as if he was an absent father on one journey of life while his family was on another.

Marie trailed him to the kitchen and watched him pull mayonnaise, mustard, pickles, turkey, lettuce, and tomato from the refrigerator. Jack couldn't find the bread. Not in the refrigerator, food pantry, or the cupboard. As his search came up empty behind each door, his anger and frustration bubbled over.

Finally, after Jack slammed the fifth cupboard door in a row, she spoke, "You're going to break the doors. What are you looking for?"

Jack slammed the sixth door so hard it bounced back at him. He grabbed it and slammed it again. "The fucking bread." He supported himself on the counter and hung his head low.

Neither knew what to say. Jack put the blame for Valerie's abduction on his shoulders.

"Jack?" Marie asked. "What is it? Talk to me?"

"Do you know where the bread is?"

"I think I put it in the microwave for some reason." She hadn't stirred from the kitchen doorway. She leaned on the doorframe.

"What the hell's it doing in there?" Jack went to the microwave and found the bread. He pulled two slices of bread from the package and spread the condiments with a knife. "There's another three TV news vans out there."

Marie approached him and gently laid her hand upon her husband's. "I saw them, too."

Jack froze. The contrast between the way he felt and her gesture of comfort was nearly disorienting. "I should have done something to stop this from happening."

"Don't blame yourself." She squeezed his shoulder, only to have him draw away from her.

"Where were we in that picture in the hall? The one with all of us in it. Valerie was wearing a blue ball cap. We all had sunglasses on."

"You took us to Sea World for her 16th birthday." Marie took the knife for herself and sliced the tomato sitting on the counter.

"Did we have fun?"

"You don't remember?"

"Did we have fun, Marie?" Jack demanded to know, averting eye contact.

"You were doing the right thing. You always do." Marie knew Jack acted the same way anytime they left the house. He spent the whole time checking over his shoulder for someone who might be following them. She recalled Sea World specifically. He didn't ride any of the rides or go inside any of the exhibits. He stood guard outside watching her and Valerie enter. Then he'd be waiting for them at the exit. He was always on guard.

"When did I stop protecting her?"

"What are you talking about? You're being ridiculous."

"I forgot the anniversary was coming. I should have known she'd try something like the newspaper articles. Why didn't I know?"

Marie went to him and took his hands inside hers, "Jack, she's moving away from us. She's a grown woman. Nothing we could have done or said would stop that process."

Jack took his hands back from Marie. "If I'd paid attention, I could have seen it coming and prepared her for the time when she'd leave us."

"Enough of this feeling sorry for yourself." Marie let go of his hands and took a firm stance at the counter. "Yes, you missed opportunities to show Valerie how to protect herself. You missed out on parts of her life because you were busy doing what you thought was right."

"I did that because I love her."

"I know you do. And I know you're afraid she is going through something terrible because that's what I'm thinking too." There was no retort to Marie's words, which only prompted her to continue. "If she's ever needed protection, Jack, it's now. You've never hesitated to act, so act." She pointed to the front door. "Go out there and use the media to get your daughter back. Make a plea to the nation for help. I've had it being a prisoner in this home, too. Our daughter needs us out there."

Again, no retort. Jack looked away from Marie, embarrassed by the scolding. Yet, he knew she was right. His nerves came to life, so as he walked to the front door, he maintained them with controlled breathing. He paused at the door, pulling his thoughts together, pushing aside his fears for his daughter, swallowing his pride and self-blame, then jerked the door open. The media monster woke sharply. Cameras flashed, microphones raised, and the crowd pushed toward Jack Hardy.

CHAPTER 23

Chief Boudreaux smiled when Gray and Parker finally entered his office.

"We can start now."

Boudreaux motioned to the other man in his office, "This is Special Agent Peter Tyler."

Boudreaux's office window exposed a view of Lake Mirror and the surrounding public gardens. The carpet was a deep royal blue color, and the LPD logo greeted entrants at the door. Boudreaux's desk was surrounded by Queen Ann style oxblood chairs and couches.

Tyler stood as he shifted files from his lap to his left hip. He shook hands with Gray and Parker as they exchanged greetings. Tyler almost lost the files at his side and quickly moved to stop their fall. His blond hair had been thinning for years, but he only looked to be about 35 years old.

"Agent Tyler flew in a couple hours ago to, one, deliver the old case files and, two, to get us caught up on the profile of the Pen Pal."

Tyler set the files on the edge of Boudreaux's desk. "Unfortunately, I've been called back to Washington on an emergency, so I won't be able to spend the amount of time I'd like to spend with you on this one. I will, however, give you as much information as possible in person, and the rest you can get from my report and the old case files."

"You've looked at last night's crime scene and compared it to your profile?" Gray asked.

"No, I haven't. I'll do that on the flight back to Washington and get it to you before tomorrow morning. I'll also, in that report, provide you recommendations on a course of action."

Tyler presented himself with strength, confidence, and authority. He passed each of the men a folder.

"Inside this you'll find the initial profile, my new profile on the Pen Pal, and key pieces of evidence, like copies of the letters for each of the girls and some other items. Quickly, it goes like this: We're looking for a white male, by now probably in his forties, lives alone, and has problems with father figures.

"The letters were meant to throw off law enforcement." Tyler paced the room as he held his folder in front of him and read from it. "The first one was written so he'd appear stupid and unsophisticated. If you look at the letter, you'll notice the simple wording, the misspellings, and the bad grammar. However, the man was cunning enough to know from where to mail the letters to each girl, so they'd all receive the letters on the same day. Hard to do when they were in each of the four time zones. This would lead us to believe the Pen Pal had done test runs with the letters and known how it would result. Also, that fact would suggest he traveled a great deal, maybe as a traveling salesman, a truck driver, or something like that.

"The second letter was written differently. Completely opposite. The handwriting was the same, but the spelling was correct, he used multi-syllable words, and formatted the letter professionally. You know the way they taught you in school. With the date. The recipient's address. The salutation. The body. Sincerely. All that.

"All indications suggest if the Pen Pal has this girl, she'll be dead in a couple days. Then again, typically a guy like this wouldn't wait ten years before acting on his threat."

Tyler paused for the first time, in thought.

"Let me put it this way. Despite an uncharacteristic wait time, if the Pen Pal has Valerie in his possession, we should fear the things he'll do to her. And we should prep her family for the worst."

Tyler closed the folder and set it on Boudreaux's desk with the pile of other information. "The local field director said he'd be in touch with you, chief. He asked me to tell you they're casting a net on the other four girls who received these letters, but he wasn't promising any results."

Tyler grabbed his jacket and slipped it on. "Now I apologize, but I must go. My contact info is inside the folders, so don't hesitate to contact me, if you have questions.

"Chief," Tyler extended his hand to Boudreaux, "nice to meet you. Good luck, and I'll be in touch."

Boudreaux thanked Agent Tyler, who then exchanged good byes with Gray and Parker.

"He's not the life of the party, huh?" Parker said with a smile.

Despite his subordinate's attempt to lighten the mood, Boudreaux didn't bite. "I heard you two had an interview in the middle of the night."

"Michael Edwards, from the newspaper," Gray said. "He's the reporter who wrote the articles about Valerie. He was more concerned about himself than her."

"That makes sense."

"What's that mean," Parker asked.

"I'd like for you two to perhaps not threaten people." Boudreaux said, not looking up from the file he was reading.

"I don't know if that's fair," Parker said.

"I get it." Boudreaux finally looked away from the report. "No more threats."

Typical Boudreaux. Only worried about the big cases. Gray took an angry shot at the boss. "No, no, chief, we didn't find Billy McGee. He's still in the wind. Thanks for asking."

"I already knew that. Close the door on your way out please."

CHAPTER 24

July 29 – 12:07 p.m.

Awake again, Valerie felt an incredible urge to urinate. She raised her arms, which sparked a flicker of pain in her left shoulder, and ran her fingers through her damp hair, brushing it off her face. *Why aren't my hands tied?*

Valerie darted straight up on the bed. She looked, without the pantyhose covering her head, at her free hands, her free feet, and her naked body. She tore at the bedspread underneath her. She pulled it and covered herself.

She remembered throwing up, remembered why instantly afterward. She had puked everywhere. Just thinking about it made her want to vomit again. Valerie smelled the bedspread now wrapped around her bare body. It smelled like it had just been washed.

The Pen Pal's a clean freak?

He cleaned the bedding. He cleaned her. The thought disgusted her, imagining his hands all over her, but she pushed that thought away, knowing she needed to take advantage of her free arms and legs, not worry about what he was doing to her.

She checked the room. A nightstand stood on both sides of the queen-sized bed, which butted against an outer wall under a set of curtains and a window. To her left was a closet with sliding doors. Next to the closet was the bedroom door. Locked from the outside. Framed charcoal and pencil drawings of various bridges hung on the walls around the room. Directly across from the bed, she saw a sink, cabinet, mirror, and another door she suspected was the bathroom. Then on the last wall, a dresser and another set of curtains hiding a window.

There were no clocks anywhere, and she wondered what time it was. What day it was. Not knowing how long she'd been unconscious, she wondered how much was left of the three-day timeline outlined in the Pen Pal's letters. Her parents would receive a letter on the third day, telling them when and where they could find her body. She had no idea how much time she had left.

She stood on the bed and checked the window above it. Maybe someone who could help her was just outside the window. Maybe a gardener or a lawn crew? Maybe the windows were unlocked and she could escape.

However, she saw no lawn crews, only the side of another house. *Maybe if I scream loud enough someone will hear me.* She decided against screaming for now. With her hair still wet and she freshly cleaned, the Pen Pal was likely still in the house. Quiet, it is then.

She bounced off the bed and checked the other window in the room. This other window's view was better. She saw a residential street and more neighboring houses. She imagined children drawing chalk hopscotch boxes in the road and hopping across them, boys riding bicycles outside, father and mothers doing yard work. *Why aren't any of them outside now?*

She also found that each window was locked and had stoppers attached by a screw on the border of the frames. That meant even if she unlocked them, the window would only rise to the stopper, allowing – in this case – less than an inch of movement.

Recalling her urgency to urinate, she hurried toward the attached bathroom where she stopped in the mirror. Her ghastly appearance caught her attention. While her shoulder was visibly bruised from the attack, she noticed her face more. She in no way was a Barbie doll girl, not prissy or high-maintenance in the least bit. Yet, she liked to look good. Thought she was pretty enough. But, now she looked rough. Tired. Weak. Puffy. A rash had developed around her mouth, dipping down to her chin and rising up to her nose circling her nostrils. Her skin was red, irritated, and a little swollen. *What's he doing to me?*

She went into the bathroom, sat on the toilet, and emptied her bladder before wiping with tissue.

She gasped.

She was shaved. Smooth. Her legs too. She sat back on the toilet and held her stomach. *He didn't just clean me.*

She was too disgusted to cry, but her chest tightened. Now she had to think about him and what he was doing to her. The thought made her dry heave, and Valerie, trembling, slid off the toilet onto the bathroom floor. She thought of his flaccid penis and figured he was doing to her while she's unconscious what he wasn't able to do to her while she was awake.

Soon Valerie pushed herself off the floor, the shoulder pain – and her whole body – numb now. She leaned against the bathroom wall and looked down at herself, picturing him on top of her comatose body, doing whatever he did to her. Her fists clinched in anger. She built the venom of hatred inside her. *He's dead.*

She rushed to the night table next to the bed, opened the drawer, and rummaged for anything that would serve as a weapon. Valerie yearned for her revolver. She slammed the drawer closed and scanned the room frantically.

She ran back to the bathroom and searched the sink counter and drawers, but found nothing. *Nothing.* Just normal bathroom stuff. Combs, brushes, toothpaste, bars of soap. *Nothing!* Valerie then looked in the cabinet underneath the sink. Same thing. No weapon she could use. She did, however, find more than 20 bottles of ether.

"The wet cloth. Son of a bitch. Not again, you won't."

She grabbed a bottle and cracked the seal. She dumped the contents into the bathroom sink. Took another, opened it and dropped it into the sink. She continued quickly, quietly until all the bottles had been opened and turned upside down. Then she turned her attention back to finding a weapon.

She searched through the drawers again. This time the bars of soap called out to her. She grabbed all the bars of soap, five in all, and moved to the bed where she tore a pillow from its case. Inside the case she dropped the bars of soap. Valerie practiced swinging it at his imaginary head a couple times. Her shoulder pain ignited again, but she kept practicing until the pain didn't matter and her movement was unhindered.

Valerie looked inside the dresser and found clothes. Her clothes. Washed and folded. Put away, like this was where they belonged. The find made Valerie look around the room again. The curtains were floral patterned, and they matched the bedspread. *Is this to be my bedroom? Was it styled for me? Is he keeping me? None of this matches my profile of the Pen Pal. How could I have been so wrong?*

A sudden, startling low thump came from outside the bedroom door. She thought so anyway. She quickly dressed then bounced across the bed, snagging her soap-filled pillowcase. She stayed in the nook created by the closet, squatting. She thought briefly about her parents, wondered how they were handling this situation. Guilt reared its head. She'd have to make it up to them, and even though she accepted she might die – expected it really – she hoped she'd get a chance to make it up to them.

The doorknob rattled. *He's using key to unlock the door.*

"Come on," she whispered, urging him inside.

The door opened and Valerie erupted. Screaming – partly due to the shots of pain from her injured shoulder and partly from her feelings of abhorrence toward him – she flung the case of soap bars at his head. She connected. Hard.

He crumbled to the floor. She had imagined him a beast, big and strong. But he wasn't. He was skinny. He looked malnourished. Weak. That gave her more strength and resolve to club his brains out. She thrust the case down upon him again, groaning with every swing. Finally, feeling she'd done enough damage, she slammed the bag of soap down on him ten more times for good measure. She screamed unintelligibly at him, like it a roar. She spat on him before jumping over his limp body darting down the hallway, literally running for her life.

She found the living room, didn't see a door, and kept going. She went through the kitchen. *No door?* The dining room. *Where's the fucking door?* The family room. *No door.* Frustration got the better of her, and she screamed as loud as she could. Somehow she found herself in the living room again. Tears built in her eyes, mostly from her aching shoulder but also because she was so close to getting away and she didn't see a door. She noticed a huge bay window and her mind shrieked at her to throw something through it and jump to safety. She grabbed a thick, black unused ashtray off the coffee table and cocked her arm, but before she could throw it, something caught her eyes and ears by surprise. Froze her.

The television ...

He might as well have been standing right in front of her.

Daddy.

The Pen Pal came out of nowhere, it seemed to Valerie, and tackled her from behind.

"Let me go!" While struggling, she immediately focused again on the screen. "Daddy!"

The kidnapper dragged Valerie kicking and screaming down the hall. He pulled her by the legs. She scratched at the floor, grabbed at the doorframe. She did anything to continue seeing the television.

"No," she screamed.

The Pen Pal overpowered Valerie, jerking her back into the bedroom. He threw her to the side, like a trash bag and locked the bedroom door. When he turned, she'd gotten to her feet and was rushing at him. He moved mostly out of her way and she collided with the bedroom door. Her left shoulder hit the doorframe, sending eruptions of pain across her body, bringing her to her knees. She connected with him too, but the strike only knocked him off balance. He was up quickly and ready for her next attack, which wouldn't come. She was on the ground, kind of in a heap. Holding her shoulder.

The tension eased for him. He noticed he was out of breath. His head pulsated. Blood streamed down his face and had stained his shirt. And his penis was hard again. He thought about trying to take her now, but he was afraid he'd lose the erection again. No, he had a better idea. That's what he did — think of better ideas. He'd put her to sleep again and then punish her. In the vilest ways he could think of. The Pen Pal stumbled to the bathroom cabinet to get a canister of ether.

"No!" he shouted, seeing the bottles of ether she'd poured down the drain.

Valerie leaned against the bedroom door. She laughed. "Looking for something?"

"You think I don't have more?"

Valerie kept laughing. "I don't care." She was tired of crying. And she'd realized by seeing her father on television that he wasn't giving up on finding her, so she couldn't give up on escaping, on killing this ugly, weak man. No matter what he did to her – awake or asleep.

It was the first time she'd gotten a good look at him. Aside from his ghoulish features, he looked young. Younger than she thought he would be.

He stepped toward her. She moved to attention, set her jaw, and readied for another fight. He stopped his advancement. Both of them now somewhat leery of the other.

"I can tear your clothes off you or you can take them off yourself. Either way is fine with me," he said.

"Then what?" she challenged him. "You and your limp dick going to do anything then?" She laughed. "Probably not, right?" She wanted to anger him. Maybe not so much that he'd find a way to rape her while she was awake – when she'd remember it – but she wanted him to come close, so she could try to kick him in the head. *Or his limp dick.*

Even though he had lost his erection, it wasn't the comment that infuriated him, it was the laugh. He charged at Valerie, who kicked out at him, trying to swipe his knee. She connected but not hard enough to break his knee. He fell to the ground though on top of her, so her plan partially worked. But she wasn't expecting that result, so she wasn't ready for it, for him to be so close – his breath smelled. She couldn't strike at him, couldn't get her arms from under him.

He recovered immediately from the fall with a great idea in order to subdue her. He grabbed her head and hair. Slammed her skull against the door. Not once but five times. Her eyes appeared to be rolling around their sockets when he stopped, and her body fell limp when she blacked out.

CHAPTER 25

Jack Hardy quickly began sweating outside his front door. The Florida climate clung to Jack's body, producing a layer of dampness all over him. The police officers stationed at the Hardy residence were asked to step aside and allow the reporters to approach.

They swarmed the father, shouted questions, which Jack ignored. He just stood there for a long time and built the strength to say what his anger demanded of him. Jack turned to find Marie, but he couldn't see her in the crowd of reporters, photojournalists. He called to her, and she slowly peered out the front door. Jack invited her to his side, asking the reporters to make way. They did, and Marie cautiously walked to her husband's side while camera flashes bounced off her ivory skin.

Past the reporters surrounding him and his wife, Jack saw his neighbors in their driveways and others looking through their windows. He didn't know what he was going to say when he came outside. How he'd start his statement. He saw the manicured lawns, the nice houses. He saw the shiny automobiles, boats on trailers parked in side yards, tire swings tied to large oak branches, and basketball hoops at the edge of various driveways. Then he knew what to say.

"Look at this neighborhood. Look at this quiet, normal city. I never thought what happened to my daughter could happen in a place like this. I apologize to my neighbors for causing the intrusion of you people into our quaint neighborhood."

Jack said nothing else for a very long time. It seemed like forever on live TV.

"I'd like to thank, first of all, the men and women who are working hard to find Valerie. Many of them have their own children, so they understand what my wife and I are going through and they're working tirelessly to find Valerie. Thank you."

Again, Jack stayed silent for a long time. Marie wondered if he was keeping his emotions in check or thinking of something to say, but Jack knew what he was doing. His eyes burned into every video camera present. His anger was apparent to every person watching throughout the city and, he hoped, across the country.

"If I am to ever get my hands on the man who's taken Valerie from me, there will be no army of men who can stop me from the pain I'd inflict upon him."

Jack's mind suddenly filled with forgotten details about Valerie. He recalled the outfit she wore the day the letters had arrived. How he had held her while she cried in his arms that night and all the nights directly after the initial threats. Her nightmares. Holding her hand. Kissing her goodnight. Checking on her every night of her life before he went to bed. Locking the front door. He even recollected the details surrounding the pictures on their hallway wall.

But the most prominent memory were the letters themselves and their wording. The reports read to him by the FBI and local police in Idaho. It all just popped right into his head, like he'd just escaped from a shell of darkness.

"There's an epidemic in our nation. Our children are preyed upon. Where we once allowed children to ride their bikes freely around cities and towns, we now limit them to boundaries identified by a parent's line of vision. We have leashes strapped to children's wrists. For their safety. I'd like to know what has happened in the heavens to allow our children to become such targets.

"I have spent a decade protecting my daughter, not from just one man that threatened her, but from all men who would potentially hurt her." Jack's bottom lip began to tremble. His face twisted. His eyes remained rage-filled, even as tears began to trickle out of them. "And I have failed. I've failed my daughter. And my wife."

The different news programs broadcast silence as Jack regained his composure; his eyes never changed, never stopped sending his message of anger to the man who took his daughter.

"And I apologize to both of them." Marie squeezed Jack's hand and leaned in close to him. "It's a father's job to protect a daughter. It's his duty." He could hear his heart beat in his ears. "I failed at my duty. I realize now that a father can never love his daughter enough, can never care for her enough, can never cherish and respect her enough."

Jack lost control of his emotions. He sobbed openly on television; shuddered even, as the cameras soaked up every emotion-filled body movement. "I should have done more. I saw it coming but didn't do anything. I should have done something to stop it from happening. Please don't hurt my baby. Don't hurt my daughter."

Three neighbors charged through the crowd of reporters and covered Marie and Jack with their arms. They led the couple into the house. The reporters followed, but the police officers at the front door stopped their advance.

With the front door closed, Jack could finally stop his act.

"Son of a bitch, that was great!" Jack shouted excitedly.

"What are you talking about?" Marie asked, wiping her eyes of tears.

Their rescuing neighbors watched Jack's mood change with shock. They stayed quiet, confused.

"No, baby." Jack gripped Marie by the shoulders and bent down to be face to face with her. "I remember. Everything. I need to call Chief Boudreaux."

CHAPTER 26

The files Special Agent Peter Tyler delivered from Washington, D.C. were spread across the conference room's eight-foot table. Gray meticulously flipped through them one by one. The Pen Pal was sophisticated enough, as Tyler had said, to try to throw off the police with the two differently styled letters, and he'd known how to ensure the letters would arrive on the same day at each of the girls' house. Plus, he'd stayed undetected for ten years. Why such a long gap between the second letter and the present day?

Parker still flipped through Valerie's journal notebooks. He stopped and rubbed his eyes. "What would you do?"

"If I were the Hardy family?" Gray set aside the file in his hands.

"Yeah."

"I don't know."

"I would have changed our names and moved somewhere like Costa Rica," Parker said.

"You'd never survive in Costa Rica."

"I'd never survive?"

"You're too big a person. They'd force you into hard labor. I'd come for a visit and find you coming down a mountain and carrying coffee beans on your back."

"Like a mule? That's nice."

Gray shrugged his shoulders like that was the only possible outcome for Parker.

"Come on," Parker said. "Really. What would you do?"

"I don't know." Gray didn't want to think about it. "It's something I'll never have to worry about."

A uniformed officer opened the door of the conference room. He seemed tight, tense. "Boudreaux wants both of you in his office now."

With Parker out the door first, Gray fumbled with keys to the conference room door.

"I'll lock it and bring you the keys, if you want," the officer offered.

"No, I got it," Gray said.

≈   ≈   ≈   ≈

Boudreaux's feet were on his desk as he leaned back in his executive chair. He had a pile of paperwork lying in his lap. His reading glasses rested on the tip of his nose, and as he watched television, he shook his head.

"Check this out," he told Gray and Parker when they entered. "It's on continual replay. He's just standing there, trying to think of what to say next."

Jack Hardy's face took up the whole TV screen. He was sweating pretty hard and looked cross. Jack spoke again, about children being prey. He went on to tell the world about how he failed his wife and daughter, that he failed at his duty as a father, and that he should have done more, should have seen all this coming. He sobbed and begged the man who took his daughter not to hurt her.

"That's a new approach for the family." Boudreaux scratched his head.

Parker sat on one of Boudreaux's couches. Gray remained standing and listened to the TV reporter reiterate what Jack Hardy had said, like the public didn't understand his words.

"The father must have read the first profile on the Pen Pal," Gray said. "He hit all the major points. He was trying to provoke him. Trying to get him to empathize. The Pen Pal had daddy issues. But Hardy is reversing the blame. He's accepting the blame. He's trying to draw him out."

"He took over his daughter's plans." Parker stood again.

"Maybe he's trying to get the Pen Pal to let Valerie go by admitting his flaws in his fatherly duties. Hardy's a smart guy."

Boudreaux's telephone rang, as he spoke. "You should go talk to him."

Parker made for the door. Gray was glued to the TV, watching the replay of Jack Hardy's speech.

Boudreaux hung up the receiver. "Head over to FDLE first. They've got some information for you off Valerie's computer."

CHAPTER 27

July 29 – 1:39 p.m.

Gray and Parker drove to the local Florida Department of Law Enforcement office, where Valerie's computer was being combed for evidence. Gray's driving was aggressive, in and out and back and forth across the southbound lanes of Florida Avenue.

"Why are you in a piss-poor mood?"

Aside from Gray's aggressive driving, he hadn't said much since Jack Hardy's press conference. Something about the story of failed parenting hit home with Gray, who cut in front of a Nissan SUV and accelerated around a Chrysler van, as they passed the arch at the Southgate Shopping Center.

"I'm just tired." He made an excuse.

Images from Valerie as a toddler jumped into his mind again. They interplayed with images from his past, and that interplay set fire to his mind. He cut in front of the Windstar and ran a yellow light at Edgewood.

"You're dismissing normal conversation. When you do that, something's usually up with you."

"Nothing's up, Jeff."

The drive for the next few minutes were silent.

Parker finally asked, "Have you talked to the department shrink lately?"

"I don't need to. You're clearly my shrink. So just file the report and let me know how I'm doing."

Parker laughed even though Gray wasn't joking. "So that's how it's going to be, huh?"

Just after Lake Miriam Drive, Gray pulled across oncoming traffic and stopped in the parking lot of the FDLE office. He jumped out of the car quickly and was inside the building before Parker closed his car door.

"Nice talk, buddy," Parker said.

≈　　　≈　　　≈　　　≈

George Nelson, the FDLE computer analyst, noticed the tension between Gray and Parker as he led the two detectives down a short hallway to his office. His office was a huge room with multiple desks. On top of each desk was, at least, one computer, some assembled, some not. Around the room pieces of computer cluttered the walkways. One desk in the far corner was bare, except for files of paperwork.

Nelson steered Gray and Parker to the desk that held Valerie's personal computer. He sat down, motioned for Parker to grab the only other chair in the room, and apologized to Gray for making him stand. Nelson pushed the monitor's power button, and his face quickly reflected the light from the computer's screensaver.

Nelson worked his way through the computer, windows popped up and disappeared as he worked.

"I haven't written up a formal report yet. Your chief said this was a very important piece of evidence in the case and he'd appreciate it if I could expedite the process. He said you'd need to know if I found something ASAP and wouldn't have time to wait on the report."

Nelson paused, made two clicks, and then started talking again.

"He seems like a cool guy. You like him?" Nelson asked and looked up at the detectives while he continued typing. "You guys aren't big talkers, are you?"

Gray finally broke. "Listen, no offense. This case is taking its toll, so could you just tell us, show us, or whatever you do. Could you just give us the information?"

"Right." Nelson looked back toward the monitor. "Here."

Nelson turned around in his chair to face them. "Briefly … You're vic liked chat rooms. She'd been in hundreds. Talked to all kinds of people. That I can find, she only revealed her special situation to one of them. I have the screenname he was using and am working on documentation to see if the online provider will supply his name. There's a lot of variables to that, mind you."

Nelson's shirt and pants were crisply starched, wrinkled at the elbows, knees, and waist. His shoes were perfect, almost pristine. He didn't see much action.

"Mainly, screennames in chat rooms are almost untraceable. Hopefully, we'll get lucky and that'll be the person's real screenname." Nelson noticed Gray looking down at the floor and leaned down into Gray's stare, "A screenname is someone's online identity. Sometimes it's — "

"I know what a screenname is."

"Good. Thought I lost you. Valerie called him David. I'll include that in my report." Nelson moved on. "One more thing, I think Valerie met someone online. Seems that way anyway."

Gray shot him a dirty look, shook his head, and tapped his watch.

Parker replied curtly, "Come on, Nelson. It's not like we got tons of time. Explain," Parker demanded.

"An online dating service. Valerie had an account. Someone paid to view her picture and profile and he contacted her. She replied. Judging by the contents of the e-mails, it looks like they arranged to meet."

"You know this guy's name?" Gray pulled a pen from his jacket and then retrieved his notepad from his back pocket.

"William Ford."

Nelson stood and made his way to his cleared desk. He opened a folder and read a little of it before answering them.

"He's from Newark, New Jersey. He gave her a whole line of crap about his identity. I don't know yet if any of it's true. But I don't think he's left the area."

"What?"

"He's been sending her emails ever since they met up. He wants to meet with her again before he leaves."

"When did they meet?" Gray asked.

"Online?"

"No, in person."

"The night before she was kidnapped."

CHAPTER 28

Via telephone, Parker filled in their lieutenant on what they'd found out from Nelson. The boss was going to pass the information on to Boudreaux, and they'd work together to get in touch with the online provider, using David's screenname to see what the company could provide about him. The boss and the chief would also get the ball rolling on warrants for William Ford's financial records to check for his billing address and hopefully a hotel charge from the night he and Valerie had their encounter.

The detectives were tasked to return to the Hardy residence. They used the drive to bounce around ideas, a ball Parker started rolling first. "Valerie's 18, right?"

"Right."

"You remember being that age?" Parker asked, receiving an annoyed look from his partner, the one he got when he couldn't figure out where Parker was coming from. "You were that age at one time, right?"

"What are you getting at?"

"Sex! Here's this girl, she's eighteen, never been out from under her parents' thumb. Means she probably never had a boyfriend. Here she is setting herself up in the paper to possibly get attacked or killed ... or she's thinking of killing herself," Parker said, listening to his words as they played around in his mind. "Now, if that was me, at 18, then I probably would want to find some chick to have sex with, you know, experience it before I die."

"And you're wondering if Valerie would think like a guy?"

"Crude and callous, but yeah. I mean, on the surface that's what it looks like … but it's not sitting with me right."

"Because she's not being led around by her dick?"

Parker shook his head. "While an obvious observation, that's a valid point."

"Her diary entries don't read like a sex-starved teen," Gray said. "She's too singularly driven for something like that,"

"I don't know if anyone is singularly driven." Parker's attention faded and he looked out the passenger window. When he turned back, he saw Gray deep in concentration. "What's up?"

"You think she's faking this whole thing?" Gray asked.

Parker shifted in his seat to face Gray directly. "Faking the kidnapping?"

"Maybe this William Ford is helping her. Remember the blood on the door of Valerie's car? Maybe it's his. Maybe she's shacked up with him right now across town somewhere."

Parker wanted to disagree but didn't. "Okay. That's a theory."

"Maybe instead of killing herself, like Edwards said she'd threatened, she decides to fake the whole thing. See if she can't force an outcome. Edwards said she wanted her case re-opened. What better way to do that than get kidnapped?"

Parker still wasn't convinced of the validity of either theory.

≈   ≈   ≈   ≈

Gray had to park more than eight houses away from the Hardy's residence because the road was nearly blocked by all the news vans. The press swarmed around Gray and Parker as they approached the house. Parker used his size to glide easily through them like a wedge. Gray wasn't so lucky. He trailed Parker by a few feet, and that distance rendered the wedge ineffective.

A bright flash blinded Gray momentarily. Upon regaining his vision and awareness, Michael Edwards jammed a tape recorder in his face and pounded Gray with questions about the case. The mass of press shifted, shoving Gray, whose mouth connected with Edwards's recorder. Pain flared across his face, which unlocked anger inside.

Gray pushed Edwards as hard as he could and yelled at him to get out of his face. The bearded, bookish journalist protested his assault, which made Gray go at him again. The cameras flashed video recorded the incident. Parker jumped to Edwards' rescue and pulled Gray away from the reporter and the cameras. Because of his size, Parker was easily able to drag Gray through the crowd of media personnel onto the Hardy's front step.

"What's wrong with you?" Parker demanded. "Every camera in the free world is out there, and they all recorded you assaulting Edwards. You think they won't run with it all day?"

Gray spun around, away from Parker, and came face to face with Jack and Marie Hardy. They looked exhausted. Worn down by stress and worry. Tattered even.

"I feel the same way about them, detective," Jack said. "Come inside."

The detectives sat down in the living room with Valerie's parents. Jack's comment put Gray at ease. And being inside the house allowed Gray to focus on the case and not Edwards or his sore tooth. When he calmed, he noticed Jack and Marie were anxious. Jack was almost beside himself with hope, and he wanted to get right to the point. Marie was more stand-offish, less hopeful, more afraid of what the detectives may tell her.

"What did you find?" Jack literally moved to the edge of his seat. Marie slid back into hers, sat on her hands.

"Have you heard of William Ford?" Gray asked.

"Who is he?" Jack answered.

"Valerie and he had a type of online relationship. She'd been communicating with him a long time."

"That damn computer," Jack said to himself. He looked at Marie, "I told you that thing was no good."

"Jack, please," she said, looking sheepish.

"No. To answer your question," Jack said, looking back to the detectives. "We've never heard of him."

Gray didn't like the way Jack spoke to Marie. "What about you, Mrs. Hardy?" Gray asked, thinking she could speak for herself, but there was something else about her demeanor that stuck with Gray.

"I haven't either."

Parker continued, "Did she ever mention anyone named David?"

"She met him online, too?" Jack asked.

Clearly he and Marie had different viewpoints about some things when it came to Valerie. It seemed that Marie Hardy was more understanding and compassionate, while Jack stuck to the rules.

"She did," Parker answered.

"Damn!" Jack was up and pacing the living room floor now. "She'd sit in her room for hours on that computer."

Marie said, "I always thought Valerie needed a connection to the outside world."

"Did these boys have something to do with Valerie's disappearance?" Jack requested.

"We don't know yet," Parker said.

"We're checking into it." Gray continued, "Tell me about earlier today and the speech on TV."

Marie looked away when the question was asked.

Jack hesitated then said, "Listen, I already got chastised by your chief. I don't need it from you two. But I'll tell you the same thing I told him. I have to do something to help my daughter. If you had kids, you'd understand."

Parker played the bad cop and sent a warning to Jack. "But if your actions impede our ability to find your daughter safely … " Parker let his voice trail off.

Jack said as he stood his ground. "Don't waste Valerie's time with empty threats towards me. I'm going to do what I need to do."

After a moment of tense silence, Gray returned focus on the topic at hand. "Valerie's plan was to get the Pen Pal to surface again after all these years, right?" He took the silence as agreement with his statement. "Is she capable of faking this whole thing?"

"What?" Marie gasped.

"Maybe she fakes the whole thing to get the Pen Pal to surface in some way. These guys typically get involved in the investigation. Maybe she thought we'd find him when he came to help find Valerie."

Marie replied quickly, "No. She wouldn't fake something like this."

Jack said dryly, "She's capable of it."

"Jack," Marie protested.

"What? Search yourself. You know she is. She's been obsessed about this guy for the last few years. And," his eyes bore into his wife's, "she's smart enough to think of a plan like that, but naïve enough to think it'd be that simple."

Parker asked, "If she was faking all this and needed a place to hide out, do you have any idea where she'd be?"

Jack and Marie both immediately began shaking their heads. "No. None."

Jack offered, "Check with that William Ford and the other guy. David, right?"

"That's being done now," Parker said. "What about killing herself?"

"No!" Marie shouted, offended but more frightened it might be true. She knew Valerie was often depressed with her living arrangements.

"I wouldn't think so either," Jack said, matter of fact tone.

"I keep thinking about all the locks on the doors in your house, the alarm system, which I suspect are connected to your windows," Gray said. "The evidence we've been able to find suggests that Valerie sneaks out of the house quite a bit."

"What?" Jack Hardy was furious. "There's no way. We never leave her alone. Either I'm with her or Marie is."

Gray was the first person to see Marie's face change.

"Mrs. Hardy?"

Then Jack saw it – guilt.

"Marie! You knew about that?" It was more an accusation than a question.

Marie burst. Tears came from her eyes. Her shoulders convulsed and her body bent. It looked like her body was pumping out her emotions.

"You knew?" Jack spoke louder and louder every time he repeated those two words. "You knew?"

Finally, Marie screamed back at her husband. "No. I suspected, but I didn't know. You don't understand her. She's eighteen. She's a woman now. She needs certain things, like autonomy."

"No, you knew." The accusation bit harder this time, more like it was a factual, judgmental statement. Then he continued, "And you allowed it by ignoring it. I can't believe this."

"All right, Mr. Hardy," Gray said, thinking the interaction between the husband and wife needed to calm down.

Tears continued to roll down Marie's face. "You know we couldn't keep her here forever. One day she was going to want a life."

"Where's her life now, Marie?" Jack exploded back at Marie. "Where's ours?"

Parker stood after Jack's explosion. Parker dwarfed everyone present. He usually did, and this time he used his physical presence and a deep, authoritative voice to control the situation. "Everyone needs to calm down."

Jack looked at him as if to say, "Don't tell me what to do." Then, seeing Parker's size and realizing he was right. Jack plopped down in a recliner.

Gray approached Marie. Sat next to her on the couch. "Mrs. Hardy, tell me about the night before Valerie was kidnapped."

Marie took a deep breath. "Valerie went to bed early. It was just a normal night. When she went to bed, I took a hot bath and read a book. That's it."

"Did you set the alarm?"

"I don't know."

"And where were you?" Parker asked the father.

Jack's voice was weak with disbelief. "I worked a double at the power plant."

Parker looked at Marie and shot her an unconvinced look. "Mrs. Hardy, you didn't know Valerie left the house that night?"

"What? No."

"Are you sure she didn't tell you she had a date and you felt sorry for her, you know, now that she's a woman?"

"A date?" Jack asked.

"Just because I sympathized with my daughter doesn't mean I would disregard her safety," Marie replied firmly.

"She snuck out that night, didn't she?" Jack asked.

"Looks that way, yes," Parker said.

"I didn't know about that, but I should've," Marie said, blaming herself.

CHAPTER 29

William Ford's hotel room was nothing to be excited about, unlike the one the night before. Based on his credit card history Boudreaux was able to obtain, Ford booked a luxury suite at the best hotel in town, rented a limo, and wooed Valerie with a fancy dinner. Today, he shared a hotel room with cockroaches, dust, and grime.

Gray had hoped to find Valerie in the small room. If Valerie had faked her kidnapping, she might have been hiding here with William Ford. But, that wasn't the case.

"I'm glad you had more class last night to take that girl to a nice hotel instead of this shithole."

"What are you talking about?" Ford asked. The curly-haired 21-year-old shook with nervousness.

"What? You don't know what a shithole is?"

"I know what a shithole is. I don't know why you're here." Ford wiped his sweating hands on his white tank-top and then stuffed them into his pockets.

"William," Parker said, "we know what you did Sunday night." Parker sat on the bed and patted the spot next to him. "Sit down. Here."

"Your little vacation's over, dude." Gray's anger prominent in his voice. "You can't come down to Florida, into my town, rape an under aged girl, and get away with it. Add on the whole Internet connection and that you traveled down here, that makes it so much worse for you." Gray grabbed him by the arm. "Come on, get up. Hands against the wall."

As Gray led him to the wall, Ford's mind spun.

"Rape? I didn't. Wait. What? No." The whole thing overwhelmed Ford.

"Hold on. Hold on," Parker said. He took Ford by the arm and led him away from Gray. "She told us you raped her. You didn't?"

"Oh, come on, you bleeding heart," Gray protested. "They always say they didn't do it. Let's take him in and go get something to eat."

Ford emphatically pleaded his case. "But I didn't. Why would I rent a limo, if all I wanted was to rape her?"

"See? That makes total sense. Let him go," Parker said to Gray. Once Ford was free of Gray's grip, Parker said, "You were just trying to impress her. You wanted your date to be special," Parker said.

"She told us all that," Gray said. "And she said when you didn't get what you wanted from her, you took it. Forcefully."

"No, no, no. She's lying." Ford didn't know what else to say.

"Of course she is," Gray said, rolling his eyes. "Come on, partner. Let's just take him in."

"No, she is. We didn't even have sex. Aren't there tests you can do to prove that?"

"Hold on a second," Parker said. "Then tell us what happened. Tell us your side of the story. If she filed a false report, then we can put all this back on her."

Ford nodded his head, then sheepishly started his story.

He and Valerie had been communicating over the Internet for months. They had slowly built their relationship. They'd exchanged pictures, talked of their dreams, places they always wanted to visit, the problems they had with their parents, and stuff like that.

"Normal stuff."

Recently, Valerie suggested they meet. Ford liked what he saw in the picture and decided to drive down and meet her. They met that night for dinner. He showed up in a limousine, took her to the best restaurant in town, and then they'd watched a movie in the fancy hotel room, and they hung out. He thought they would have sex, but they didn't. Then around two a.m. she went home. He tried to email her a few times since the encounter, but she hadn't replied.

"Where were places she wanted to visit?" asked Gray.

"What?" Ford asked, unsure what that had to do with anything. "Germany, Italy. Normal places people want to go."

"Nothing around here?" Parker asked.

"No," Ford said, confused.

"You watch the news, kid?" Gray asked.

"The TV's busted. Can't watch anything."

"William," Parker said, "we think Valerie's been abducted. You were one of that last people to see her."

"What?" He sounded concerned. For her, not for himself. He sat on the bed, weary by the news. "So she didn't say I raped her?"

"No, she didn't." Gray turned off the bad cop routine and sat in a weak-legged chair across from the bed. Stared intently at Ford as he spoke. "Tell us more about the things Valerie told you."

It took a minute, but Ford pulled himself together after the change in his circumstances. Relief overcame him, and he was happy to tell them what they wanted to know. "She wished she had more time to take pictures." He thought more about it. There just wasn't much to tell. "Really, we just talked about normal shit."

Parker asked, "You can't think of anything that might help us?"

Gray led Ford. "Right, maybe she told you where her favorite place was. You know, somewhere she liked to go to by herself."

Ford just shook his head. "No, nothing like that. I will tell you," he paused, as if all he and Valerie's conversations were replaying inside his head, "I tried to make arrangements for another meet up, but she said she didn't want to talk about the future. She said she didn't know what the future held. She said we'd take it as it came. Then I never heard from her."

CHAPTER 30

July 29 – 5:59 p.m.

The calls crime scene technician Maddy James's made to Parker went unanswered. And calling Gray didn't appeal to her at all. *The guy's rude.* Maddy knew the information she had in front of her was important to their case. *Is it so important I can't wait for Parker to call me back?* She decided she could wait and then moved on to different tasks. Soon though she felt guilty, like she was letting down the victim and the family by waiting. She tried Parker again, hoping he'd answer, but he was unavailable once m ore.

"Dammit."

Maddy contorted her face in unease before dialing Gray's number.

"Gray."

Of course he'd answer. "Detective Gray, it's Maddy James … in the lab."

"Okay."

What an asshole. "I have some information on the Hardy case I thought you and Detective Parker would be interested in."

After a short wait, Gray asked, "You want to give it to me?" His lack of sleep over the last 33 hours was starting to show.

"I thought you and Parker would want to come down here and check it out."

"Right. That's exactly what we want. Why just file it in the computer system, when you can have us come down to the lab?" His tone dripped with sarcasm.

≈   ≈   ≈   ≈

In the elevator, Parker noticed Gray's mood had changed again. Earlier at the FDLE office, Gray acted agitated. Now he seemed more pensive.

"You look tired," Parker said, hoping to draw out of Gray whatever was bothering him.

Gray leaned against the wall. "I really thought she'd be with William Ford."

Surprised Gray opened up so easily, Parker said, "I know you did."

"I don't think she faked it."

"I agree."

"It seems like we're back at zero."

"That's just you being disappointed. The dump of her cell phone came in."

Gray pushed off the wall, stood on his own, a little more excited than before. "And?"

"There are nine different phone numbers in the call log. Most of them outgoing."

Gray thought about that, then said, "Here's this girl. The parents' assumption is she has no friends, no contacts outside of them, but we already know that's not the case." He counted on his fingers. "Edwards. Ford. I'm not surprised there are more."

"Exactly. Those numbers are on there too. Boudreaux asked Gorski and Burrell to work on identifying the others." Gorski and Burrell were detective peers of Gray and Parker. Boudreaux was using them to do investigative leg work, while Gray and Parker were chasing down other leads.

The elevator doors parted, and Gray and Parker exited between people waiting to board. Parker pulled the lab door open and held it for Gray.

They weaved through the lab, around workstations and technicians, looking completely out of place. Their own colored clothing a disparity against the technicians' white lab coats. Physically they seemed uncomfortable, not wanting to touch anything, get in the way of work being performed. Plus, the low temperature in the lab gave them the chills.

"That didn't take long," Maddy told the detectives, though she was really just speaking to Parker.

"I heard you wanted to see me, so I rushed down here," Parker playfully replied.

Maddy placed her hands behind her back, opening herself up to him, and giggled at his comment.

Gray pushed the conversation along, again annoyed at their flirtatious relationship. "What did you find, Maddy?" His annoyance clearly in his tone.

"Actually, I have quite a bit to offer."

Gray wondered if that was an innuendo meant for Parker.

"We'll start with the tire casts," she continued.

She led them to a worktable. Her colleague stepped aside while Maddy provided the results of their tests.

"One of the casts I took from the crime scene gave us a return."

She pulled the mold across the table and showed it to the detectives. The tread was plainly visible, like she took the mold directly from the tire.

"I narrowed the search down to a couple of car models." She handed the folder to Parker. "Here's the report."

He looked through it then handed it to Gray. "Narrowed it down, I'd say," Parker complimented the technician as Gray took the folder and skimmed through it.

"Initially, it seemed like it could be one of 15 or so. I compared the other tire molds from the scene and was able to find the rear tire width. Compare that to the tire and all the possible cars I came up with a Chevy Nova."

"What year?" Gray asked.

"It says right here," Maddy stepped closer to Gray than she wanted and pointed to the information in the report. She relished being able to point out that he overlooked the information.

"I see it." He read. "Late sixties."

"I'd stick with 66, 67, 68, or 69, personally," she added in an attempt to be helpful.

"So ... late sixties?" Gray replied, purposely demeaning her.

"I mean," she tried to ignore him, "I wouldn't be looking for anything before 1966. The Nova didn't cross over from a standard car to more of a muscle car until then. Greater tire width was needed at that point. And, since this case is time sensitive, I was helping you do your job. So, you're welcome."

"Thanks." Gray said sarcastically then closed the folder. "Late sixties. Got it."

Such an ass. "Also, I scraped enough paint from Valerie's car that I could tell the Nova's color is dark blue. When you compare the samples to the paint codes for the car, the color is called Danube blue."

"That does help." Parker overcompensated for Gray's rudeness.

"Next," Maddy said, moving to another table. "Valerie's gun. It's been fired quite a bit. Probably never been cleaned. But it hasn't been used recently."

"Good stuff. What's next?"

Parker elbowed Gray and gave a look that said, "Lighten up."

Maddy appreciated Parker sticking up for her by elbowing Gray, but she knew what to expect. She tried not to let it bother her, but sometimes he won and managed to irritate her. She wasn't going to let him win today. She glided down the length of the table and on to her next topic.

"The crowbar is common. No need to think tracking its retailed location will help in the investigation. Plus, the store where it was bought is probably closed. This thing is old. There's a large amount of rust on it. Maybe even came with the car. No prints."

"Perfect," Gray stated.

Maddy stopped leading them to tables. The faster she gave them the rest of the information, the faster Gray and his attitude would leave her lab.

"The substance on the rag you found at the scene was ether. Knocked her right out. Well, kind of. You have to hold it on there for a few minutes. Not fast acting, but it is effective. Though, if Valerie's adrenaline was kicking and she was respiring quickly, it'll probably kick in faster."

Parker looked at Gray and said, "That's how he got her to his car."

"Anything else?" Gray asked.

Maddy shook her head. "Nothing now. I should have the results back from the blood found on her car door soon."

"Sooner the better," Gray said on his way out of the lab.

When the door clicked behind Gray, Maddy stared at Parker, speechless. Her face asked, "What the fuck?"

Parker chuckled. "I'm sorry he's," he thought of the right word, "abrasive."

"Is it me?" she asked.

"Probably." Parker smiled ruefully.

She checked her watch. "It's been a long day. You want to grab something to eat after work?"

"Just ate. Besides, someone has to watch Gray to make sure he doesn't piss anyone else off."

"That shirt's a good color for you," she said, ignoring his rejection and wisecrack about Gray.

"Thanks. I'll talk to you later. Let us know about that blood."

"You'll be the first call." Then as Parker left the lab to catch up with Gray, she said to herself, "Because I won't call Gray again."

Parker caught up to Gray, who was waiting for him at the elevator.

"You like it, don't you?" Parker asked him.

"Like what?"

"Fucking with people? You know she's intimidated by you, and you like it. That's why you turn it on around her and act like a bigger jerk than usual."

The elevator doors opened. Parker followed Gray inside. Gray pushed the button for the second floor and the doors quickly closed.

"I'm trying to lead by example. You should adopt more of my attitude around her."

"She asked me out again," he said.

"You like it, don't you?" Gray asked, turning the tables on Parker.

"What? Her asking me out, no? She doesn't get that I'm married. Can't a man and woman just be friends?"

"Maybe you should stop flirting with her."

"We're not talking about me right now."

"I see how it is. We only talk about what a shit I am."

The doors parted and Parker followed Gray down the hall toward the conference room.

"We *were* talking about you. You should be nicer to people."

"Why? So people will think I'm approachable? That'll just lead them to asking me questions. Why don't you sleep at home? Why do you drive your car all night long? Are those the same clothes you wore yesterday?"

He opened the conference room door with a key and then went inside.

"I don't mind when you ask. But it's no one's business."

Parker's cell phone rang. He waited to answer it and instead said, "I have asked you that stuff a hundred times. You haven't once given me an answer."

"I know." Gray sat down at the table.

Parker accepted Gray's response then connected to the incoming call. Meanwhile Gray flipped through the file Maddy James just provided them. Parker ended the call.

Parker said, "Patrol found Valerie's wallet. Let's go."

CHAPTER 31

Lakeland is approximately 11 miles long north-to-south, and it can take 45 minutes to get from one end to the other. Gray and Parker were half the distance from where the wallet was found. The drive acted as a dark reminder of the grave circumstances of the case. Everything they did had to be vital to the case, had to amount to something, if they were to find Valerie before the Pen Pal's third letter on the third day arrived at the Hardy's home. Gray drove as fast as he could through the thick traffic, but it didn't seem fast enough.

Parker sat hunched over in the too-straight passenger seat and rubbed his forehead, overwhelmed with worrisome thought. Gray knew what he was thinking because he was thinking it, too. Where the wallet had been found – a truck stop in the northwest corner of the city limits – was a considerable distance from the crime scene, as well as being only a mile or two away from the interstate. Did Valerie somehow drop it as a clue? She's smart enough to do so. Did the Pen Pal drop it there as a distraction? He was prone to trying to distract law enforcement. Or, was the wallet dropped accidentally? But most importantly, what would the wallet tell them?

The truck stop was busy. Rigs pulled in and out of the place every few minutes. Gray counted 13 trucks parked there when they got out of the car and approached the restaurant. They could see men and women inside eating, drinking, resting, reading, watching TV, or dozing.

Could the Pen Pal be a trucker? Special Agent Tyler said that the Pen Pal was someone who traveled. If that was the case, then the Pen Pal could be in another state already.

The uniformed officer, Marcus Renfroe, a crop-topped gray-haired officer, leaned against his car with a man whose clothes were tattered and dirty, whose hygiene left something to be desired. He needed a shower.

The wallet, a credit card sized coin purse, was set on the hood of Renfroe's cruiser. The homeless man eyed the wallet, like it was gold.

"How many people touched it?" Parker pulled rubber gloves over his big hands.

The uniformed officer spoke with what sounded like a lisp. "Since I found it, no one. Before that, you'll have to ask, old Freddie, here."

"Freddie, where'd you get the wallet?" Gray asked.

Parker unzipped the wallet and examined the contents. He placed each item, after studying it, into a separate plastic bag.

"That's mine," Freddie protested and lurched toward the coin purse. Renfroe grabbed Freddie and held him.

"No, it's not, Freddie," Gray barked at him. "Now … where did you find the wallet?"

"That's my wallet." Freddie looked hypnotized by the coin purse.

Renfroe was familiar with Freddie. "Just tell him, Freddie, then we'll go inside and have something to eat."

"My wallet," Freddie repeated to Renfroe.

"Christ, Freddie," Gray exploded. He tore into his own wallet and handed Freddie a ten-dollar bill. "You ready to talk to me?"

Freddie eyed Gray's wallet. "That's a nice wallet."

"He doesn't care about the money, detective," Renfroe said.

When Gray was a patrolman, there were always homeless men coming and going, creating nuisance situations. The stereotype that they were all schizophrenics wasn't true. Some were put together people who the world simply overpowered. He remembered only a specific few now, and Freddie reminded him of them.

Gray put his wallet and money away. Then he stealthily dipped his hand into Parker's back pocket and pulled out his wallet.

"What are you doing?" Parker objected.

"He's helping us."

"I know, but what are you doing?" Parker had his hands occupied, going through Valerie's wallet and protecting the content, so he couldn't fight back.

Gray emptied the contents of Parker's wallet, pushing them into Parker's front pocket.

"Gray?" Parker protested.

Leaving some money in the wallet, showing that to Freddie, Gray held it out in front of him.

Excited, Freddie finally made eye contact with Gray, who asked again, "You want this? I'll give it to you if you tell me where you got that wallet?"

"Wait. What?" Parker said.

Freddie pointed toward Parker's wallet. "That one?"

"Yes, Freddie," Renfroe confirmed, amused by the interplay between the detectives.

Freddie pointed across the busy street.

Gray followed the man's directions and asked, "At the gas station? That one with the red sign?"

Freddie nodded his head and held out his hand expectantly.

Across the busy boulevard, a brightly-decorated gas station and convenience store buzzed with activity. The fluorescent lights flickered to life to fight the pending night as the sun moved toward the horizon.

"Who dropped it?"

Freddie shook his head. He didn't know.

"Help me out Freddie. Don't make me put this wallet back in this guy's pocket. Tell me what happened when you found the wallet."

"I kept it." Freddie's timorous but distant voice cracked when he spoke.

Gray laughed at himself. *Ask a dumb question, get a dumb answer.* He made sure his next questions were concise and simple.

It took Freddie a few minutes to muster up the words, but he finally did. He told Gray and Parker he found the coin purse late the night before after a man stopped to get gas. A white man.

Gray asked, "What kind of car was it?"

Freddie shook his head, "Green."

"How many doors did the car have?"

"One," Freddie said.

"One door. Green. That totally helps," Parker snapped.

Renfroe interrupted for the first time. "Wait a minute. Freddie, where were you standing?"

Freddie pointed at the dumpster at the right hand side of the gas station.

"So, from there, you saw one door."

"Yes."

The officer turned to Gray and Parker, "It was a two-door car. He said he saw one door." He turned and pointed to where Freddie had been standing the night before. "From there."

Parker said, "I got it." He was grumpy now about losing his wallet to Freddie.

Gray held out Parker's wallet to Freddie, who eyed it hungrily then snatched it from Gray's hand.

"Thank you for your help, Freddie," Gray said. Then to Renfroe, "Go get him something to eat please." Gray patted Freddie's back.

"Thank you," Freddie said over his shoulder to Gray.

Parker finished going through Valerie's coin purse and sealed its contents in individual plastic evidence bags.

"What am I going to do for a wallet now?" Parker asked, still protesting.

"Don't be such a victim," Gray said.

"And how much money did you give him? Karen keeps me on a budget."

Gray ignored Parker's question. "The wallet was found around one a.m."

Parker filled in the blank. "That's only a few hours after Valerie disappeared."

"And the green car color ... under those," Gray pointed across the street at the gas station, "huge neon lights."

Parker finished his thought thinking of the identified paint color of the Nova involved in Valerie's abduction. "Blue might look green under those lights."

"Exactly."

"Look at this," Parker said. "Valerie had a couple of credit cards, a library card, some book club cards, and this." Parker held up a piece of paper with a telephone number written on it.

Gray pulled Parker's cell phone from Parker's shirt pocket.

"And now my phone? Who are you giving that to?"

He dialed the number and waited through for ringing, but he only heard a message indicating the number had been disconnected.

"No good," Gray said, slipping Parker's phone into his own pants pocket.

"Give me back my phone," Parker demanded jokingly.

"Finish up with the evidence, will you?"

Gray and Parker turned to leave and saw Michael Edwards staring them in the face. "Hey guys," he said, like they were old friends.

Gray spoke up first. "What are you doing here?"

"My job. What did you find? Something on Valerie?"

"You don't seem as shook up today as you did last night." Gray charged passed him and drove his shoulder into Edwards' chest. "Excuse me." Gray apologized for bumping into him.

Edwards was throttled backwards. "That was a mistake. I'm going to file a complaint."

Parker leaned threateningly in toward Edwards' face. "While you're filing a complaint against him," Parker shoved Edwards in the chest, "file one on me, too."

Edwards almost fell to the ground but was able to keep his feet under him. Parker hadn't pushed too hard. If he had wanted to, he could've sent Edwards flying across the truck stop diner's parking lot. "You did that in front of a restaurant full of people. I think I will file a complaint. I have plenty of witnesses."

Parker said, heading toward the cruiser, "Those truckers don't give a shit about you."

"Be careful," Gray called out before getting into the car with Parker, "if they get to know you, they may hit you, too."

Gray slammed the car door. "I hate that guy."

Parker handed Gray the evidence bags and snatched a photograph of Valerie from the file on the dashboard. "I'm taking this inside and showing the staff. See if they saw her." He held out his hand. "And give me my damn phone."

"Look at my hands." Gray held out his hands, which trembled with anger.

CHAPTER 32

Jefferson City, Missouri
July 29 – 6:10 p.m. Central Time

Samuel Hubbard punched keys on the keyboard in front of him. He'd learned to type between the ages of 20 and 26 when he worked with a traveling evangelist named Reverend Willie Hindman.

That seemed like a long time ago.

Hubbard had lived many different lives in his short 34 years of life. He was currently living the quiet life. A stark contrast to his childhood.

His cubicle had no personal effects. Just plants. A stacked flowerpot planter contained numerous well-watered, vibrant geraniums with blooming purple flowers. His co-workers thought he was strange, so they didn't try to talk to him much, which was good because he didn't' want to talk to them anyway. Hubbard had learned over the years that most people weren't worth his time. That's why working for a closed captioning company was perfect for him. No people to interact with. All he had to do was show up for work, type well, and everything in his world would be fine.

On the glowing console in front of him, Hubbard watched the lead-in to a special report news briefing. He quickly typed in the words MUSIC PLAYS in brackets. His hands stayed ready. The perfect-looking female news anchor began speaking and Hubbard began typing. The words flowed out of her, into him, through his hands, and back onto the screen. He wasn't even listening to what the anchor was reporting, just the individual words.

The report switched from the anchor to a live press conference. Again, the words were important, singly, not collectively. He watched the screen for misspellings. He competed against himself when typing. He always strived for fewer typing mistakes than the day before. For a week straight he had no mistakes.

The inherently strong man on the screen seemed weaker in his circumstance. The man cleared his throat, which began the press conference. The media present quieted down. Then he spoke to the world.

"Good evening. Thank you for coming and watching. I'm announcing a $750,000 reward for specific, verified information leading to the return of my daughter, Valerie Hardy, or for the capture of the man the media calls the Pen Pal."

Hubbard's fingers froze. His eyes slowly cast from his keyboard to the glowing console just above his eye line. The man on the screen continued, "I am also offering $50,000 to any person who puts me alone in a room with this man. I don't care about the legal implications of this separate reward. What I care about is getting my daughter back and making sure the man responsible pays dearly for what he's put her through. Please continue circulating Valerie's picture. She's a smart, funny, beautiful woman despite the hellish childhood she's endured because of the threats made by this man, stupidly identified as the Pen Pal."

Hubbard sat stunned frozen. The female news anchor returned to the screen when Jack Hardy finished his speech. She moved on to extended coverage of story while Valerie's photograph displayed at the screen's bottom corner. Although the female anchor continued to talk, her voice ceased to register in Hubbard's mind. As he watched the screen became grainy, replaying video footage from ten years ago after the letters first arrived at the girls' homes.

"Valerie Hardy, a free-spirited eight-year-old girl, has been threatened by two letters written by a mysterious man. Cruel and horrific? Yes."

Not cruel, not horrific. Protective is more like it.

"But what's more horrific is four other girls received the same letter today, and their residences are spread across the continental United States. At this hour, we have little to go on, as all the families have only been aware of the threats since they received their mail just hours ago."

Hubbard scrolled up the screen of text he'd typed. All the way to the beginning of the special report, when he was only listening for words, not substance. There, he found what he was looking for: the reason the images from the past were replaying on the console in front of him, the reason his plan was unraveling.

Valerie Hardy had been kidnapped.

Fates of the other four girls unknown.

PART II

CHRIS WENDEL

CHAPTER 33

Lakeland, Florida
July 29 – 7:20 p.m.

After Gray and Parker pulled out into traffic from the truck stop parking lot, Gray made a U-turn and veered into the gas station's entryway. Two cars drove off, two more took their place in the filling lanes, while one waited to get next position at the gas pump. Just like the truck stop, so many people come and go at this gas station that the Pen Pal could have been there with Valerie in the car and no one would have ever noticed.

Parker asked, "Do you always use the gas station closest to your home?"

"I drive all over, so, no, I don't."

"I do. I think most people do." Parker said, thinking about the situation. "Wouldn't you have gassed up before you kidnapped her?"

"That doesn't make sense, does it? All this time to plan, and he forgets to gas up?" Gray shook his head, confused.

"And he leaves a ton of evidence at the crime scene – the blood, the ether, the tire jack – when ten years ago he didn't leave so much as saliva on the envelope?"

"And now Valerie's wallet is found on the ground?"

"Exactly!"

"We're not dealing with the Pen Pal, are we?" Gray asked.

"And she didn't fake this," Parker said.

"Someone else has her."

≈   ≈   ≈   ≈

Inside the convenience store, the fluorescent lights gave the store more of a clinical feel than a natural setting. Outside, nightfall approached, and as it did, news commentators would say Valerie's time may be running out. The longer the investigation took, the higher the likelihood she'd be lost forever. However, optimists would cite the Elizabeth Smart case, where it took nine months to find her ... still alive.

The clerk at the register, crowded by displays of cigarette lighters, candy bars, Florida lottery signs, and of course the typical "Help the Children" collection pot, didn't recall specifically seeing a green or blue late sixties Nova. And, how could he? The clerk, an immigrant from Vietnam who barely spoke English, saw hundreds of cars every day. He called to his cousin and coworker, Vu, who was better with the language. Vu told Gray and Parker both he and his cousin were working last night. Vu did not recall such a car either.

"Many people pay credit," he said, referring to the pay-at-the-pump capability. "We never see them."

"That's a good point," Parker said to Gray.

"We'd like to get a copy of the video surveillance from the last two days."

Vu explained Gray and Parker's interest in the surveillance video to the clerk, who apparently was the owner and named Tran. The two men spoke back and forth in their native language for nearly five minutes before Tran agreed to hand over the tape. Vu led Gray and Parker to a little office in the back of the store. The room was hot, small, and smelled like wet cardboard boxes. Vu didn't seem to notice the odor. He pulled the wooden chair from under the desk and sat. Vu shuffled stacks of paper on the desk and uncovered a video recorder.

"Here it is. I'll make you a DVD."

Parker said, "Thanks."

"Will we be eligible for the reward?" Vu asked.

"What reward?" Parker asked.

"From the TV," Vu explained.

He turned on the TV in the office, and the news anchor was recapping a news conference given outside the Hardy house moments before. Then they replayed the highlights, which included a replay of Jack Hardy offering a $750,000 reward.

After they listened, Parker told him, "We'll see. I don't know anything about it."

"That'll muddy the water," Gray said.

CHAPTER 34

Jefferson City, Missouri
July 29 – 6:23 p.m. Central Time

When the female news anchor finally did move onto her next story, Samuel Hubbard leaned back in his chair. He felt lifeless, thought his body had lost all its form, like he was slowly seeping down into a puddle of liquid.

Hubbard's supervisor barged into the cubicle. "Why aren't you typing?"

He looked back to the screen where the cursor blinked waiting for Hubbard's next entry. Hubbard's temper, which had been dormant for so long, burst to life. He grabbed the keyboard, ripped it from its port, and slammed it into the console monitor. The LCD screen flashed a rainbow of colors and fell from the console.

Hubbard gave a guttural scream as he thrust the keyboard at his boss, who covered his face with his arms just before the keyboard struck him. He fell back, hit the cubicle wall, and landed on the floor. Hubbard kicked him repeatedly, not wanting to stop. The outburst felt so good. *It's been so long.*

Once he did stop, Hubbard scanned his workspace in a rage. Co-workers gathered but none attempted to stop him. He growled at them, warning them to stay away, then grabbed his beloved Boston fern and slammed it down on top of his boss's head. He gave a horrendous scream before he ran out of his cubicle and barreled through a crowd of workers who'd left their monitor screens to investigate the commotion.

≈   ≈   ≈   ≈

Hubbard made it onto the street and ran as fast as his legs would carry him with no particular destination in mind. Nothing made sense. His vision blurred, making the clouds look like they were melting and the sky appear to spin above him. His galloping stride was a laborious effort, like he was running in 4 feet of water instead of on concrete sidewalks.

He stopped at the corner as cars sped through the busy intersection. A few droplets of rain fell around him then ceased. Hubbard waited for a break in traffic and then sprinted across the street. He kept going as fast as he could for as long as he could. Droplets began again then turned into a light drizzle, and two minutes later Hubbard's clothes stuck to his skin.

Running didn't make the memories or the questions stop traversing Hubbard's mind. Everything good and bad. Why had all this happened? How? Where was Valerie's father to let this happen? Would Amanda, Melinda, Maria, and Tiesha now somehow be targets? Would the media find them? Would their secure lives now be threatened?

What would Reverend Hindman think of him now?

CHAPTER 35

Lakeland, Florida

At police headquarters, Gray and Parker found Maddy James at her desk. All the lights in the laboratory were off, except for her desk lamp. She was taking advantage of the quiet and studying the contents of a file, making notes. She looked up at the approaching, worn out detectives and smiled when she made eye contact with Parker.

"You two look like hell," she told them.

"We've been out busting our asses to find more evidence." Parker paused before continuing. "Just to come back and see you." He placed a brown paper sack on Maddy's desk.

"Who said you need an excuse?" she replied.

Gray shot Parker a confused look. Their flirting was obvious. *Obviously gross*, Gray thought. *And not even good flirting. It's like middle school type flirting.* Gray was sure it was innocent on Parker's part, but it didn't fit with how much he loved his wife, Karen.

"Do you have anything new for us?" Gray asked, hoping to move beyond the flirtatious conversation.

Maddy lost the smile quickly when Gray spoke. "Just that the blood in the car didn't belong to the victim."

"She has a name," Gray said. "Did you run it through the databases?" Gray asked.

She turned to Parker and gave him the report, ignoring Gray. *He can be such an ass sometimes.* "We ran it through the database. No match on file anywhere."

Gray nodded and turned to leave the lab.

"What's in this bag?" Maddy asked, shaking her head behind Gray's back. She opened the paper sack on her desk.

"Valerie Hardy's wallet. Gotta go." Parker smiled before catching up with Gray.

≈   ≈   ≈   ≈

Gray and Parker knocked and then entered the chief's office. Boudreaux sat on the corner of his desk, speaking to someone. A photographer snapped an occasional photo of the police chief. The conversation stopped when Gray and Parker entered.

"Look who's here," Boudreaux said and raised his arm to welcome the detectives. He seemed uncharacteristically cordial.

The person Boudreaux was speaking with turned in the chair and smiled at Gray and Parker. *Michael Edwards.*

"Gentlemen, sit." Boudreaux said it like an invitation, but it was a command. "I was just telling Mr. Edwards what we'd all discussed earlier."

Gray and Parker's faces blanked.

"Our commitment to finding the person responsible for abducting Valerie Hardy. In fact, Becker, in a moment maybe you can elaborate more for us, but first I was telling Mr. Edwards about your personal commitment to this case."

Gray tightened his brow. Boudreaux had never called him by his first name. Plus, he had no idea what Boudreaux was talking about.

"Why don't you go ahead, chief."

"You see, Mr. Edwards, due to promotions, retirements, and transfers, Detective Gray is one of only a small percentage of LPD resources that was actually with us ten years ago when the Pen Pal sent those letters to the five girls. He, for motivation he still hasn't explained, became extremely interested in the case and even requested to be sent to one of those five cities to help with the investigation.

"Now present day situation with Valerie," Boudreaux continued, walking around his desk to sit in his chair, "I'm sure you can understand that he's been on edge about this whole thing. I mean, he got what he wanted, right? And, now he's faced with the task of, not just finding the man responsible for this, but for getting the girl back alive. I'm sure, after ten years, this case has festered inside him a bit, and right now there just aren't enough hours in the day for him."

Edwards smugly jotted it all down, ate it like chum.

Parker would look at Gray differently if Boudreaux's statement were true. It may be. It'd be like Gray to not level with him, but Parker smelled a lie.

"So Detective Gray feels like it's him versus the letter writer?" Edwards asked.

Boudreaux replied, "Ask him yourself."

"That's right." Gray knew to go along with whatever Boudreaux had going.

The camera snapped in Gray's eyes. The photographer got two or three good headshots of Gray.

"It's personal," Edwards uttered as he made a few final scratches in his notepad.

When Edwards finished, he stood up and shook Boudreaux's hand and thanked him. Then he shook hands with Gray and Parker. He told

Gray that he'd be in touch and thanked him again. Edwards and the photographer departed the office.

As soon as the door closed, Boudreaux lost the friendly tone he used with the reporter. "What the fuck are you two doing out there? I've gotten numerous calls on you two today for assaulting reporters. How many more will I get before I go home?"

He didn't expect them to answer, and they weren't going to.

"We can't afford to have Michael Edwards sue the department. Not now. So ... Edwards gets the exclusive on everything, you got it? He'll be riding with you if and when we can make a bust on this case. Plus, he's doing an exclusive on you, Gray."

"He's doing what?" Gray objected.

"Agent Tyler faxed us his analysis of the crime scene and compared it to his profile. You'll find it interesting. He made recommendations for us. One of those recommendations was to use the media and pit one of us against this Pen Pal guy. Since you pissed me off today, I decided that person should be you.

"That's where my deal with Edwards comes in. He gets full access, and we don't get sued or crucified in the paper because of your belligerent behavior toward him and other reporters. Tomorrow, in the newspapers across America, there's going to be an article about you and this case. I worked with Agent Tyler on the profile to be portrayed of you, and I supplied Edwards with it."

Shock overtook Gray to the point of numbness.

"I don't expect this to distract you from the case because, after all, the profile Edwards has isn't really you, so don't get all bitchy on me about this. It's the best road we can take to draw out the Pen Pal."

"That asshole has it in for me," Gray protested. "He's going to dig into my past and find real things to include in your little bio. He'll search through my professional records and question every action I made as a police officer. He won't just stick to the profile you gave him."

"Then if he does that, the deal's off." Boudreaux compromised even though he didn't want to, but he knew what point Gray was really trying to get across. He remembered. *How many years has it been?* Gray hadn't been the same since.

"You didn't even ask me." Gray's voice was low and soft. His lip trembled, anger coursing feverishly through his veins, quickly replacing cool shock with heated rage.

"Wasn't your decision." Boudreaux shifted in his chair.

Parker knew Gray was losing this battle, so he piped in and changed the subject.

"So we've had an interesting evening. We have a wallet that looks like it belongs to Valerie Hardy."

"Where'd you get that?"

Parker kept talking. Gray's jaw was set in anger. "You know that truck stop on 92? The gas station across the highway? There. A homeless guy picked it up for us."

"Why would it be there?" Boudreaux asked, leaning forward to listen.

"Don't know exactly. We've been batting around some theories."

"But you don't want theories, do you? Or, detectives who actually think. You just want men who do what you say." Gray finally spoke. Disgust in his voice.

Boudreaux's blood pressure visibly rose. Gray's tone reminded Boudreaux of how his teenage daughter sometimes talks to him. He tried to ignore it. Unlike is daughter's tone, he knew why Gray was angry at him. "I don't mind theories, but what do you have to support them? That's what I care about. *The evidence.* You remember what that is, Gray? Bring me a theory clearly supported by information, and then we'll discuss them together."

Parker quickly jumped into the conversation, forced to be the buffer between Gray and Boudreaux. "We have the security video from the gas station, so we're going to watch that. See what we see."

"Good. Listen, investigate what you need to. I'm not tying your hands here. But, bring me facts. And hurry the shit up."

He changed subjects. "That reminds me." Boudreaux uncovered a file on his desk. He handed it to Gray, who didn't take it so he pushed it Parker's way. "These are the Hardy family financial reports. And these …" He combed his desk before finding another file. He pushed it to Parker too. "… are the call history reports for the Hardy's telephone."

"We'll review them, thanks," Parker said.

Boudreaux leaned forward on his desk, supporting himself on his elbows. "We've had over 700 tips nationwide so far. FBI has been helping us when they can. We owe a bunch of local police and sheriff's offices favors now for helping us check them all out. I should be getting a report soon, but I've had Burrell and Gorski interviewing the Hardy's friends in Lakeland. I don't think they've been much help."

He turned to Gray and asked, tired of him not joining in, "You're watching the store's video tonight, right?"

Parker looked to Gray to answer, but Gray wasn't going to.

"We will," Parker said, "and we'll let you know what we find."

Boudreaux's direct phone line lit up and rang. He recognized the number. "Goddammit. If Malcolm Turner's mother doesn't stop calling me and crying about her baby's safety, I may shoot myself right in the face. No less than a dozen calls today from her." He pressed the ignore button on the keypad.

"Where is Turner?" Parker asked.

"The facility in Frostproof. In solitary. He's pissed. His mom's pissed. That's what I've dealt with all day – people are either pissed at me or pissed at you two. I don't do police work anymore. I just try to keep things balanced." He sighed. "You two can go. Let me know about the results on the security video."

Parker stood. Gray didn't move. He scowled at Boudreaux.

"Gray," Boudreaux said, "I'm glad you pushed Edwards. Next time punch him. And don't do it in front of news cameras." Then he went back to work, dismissing Gray and Parker without saying so.

Parker touched Gray's shoulder urging him out of the office before something irreparable happened. Gray yanked his shoulder away. He stood up quickly and the force threw the chair off balance. It toppled over. Boudreaux didn't look up from his desk. Gray shook his head and followed Parker out the door.

"Son of a bitch!" Gray exploded in the hall. "I don't want them writing about me in the paper. Dammit."

Parker didn't know what to say. What Boudreaux did was a horrible thing, but it was for the case and it wasn't really Gray they'd be portraying. "It's all fake, man. A made-up profile." He wasn't sure why Gray was so mad.

"You don't understand."

"Tell me," Parker demanded.

Gray paced in a small circle, ran his hands through his hair. His eyes scanned all around him as if looking for an answer. "Son of a bitch. Son of a bitch," he kept muttering over and over.

"You need to calm down," Parker finally said. "We have to work this case. We've got to find Valerie. Isn't that first and foremost?"

"I can't think now," Gray shouted.

"Let's go get something to eat then. Calm down a bit."

"No, you go. I'll be fine. I have to … go … take a piss." Gray stomped down the hall and disappeared around the corner.

CHAPTER 36

July 29 – 9:45 p.m.

Valerie couldn't scream loud enough. Her vocal chords felt damaged, and she sounded hoarse. The rash around her mouth stung, stretching skin as she yelled. Her shoulder constantly hurt now instead of only when she moved it. And she had a splitting headache. She had no idea how long she'd been yelling, what time it was, or even what day it was. However, she was determined to get her captor back into the bedroom. She had to talk to him. She'd convinced herself that her captor was not the Pen Pal – a good and bad revelation.

She took a deep breath and let out another shriek.

Why wasn't he trying to stop her yelling? Why wasn't he storming into the room to cup his hand over her mouth? She'd seen the house next door, the street outside. Anyone might be passing by and hear the screams.

Is he not home?

Bound to the head and foot boards, on her stomach, and hooded, Valerie thrashed her head about, trying to edge the hood off her head so she could see, but it hadn't yet worked. She rested, out of breath again. The binding on her hands seemed to tighten with her every move, and her feet were tied to objects at each side of the bed, which left her spread eagle. She knew she was naked. By now, that was expected, but she hated it.

Unbeknownst to Valerie, her captor was in the room. Positioned at the end of the bed. He sat in a chair, himself naked, fondling his genitals as he watched Valerie thrash about on the bed. Her muscles contracted as she writhed fighting her binds. Then they'd relax as she caught her breath. *Such a lovely girl.*

He watched, aroused by her and empowered by his cleverness, biting his lip so hard he tasted blood. No one had a clue she was with him. As every news report grew more focused on the Pen Pal, his confidence intensified that no one would ever find her. The police would continue to look for the Pen Pal, and if they were ever to find him, he'll tell them he knows nothing about Valerie's abduction. The truth would be he actually would know nothing. Even better, they wouldn't believe him, which would feed right into his overall plan perfectly.

It was the perfect plan. *Brilliant. Genius.*

She would be his forever. He laughed to himself.

Valerie thought she heard a quick, soft noise, like a breath or a sigh. She immediately froze, listened as intently as she could. Tingles spread across her back, fright seared into her mind. She could hear the air-conditioning running, a large truck drove near, birds sang, and her heart drummed in her ears. Was she mistaken? Was she hearing things?

Or is he in the room?

"Are you there?" she asked in an angry voice.

Nothing.

"You are there, aren't you?" She waited, then shouted, "Say something!"

She listened to the room for what her internal clock thought was almost five minutes, all the while hearing nothing.

"I know you're not the Pen Pal." She waited, but no reply. "If I figured it out, then you can bet the police know."

She paused again, heard nothing but the air-conditioner cut off.

"You're nothing but an impotent fool, trying to get his rocks off," she said, purposefully trying to make him mad. Even him striking her out of anger would be better than this silence. At least she'd know she was getting to him.

"Why don't you tell me why we're here? What are we doing?"

Another minute passed.

"What are you're going to do to me?"

With each passing minute, her anger and rage amplified. She was ready to kill him.

"Don't ever free my hands," she warned. "I will pull your spine out through your eye sockets." Valerie's voice was rough with exertion and fury.

"I won't," a male's voice replied.

Valerie jumped with fright, then she heard the bedroom door close.

CHAPTER 37

July 29 – 10:12 p.m.

Parker was right. Finding Valerie was the most important thing. Nothing else could interfere. Gray sat behind the table in the control room, Valerie's case files before him. He needed to focus. Nothing mattered except for Valerie, not even what Edwards might find out about him.

He wished he believed that.

Gray buried his head in his arms on the tabletop. Anger and fear needled through him, building to a snap. A snap which culminated in a release of frustration. Gray slammed his fist down onto the table, sending vibrations rippling across the table and causing items stored there to shift. He had stuffed his past so deep inside him that he thought he didn't have feelings anymore. He certainly didn't want them anymore, and he did everything in his power not to feel.

I've been doing a damn good job of it, too, he thought. When he succumbed to the urge to feel, things tended to unravel. The world seemed crueler and colder. He would realize how the world and God took from people, took from him, and neither gave much back in return.

And when he would see all that – when he felt – he drank. *And when I drink …* So to combat living in a bottle, he eventually decided to remove himself from the human race and not feel. Indifference as his offense.

No one needed to know what he'd been through, and he made sure anyone who might remember never talked about it. However, the world might open tomorrow's paper and find out. He was scared that even he'd open the paper and find out too. His fortress of indifference had allowed him to act as if nothing had happened, as if not a shred of it even existed, but if he read it in the paper, it would show it did exist and it had happened. What would he do then? How could he handle it? Why would God make him relive it?

Why should anyone be forced to relive something like that?

With that question hanging in the air, his thoughts turned to the McDonough case. Malcolm Turner stirred up the Timothy McDonough investigation with the revelation that the boy's friends had killed him. Until then, everyone had believed Timothy accidentally shot himself.

Why would God allow that?

Gray admired Frank McDonough, his efforts to help, his ability to be the rock for his family. The strength the man must possess. Gray knew he didn't possess that strength.

But what if he did? What if he could be like that? Gray had always admired McDonough, but he'd never consciously thought about emulating him. *What if I did?* He sat up straight in his chair, knowing his thoughts were foolish. Nonetheless, he said it anyway.

"I just need to be like Frank McDonough."

And that was that. The worry subsided. Gray pushed it away like he had done with every other feeling he'd had for the last eight years.

Time to work again.

Gray decided background noise would help. The more noise that pumped into his brain, then the less thinking that might occur. Silence always yielded bad memories. Gray picked up the TV remote, pressed the power button, and the all-news channel played instantly. He grabbed Agent Tyler's new profile and began reading through it. The unknown subject who kidnapped Valerie appeared disorganized, almost unsophisticated. The actual abduction event appeared inadequately planned, abrupt, almost juvenile. If the UNSUB was the Pen Pal, the amount of time s/he had to plan an abduction that s/he'd promised in the letters would have yielded a more elaborate kidnapping.

Gray flipped through his own notes. The UNSUB left blood at the scene of the crime. He needed to get gas after he'd abducted her. Losing Valerie's wallet. Tire tracks left at the scene. Not to mention the crowbar and the ether soaked rag. All of it fit the unsophisticated, immature, and poorly planned kidnapping of which Tyler wrote. Why would the Pen Pal, who'd had ten years to plan, have to rely on a car collision to approach Valerie?

He turned to the next page of Tyler's report. Tyler reasoned the hasty kidnapping came because the Pen Pal was taken off his timetable by Valerie going public, and this caused him to speed up his work. In the rush to fulfill his fantasy/mission, he became disorganized. Tyler thought, because of this, the Pen Pal would be moved by media coverage. He'd be unsure of his plan. He'd be paranoid he had made a mistake because he had to kidnap Valerie quickly and not the exact way he had planned. Pitting an officer of the law against the Pen Pal would escalate the Pen Pal's nervousness.

Gray considered the information further. Tyler's report, while Gray understood the thought process, didn't take into account any other version of the events. Like the notion that someone other than the Pen Pal may have abducted her.

Jack Hardy's voice from the television speaker caught Gray's attention. The all-news channel was replaying his speech from earlier in the evening. The news anchor then explained that Jack and Marie Hardy had granted an exclusive interview with the all-news channel. Then, a reporter introduced the Hardy's. The scene changed to the inside of the Hardy house.

"I've been asleep at the wheel of Valerie's life," Jack told the reporter. "I never imagined the man would be successful in finding Valerie. However, I never imagined she'd essentially hand herself over to him."

"So you're angry with Valerie?" the reporter coaxed.

"Extremely." He shrugged his shoulder. "I blame myself though. We came to this city and became complacent. Felt too safe. We forgot about what Valerie was going through. Essentially, the bottom line is, I was a horrible father."

The interview went on like that. Jack beat himself up and the reporter encouraged him by asking leading questions. Jack ended the interview by saying, "I've never known loss like this. My whole world is shattered. It's dark and foggy. It's never seemed smaller. I can't see anything but my pain. I'd give every cent I have for a chance to protect Valerie again, to save her."

Background noise had been a bad idea. Gray turned off the TV, and his worries about Edwards digging into his past quickly returned. He thought about getting a drink, as he began hyperventilating. Weakness set in and the impulse to get a drink grew stronger. He thought about the bottle of Jack Daniels whiskey in his duffle bag, and he suddenly became aware of perspiration breaking out across his body.

Parker entered the room. Gray pushed out a heavy breath of relief. As long as Parker was around, he'd be fine. He just needed to be with him and to keep being strong like Frank McDonough. The impulse would pass. It always passed.

I hope.

CHAPTER 38

Parker dropped a box of pizza on the table, threw back the lid and dug in. His face contorted and he shook his head like crazy, waving his hand in front of his face. Parker moaned and swallowed the pizza without chewing.

"Need a drink?" Gray asked.

He sucked in a few more breaths of cool air. "I think I'm all right. Shit, that was hot." Parker wiped his tongue with a napkin he produced from his pocket. "You feeling better?"

"Am now, yes."

"I figured. Lack of sleep and all. Maybe we're both not thinking straight. You with the newspaper profile. Me with the pizza."

Gray smiled politely at his partner's attempt to explain it all away. Parker was always trying to put a nice, simple bow around everything. "Maybe."

The pizza smell filled the small conference room, and along with Parker's presence and dialogue, it wafted away Gray's sense of doom. Gray pulled a slice of the pie from the box and took a nibble from the tip to test the temperature. He laid the piece down on a paper plate to wait for it to cool. Parker sat across from him at the table.

"Tyler surmised that Valerie's article and the subsequent media blitz to cover it made the Pen Pal go into hurry-up offense. And that hurry-up made him sloppy. That's why he left blood at the scene. Why he crashed into Valerie's car. And why he dropped her wallet at the gas station."

"As a theory," Parker said, "I could buy it, but what about our theory?"

Gray shifted in his seat and leaned his elbows on the table. "Tyler can't be right. The guy's had ten years to plan. How much longer did he need to be organized? No one's that slow of a planner. With as much time as this guy had, I picture him being able to steal her out of the communion line during Sunday morning's 10:30 Mass."

"That's exactly what we were talking about earlier. That this wasn't Valerie setting the whole thing up. That this wasn't the Pen Pal." Parker said. "At least we're on the same page." Parker took another bite of his pizza and spoke while chewing. "We should tell Boudreaux even though he doesn't want to hear it."

"No, Boudreaux's right."

"That's a surprising statement from you," Parker quipped. "I thought you'd be all," he changed his voice for affect, "'Fuck him. Let's go tell him he's wrong.'"

"We don't have anything to back up our theory. Not really. And he's stuck to the FBI's profile anyway. We won't be able to convince him of anything else right now. He did say though that we can investigate whatever we think is right."

"I don't know what to do with this?"

"What are you talking about?" Gray asked.

"I don't know. I'm trying to figure out how this helps you get him back for putting you front and center in the newspaper?"

"That's not what I'm doing. I'm not that petty."

Parker smiled good-humoredly. "I think you might be that petty when it comes to Boudreaux."

"I just want to get Valerie home safely, and I want to look at every option. You said the same basic thing before you went out for pizza."

Parker shrugged, not remembering what he had said before then. "You sound defeated."

"Do I?" Gray asked. "I'm sure I'm just tired."

"A lot's happened tonight … with Edwards. You want to talk about it?"

"No," Gray said, realizing Parker's presence was a double-edged sword. He provided Gray relief, but he'd keep pushing to find out more. And Gray just wasn't ready to face it yet.

"You said earlier I wouldn't understand why you were so upset. You sure you don't want to try me?"

Buzz.

Gray was saved from continuing the conversation by Parker's text alert sounding.

≈   ≈   ≈   ≈

Boudreaux offered Gray and Parker a different view of him than they'd seen just a couple of hours ago when Edwards and the photographer were there. Boudreaux's tie and collar were now sitting loose around his neck. His usually straight posture slouched. Puffy skin weighed heavily under his eyes, which made him look older in the dim office lighting.

"It's almost eleven, chief. What are you still doing here?" Parker asked.

"I just dealt with two phone calls," he told his two detectives. "Neither one of them I wanted to deal with."

"Edwards again?" Gray asked, the same teenage disgust in his voice.

"No," Boudreaux said. "Have a seat, if you want."

"I spoke to Jack and Marie Hardy. I chastised Mr. Hardy for his offer of reward money. Did you two see his statement? Offered fifty grand for anyone who puts him alone in the room with the Pen Pal. Nice, huh?"

"It seemed like an over the top response." Parker said.

Boudreaux shrugged his shoulder. "Unnecessary to say the least." He grew quiet, like the conversation, tapping his fingers on the desktop before him. "Are we going to get Valerie back?"

"We're trying," Parker said.

"I know you're trying. Are we going to get her back?"

"Do you want to hear our theories?" Parker asked.

"You going to tell me she faked the whole thing?"

"No," Gray said. "We don't think the Pen Pal took her. Maybe a local opportunist."

Parker said, "We know Tyler thinks the hurry up and sloppiness is because Valerie put herself out there in the newspaper and the Pen Pal had to act fast. We think that sloppiness is because someone else had to act fast."

"What do you know?"

Parker said, "The blood found at the scene on Valerie's car wasn't hers. The lab ran it. No hits in any of the databases. We have vehicle make and model we're looking for. We've ruled out quite a bit."

Boudreaux tilted back into his chair. "Keep me posted."

"You said two calls, chief. What was the other one?"

"The other call I got was from the FBI in L.A. Two things. One, the FBI hasn't found any other occurrences similar to this one that they'd say may be Pen Pal related. Meaning, they don't think he's sent letters to anyone else. Not that they know of, at least. And, two, speaking of the letters, there were four other girls besides Valerie Hardy who received threats from the Pen Pal. Melinda Tillman, Marie Vasquez, Tiesha Knight, and Amanda Richards. The FBI just told me that two years ago one of the girls was found dead. Murdered. The parents didn't receive a letter."

"So it's not related," Gray proclaimed.

"Maybe someone else is targeting all the girls that the Pen Pal wrote to." Parker said.

"They're faxing the report to us now. We'll see."

"And they're looking for the other girls, right?" Gray said. "Make sure they're okay?"

"They are," Boudreaux said. "I haven't heard anything on them yet."

Gray said, "I read that when the letters arrived, Amanda Richards' mother accused the karate instructor of sending them, but that didn't pan out. Amanda's parents divorced right after the letters arrived. Dad ran off, left mom with nothing. No job, no savings. I guess it didn't get better after that."

The fax machine in the corner of the office came to life. The papers from the FBI in Los Angeles spit slowly out of the device. The three police officers surrounded the machine.

Two years ago, Amanda Richards, at the age of 16, was found dead in a Los Angeles night club. The staff at the club were cleaning after business hours when they came upon her body. Amanda had been raped and stabbed six times in the VIP room of the club. The killer had never been identified. The toxicology report indicated that cocaine and alcohol were in her system at the time of her death. Coroner report showed a history of drug use by way of the affects it had on her body.

It seemed abnormal to be relieved. A girl lost her life and went through hell on the way out. However, there was no reason to believe, based on the report, that Amanda's death had anything to do with the Pen Pal. And that was a good thing.

CHAPTER 39

July 30 – 11:55 p.m.

Sleep should've been easy, but it wasn't as usual. Gray stayed at the department after Parker went home. Parker left under protest. He tried to stay with Gray, didn't want him to be alone, but Gray insisted Parker go home to his wife. Gray pretended to be feeling better, to be calmed down, to not be so worried about the article. Behaving that way was the only way he'd convince Parker to go home. *Pretend being the key word.*

He was still upset about the news article, about Edwards digging through his past. It was the worst thing Boudreaux could've done, siccing Edwards on him. So Parker going home was important to Gray. He really needed to process the whole situation. He needed to stay focused on Valerie's case. He preferred to stay busy rather than driving all night and fighting the urge to drink, and he didn't need Parker around for all that. At least, he thought so anyway.

Gray, coffee in hand and a notepad in his lap, sat before a television and DVD player. He loaded the player with the DVD from the convenience store security system, and as he leaned back in his chair, he used the remote control to advance the video recording. Cars zipped in and out of frame in fast forward, and people rocketed from their cars into the store and then back again. Gray slowed the video when it neared one a.m. He set down the remote and watched closely for the Nova. Within ten minutes the green looking Nova stopped at pump 15.

A male threw the driver's door open and then emerged from the car. He pulled out his wallet and checked its insides. He looked confused and began looking harder at the wallet, pulling and tugging at the pockets.

He didn't have any money or credit cards? Gray carefully observed the man's reactions.

He stuffed the wallet back into his pocket, clearly frustrated. He scanned the other cars and the parking lot, completely turning in a circle. Then it looked like an idea hit him. He hurried to the passenger side and opened the car door. The interior light turned on and outlined something slumped over in the front passenger seat.

"Is that a body?" Gray wondered aloud.

The driver fumbled around before standing up and producing a credit card size wallet. He closed the door, looking around him and making sure no one noticed what he'd been doing. He looked through the coin purse and found a credit card. After placing the coin purse on his car roof, the male slipped the credit card into the gas pump, waited for approval, and then began pumping gas into his car. When the full tank cut off the gas flow, he replaced the nozzle, sealed the gas tank, took one final look around the gas station for anyone who might've spotted him, then finally climbed back inside the vehicle and drove off.

"The son of a bitch used her credit card."

Gray tossed aside the notepad and dropped the coffee into the trash, heading to the other end of the conference table. He rummaged through the mounds of files. Soon Gray found the folder he was looking for. He laid out the papers and began running his finger down the list of transactions. Eight pages and a few minutes later, Gray raised his head.

"He did." He laughed. "That *was* Valerie's card."

He turned, expecting to see Parker just as excited about the development as he was, but he realized he was in the room alone. A sense of loneliness set in. He wished now that he hadn't pushed Parker to go home.

But he stayed on task, buried himself in work. After retrieving his notepad, Gray jotted down notes before the thoughts went away, before his concentration faded, before he started thinking about a drink again.

Someone took VH, knowing we'd look for the PP.

Someone local.

Supremely disorganized.

How'd he find her?

Newspaper? TV news? Had he seen her before?

Criminal record? No, per Maddy James. Prints not in database.

First abduction? First assault? Likely no, but see above.

Gray pushed the notepad aside. Studied the paused, grainy image of the male on the television, wishing he could see the face clearer.

The car. He scribbled the note on the paper before him.

Chevy Nova. That's the key.

CHAPTER 40

Jefferson City, Missouri
July 30 – 10:55 p.m.

Samuel Hubbard woke up in an abandoned building. He checked his watch. It had been over four hours since finding out Valerie had been kidnapped. The grit and dust from the construction site covered his clothes. Once on his feet, his head spun, dizzy at his sudden rising. He supported himself against a damp wall.

The coolness of moisture became apparent, spread across his left side. He dried his wet hand on his pants while looking around. The dark, dank place remained lit only by the full moon and street lamps outside the building along the busy city street. The whole space was pretty much hallowed out. The only things he saw were steel support columns and a collection of construction equipment off to the right – ladders, scaffolding, buckets, portable lights, tool boxes and the like. Streaks of water trickled down the wall to his left. Gathering rainwater leaking through the old, decaying ceiling.

The place reminded him of his past. He'd lived on the street for almost a year when he was 17. He'd slept in places like this dozens of times, when he couldn't find a bridge to sleep under, a shelter to sleep inside, a dumpster to shield him from the cold wind, or a jail cell. If he applied his imagination, it also reminded him of the places he'd traveled with the Rev. Willie Hindman when he was 20 years old. This place in its heyday, it must've been a regal building with plush red carpet, grand mahogany on the walls, and exquisite furniture lining the lobby. Decadent and majestic.

But the trip down memory lane led him to Valerie. And Amanda, Melinda, Marie, and Tiesha. *And my plan.*

Hubbard coughed and dust shot out of his mouth. It disgusted him. He hated being dirty. He thought he'd left dirt and dust behind him, but here he was right back in it again. That's how his life had been. Knocked down, get up only to get knocked down again. Along with the dust clinging to his body again, was the reemergence of his anger. That's how his life had been too. Anger always there. Even when it was dormant, like it had been for more than ten years, it was there. Waiting. Lurking. Knowing its day would come again.

Hubbard exited the building and headed north to the bus stop. He grabbed the 11:15 p.m. city bus and transferred at the station to the bus that would deliver him one block from his apartment. Once off that bus, he proceeded through the restaurant district and into his apartment building. He punched in the security code to his building. The door buzzed. He entered and traveled to the fourth floor by way of the stairs.

Apartment 403 appeared before him right next to the staircase doorway. He slipped his key into the lock and entered his safe place.

The room was spotless. Nothing dirty, dusty, or out of place. Of course, he only had a few things. No TV, a small couch that pulled out into a bed, and a table. All around the room books were set in stacks, some several feet high. No pictures hung on the wall, and the kitchen appeared never used.

He hurried into the bedroom, which had no bed. He used the room to stack more books, just like in the living room. They were stacked against the walls, leaving the whole middle of the room empty. He usually only came in the room to place a newly read book on the next stack in the rotation around the perimeter of the room. Sometimes he'd lay in the center of the room and imagine all the words inside those books flying, floating, soaring above him in a chaotic tornado of literary meaning only known to him and the universe. Today was different. Today Samuel Hubbard entered the room to retrieve the past.

Hubbard opened the closet and seized the only item inside – a cloth sack. A large sack with drawstrings at the top. Half empty. Tugging at the mouth of the bag, Hubbard opened it and then emptied its contents onto the floor. Photographs, papers, notebooks, drawings, a bible, magazines, loose cash, and a gun and knife all rattled down ono the floor at Hubbard's feet. He folded the cloth sack in half and then rolled it up, placing it on the shelf in the closet.

Hubbard sat down on the floor, crossing his legs and tucking them under one another. All the photographs went into one pile, all the papers the same. Notebooks drawings, magazines and cash, all were stacked. Then Hubbard went back through each of the piles and organized them by size. For the cash, he organized by denomination. He stacked the bible, gun and knife – bible on the bottom, gun and knife next to one another.

He thumbed through the drawings. Most of them were crayon-drawn. Stick figures. Houses and dogs in the background. The sun was a circle with five to eight lines coming out of it. Some suns had smiley faces in them. These were particularly cherished items for Hubbard. He'd had a troubled youth, of which he never told the stories. He figured his experience wasn't all that unusual. *Shitty parents do shitty things to kids*, he'd say when asked specifics. And that *shittiness* led him to jealousy of families who seemed to have it all, and then ultimately to jealousy and violence. He wouldn't talk about that either.

But then he met Reverend Hindman. He was truly a good man. Someone who cared for Hubbard without any strings attached. Very much a father figure. Sure, he scolded Hubbard when he chose incorrectly, but he didn't do it in a way that put Hubbard down. He didn't speak to Hubbard in a way that made him think he was bad. *You aren't bad,* Hindman would say, *but the choice you made was bad.*

They had a business relationship too. Hindman was a travelling evangelist. Hubbard went along as his assistant. They'd visit churches, speaking the word of God. Hubbard's job was to essentially be the business manager, the janitor, the teacher, the coordinator, the everything. And he loved it. He had a sense of purpose, of value, and of peace. All things he'd never had before he'd met Hindman.

He moved the crayon drawings away and then thumbed through the photographs. There were eight in total. Two of him and Hindman. He nostalgically studied the photographs with Hindman, the man long dead now. Hubbard felt like those were the best years of his life, and thinking about them – he hadn't in quite some time – brought a smile to his face. One was of his mother, which he'd forgotten was even inside the bag – he crumpled that one into a ball, tossed it aside. And five others. Each of those five was a photograph of a little girl about the age eight years old. In front of him, he laid out each of the remaining five photographs. Innocent girls' smiles staring back at him.

Hubbard moved on to the notebooks. He flipped randomly through the pages. This is where he kept his notes from Hindman's teachings. His notes on bible study. He read them again, remembered writing each one of them. *Children are a gift from the Lord. They are a reward from him.* And then, *Psalms 127:3.*

One of Hubbard's tasks was to teach what Hindman called the Early Gospel Class. At each of the church stops, Hindman would take the parents, and Hubbard would take the kids. Hindman liked doing that – from a business standpoint – because the parents would have free hands to write a donation check, if the kids were occupied. *Be strong and courageous. Do not be discouraged. For the Lord, your God, is with you wherever you go*, he'd written. *Joshua 1:9.*

That's where the crayon drawings came from. Hubbard loved that part of his job with Hindman. He believed the reverend when he'd say it was everyone's responsibility to protect the children of this world. *If you can protect even one child,* he'd say, *from the harm of the evil, then you have saved Jesus Christ, our savior, just as if you feed the lowliest of souls on this Earth so, too, do you feed Him.* Hubbard took that to heart. And he looked at the five photographs before him. *And, as parents,* Hindman would say, *you have the ultimate responsibility in this protection, in this rearing of God's children. If you don't take that responsibility to heart, then the children's hearts will be taken elsewhere.*

At first, when he had just met Hindman, Hubbard would always think of his own parents when Hindman said this. *Why didn't they do that?* But, after time, that morphed into his own feeling of responsibility. Into his own sense of protecting the children he taught. *For my father and my mother have forsaken me, but the Lord will take me in.* Hubbard flipped further through his notebook. *And, ye fathers, provoke not your children to wrath.* Then he looked again at the five photographs before him.

He said, "See, I am sending an angel ahead to guard you along the way."

Hubbard got to his feet. *Valerie needs me.* And he only took the money, gun, and knife with him.

CHAPTER 41

Lakeland, Florida
July 30 – 12:52 a.m.

The effect of having little sleep finally caught up with Gray. He couldn't remember things he'd just written down. His vision blurred. His thoughts vacillated between missing the company of his partner and not wanting to succumb to the false comfort offered by the bottles of whiskey in his duffle bag. He fought both his loneliness and his fear of slipping again.

He needed to leave work, to take a break, so he hurried to his faithful Honda Accord. He pushed aside the notion to call Parker. He wanted to, but he didn't want to bother him either. Tough place to be, needing someone and not wanting to ask for help. Gray started the car and drove out of the police department parking area through the electronic gate, headed north toward the interstate because he knew going to home to sleep wouldn't be successful. Not until he could turn off his brain. But then he was struck by a thought – *the gas station.*

If Valerie's captor was local, then maybe, Gray surmised, he lives near that gas station. He checked his watch, and the time neared one a.m. He wouldn't be falling asleep any time soon, so Gray convinced himself that maybe the guy would come again to that filling station. Maybe he was a regular there.

Gray rubbed his eyes.

Gray turned his car around and headed east to the gas station, where he parked at the edge of the property hoping to hide in plain sight. Anyone driving through, he expected, would think the car belonged to an employee. Business wasn't as demanding as it had been the night of Valerie's abduction – one car after another, almost in a line – but approximately every quarter hour someone would get gas or go inside for a late-night purchase. That pace was fine with Gray. *Maybe I can get some work done.*

Not wanting to use his interior light and ruin is hiding, Gray angled the case files so he could read them against the lights of the gas station. He stopped thumbing through the file when he came to a photocopy of the scrap of paper bearing a phone number that Parker found inside Valerie's wallet. He flipped back to the phone records from the last six months and found that listing on the fourth page. Not once or twice but 47 times. They all occurred within a two-week period two months prior. But the number wasn't listed in the logs again after that.

He reviewed the rest of the pages and found the same pattern having occurred four other times with four other numbers. Although further examination of all those phone numbers perked something in Gray's mind, he didn't have time to process it. He noticed a car turn into the parking lot of the convenience store. The lanky driver got out of the car and walked toward the entrance. Gray set the papers onto his lap and curiously watched the man. *Where have I seen him before?* Gray thought.

He knew he was beyond fatigued and he could be mistaken, but he swore to himself he knew the man who had just walked into the store. Gray watched as the guy made his way to the ice cream freezer and then over to the beer refrigerator. *Who is this guy?* As the man shuffled to the cash register to pay for his snack, Gray looked at the car again, and it, too, looked familiar.

Holy shit. Billy McGee.

Pushing aside the file and phone records with one hand, Gray pushed open his car door with the other. McGee exited the store and walked nonchalantly to his car. Gray increased his pace, resting his palm on his holstered gun.

McGee saw a man advancing toward him across the dark parking lot, saw his hand on a weapon. He panicked. He dropped his beer and ice cream and exploded into a run toward his car. Gray hurried and was close when McGee jumped into his car and started up the engine. McGee jammed the car into REVERSE, but before he could slam on the gas, Gray used the butt of his gun crack the glass window.

At first, McGee thought Gray had shot him, but he realized he wasn't hit and that the loud crack was his shattered car window. He frantically looked around but didn't see the gun-wielding man anywhere. McGee had stolen drugs and money from some bad people, and he'd been in hiding. He figured someone would eventually find him and probably shoot him, but that didn't mean he wanted that outcome. So, not seeing where the man got off to, McGee decided to get out of there immediately. He turned the wheel hard but before he could press on the gas, he heard "Police!" shouted from outside the car. McGee looked up and saw Gray standing in front of the car, his weapon leveled right at McGee's face.

"I'm happy to find you, Billy," Gray said.

McGee put the car in PARK and raised his hands in the air. "I knew someone would sooner or later," McGee muttered to himself.

CHAPTER 42

By two a.m. Gray found himself back at the gas station. Billy McGee had been booked and put in a holding cell, where he told Gray everything about getting the gun for his cousin and his friends. The kid was remorseful, eaten up with guilt. He agreed to help with the case and do whatever he needed to do to make it right. All of which was good. If he'd been a jerk about the whole thing, Gray may have laid him out.

Gray didn't know where else to go. He didn't want to drive on the interstate. He didn't want to go home. Or stay at headquarters. So, he went back to the gas station. And he was glad he did. He expected to review case files, maybe get some sleep, but instead he received interesting news from Tran.

As Gray was reviewing the case files, a hollow clank rapped against his car window glass. Gray startled, expecting to see Mike Todd, the highway patrolman who wakes him most mornings by knocking on his window. Instead Tran stood there.

Gray turned the key in the ignition to get some power then rolled down his window. Tran moved in an animated fashion, frantically pointing at a grainy picture of a Chevy Nova. Gray had given the store owners a copy of the photo, so they could keep a watch out for it. Tran handed Gray a cell phone and gestured for him to listen to the person on the other line.

"Detective?"

"What?" Gray asked.

"My cousin thinks he saw the car you're looking for. He said the guy came by while you were gone."

"Is this Vu?" Gray asked.

"Yes. My cousin asked me to talk to you."

"Did he see the man driving the car?"

"I don't know. I didn't ask," the cousin replied.

"Ask him now," Gray said sternly before handing the phone back to Tran. Gray got out of the car and stretched his back while Tran spoke his native language to Vu.

The owner gave Gray the cell phone so he could talk to Vu.

"What'd he say?"

"He said he saw the guy. He came in and bought eggs and bread," the cousin said. "He asked about the reward again."

Gray watched a minivan roll to a stop by the newspaper machines.

"Listen, I'm not going back and forth anymore. You and your cousin need to come to the police station and meet with a sketch artist."

"He'll say no."

"Not an option," Gray said. "Be there. Nine a.m. and ask him to go back inside and get me a copy of the surveillance video."

As Tran listened to Vu's instructions, Gray watched the minivan driver pull a bundle of the day's newspaper from the back and load the newspaper vending machine. Gray watched as Tran walked inside the store looking quite unhappy about the request to retrieve the video.

Gray walked across the parking lot to where the delivery guy dropped off papers. After plugging in coins for the daily newspaper, he went back to his car. He scanned the front page for the big story about him, but it wasn't on the front page. A story about Valerie and her case took up most of that real estate.

Then Tran reappeared with a DVD and his cell phone.

"No. No. No come." Tran said as he shook the phone at Gray.

Persistence might work with some, but not with Gray. "I'll come get you, if you don't show up. I know you understand what I'm saying. Be there." Gray snatched the DVD and returned to his car so he could drive to a quiet place and read the newspaper.

CHAPTER 43

July 31 – 6:37 a.m.

He sat in his car, but this time on a street off Lake Hollingsworth, where morning joggers and walkers would soon pass every couple of minutes. When Gray woke from two hours of restless sleep, the distant sky turned orange and purple as the sun slowly began its ascent.

Still too dark to read the article about himself that he'd found on page 1 of the local/state section of the newspaper, Gray refused to read by interior light. Perhaps it was a stall tactic as much as anything. He had done so in many instances of his life He'd put off marrying Denise until she was pregnant. He'd put off finishing college until he was refused employment because of it. He'd put off his effort to stop drinking until his life crumbled around him. The accumulation of each resulted in his isolati on from the rest of the human race to the point he didn't have any feelings left.

A woman running the lake with her dog in tow stopped for a breather. A couple people passed her before a man stopped to extend a greeting. Gray imagined the conversation. A quick catch up. Neighbors who didn't see each other much. Business associates maybe.

Gray thought back to last night in the conference room. Noticing Parker's absence had created such a weird feeling of loneliness. He trained his eyes on the people by the lake, and thought how long it had been since he ran into someone he knew.

As the sun floated above the trees, its morning rays were especially bright cutting through the sleek, thin clouds smeared across the new day's sky. They offered enough light for Gray to read. Reluctantly, he placed his now cold cup of coffee in the holder between him and the passenger seat, realizing this whole time he'd forgotten he was even holding it. Pulling the paper from the passenger seat, Gray spread the newspaper evenly across his lap, a photograph of himself on the page looking back at him. His tentative sigh turned into a yawn.

Don't read it. That wasn't an option, he knew. But, he could stall a little longer.

Gray pulled the national section from the pile of newspaper, unfolded the paper, and saw Valerie's picture at the bottom of the front page. The article described developments in her kidnapping investigation. Boudreaux was quoted a dozen times, which brought a grimace to Gray's face. That man was always being quoted by the media. On the opposite side of Valerie's photograph, Gray noticed parts three and four of her story were printed after a day's break, which he read through.

Edwards' writing at times was flowery and overly dramatic, while at other times was dark in its detailing of her feelings of isolation, despair, and depression. But later in the fourth article, Valerie's quotes sounded hopeful. She wanted the Pen Pal arrested. She wanted her life back. She'd hide no more. All in all, after reading the four articles Michael Edwards wrote for Valerie, Gray understood Valerie's frustration with them. It was a good start, but they didn't have much teeth to them, which confirmed for Gray his dislike of Edwards.

Tossing aside that section of the paper, his eyes landed on the major headline in the local/state section – DETECTIVE: MISSING

GIRL'S CASE PERSONAL. Michael Edwards' name in the byline, which made his stomach turn.

Read it later.

Gray started his Honda Accord and drove to the stop sign at the end of the road, steered the car toward his apartment complex. Finding some comfort in his apartment, he bathed in his own shower, brushed his teeth at his own sink, dressed from clothes out of his closet instead of a duffle bag, drank coffee from his own coffee pot in his own mug instead of a Styrofoam cup. He paused at the apartment door before leaving. It might have looked like a shell of a home, but he didn't want to leave its comfort and safety today.

Back inside his Accord, Gray held the local section of the paper in front of him, still not wanting to read the article. A drink would help build his courage. Another sigh turned into a yawn.

Just read it.

He spread the paper across his steering wheel. Smoothed it with his hand. And read. Paragraph after paragraph, Gray read about his police officer life, the one made up by Boudreaux, that is, but there was nothing else. Nothing about his real life, his personal life, which allowed Gray to hold out hope Edwards hadn't researched Gray's past in great detail. The article continued on page B5. Gray turned the pages and then saw it.

"Edwards, you asshole." He had done his research after all.

In the corner of the page sat two articles which filled Gray with rancor. One written by Michael Edwards and the other by Belinda Abeline. He'd expected to see Edwards' byline throughout the newspaper, but Abeline's was a surprise. She'd been the reporter who befriended Gray a long time ago, who'd drawn him out of his shell and convinced him to talk to her, who'd won his trust, who'd then turned around and betrayed their off the record discussions, betrayed their friendship by never calling him again after she got her story. *Never apologizing.* Clearly, she and Edwards went to the same journalism school, the one that extolled the only thing that mattered was the story. *Fuck the people, just get the story.* And if the article written by her had been pulled from the newspaper's archive for publication, then so had –

Bitterness cemented inside his chest, building a monument to his past. A small picture of Gracie's toddler face confirmed everything he needed to know about the contents of Edwards' side article.

He crumpled the paper into a ball, crushing it between his two hands, squeezing it until his fingertips went cold, trying to control his loathsome thoughts about the reporters and Boudreaux. Gray knew this would happen, knew his past would be exposed. He had tried to tell Boudreaux. He didn't know, though, what would happen now. Or maybe he did know. Either way – he squeezed the ball of paper tighter – it left him unnerved.

CHAPTER 44

Parker made it to work earlier than usual. Because of the Gray. Parker couldn't sleep and woke early. He dressed and drank his coffee while reading the day's newspaper. He stood stunned for a long moment after reading the articles about his friend, but he soon took off in a hurry, worry filling his heart. The newspaper discarded on the floor and his coffee cup tossed, broken in the sink. Attempts to reach Gray by cell phone proved futile. Parker drove by Gray's apartment to find him, but the Accord wasn't home. He went to the restaurant where Gray often ate breakfast, but no one had seen him. He now moved quickly through the police headquarters building, his face chiseled in concern, asking anyone he passed whether they had seen Gray. But, no one had.

He stomped up the stairs from the lobby to the second floor. He checked the locker room, the fitness area, and the conference room for Valerie's case. Gray was nowhere to be found. Parker had never been so worried about Gray, and, worse, he didn't know where else to look for him.

Parker sat at the table in the command room and eyed the massive amount of information stacked an strewn upon it. He saw Gray's notepad. Read the scribblings he'd made.

Boudreaux entered the conference room. "Parker, where's Gray?"

"I don't know," Parker replied.

"Did you know he brought in Billy McGee last night?"

"What?" Parker stood. "No."

"Find him." Boudreaux said, leaving the room.

"Chief, will you have someone search for the car in the case?" Parker found the car details in a stack of files on the table. "They should start with a five, maybe ten-mile radius of the gas station. Address is here." He pointed to a second piece of paper.

"Sure, Parker. Anything else I can do for you?"

Parker ignored Boudreaux's sarcasm. "Have you read the newspaper?"

"No. I do that at nine. It's not nine." He stepped away from the door.

"Chief," Parker called to him and met Boudreaux in the hallway outside the conference room. "You knew what it would do to him."

Boudreaux sighed, annoyed at Parker. "No, I didn't."

Parker sighed back. "You knew what it *could* do to him."

Boudreaux didn't sleep well the night before, thinking of Gray. He and Gray hadn't always butted heads. A long time ago, they were friendly. What Gray went through surrounding his daughter's death, and probably what he was currently going through, wasn't lost on Boudreaux. He wasn't a monster.

"We could've figured out a different way," Parker said,

Boudreaux decided against making excuses, saying the decision was time sensitive, blaming his position, blaming the case. "Maybe."

≈   ≈   ≈   ≈

Morning traffic was awful. Stop, start. Start, stop. People cut off other drivers. They ran red lights. They increased their speed when the light changed to yellow. They didn't stop for stop signs.

And among the worst driving offenders this morning was Parker.

Parker had read the articles about Gray. There was no doubt why Boudreaux's idea about the profile in the newspaper made Gray so mad. But they also shed light on Parker's partner. He didn't know about Gray's daughter, Gracie, but it explained Gray's sleeping problems. And why he retreated from personal relationships, and especially hated cases with child victims. Parker wanted to just reach out and hug him.

Soon Parker arrived at the only other place he thought to look for his partner. Frank McDonough's neighborhood streets were canopied under enormous trees. The yards were well kept. Most of the residents were major players in the city or county, as Frank had been before his son was murdered.

Parker drove slowly through the streets, careful of the numerous people out for a walk. He rounded the bend in the road and saw Gray's Accord parked a few houses down from the McDonough residence.

Gray, in the rearview mirror, watched Parker walk to the Accord's passenger side of the car. Gray pressed the unlock button, and Parker folded himself into the car.

"Good morning," Parker said, eyeing the crumpled newspaper in the passenger floorboard.

"Hey," Gray said, not taking his eyes off the McDonough house.

"What are you doing?"

"I don't know."

They sat in silence for a while.

"I got Billy McGee last night," Gray finally said.

"I heard."

Gray shook his head, almost laughing. "At Vu and Tran's store."

"And you were there?"

"Was hoping your Pen Pal-copycat would stop at the store for more gas or something. Maybe I follow him back to his house."

"But he never did?"

"He did actually." Gray's voice was cold, monotone, and matter of fact. "While I was booking McGee." He paused and then asked, "What time is it?"

Parker checked his watch. "Eight eleven."

"Tran, the convenience store owner, saw him. Says he saw him anyway. He's coming in to do a sketch."

"That's really great news."

"It is," Gray replied. "I have the surveillance from inside the store, too. While the guy was there, you know?"

"You've been busy?"

Gray nodded his head. "I guess so."

Parker settled in the seat and watched the house with Gray, but it wasn't long before he broke the silence.

"Did you get any sleep last night?"

"You said it's eight eleven now? A couple hours."

"You need more than that."

"I know," Gray said.

"Good. What are we doing here? Shouldn't we be watching the video or something?"

"None of us know when we wake up what's going to happen that day. Not really. You and I see that shit all the time. So, I'm just sitting here, wondering. Inside that house, whatever's going on won't matter when we tell them their son was murdered because of the stupidity, negligence, and help of one of their own family members."

Parker decided not to reply. See if Gray will keep talking.

"I just want to see them doing something normal, like taking out the garbage," Gray said. "I want to see what I'm about to ruin."

"Why would you want that?"

"I don't know."

"Yes, you do," Parker said.

"I'm just trying to remember."

"Remember what?"

"Before."

Parker reached out to Gray and squeezed his friend's shoulder. "Why don't you go get some sleep? I'll handle this with McDonough. Come in after lunch and we'll get caught up on Valerie's case."

"Ever wonder what makes a person strong?" Gray asked, ignoring Parker's suggestion.

"Faith. Family. Self-esteem," Parker speculated.

"Indifference." Gray sat up and turned the key in the ignition. His Honda hopped to life.

"You're not indifferent, Becker. If anything you're the opposite. You feel too much."

"I'll see you at the station." He waited for Parker to get out of the car.

CHAPTER 45

July 31 – 9:22 a.m.

Although Gray and Parker planned on staying with Tran and Vu as they sat with a sketch artist, they found it difficult to focus on the sketch while the trio sorted through a language barrier. Instead, the detectives headed to the conference room to watch the video of the night before.

Patrolman Emilio Sanchez rounded the corner and caught up to Gray and Parker. "I hear you were looking for me."

"I was," Parker said. "Boudreaux said he asked you to get some info on a car for me."

Gray listened, watching the floor, looking toward Sanchez only periodically. Never making eye contact. He assumed everyone had read the articles about him and knew his past. The last thing he wanted to do was encourage people to talk to him about it.

"I left the results with my sergeant," Sanchez explained.

"A phone message would have been nice," Parker said. "I didn't see your sergeant, and he didn't come looking for me."

"Next time I'll just hunt you down. How about that?" Sanchez fired back, defensively.

"Thanks so much for your magnificent follow through. We're only trying to save a girl's life," Parker replied.

"I did my job," Sanchez declared. Sanchez looked to Gray and put his hand on Gray's shoulder, "I saw the article, man. I feel for you."

Gray thought of jamming Sanchez in the throat and tossing him down the stairs. Instead, he said, "Why don't you go get that file for us." *And take your sympathetic face with you.*

Sanchez nodded and left to get the report.

"I thought you got along with everyone," Gray commented, his voice still low, weak, and monotone.

Parker pushed open the conference room's door, then rounded the table and slid the newest surveillance DVD into the player. "I haven't slept much and am grouchy as hell." He turned the television on. "I don't know how you do it."

Gray's cell phone beeped. He checked the incoming call, noted the number, and hit the silence option.

"Important call?" Parker joked.

"My brother. Did you hit play?"

"You should take the call," Parker suggested.

"Later maybe."

Parker moved on not wanting to involve himself in Gray's family life at the moment and pressed the play button on the remote. He used the remote to forward the tape to the time when Tran stated the copycat entered the store, then they watched. The white male had something wrapped around his waist and hanging down the front of his legs, and he had on a ball cap. The cap had a letter or a logo emblazoned across the front. They couldn't tell hair color. The guy was very thin. His T-shirt had writing on the front and back, but none of it was extremely clear.

The white male finally made it to the register where they could make out his face: deep eye sockets, darkened by the brim of the cap, small nose, a wide jaw, and a distinguished chin. He appeared timid in his walk and movements. They saw no scars or tattoos. To their disappointment, he was just a normal looking white male between the ages of 20 and 30.

Gray's cell sounded again. He checked the number and ignored it.

"Your brother again?"

"No, my dad. Let's watch the outside video."

"You sure?" Parker asked.

"Yes, let's watch the other video."

Sanchez knocked then entered the room with a file. "Here's those results," he said from behind them. "I gotta run." He set it down on the nearest chair and left the room.

"Asshole," Parker said as he went to the file and retrieved it. "He couldn't have handed it to me? Had to drop it on the chair farthest away?"

"What's your beef with him?"

Parker looked confused. "I don't know. I guess you're rubbing off on me. Look at this," he said.

Gray moved closer, and they reviewed the file together. Four men within a five-mile radius were registered as owning a late 1960s Chevy Nova. Two of the men had a previous record – one for marijuana possession, the other for aggravated assault.

"None of these guys are the kid in the video," Gray said, evaluating their physical descriptions from the arrest log. "Watch." Gray pressed the play button.

A dark Nova rolled into frame. The driver parked the car, got out of it, and went inside the store. Gray noticed the passenger side rear taillight was damaged. He paused the video.

"Did you see that on the first video we have?"

"Not that I recall," Parker said. "Look at the license plate. Is that a T or a 7?"

"Not sure."

"I'll take these DVDs with me and see if Nelson from the FDLE can help clear them up," Parker told Gray.

"I'll stay here," Gray replied.

Parker stopped at the door. "You should get some sleep. Try to, at least."

"Won't happen," Gray replied.

CHAPTER 46

July 31 – 9:53 a.m.

After Carson Anderson woke, he sleepily shuffled into the hallway to Valerie's bedroom door, unlocked it with a key, and pushed the door open. Valerie was still asleep. Carson noticed gleefully how her naked body shined in the morning sunlight. He smiled proudly at his accomplishment of having Valerie in his possession. *Now to feed her!*

He turned on the television. Voices appeared before the picture did. He moved to the stove, twisting the knob, alighting the blue flame of the front burner. Carson placed a pan on the rack and waited for it to heat. He increased the volume on the kitchen television and then changed the channel to the local all-news network.

As the female anchor spewed the news like a robot, he moved about the kitchen preparing breakfast for Valerie. He went to the refrigerator for the eggs and bacon. He hit the pantry for grits, and from a plastic bag on the counter, Carson pulled the bread he purchased at the convenient store the night before. The bacon was quickly sizzling in the frying pan and the grits bubbled in their pot on the back burner. He whipped the raw eggs in a bowl and waited for the bacon to finish cooking, so he could use that pan.

At the top of the hour, the headlines replayed, and the female anchor began with a quick recap of Valerie's case. The news station had a creative logo and theme music to go along with the case news. He stopped whipping the eggs and sat down in front of the television to listen to the report.

"Police still seem baffled by the case, which began ten years ago when five girls, living all across the United States, received the same two letters from an unidentified person. The letters threatened the safety of one of these five girls, saying the author would pick one of them to perform unthinkable acts upon. The author gave no indication who he would select. Or when for that matter.

"While the police in Lakeland insist leads are continually coming in, they have not made public any list of suspects or any of the directions the case is taking. Wilson Harris, a retired FBI agent, is here with us to discuss why the police are being so secretive."

The screen changed to show a studious man. The anchor immediately started a dialogue. "Thank you for joining us, Mr. Harris."

"My pleasure," he answered, his voice strong and authoritative.

"Sir, because of the age of the original case, some experts say the case is too old to solve. Sources say the perpetrator has had too much time to plan. But isn't it possible that Valerie Hardy's recent abduction could be the catalyst for capturing the man who wrote the letters?"

"The police collectively work in a reactive environment most of the time," Harris said. "But — to answer your question - there is a possibility that police can react to something quickly even if the abductor has had ten years to plan. The resources available to today's police force were unimaginable ten years ago. I have faith in the police, their processes, and their abilities. However, for all we know the abductor in this case — the Pen Pal, he's called — has carried out this plan dozens of times across the

United States in order to perfect it. And, this may be his masterpiece. And he may not be caught."

"But time is a major obstacle?"

"It is, as with any abduction case," Harris said. "With this case, in particular, the police face a specific deadline issued by the Pen Pal. In the letters he sent, he wrote that on the third day of the abduction, the family would receive a third and final letter. Inside that letter, he'd tell the family where they could find all the pieces of their daughter. That indicates a terrible end to this young woman, if the police aren't able to discover her whereabouts. I know they're doing everything they can. And I understand why they haven't released much information about the case."

"I'm sure they are too," the anchor said, her tone unclear if she meant that or not. "One advantage the police are excited about is their lead detective on the case." A small box enclosing Gray's face appeared to the left of the female anchor. "According to police officials, Detective Becker Gray was a patrol officer ten years ago when Valerie and four other girls received letters from the man they have yet to identify. Detective Gray reportedly took the case very seriously. Although the cases were far from his home in Lakeland, he requested a transfer to any of the five different cities to help with the investigation. In a strange twist of fate, here he is investigating the very case he so desired to help with a decade ago. It seems he was destined to work this case.

"Here with me now is Michael Edwards from the local newspaper in Lakeland. Mr. Edwards is the same reporter who wrote the articles about Valerie Hardy that are now appearing across the country and that seem to have set this whole thing in motion. He has spent time recently with Detective Gray and subsequently has done an astonishing job covering the detective's life and why he's taking this case so seriously." She turned to him. "Michael, thanks for being with us this morning. Can you tell me what you learned about Detective Gray?"

"Happy to be here. I think the most important thing about him regarding this case is the death of his daughter, Grace, who was killed in an auto accident when she was just two. Almost eight years ago. It's true that the birth of Detective Gray's daughter coincided with the delivery of the Pen Pal's letters ten years ago, and his deep devotion to his own daughter drove his personal connection to this case. I've never seen anyone so determined. I don't know if he works every case as he is this one, but if he does, I have to tell you, if I was murdered, I'd want him working my case."

The aroma of bacon drifted around Carson, along with smoke which was immediately followed by the stench of burned meat. Carson had forgotten about the breakfast. He jumped up and tended to the food.

"They don't even know who they're looking for," he chuckled to himself.

≈ ≈ ≈ ≈

Miles away – on 331 outside Enterprise, Alabama – the passenger bus stopped for gas. Many of the other passengers got off the bus and wandered around to stretch their legs. Samuel Hubbard headed off the bus straight into the store, where he purchased a drink and a newspaper. The clerk was watching news coverage when Hubbard walked to the counter.

"Holdonaminute, hon," the clerk said, four words meshed into one. "Have you heard 'bout this?"

"Turn it up, so I can hear it please," Hubbard requested to the clerk.

"Sure, hon."

The news from Florida was spreading quickly across the country as interest in Valerie's story grew. A local reporter named Michael Edwards described the dedication and motivation of the case's lead detective. When Edwards finished talking, the clerk turned the TV volume down.

"That poor girl," the clerk said.

Hubbard nodded and stepped out of the store.

"Detective Becker Gray," Hubbard whispered to himself. "We need to talk."

CHAPTER 47

There it was on television. Right in his face. Undeniable. Gray lifted the remote and powered off the television in the conference room.

We called her Gracie, not Grace.

Then his anger popped. Gray hurled the remote directly at the television screen, causing the remote's plastic casing to shatter. He wanted to scream. Wanted to grab the set and throw it to the ground. To push away all the chairs and flip the conference room table on its side.

"Do it," Parker said.

Gray whipped around, surprised by his presence.

"You deserve it. Grab that chair and throw it against the wall. Do it."

Gray seriously considered it.

"Last night when you were mad about the article ... I didn't know this was why."

Gray seethed. "Boudreaux knew. And he did it anyway."

"I'm sorry, Becker."

"I told him this would happen," Gray said as he leaned on the table. "And now I have to work this case and deal with this bullshit." He slammed his hand against the table.

Parker gave him time. Didn't push or ask questions. But he wanted to ask questions. *Why hadn't you ever told me?* But that made the situation about Parker. *That's not what I want.* He just let his friend wrap his mind around the morning's revealing events. Gray had been completely exposed. All the things he'd clearly been hiding had been brought out into the open. The man was unprotected and flanked on all sides by the truth he fought so hard to ignore.

Gray finally walked to a chair and set himself down. Energy sapped. "I don't think I can do this today."

Parker didn't know about Gray's daughter before reading it in the paper, but he did know about Gray's fight against alcohol. With so much pressure mounting, this seemed the ideal time for someone like Gray to drink. And because of that, he didn't want Gray to be alone.

"I need your help today, Becker," Parker said.

He stood. "I need some time."

"I know you do, but Frank McDonough is downstairs waiting for both of us."

"I can't."

"Yes, you can."

Parker knew how Gray felt about McDonough. Deep down, Gray would want to be the one who told him what they'd learned about his son's death. Parker also knew Gray would regret it if he wasn't a part of that conversation. And McDonough being there might be the only thing that would keep Gray engaged today.

≈ ≈ ≈ ≈

Parker held the door for McDonough. They moved from the waiting area of the Criminal Investigations office to a quiet room where they wouldn't be disturbed.

- 215 -

"Thanks," McDonough said to Gray. "I mean, for taking such an interest in my son's case, detective."

Gray patted McDonough's shoulder, gave him a quick empathetic nod, disliking what he had to tell the man he so much admired.

"I saw the paper and the news coverage on this missing girl's case. It's apparent you put more into your cases than other detectives."

He avoided eye contact. "Here. Have a seat," Gray said, keeping the focus on McDonough. He pulled out a chair for McDonough. The two detectives sat at each of McDonough's side.

"You may know," Parker began, "we arrested your nephew, Billy, last night."

"I didn't know that. It's a shame. He hasn't been well for some time, so I can't say I'm surprised. But, that can't be why you asked me down here."

"It's not," Gray said. For Gray, putting on a work persona helped him not worry solely about his own predicament. "Billy confirmed information which we'd recently collected about your son's death."

McDonough froze, surprised. "It's been over a year." More of a question.

"It has."

"What else could there be?" McDonough asked.

"Do you know Aaron Johnson, Mario Beasley, and Paul Scarborough?" Parker asked.

"Why?"

"They were Timothy's friends, weren't they?" Gray asked.

"I'm thinking you're about to tell me they weren't."

"This isn't going to be easy to hear, Frank," Gray said.

"Just say it."

And that's how Gray would expect McDonough to respond. Strong. Stoic.

Parker stayed quiet on purpose. He believed the scene before him was just as much about Gray as it was McDonough.

"Those three boys, along with Timothy, had formed a group they called G2. It was their version of a gang."

McDonough stayed silent during Gray's pause, listening, waiting for the blow.

"Billy procured a gun for them, and they used it to," Gray paused again, thinking of McDonough, whose world was about to change. Gray wanted to be sensitive to that. "Frank, the boys held up convenient stores. They killed animals with the gun. They carjacked an elderly woman."

McDonough swallowed hard, hearing the information. His mood remained unchanged.

"And you can prove all that?" There was defiance in his voice. Disbelief. A challenge even.

"We've arrested Aaron Johnson and Mario Beasley." Parker finally spoke. "They confirmed those things."

McDonough sighed at the destruction of the image of his son he held so deeply, so preciously in his mind and heart. He muttered, saying what he felt was the appropriate response, "Good. I'm glad you were able to find the truth."

Truth is a bitch, Frank. "There's more," Gray said.

"What do you mean?"

Parker again stayed silent and forced Gray to talk.

"Timothy didn't like what the boys were doing, so he told them he wouldn't do it anymore and he was leaving their G2 group."

Gray detected a sense of relief in McDonough's posture. *Please stay strong.*

"The boys didn't like that idea. They thought he'd turn them in."

McDonough felt the blow coming.

"Timothy didn't accidentally shoot himself playing with a loaded gun," Gray said. "One of the boys shot him to keep him quiet."

And with that, the room became a vacuum. All the oxygen sucked out. McDonough's chest burned to breathe. His vision blurred and twisted. But he held it all in. No tears. No break down. Just strength.

He finally spoke. "Paul did it, didn't he?"

Neither detective confirmed or denied McDonough's question.

"Bring him in," he said. "Make him pay. Make all of them pay."

CHAPTER 48

"How'd it go with McDonough?" Boudreaux asked from behind his desk. He stood as a courtesy to Gray and Parker.

"It was pretty awful," Parker replied, thinking more of Gray than McDonough.

"He's strong," Gray added.

"I hope so," Parker said to himself.

Boudreaux motioned toward the seats in front of his desk then sat again. Parker took a seat then, reluctantly, almost grudgingly, Gray sat. His anger over Edwards's article churned deeper at the sight of Boudreaux.

"Gray," Boudreaux said, "I've scheduled us for an interview tomorrow with Dateline on NBC."

"Us? The two of us? Me and you? No, you can do it on your own. I'm not doing it."

"Yes, you are." Boudreaux rounded his desk and snatched the coffee pot from his private machine. He poured the black liquid into a coffee mug and then doctored the drink with sugar. "You're the out-front guy on this one. You know sometimes we use the local media for this sort of thing. This," he tasted the coffee, "is the same thing. The platform is just bigger this time." He added more sugar to the drink.

"I'm not doing it," Gray repeated.

"You are, and there's no more discussion on it. They'll be here tomorrow morning to tape the interview. You'll be fully rested, which means go home and sleep in your bed tonight, you'll be shaved, in your uniform, and punctual. I'll have a script drawn up for some of the answers."

"A script?" Parker knew he had to get involved in this conversation. Boudreaux and Gray communicating on this subject, unmoderated, would result in a full-blown yelling match. "I'll do it."

"No, it needs to be Gray. I've been working with Agent Tyler on every move we make. This is the best way for us to operate publicly right now. You've read the profile in the paper, right? Edwards did a good job. It's meant to provoke the Pen Pal, which I think it did, and the TV interview is the next step in that."

"What happened to maybe the Pen Pal not having done this?" Gray asked.

"You haven't shown me any real proof of that."

"We have a vehicle identified," Gray started. "A Chevy Nova. Late sixties model. We have a lead on one that's repeatedly going to the gas station where Valerie's wallet was found. We have a sketch of the guy who drives the vehicle. We think he's stolen the car or something because the car isn't registered to him. And he looks too young to be the Pen Pal. We have examples of the disorganized manner of the abduction and the man's actions afterward. We have blood from Valerie's car."

Boudreaux looked confused and cut off Gray's argument. "Look, I'm sorry. Does any of that directly point to someone who may not be the Pen Pal?"

"We think it does," Gray pressed.

"None of that does. There's no solid information there."

Gray's frustration level peaked at a new high. "It's not the Pen Pal."

"It may not be, but the investigation needs to go in a direction. This is the direction … until it's not." Boudreaux said.

"He's right." Parker agreed. But only to end the conversation. He knew Boudreaux wouldn't change his mind about the television interview and Gray would continue saying whatever he could to get out of the interview.

"He's not right." Gray left his chair and paced across the carpeted police logo on the floor of Boudreaux's office. "You know he's not right."

Parker shot Boudreaux a look, telling him to change his approach.

"I've known you a long time, Becker, and I know all about your past. I'm one of the few around here who didn't need to read it in the paper. I'm sorry it's working out like this. You were right. I didn't think about that when I had this idea. I'm sorry. But this case is bigger than your inability to deal with your grief."

"My grief?"

Parker shot Boudreaux another look – *wrong approach again.*

"I know it's bigger than that," Gray said. "And kiss my ass, talk about my grief. You don't know my grief."

"All right." Boudreaux was done. "Tomorrow morning. Ten a.m. In my office."

Parker stood slowly, shaking his head in disapproval of both of them.

"Gray," Boudreaux called to him, "I really do empathize. I remember what you went through."

Fuck you. He wanted to say it out loud. Gray exited the office and found Parker waiting in the hall.

"I am so sorry he pulled that shit on you," Parker said.

"You agreed with him."

"I had to. I know we're right about the case, but we don't have what we need to convince him otherwise right now."

"Then let's go get something. If I get something, I won't do the goddamn interview. I won't."

As Parker chased Gray around the corner, he saw that officer Emilio Sanchez had stopped Gray in the hallway, and he wasn't standing there alone. A woman stood with him, smiling empathetically at Gray.

"Hi, Beck," she said.

A breathless, almost awkward silence filled the hall and engulfed the four of them.

"No," Gray said. "What are you doing here?"

The smile faded. She knew he was still mad at her. After all these years even. She knew. "I thought we should talk."

"Take her in the conference room ... Beck," Parker suggested, emphasizing the woman's nickname for his partner. "Have some privacy."

Parker squeezed between Gray and the woman, tapping her arm as he did so. "It's right here," he told her and opened the conference room door.

The woman followed Parker's suggestion and entered, but Gray didn't move.

"Beck," Parker said, motioning him forward, enjoying the situation. "Come on."

Gray sighed and walked past Parker. "This is no good." Gray closed the conference room door behind him. Locked it.

Parker turned quickly to Sanchez, losing the grin and dismissing his enjoyment. "Who the hell is that?" Parker asked.

"She said she was Gray's wife. Is he married?"

"No," Parker said, looking at the conference room door, curious about what is happening behind it. "I don't think so."

CHAPTER 49

Gray hated bad dreams, but at least he could wake up from them. But now he stood in a room with one of his bad dreams coming to life.

Denise Gains flashed the same smile she gave him every time there had been an awkward moment between them. It made his eyes water and his stomach hurt.

"Your hair's shorter." His voice broke with overwhelming shock.

She touched her hair. "I guess it is."

Denise crossed her arms in front of her chest, then let them slide down and clutched them, interlocking her fingers, in front of her body. Uncomfortable. Nervous. Vulnerable.

"It's been a long time," she said.

Gray snapped out of the clouded daze caused by her presence and shuffled close. They exchanged an awkward hug. The top of her head came up to Gray's nose, and he could smell her fruity shampoo. He breathed deeply. She had always smelled so good.

She gently pulled away from him. "Sorry to just show up on you like this. I mean, without calling."

Gray stared at her, seeing their daughter's bright, shiny face in hers. But he couldn't find any words to share.

And Denise recognized that. "I'm sorry, Beck." She placed her business card on the table. "I should go. I can see it's too much for you right now. I just saw the article today and thought I'd reach out. Sorry. Call me, if you like." She turned to leave.

"Are you," he cleared his throat to speak in a normal tone, "in town?" He noticed she wasn't wearing a wedding ring.

She turned, tears welling in her eyes now. Talking seemed to help her control them. "Have been for a couple months. Selling real estate."

Gray let that hang in the air, unsure if he would've wanted to have known that or not.

"I didn't think you'd want to see me. I wanted to see you, please don't think I didn't. Plus, I was ... getting settled here, starting my own business and all. I was pretty busy."

Her emotions began to get the best of her. "God, Gracie looked like you." Tears slipped out of her eyes and glided down her cheeks. She wiped them away quickly, saving her pride and makeup.

Gray placed both hands on the conference table and leaned on his arms. He dropped his head, hiding his own tears.

"I'm sorry I ran," she told him. "A day doesn't go by when I don't think about it. It was a shitty choice I made."

Gray stood up in a thrust, like he was heaving the weight of all of this off his shoulders. Wiped his eyes. "This is too much right now."

"I'm sorry."

"I've got a huge case and the media's all over me. And Gracie's been on my mind a lot lately, and now ... you. I can't, Denise."

"I understand."

"I mean, did you think it would make everything all right, if you came here?"

"What? No."

"You just show up out of fucking nowhere?"

"I said I was sorry."

"Were you hoping to get your picture in the paper, too? Maybe help you sell a couple more houses?"

She shook her head. "You're an ass."

"The last thing I remember about you is your selfishness. I don't know what to believe."

"And fuck you, too. You feel better now, Becker? Got all that off your chest? You happy? Did you want to make me feel like a piece of shit? Well, way to go. I feel like shit. You feel better?"

"I don't feel anything. I haven't felt a goddamn thing since the day Valerie died, and I'm not trying to make you feel like shit either."

"You," she started but couldn't continue. Her demeanor changed.

"What?" Gray asked.

"You said Valerie. 'Ever since *Valerie* died,' not 'since *Gracie died*.'"

Gray hadn't noticed the misspeak, and he wouldn't want to admit it, if it were true. Not to her. "I'm under a lot of stress, Denise."

She seized her business card from the table. "I'm going."

"Leave it," he demanded. And then, with a voice that sounded vulnerable, weak, and calm, he said, "Please."

She turned and looked him in the eyes. No one had done that in a long time. She saw all his pain. She knew it would be hard, but she could help him. The way she should have a long time ago. Denise returned the business card to the tabletop.

"Don't call me if you're going to yell at me."

And with that, the only woman he'd ever loved walked away from him for the second time.

Once the door closed, Gray fought a losing battle with himself. He finally erupted and slammed his fist onto the table. Not enough of a release, he snatched up a metal folding chair and threw it against a wall. Gray grabbed another one and threw it at the door. Gray lost a battle with balance too and he fell backward against the wall and slid against it to the floor.

"I'm sorry, Gracie. Gracie. Gracie." He repeated her name, like he'd betrayed her by interchanging Valerie's name, like saying it over and over would correct the mistake.

Parker cracked the conference room door after hearing the commotion inside. Gray looked dead tired. He saw the chairs and the marks one had left on the wall.

"You want me to come back later?"

"No." Gray, although a struggle, got to his feet. He looked at his watch. "I need to work."

"You want to talk a bit?" Parker closed the door behind him. "Maybe catch some sleep before we work?"

"No. Neither one. What's that?" Gray motioned to the folder Parker was holding.

"You'll have to get it off your chest at some point, Becker."

Gray leaned on the table again and looked at Parker. "I don't even know what the fuck just happened, so let me figure it out before you start drilling me about it."

Parker knew he wouldn't get anything out of Gray, so he moved on. "All right."

Gray sighed, wanting desperately to change the subject. "What's in the file?"

"The sketch." Parker dropped the file on the table.

Gray opened it and examined the drawing of the Nova driver, as described by Vu and Tran.

"The sketch doesn't match any of the Nova owners' license photos," Parker said.

"We only searched a small radius around the store, right?" Gray closed the file. "Let's widen it."

CHAPTER 50

July 31 – 2:33 p.m.

It took more convincing than Parker expected, but he was finally able to talk Gray into taking some time to himself. But not before they planned the rest of the day. While having lunch, Parker agreed to pull the information on Novas registered to anyone in Polk County so they could perform a comparison against the sketch, which extended the range of the first search that only included the area around the convenience store. Next Parker would get with George Nelson from FDLE, asking him to review the video. Maybe he could clean it up, make grainy portions more clear. Then Parker would wake Gray.

As Gray laid in the rack, he thumbed Denise's business card. For the longest time, no thoughts flowed through his head. He just flicked the corner of the card with his thumb. Too tired to think. Too numb. His breathing eventually slowed, and he fell asleep. But only for a second. His breath caught, stopped short, like his heart skipped a beat. Then his breathing quickened. And thoughts began flowing again. He flicked the card one more time, looking at the name printed on it. Denise Gains.

Gray pushed himself up off the rack. Elbows on his knees, head hung low. His ex-wife had a new last name. And more names flooded his mind. Valerie. McDonough. Jack. Edwards. Amanda. Tiesha. Marie. Tran and Vu. Melinda. McGee. Denise. Gracie. Over and over, like a carousel.

Names …

The door opened.

"You're awake?" Parker asked.

"I don't think I slept."

"What have you been doing? You've been in here almost two hours."

That didn't seem possible. "Where are Valerie's call logs?

"In the conference room, I guess. Why?"

"Names." Gray stood and marched past Parker. Gray continued talking as he rushed down the hall to the conference room. "Remember that FDLE guy? What was his name?"

"George."

"Right. George said Valerie was instant messaging a person named David about being one of the five girls the Pen Pal targeted?"

"I remember that."

Gray entered the conference room and began looking though files. Parker joined him.

"There was a David on her phone log."

"Here." Parker handed him the folder.

Using his index finger to scroll down the list of names, Gray continued through the pages. "There it is. David Kilborn."

"Call the number."

Gray beat Parker to the punch. He was already punching David Kilborn's number into his cell phone's keypad. Three rings and then: "You've reached the offices of David Kilborn, private investigator. I am currently out of the office on an investigation, but please leave me a message and I'll quickly get back to you before the end of business today. Thanks."

"Mr. Kilborn, this is Detective Becker Gray from the Lakeland Police Department. I'd like to speak with you as soon as possible regarding a case here in Florida." Gray provided his cell number. "Please call me as soon as possible. This is very important."

"Voicemail?" Parker asked.

"He's a PI."

"Why would she call a PI?"

"She had to be looking for the Pen Pal," Gray said.

Parker's demeanor changed. "Speaking of the Pen Pal."

"What?" Gray said, realizing Denise's business card was still in his hand. He stuffed it into his pants pocket.

"Chief called. Said something about a third letter."

"What?"

"He wants us to head to the post office. That's why I came in to wake you up."

"A third letter? But the Pen Pal didn't take her."

"I know," Parker said.

"Then why's there a third letter?"

CHAPTER 51

The community interest in Valerie's story caused the media to go into a frenzy and over-report the story. Well beyond simple updates to the events, human interest stories were pushed out ad nauseam in an attempt to continually hook viewers on the headline and keep the story alive.

The Pen Pal's three-day deadline only heightened the frenzy. The media had been talking about it nonstop since the abduction. And, here it was – day three. Inestimable news outlets were offering live news coverage outside the Lakeland mail processing center, outside the police department, and outside the Hardy's home. It was ridiculous, stupid, and, Gray thought, obstructing the job he and Parker needed to do.

Additionally, the regurgitation of Gray's fake profile in the paper and the story of his daughter's death made it infinitely deplorable.

He couldn't even find solace in radio stations. Hearing yet another report over the radio airwaves fueled his annoyance. Gray punched the radio knob, turning off a talk show.

"This traffic sucks," he said.

"Schools are letting out," Parker replied. "We got the results from the DMV search. The sketch didn't match any of the photos on file."

"Dammit. And George Nelson?"

"The FDLE guys are looking at the video now for frame-by-frame image enhancement. After they looked at the first couple frames, they said to not hold your breath on getting much from it."

Gray grew more annoyed and frustrated as their progress slowed and even stopped at certain points. Or maybe it had been the information Parker had just relayed to him. Progress then roadblock. *This traffic is just like the case.*

"Do you want to talk about that woman who came to see you?" Parker asked.

"Not particularly."

"Sanchez said she was your wife."

"Sanchez should shut his goddamned mouth."

"He should. You're right. If you decide you want to talk ... "

"Thanks."

When they arrived at the post office, Gray and Parker were led through a maze of reporters by four uniformed officers. Once inside the building, two other uniformed officers took over so the four could block reporters from entering behind them. Gray and Parker were led to the bowels of the building where they found a sea of postal workers, a couple dozen uniformed officers, Boudreaux, a few detectives, Maddy James, and Michael Edwards. All of them waited anxiously.

"What the hell is Edwards doing here?" Gray mumbled to Parker.

"Don't talk to him."

"What I want to do to him doesn't require talking."

Boudreaux approached. "Over here." He pointed to a table, which had been cleared of everything except one thing.

Maddy James stood beside the table, hands gloved, flashing a friendly smile at Parker. Then she looked at the object on the table, her smile fading. Parker followed her eyes. The third letter had arrived. Right on schedule, per the Pen Pal's original correspondence ten years ago.

"This doesn't make sense," Gray said.

"I know," Parker replied.

The envelope was a plain No. 10. Just like before. Valerie's name and address had been printed on the front. Gray thought the handwriting looked different, since he'd studied the first letters' handwriting technique so closely, but different was how the Pen Pal worked. Gray remembered the differences between the first and second letter. It'd be naïve to think the third would be anything like the first two letters. The stamp on the envelope indicated the letter originated in Lakeland. It was sent the day before.

Did the copycat send it to try and throw us off? Or is that too organized for him?

Michael Edwards joined Boudreaux, Gray, and Parker at the table. He stood next to Gray.

"Switch with me," Parker said, grabbing Gray's arm and sliding between him and Edwards.

Maddy James began to methodically open the envelope. The uniformed officers crowded behind, creating a human wall of privacy between them and the postal employees.

Once the envelope was finally opened, Maddy used tweezers to remove the letter. It was a single sheet of paper, loose leaf. She peeled back the outer flap then the other. She used a camera and took numerous photos of the letter. Boudreaux leaned over the letter and read its contents quickly. Too quickly for anyone else to read it. Gray caught words here and there, but nothing of substance. Boudreaux nodded to Maddy James, who immediately folded the letter and slipped it into an evidence bag.

"Wait," Edwards protested.

"You three, come with me." Boudreaux pointed at Gray, Parker, and Edwards.

Gray was the last of the three to follow Boudreaux. He watched Maddy do her job.

"Will you send me and Parker one of those pictures? I'd like to read the letter."

"Of course," Maddy replied.

Boudreaux turned to Edwards. "Here's what I want you to write."

Michael Edwards scratched his white beard. "Writing what you tell me to write isn't an exclusive."

Boudreaux stepped forward, leaned into Edwards' personal space. He spoke slower, stronger, deeper. "Here's what I want you to write: According to a source close to the investigation, the third letter arrived right on schedule, just as the Pen Pal promised. Details were not immediately verified, but the source reported the letter contained specific details about Valerie Hardy."

Boudreaux continued, as Edwards made notes in his notepad.

"The Hardy family is being notified of its contents. Official word has not been released. A press conference will be scheduled."

Edwards looked up, almost glassy-eyed. His voice cracked when he spoke. "Is she dead?"

Boudreaux stepped away from Edwards. His intimidation had worked. "Just write what I told you."

As Edwards ran off to file the story, Gray's blood boiled. Boudreaux motioned them to follow him. Boudreaux stopped a postal worker and asked for an empty office or room. The postal worker pointed to a small storage area at the end of the huge sorting room.

"You two, come on."

Boudreaux led them into the room and then closed the door behind them.

Gray crossed his arms in front of his chest and locked his jaw. A snarl lifted his right cheek. "Edwards is a piece of shit. Why are you still dealing with him?"

Boudreaux looked them both in the face. "I wrote that letter."

Parker's breath lodged in his throat and forced him to cough. Gray's arms fell to his side. A different anger filled him, even as confusion seeped through his mind.

"Let me explain." He held up his hand to stop the protests he knew were coming. "I couldn't tell you because I needed your reactions to be genuine. All those people out there saw your reaction. All of them will tell someone, hopefully the media outside, exactly what they saw. That's partially what I need."

Gray protested. "You interfered with the investigation."

"Let me finish. After Parker told me about the copycat theory, I ran it by Special Agent Tyler. We examined the theory, and it seems probable. So, we asked ourselves: what if everyone's theory is correct? What if the Pen Pal is still out there? What if Valerie was abducted by someone pretending to be the Pen Pal? What if she faked her own kidnapping? The media will help us get the word to all who might be involved that Valerie's dead and that part of the investigation is over."

"Not a great plan. If the Pen Pal killed her, he's gone. He's got nothing to worry about." Gray shrugged his shoulders and shook his head in disbelief.

"No," Boudreaux replied, "the Pen Pal's got a message in all this. He's not going to kill Valerie and disappear. That's not what it's about for him. If it was, he'd have done something a long time ago. His letters aren't about action. Not his anyway. And if it's a copycat, and he hasn't killed her yet, then we've still got time to catch him. He'll think he's home safe. If he's as disorganized as you two say, then he'll make a huge mistake soon, and we'll catch him."

"And what if she faked it?" Gray asked, wanting to know the thought process more than believing the possibility.

"Then she'll have to contact her parents. She can't have them thinking she's dead. She's pissed about being locked up in their house, but she doesn't hate them and doesn't want to cause them pain."

"I don't like it," Gray said. But he had to admit to himself that Boudreaux's gamble made sense.

Then again, I'm sleep deprived and may not be thinking clearly.

"Since you brought it up, what about the Hardys?" Parker asked.

"I've already spoken to them. They're willing to give us until tomorrow morning before resuming their campaign in the media."

Parker spoke softly, "This could make whoever has her feel like he's being played. Maybe he kills her and we never find her or him."

"It's not brilliant, but it's a course of action that gives us the upper hand." Boudreaux's reply was filled with guilt. It was something he'd already considered and for which he already accepted responsibility.

CHAPTER 52

George Nelson from the FDLE was waiting for Gray and Parker at the police department when they returned from the post office. Laptop resting on his legs, working. He looked thrilled to be a part of something as exciting as Valerie's case.

"I heard about the letter. It didn't sound good," he said. "I have something. Three somethings actually."

Gray and Parker rushed him into the conference room, where all the information for Valerie Hardy's case had been stored. Boxes stacked around the room. Files all over the table.

"You guys thought about going paperless?" Nelson asked.

"Maybe one day," Parker politely replied.

"What'd you find, George?" Gray asked not at all politely.

Nelson booted his laptop again and situated himself at the table, his finger pecking away at the keyboard. Quickly he was ready to show them what he'd learned.

"I can't blow up these still-frames, like zooming in on the guy's face, and clear out the blurriness. That doesn't work. I can only work with the data stored in the image. So, that's what I've done."

He pointed to the picture of the passenger side, right quarter panel. "This one is an obvious result of a collision, like the one described in your reports. It supports what happened at the crime scene." Nelson turned the laptop around and showed the detectives.

"This next one," he turned the laptop toward himself and switched to the second image, "is the logo on the hat worn by our suspect while inside the convenience store. It's an H, embroidered here." He turned the laptop again and pointed it at Gray and Parker. "If you remember, he was wearing what looked like an apron. The time stamp is 1:22 a.m. Maybe he works at a restaurant. Closed it down, cleaned up, and is making his way home."

"Makes sense, Nelson," Parker said.

"Keep going," Gray said, hoping the third something was the big clue, hoping Nelson had saved the best information for presentation last.

"And the final one," he pulled and turned the laptop toward himself again, "is the license plate."

"No shit." Parker said. He bent to look closer at the laptop screen.

"Clear as day," Nelson said. "The information was there, it was just kind of caught in a shadow, so I enhanced it and there you go." He was clearly proud of himself.

Parker laughed and patted Nelson on the back. "Great job."

"Print that out, will you?" Gray asked.

"Here," Nelson said and snatched his bag onto the table. He pulled out two copies of each picture and handed them to Gray.

"You may have just solved this case," Parker said, stroking Nelson's ego, stoking his enthusiasm.

Gray was already at the other end of the table. On his own laptop. He typed in the six digits and clicked the search button.

The computer in front of Gray beeped. The search had completed. Gray hit the print option, and the printer fired up and quickly spat out the results of the search. Parker looked over Gray's shoulder at the results.

The car was registered to Carla Jansen. Further review showed Carla Jansen had been deceased for seven years. And the license plate was registered for a 1988 Cutlass Supreme. Not a Nova. After her death, the Cutlass had been transferred to her son's name. He sold it at an auction a year later before he moved to Asia to teach English. How could the car be gone for six years, but the license plate showed up on a car that they suspected was involved in a kidnapping?

Parker took over the computer controls, and Gray watched as Parker punched criteria into their database search field. Using the H that George Nelson had provided them, Parker searched for restaurants.

"The path of least resistance," Parker said.

After a few seconds, the search returned results listing five restaurants. Each of them open until either 11 p.m. or 12 p.m., which could match the time stamp on the video, if Valerie's abductor worked at one of those restaurants.

"Get the sketch. Let's go get something to eat."

CHAPTER 53

They had visited three of the five restaurants in town with an H in their name. This was the fourth stop, and the parking lot at Hill's Bar and Grill was so full that Gray and Parker had to park across the street in a strip mall of staffing agencies, dentist offices, and small businesses. As they carried themselves toward the crosswalk, Gray noticed the sky had turned dark, but the sun hadn't fully set. Hidden behind the clouds that had rolled in during the late afternoon, the setting sun colored the sky with shades of orange, red, and purple. Seeing another day come to a close caused his weariness to intensify, edging him ever closer toward exhaustion.

"Come on," Parker said as he nudged his partner's arm. A break in traffic had spread out before them, allowing them to cross the street.

Gray leaned over the bar and motioned for the bartender. She waved an index finger at him to let him know she'd be right there. Gray waited and observed how Parker checked out the place.

The bartender arrived. "What can I get you, hon?" she asked in a sweet, flirtatious voice.

"The manager," Gray replied.

"Sure. Hold on." She slipped through a nearby opening that led into the backroom of the restaurant. When she came back out a minute later, she said, "He'll be out in a minute. Sure you don't need anything?"

Parker leaned in next to Gray. "I'll have a sweet iced tea and a burger."

She moved to the computerized register and punched in his order.

The manager appeared from the backroom doorway. He asked the bartender who wanted to see him, and she pointed at Gray and Parker. He made his way over to them.

"Hey, guys. What's up?" he asked.

Gray showed his badge inconspicuously. "Can we speak with you outside please?"

"Sure."

The cars from the nearby busy main street forced the three men to speak louder than usual. They stood in a triangle out of the way and earshot of customers coming and going.

Parker began. "We have reason to believe someone we're very interested in speaking to may be working for your restaurant."

"What?" He seemed like he'd had this conversation before. "Is it Shelly? That girl gets into so much trouble."

"It's actually not her," Gray said. He handed him the artists' sketch. "We're looking for this man."

The bartender came out of the restaurant with a plate of hamburger and fries in her hand and delivered it to Parker.

He laughed. "Now that's service." And she went back inside. He dug into the food. Gray gave him a dirty look. "What? I'm hungry."

The manager took the sketch and reviewed it closely. "My God, I think that's Carson." He looked up at the detectives. "He's off tonight."

Parker, with grease on his lips, said, "Carson who?"

"Anderson."

"We'll need his address," Gray said.

As the manager rummaged through his file cabinet in search of Carson Anderson's personnel file, he told Gray and Parker about Anderson. "He's a quiet guy. Good worker. I kind of wish I had more staffers who worked as hard as he does."

"Who was he friends with?"

"No one here. Wasn't exactly a people person," the manager said. "He didn't get along with staff. Didn't even try."

Gray asked, "How'd he get past the interview process, if his social skills were so lacking?"

The manager shrugged his shoulders. "Kids. None of them want to wash dishes. He was the only applicant for the position and I needed someone really bad." He found the file. "Finally," he said and handed the file to the detectives. "There's one waitress you may want to speak with."

"A girlfriend?" Parker asked.

"More like the only person who felt bad enough for him to even try to talk to him."

"What's her name?"

The manager led Gray and Parker through a short maze from his office to the kitchen. Across the epicenter of this business at a salad-making station, Marisa Hightower, a petite, short-haired 20-year-old, mixed the contents of a Caesar salad. The introductions were short, but Marisa responded without much prompting.

"I'm sorry," she told Gray and Parker. "I don't know that much about him. I tried to be nice to him. He didn't have any friends here. I'm not sure he had friends anywhere."

"Why do you say that?"

"No reason. Just a feeling I have. Is he okay?"

Parker replied. "We just have a couple questions for him."

"Have you ever been to his house?" Gray asked.

"What?" She laughed. "No way. I wanted him to have friends, but I didn't want to go to his house. I don't do anything alone with any guy unless I have to or want to, like the time he drove me home. That's the only time I was ever alone with him. And it was only because I had to. My car broke down. Otherwise, there'd have been no way. He's nice and all, but he was a little, I don't know, aggressive with me that night? I swore I'd never be alone with him again."

"He touched you?" Parker asked.

"No, maybe that's the wrong word. He was," she thought about the right word, "inappropriate. Just awkward. I didn't think anything of it because he's never been that way since then. Or before. He just, kind of, propositioned me. It happens a lot. A guy like him. A pretty girl that's nice to him. Guys misunderstand. They think being nice is flirting. I don't know. It was nothing. Like I said, he's never been that way other than that one time."

"What kind of car does he drive?" Gray asked.

"Some old car. Dark blue."

Gray pulled out his cell and searched images of a Chevy Nova. Once he found one of a dark colored Nova, he showed Marisa the image.

"Does it look like this?"

"Pretty much exactly like that," she said.

Gray looked to Parker, who was having a hard time containing his excitement.

They had him.

And hopefully Valerie, too.

CHAPTER 54

The cruiser raced down suburban, tree-lined roads that grew more residential the farther they traveled from Florida Avenue, the carotid through Lakeland. Traffic dissipated as well, so Gray was making excellent time. Parker set down his notepad and returned his pen to his shirt pocket before going for his cell phone.

"Who are you calling?" Gray asked.

"Boudreaux."

"Wait," Gray burst out. "If you call him, he's going to slow this whole thing down. We'll have to hook up with Edwards from the paper, the media's going to be out here. It's going to be a damn circus. A damn *slow* circus. Don't we owe it to Valerie to get her out of there as soon as we can?"

Gray's argument made sense, but it wasn't protocol. But Parker knew cops had to do what felt right, even if it meant ignoring the rules. "All right," Parker said, as he clipped his cell phone onto his belt. "I don't like it though."

Most of the houses in the Lake Morton Historic District had been renovated and restored to their historic greatness, but there were a few holdouts. Carson Anderson's house was one of the holdouts. The decay was evident even at 10:30 at night with a waxing crescent moon above.

Even the fence boundary around the house bent and swayed. Grass and weeds were overgrown, vines climbed tree trunks and the house walls, curb appeal completely ignored.

Gray, Glock in hand, crept in the shadows, moving in a crouched position. Aluminum foil obscured Gray's view of the first window he came to. He wondered if that was the room where Valerie waited to be found. At the next window through a ripped hole in the curtain, Gray could see what looked like the living room. Seeing no movement inside, he signaled Parker who then skulked along the decrepit fence boundary and disappeared past the corner of the house.

At the front door, Gray checked the knob, but it didn't turn. He stood upright and looked into the small window at the top of the door. The living room was littered with garbage. A cat jumped through the room onto and over fast food wrappers, soda bottles, beer cans, and an exorbitant amount of other clutter.

Gray checked his watch and waited for the synchronized time he and Parker had agreed when Parker would enter through the back door and Gray through the front. When the minute hand clicked to the designated minute, Gray began banging on the front door relentlessly. A light turned on inside the rat's nest of a home. Gray's exhaustion faded away, as focus on the situation took over.

Finally, the living room light came on and the door locks rattled. When Gray heard the doorknob move, he rushed at the door, slammed it open.

"Police," he announced.

The woman, thin and clammy-skinned, wearing only a shirt and panties, shrieked in fright, fell to the ground. She stunk of body odor and looked high.

Parker emerged from the back of the house.

"She all right?"

The waif saw Parker and curled into a fetal position and started crying. "My baby. My baby."

Gray asked her, "Is there anyone else in the house?"

"My baby," she said again.

"I told you to be quiet." The shout came from down the hall, behind them.

Parker raised his weapon. Gray spun around, his back now to the waif, and leveled his Glock at the hall too. A large man, rivaling Parker's size, made his way down the hall, wearing only a pair of underwear.

"Who are you?" he shouted.

"Police. Stop right there," Parker answered.

Gray stepped back and to his left, so he could see the man in the hallway. And so the man could see him. *That's not Carson Anderson.*

"You get out of my house," the man demanded.

"Get down on the floor," Gray commanded.

"Get down," Parker said.

"Make me."

"Somebody get my baby," cried the waif.

"You take another step, and we'll shoot," Gray said.

There really wasn't a choice to be made in Gray and Parker's eyes. Living is always the right decision, but the man of the house took a long time deliberating before finally kneeling in the hallway.

"Don't believe that bitch," he said, and then laid down on the floor, hands on the back of his head.

The waif launched into a run, ran at the man on the floor. She kicked him with her bare feet then jumped over him and ran down the hall.

"Stay on the ground," Parker commanded.

Gray ran after the girl, cautiously stepping around the man. He inched his head around the bedroom entryway, afraid she'd rushed in the room for a weapon. But she hadn't. He turned back to Parker and nodded, giving him the approval to cuff the man on the floor, before entering the bedroom the waif had rushed to. His gun still at the ready but not pointed.

The waif held an unclothed child, two or three years old. She cradled him, both on the floor in an embrace. The room smelled of urine and feces, which, in fact, were each littered about the room in stains on the carpet and hard black mounds.

"What happened here?" Gray asked.

CHAPTER 55

July 31 – 10:51 p.m.

Counting the billboards along Interstate 4 didn't distract Gray the way he'd hoped they would. The way they usually did. His mind kept racing, maybe still fueled by adrenaline from the raid on the house thought to be Anderson's residence. Maybe the waif. Maybe the baby.

The conditions of the room were horrid. After calming the waif and carrying off the man, Gray found out the baby had been locked in that room for four days. Barely fed and tended to. Gray frowned at himself because he'd stopped asking why these things happen a long time ago. Stopped asking who could do such a thing. But tonight the baby meant something else to him.

Valerie. Denise. Gracie.

Gray's mind veered back to Denise Gains and how simply stunning he thought she looked standing in front of him. Her light eyes and dark hair. Round face. Warm smile. And how did he react? *I barked at her. Why?* What he really wanted to do was grab her, hold her.

But that's not who he was.

With Denise's visit fresh in his head, Gray's loss of his daughter magnified. Seeing Denise made him wonder whether Gracie would have grown to look like her mother. Would she have dark hair? Olive skin like him or fair skin like Denise? Tall? Short? Whose sense of humor would she have had? What outlook would she have had on various life events? Positive, negative, cynical, carefree? Would she have been creative or analytical?

He hadn't considered those things before tonight.

He lowered his head, mad at himself, drained from doing all of this yet again. He wondered why he tortures himself with those thoughts.

Six more billboards, he counted, but he stopped, had had enough. Turned the car around at the next exit. Gray couldn't take the silence in his car or the noise in his head.

The ride back to Lakeland only took 20 minutes. Gray grabbed a burger from a fast food place and ate while he drove around the city, trying to turn off his thoughts. After another half hour, he steered his car to Orange Street. He pulled off the road into a parking lot outside Hollis Gardens, home to 10,000 flowers and ornamental shrubs just off the promenade at Lake Mirror. Gray leaned his chair back and closed his eyes, knowing he should sleep, knowing he needed sleep. His thoughts still churned actively, but he was too tired to drive anymore.

He may have dozed off. He may not have. Either way, he eventually kicked open his squeaky car door went for a walk. The events, frustrations and revelations of the last few days opened the floodgates on Gray's own loss. And he had no idea how to handle it all. He jumped the waste-high iron fence to gain access to the garden.

The Rosette fountain, which acted as the heart of the garden, wasn't flowing. Gray missed the noise of the water's movement. The flowers and shrubs, coupled with a grand gazebo and trellis, made for a perfectly peaceful, visually stimulating botanical paradise. Even in the moonlight, when the garden was closed to the public, it seemed like a pristine paradise.

But tonight it was too quiet. With headquarters a short distance away, he got back into his car and headed to the office. Gray tried to stay focused on Valerie's case – Carson Anderson, Carla Jansen's license plate, and the Pen Pal – but his brain kept veering away from it to Denise, Gracie, tomorrow's Dateline interview, and Frank McDonough. Thoughts of Denise took most of his time and energy.

He climbed the stairs to the conference room around 12 a.m. and then trekked through the maze of the building. He fired up his laptop and, almost involuntarily, typed his ex-wife's name into the database. Her residence address appeared on the screen. Gray scribbled it down. Maybe he would stop by her house someday.

I need to do something to get her off my mind, he thought. *I should sleep.*

Gray flipped open his notepad and read the details he'd recorded about Valerie Hardy's disappearance. He read through files of hers again before pulling his laptop closer to him and running Carla Jansen's license plate number through the search. He kept coming back to the car and the license plate. He scribbled down her last known address. Then he searched for any reports of stolen Chevy Nova's in the last two months but found no reports of stolen Chevy Novas since early the previous year.

Gray used the computer database again to search all known cases of abductions or attempted abductions with similar characteristics to Valerie's abduction, carjack style. Blitz attack. The results showed a multitude of incidents, but Gray only saw accidents, road rage assaults, and the like, which only helped Gray believe his theory that Valerie was taken locally.

CHAPTER 56

Gray's steering wheel seemed heavy to maneuver. His lack of sleep had resulted in a foul mood, aching body, and a blurred mind like the fog setting in over the streets. Yet he knew his body. He was nowhere near falling asleep.

The streets seemed desolate except for an occasional car, which became more pronounced the further south Gray drove. When Gray drove through Mulberry, a neighboring town of Lakeland, he turned around and headed back north. A whole ten minutes had passed. What a way to spend the night.

Gray turned into a gas station on South Florida Avenue and parked near a gas pump. His weary body made its way around the car as muggy air hugged him while he filled his car with gasoline. After replacing the pump, Gray decided to get some coffee. A buzzer announced his entrance, and after nodding to the clerk behind the counter, Gray was surprised to see a familiar face.

Gray wanted to turn and leave when he saw Frank McDonough, but McDonough turned slightly and noticed Gray. He stumbled toward the detective, tripping over his own feet. Gray reacted and stopped McDonough from hitting the ground.

"Sorry." McDonough's breath smelled familiar. McDonough wobbled when Gray let him go.

"Are you drunk?" Gray asked.

"No." McDonough spoke angrily, slowly, as he put a six-pack of beer on the counter.

The clerk was ready to ring it up, but Gray put his hand on the alcohol. "He doesn't need that."

"What are you doing?" This time when McDonough spoke, his words slurred all together. "No, I want the beer," he told the clerk. "And who the fuck do you think you are?" he asked Gray.

"I'm your friend. Let me drive you home."

"My friend!" McDonough belly-laughed. "My friend?" He stopped laughing and his face creased in anger. "Well, *my friend*," he grabbed Gray by the shirt, "my son is dead." His face suddenly bent in pain and loss, tears filling his eyes. "I can't pretend anymore." And with that, he pushed Gray as hard as he could.

Gray's footing slipped on the slick floor. He toppled over and landed hard on his elbow. Pain shot up through his arm.

McDonough threw down a $10 bill at the clerk, snatched up his beer. "Stay away from me." McDonough threw the door open and hurried to his vehicle.

Gray struggled to get to his feet. His elbow hurt like hell. He checked it for a cut but found none.

The clerk came from behind the counter to help Gray stand. "You all right? Need me to call the cops?"

"No. I'll handle it."

≈   ≈   ≈   ≈

Thinking McDonough would probably go home, Gray sped to the McDonough residence. His hunch paid off. McDonough's car was parked, albeit crooked, in his driveway.

Gray parked his car in the street, grabbed his Surefire L4 and used the flashlight to shine his way up the driveway to McDonough's car. It was unlocked. Gray opened the door and popped the hood. After finding the engine's fuse box, he disconnected the starter relay so McDonough could no longer drive it while intoxicated. The only thing that would make McDonough feel worse was if he hurt someone while driving under the influence. Gray closed the hood as quietly as possible, and placed the relay on the driver's seat.

He went back into his car, but before driving away Gray looked at the house. Red brick exterior. White shutters that matched its front door. Beautifully landscaped yard. Frank McDonough and his wife were good, successful people who seemed to have done everything by the rules. Perfect life. Marred by a needless tragedy.

Massaging his aching elbow, Gray wondered if someone as strong as McDonough couldn't handle his family's tragedy, then how could he? Gray sighed, struck by his own inevitable fate.

Gray's trepidation caused trembling. It was as if it had already been decided that he'd drink the whiskey inside his duffle bag, and there was nothing he could do to stop it. Gray's mental state allowed for no other solution, but his shaking displayed his fear of the consequences of those actions.

He reached into the passenger seat and opened his duffle bag. A picture of Gracie appeared in his mind, followed by an image of Valerie. Gray pulled the small bottle of whiskey from the bag. Behind his watery eyes, he imagined Denise's beautiful face and then he remembered how he looked in the mirror that morning. What a contrasting difference in the way they'd aged.

The media was circling his life like vultures over roadkill, which resulted in him having to face his daughter's death in a public forum, something he couldn't even do in private. The smell of the whiskey stung his nose and made his body shiver. It was the enemy to which he had to surrender.

CHAPTER 57

Gray tried to ignore the bottle's power over him by forcing his mind toward Valerie's case. The last known address for Carla Jansen was across town. Gray decided to check out the house, figuring the longer he drove, the more mentally active he would remain. And the less the likelihood the bottle would win tonight.

A few cars drove in a loose pack in the opposite direction. It was funny how the only other three cars on the road at this time of night, after one a.m., drove so closely together. You'd think they'd be spread out, one at a time maybe, and going in different directions.

That's it, keep thinking about other things. Anything but Denise or Gracie.

Gray stopped and ordered coffee from an all-night doughnut shop, glad he had it to sip as an alternative to the whiskey. And he didn't care how hot the cup was growing in his hand, he wasn't going to set down the cup. One hand on the wheel, one on the coffee cup. Both occupied. Neither could reach for the bottle.

Once at Jansen's old house, he realized there was no logical reason for him to be there. It wasn't to prepare for the next day, as he'd told himself. It was just something to do, somewhere to go, something to keep him occupied.

Jansen's house had been built in the fifties. Cinder block, carport, and jalousie windows. Three huge cypress trees set in the backyard towered over the house like guardians. They must've kept the house cool during the summer. The front porch light was illuminated. The light cut through the night's darkness and displayed a small sign in the front flowerbed informing would-be intruders of an alarm system. The yard was well-manicured. Two cars rested under the carport, a Jeep Cherokee and a Pontiac Grand Am. They glistened in the light, like they'd just been waxed.

Gray surmised instantly that this house and the people inhabiting it had nothing to do with the investigation. He wondered how many of the neighbors are still here that may have known Carla Jansen and her son. Maybe one of them would know how to reach Carla's son. And then he wondered if any of it even mattered.

Nothing mattered.

The single, depressive thought creeped into his subconscious leading Gray to think about other things. He and Denise. Gracie. Valerie. His desire to drink. Valerie's family. Tomorrow's interview. All of it. In the grand scheme of things, none of it or them truly mattered. The next question that popped into his mind was inescapable.

So why not have a drink?

CHAPTER 58

Leaving his Accord behind in the driveway, Gray hesitantly made his way up the drive to Denise's front door. He paused before knocking. *What am I doing here?* He pulled his arm down and turned.

The other houses in the neighborhood were dark inside. Some had porch lights lit like Denise, others didn't. A sprinkler system kicked on four houses away. Gray could barely see the mist in the distance, but he could hear it perfectly. A dog barked at the sudden noise of the sprinklers.

Gray knocked. His finger mashed the doorbell, then he knocked again. He waited and got nothing. After another minute of waiting, Gray knocked again. Three hard raps on the wooden door. He stopped when he heard from inside the beeps of an alarm system number pad.

Denise opened the front door. She didn't look like she'd been awake or that she knew how to feel about his visit, but she didn't protest, didn't say anything at all.

"Sorry," Gray broke the silence.

She had on a T-shirt and pajama pants. Her hair was messy and her face puffy from sleep.

"When I said call me, I meant on the phone and during the day," she said, tilting her head and revealing a thin smirk. Both were familiar. "You need to talk?"

"It's been a long day."

"Come on in." Denise stepped aside and opened her front door.

He followed Denise through her family room, but never took much notice of the hardwood floors, the paintings on the wall, the cherry wood dining table in the dining room adjacent to the kitchen, or the cat resting in a recliner. He only saw her, shuffling into the kitchen, moving before him, more mature, but yet familiar.

"It really was good to see you," he told her while she made a pot of coffee.

Denise turned on the coffee machine and faced him. Although she felt awkward, her thin smile morphed into a larger grin. The entire situation seemed awkward. Despite their history, because of it rather, they found it hard to communicate with one another. She knew there were a million things that needed to be said, but neither could speak the words.

"It's funny you say that. I didn't think at the time that you thought it was a good thing."

"My response was … I was a bit overwhelmed."

She nodded, letting the admission hang in the air.

"It's a nice house," he pretended he had noticed. He scanned the kitchen as he spoke. The refrigerator was decorated with dozens of magnets holding various drawings and photos of a boy. Gray approached the refrigerator and tilted one of the photographs. "Cute kid."

A bizarre feeling of guilt swept over Denise. She didn't reply until Gray turned to her expecting an answer. "You take sugar and cream?"

"Sure."

Each holding a mug of brew, Gray and Denise moved to the sitting room. A round coffee table acted as the sun of the room and everything else revolved around it. Two couches lined the outside walls of the room. Three bookcases took up the rest of the room along the walls.

Denise sat on a couch, her legs curled under her, while Gray sat at the other end of the couch.

"Why'd you come here, Beck?"

He thought about it. "I wish I knew."

"You know."

Gray nodded. He did know. "Thanks for the coffee. It's good." He took a sip. "When did you get into real estate?"

"Becker ... Why'd you come here?"

"Why'd you come to see me today?" he asked in response.

She collected her feelings before speaking. "Seeing the articles in today's paper ... I kind of felt like Gracie was *our* loss, but we didn't do well with coping together. I thought maybe I'd make up for it or something. Be there for you, I don't know. It's stupid." She barely made eye contact, consumed by vulnerability.

"It wasn't stupid."

They sat across from each other in the sitting room, drinking their coffees. Silent. Not saying what they needed to say. Gray took stock of the house. How it was amended. The warmth of the decorations. The cat ambling in from the other room to check out the goings on. The photo of a boy on the end table.

"Is that the same boy as on the fridge?" Gray finally asked.

Denise felt that sense of guilt again. She nodded.

"Is that your nephew? Matthew's son?"

Guilt turned to dread. "No, that's my son."

"Your son?" His tone mixed confusion and surprise.

Gray set his coffee on the table in front of them and made his way to the table, picking up the framed photograph. Examined it closely. The 4-year-old boy had a head full of curly black hair. He hadn't yet grown into the size of his mouth and ears, yet he was a handsome boy.

She uncrossed her legs from under her and scooted to the edge of the couch. "His name's Jeremy. Jeremy George."

"You had another child," he said, kind of like a question.

Denise tugged on her lip with her fingers and her eyes averted his eyes, as they got watery. "I did."

"I didn't know." He swallowed hard.

Wiping the tears building in the corner of her eyes, Denise chuckled awkwardly, "How would you?"

Gray floated down onto the couch, breathing almost like he'd had the air knocked out of his chest.

"You didn't have children, Beck? Did you re-marry?"

"How could I?"

"I'm sorry I ran the way I did. I know it was shitty."

Gray chuckled and fought back tears. "Yeah."

Again silence filled the room with awkwardness. She'd seen that look on his face before. He was ramping up for a fight, but Denise didn't want that. Or maybe she did because he'd made her feel guilty about having a son, something she never imagined that she'd feel guilty over. She stopped herself, realizing she was ramping up for a fight, too. And she really didn't want to fight.

"Maybe we should meet for lunch tomorrow. Talk about this more. I'd be all right with that, Beck. I just don't know if now's the best time. I mean, it's almost two in the morning."

Is she trying to run from me again?

"You're right." He stood. "I don't want to disrupt your perfect new life you have here."

"What are you talking about?"

"Your new house and business. Your son and husband. Everything. I'd hate to ruin it all. I mean, you ran far away to build this world."

She had wanted to avoid a confrontation, but there was no stopping Becker Gray when his feelings were hurt. He hadn't changed. In all these years. It was his feelings over everyone else's. "It's time for you to leave."

She started toward the kitchen to lead him to the front door, but her anger spun her around.

"You know what?" She turned and pushed him. "You want to know about my perfect world, Becker? My husband cheated on me with a 27-year-old dental hygienist, my son is a thousand miles away from me because I can't afford a decent divorce attorney, and I haven't sold a house in four months. So fuck you. I won't apologize for having a son. I won't apologize for trying to live my life. Gracie lost her life, I didn't. I miss her every day. I think about her all the time. You think raising another child doesn't make me remember all the things we did with her? And don't you think I see her when I look in the mirror? Fuck you and my perfect world, Becker. Did I wallow in self-pity like you apparently did? No. But I don't have to explain any of it to you. I reconciled my actions with myself, my God, and Gracie in my own way."

She breathed in and out quickly, like she'd just run five miles, and anger shot from her eyes at Gray.

"As long as you're all right with it." He moved beyond her toward the door.

Denise grabbed the nearest object, an artichoke finial accent piece, and threw it at the front door. "Why did you come here?" She continued, sobbing as she spoke. "Did you want to make me feel like shit? Well, you did. You happy?"

"I just wanted to see you," he shouted, turning and making sure she wasn't going to throw anything else at him.

"Here I am. Happy? Everything you thought I'd be?" Yes, she wanted to cry her eyes out. Yes, she wanted to rage. But somehow she knew she had something far more important to say to him. Something she should've told him a long time ago. "It wasn't your fault, Becker. Live your life."

Gray's heart dropped down into his stomach. Nothing prepared him for that comment, and he reacted per the norm. "It was my fault, Denise!" He was so filled with anger. At himself. He stuttered on the words he hadn't dared to say aloud in eight years. "I was the one driving. I was the one who fell asleep." Then he screamed unintelligibly, as the words released something long repressed inside him.

Gray fell to his knees and wept.

Denise took a deep breath. Shock of his words momentarily ceased her own tears. She wiped her face with her hands, drying them on her pajama pants, but her tears started again. Here they were together sharing the pain, hurt and grief of losing Gracie. She walked to him, pulled him close. For a moment he didn't reciprocate, but he eventually wrapped his arms around her waist and heaved heavier, from deeper inside.

"It's all right," she kept saying to him, comforting him.

Her words finally registered. They gave Gray pause. Shock and horror really. He collected himself, and rose from his knees. Still in an embrace, although loose, the two old lovers looked deep into one another's eyes. His eyes were filled with an alchemy of guilt and anger and hers with nurturing reassurance. She touched his face, dried his cheeks tenderly.

"How can you say that?" he whispered to her.

Then, without another word, he broke the embrace, walked to the front door and left Denise's house.

Denise's body shook with emotion. She went back to the couch and allowed herself to cry.

CHAPTER 59

How could she fucking say that?

Denise's words — "It's all right" — floated in Gray's head.

It's all right? How could it be all right? He had killed their child because he fell asleep driving the three of them home from a movie.

How was it all right that when he pulled himself from the wreckage that night his daughter was nowhere to be found?

How was it all right that Gracie had been ejected from their car and found 50 feet up a tree?

How was that all right, Denise?

The cap to the whiskey bottle couldn't come off fast enough. The liquid stung his mouth and throat like acid, but that didn't stop Gray from gulping it down until it was gone. He threw the bottle out of his open driver-side window.

Gray wiped his mouth and then started his car's engine. He quickly drove away from Denise's perfect home and quiet neighborhood.

The next hour and a half grew increasingly blurred. Gray's thoughts veered between anger, pity, grief, despair, hatred, envy, betrayal, and every other self-loathing thought a person could have.

Visions played in his head, churned his emotions. A younger Denise above him as they made love. Her silky smile slipped back and forth between ecstasy and happiness. Then Denise walking away from him a month after Gracie's death, her eyes filled with tears, confusion, pain, blame.

That winter day leaves blew around them while cold air bit at their skin. Gray's heart had felt nothing since.

Then his mind focused upon Gracie playing with dolls. Him on the floor next to her, wanting to watch television, but Gracie demanded his attention in her own sweet, innocent way.

She had her favorite stuffed teddy bear with her the night of the accident. He remembered finding the bear before he found his daughter.

Gray slammed on the brakes in the middle of the street. He didn't even know what street he was on. Truly had no idea where he was or what he was doing or how he'd gotten there safely. He found himself out of breath. Sweat had broken out all over his body. Tears on his face. He couldn't take it anymore. He checked all his mirrors. There wasn't a car or another person in sight. He was alone again and nothing mattered. The world was so much simpler and more manageable when he thought God was singling him out, when it was Gray against the whole world, when it was him against God.

But now ... now it was just him. He didn't know what to do. At least before he knew God cared enough to inflict pain and hurt on him. Now he knew it wasn't God's doing. It was just how his life had been. God didn't even care enough to persecute him.

Gray's temper flared, and he struck his steering wheel repeatedly until his hand hurt and he couldn't punch anymore. Tears rolled uncontrollably down his face and a violent screech came from his mouth.

A car passed, honked its horn, and made Gray lift his head. He needed more to drink.

Despite the whiskey's effect on his brain, he made it to his apartment. It took what seemed an eternity to get the door unlocked. He found a half bottle of whiskey right where he'd left it the last time he'd fallen off the wagon. He unscrewed the top and drank heartily from the bottle.

Dull the pain. Dull the pain.

Gray tripped inside his bedroom on a pile of dirty laundry. The bottle slipped from his hand and much of it spilled onto the carpet. He quickly crawled to the bottle and rescued the rest of the liquid.

His breathing labored and his body numb, his brain continued to swirl painful images. All of them kept spinning in his mind, like it was their mind to control and not his.

He screamed at the insanity of it all. Valerie's complex case. Fucking Denise's reemergence in his life.

He eyed the bottle of liquor and wanted more. But the room spun, and it made him tired. *Tired* ... He was finally tired.

Gray left the bottle on the floor and struggled to his feet. The bathroom light bit at his eyes, so he shut it off. He found his way in the dark of the bathroom into the medicine cabinet. He was going to sleep tonight. Inside the cabinet, he found a box of over-the-counter sleeping pills. He took three, washed them down with whiskey.

He staggered back to his bed, sat on the floor against the mattress and gulped again from the bottle. Twenty minutes later, he passed out.

It was a temporary peace.

CHRIS WENDEL

Part III

CHRIS WENDEL

CHAPTER 60

August 1 – 3:55 a.m.

"Becker. Becker. Becker."

The voice came from a million miles away and slowly entered Gray's consciousness. The pattern was consistent, passionate, strong, inviting.

"Becker."

Gray wanted to follow the voice but couldn't get his legs moving.

"Becker. It's time, Becker."

Gray reached for the voice, but he didn't open his eyes.

"Becker."

Gray finally wanted to see the origin of the pleasant voice. His eyes flickered, wanting to come to life, but he couldn't open them.

Screaming this time. The pleasant tone was gone, "Becker!"

That did it. Gray's mind and body awoke. He was groggy, yet his instincts were to jump to attention, but his arms and legs were paralyzed. He couldn't move an inch. Reality came quick. He wasn't paralyzed. He was captive. Bound up tight like an animal, lying on his own bed. Mouth gagged. Darkness surrounded him. As sure as he was of those particulars,

Gray struggled, unsure of his predicament. Whatever it was, wasn't good. His mind still felt cloudy from drinking and sleeping pills.

"Settle down now, Becker." The mystery man's voice resumed a gentle tone. "Relax."

But Gray continued to fight the binds.

"This can be easy or it can be hard. It's up to you, but we're essentially on the same team right now, so let's shoot for easy. All right?"

While thrashing, Gray raced to figure out how to get free. As he did so, he responded to whoever had entered his home and captured him, but his words were muffled by the tape.

"If you just said you're an officer of the law, I know already," the man said. "You're all over the news." The man behind the voice grew tired of Gray's movement. He yelled, "Stop moving!"

Gray froze. The man's breath warm against him. The closeness frightened him.

"Thank you. I've come a long way to see you, Becker, and I hope our time together is productive and peaceful." He paused. "You maintain the productivity, and I'll maintain the peace. Are we clear, or do I need to be more explicit?"

Gray responded in grunts and incomprehensible words, nodding his head.

"I think I should though." The voice turned to a whisper, and the man said into Gray's ear, "So to be clear, by saying I'll maintain the peace, I mean I won't hack you to death."

Gray nodded. Even drunk and sleepy, he knew he was in a bad situation and the best thing he could do for now was to go along with whatever this man wanted.

"Good, Becker. Now, we're going to move fast, so stay with me. Valerie Hardy made a vital mistake, which has put a number of people in danger."

What did this have to do with Valerie? Gray tried his hands again. Tried to focus his eyes on the man pacing.

"First and foremost, you. It then extends to Michael Edwards at the newspaper, her father. Your police chief for that ridiculous news story about the third letter being delivered. I mean, come on. And then there's the son of a bitch who has Valerie."

What did he just say?

"Now, I've found you. I know where to find Michael Edwards and Jack Hardy. The only thing I don't know is where to find Valerie. And I think you know where she is. So, here's what we're going to do. You'll tell me. And I'll go get her and bring her to safety in a way you cannot. She'll win her safety, others will be punished for allowing her to make this mistake, and you'll stay here, tied to your bed until someone finds you."

The man sat down on the bed.

"Do we have a deal, Becker?"

Gray didn't respond. He sucked in air through his nose, which made a slight whistling noise.

"Becker, we both want Valerie to be safe. Help me help her."

Gray didn't respond again. Just tried focusing his vision through the darkness.

The man was quiet for a long time as he sat next to Gray on the bed. Gray cursed himself for drinking. This never would have happened had he just refrained.

"Let me help Valerie, Becker," the man finally said.

Gray muttered something, so the man slowly took off the tape from Gray's mouth. "Go ahead, Becker. I'm listening."

Gray breathed heavily as he spoke. "You're about a day too early."

"Bullshit!"

"No. I'm … being … serious." Gray was still slurring his words. "We have a basic area of town … he's from. … We think. … We truly don't know anything. … It's all speculation at this point."

"Again bullshit!" The man slid a sharp knife against Gray's neck and pushed hard. "Maybe death would be better than the shitty way you're living now. You can't hide in the bottle from your daughter's death, Becker. Just be glad she's not preyed upon by evil men."

"Don't talk about my daughter," Gray warned.

"Tell me where Valerie is, or I'll ease your pain by slitting your throat."

"Okay. But take me, too. Please. You don't know how to get there anyway. I'll show you."

Hubbard took the knife away from Gray's neck. He chuckled. "I have a map." Hubbard moved away from Gray and turned on the bedroom light, blinding Gray momentarily.

"I need to see her safe too," Gray slurred, hiding his eyes.

"Okay, Becker. You can come but not because you asked. I'm taking you because I'm not finished with you."

He moved over to Gray and stood directly in front of him. Gray's eyes finally adjusted to the light, and his vision focused but not on the man's face or his knife. His eyes went right to the bottle he was holding.

"First, drink."

Then Samuel Hubbard forced whiskey into Gray's mouth.

CHAPTER 61

Hubbard checked the clock in the dashboard. It was 5:08 a.m. He didn't have much time before people would be up for the day and possibly outside, which would make his job nearly impossible to do undetected. He'd reached Carla Jansen's house and set the map of Lakeland on Gray's lap. He checked to make sure Gray was still breathing and then got out of Gray's Accord, slowly closing the door to avoid the squeak of the hinge.

Hubbard walked gently toward Carla Jansen's old house. The two cars under the carport puzzled him. He slipped into the shadows from the front porch light and examined the cars. The Jeep Cherokee was messy inside. Old newspapers were in the passenger seat, and the car hadn't been vacuumed in quite a while. The Pontiac Grand Am had a woman's makeup bag on the dashboard. It didn't make sense to him that Valerie would be held here against her will. He figured that the man who took her wouldn't excel at intersexual relationships.

Moving quickly to the front of the house, Hubbard verified the address number matched what Gray had told him. It did. So had Gray given him a bogus address? Had Gray lied to him? Hubbard scanned the neighborhood. The houses on the block were very similar to this one. The carports all had two cars under them. Now that didn't mean the man who took Valerie didn't have two cars, but two cars usually meant more than one person. Plus, many of the cars were SUVs and vans, and the news had reported the police were in search of a Chevy Nova.

Across the street, two houses down, under a group of huge oak trees, there sat what looked like a Nova. Hubbard looked around the neighborhood for people out walking or putting out the trash or leaving for work already. He saw no one, so he ran through the shadows to the car he thought was a Nova. Sure enough, it was.

Hubbard knew he had the right house. He could feel Valerie inside. He rounded the car and saw that the rear quarter panel on the passenger side was crunched and dented. This had to be it. Hubbard checked the neighborhood again. Still no one was out and about.

CHAPTER 62

Something – a premonition, a gut feeling, or maybe a dreaded nightmare – told Valerie that today would be the day she would either get her freedom or die. She hoped they weren't one in the same.

She hadn't been able to go back to sleep since she had woken over an hour ago, and the sun still hadn't risen. In the meantime, she'd been working on her bindings and had successfully freed one leg. She was still working on the other when she thought she heard footsteps.

But not from inside the house.

She froze and listened harder. Had she actually heard anything? Was it a dog? Or a cat? After the sounds silenced, she went back to work freeing her leg. If she could just get free before he woke up, she could try the windows again and make a run for it, maybe break one.

What the hell kind of knot did he tie?

She stopped again. She thought she heard something outside the house, but after she heard it, it stopped. Whatever it was, she prayed it didn't wake up her captor in the other room. If he caught her trying to get free, he'd flip out on her, hurt her or even worse. And, that made a sudden rush of guilt and anguish consume her. She thought of her mother and father. Valerie wished, hoped she could see them both again.

Thud!

She froze again. *Okay, that's definitely outside the house,* she thought. *What is going on? Who is out there?*

The noise sounded and felt like a bass note from a rap song. Then a succession of bass notes pounded throughout the house. At least, she thought the sounds now came from the inside the house.

What the hell is going on?

She tore at the knot frantically. *Hurry!*

CHAPTER 63

Gray's eyelids parted, but when the streetlights shined into his eyes, his brain felt like it was splitting wide open. He felt thick mucus accumulate inside his mouth and involuntarily his body lurched forward as he threw up inside his car. He pushed aside the map in his lap, as the smell overcame him and he threw up again.

His shoes were soaked in vomit. He kicked them from his feet and, with his bound hands, removed his socks. He then crossed his legs, tucking his feet under him. Gray reached down to his right and fumbled until he found a latch. He pulled it and the seat reclined with a jolt. He passed out again.

≈   ≈   ≈   ≈

The thudding noises jarred Carson Anderson from his sleep. His first thought was of the possibility of Valerie trying to escape again, but he'd tied her up pretty good. And his room was across the hall from hers, so he figured the thudding would be louder. *It's something else.* He sneaked through the house, masked by darkness.

It's surreal to see someone, an unknown person, climbing into your house. The thudding noise must've been from him kicking the house, as he propped himself on the window sill and tried to pull himself inside. There's a feeling of fear that comes from seeing this image. A feeling of ange r. And a ton of thoughts that accompany those feelings. Luckily for Carson, his thoughts were typically brilliant and fast and spontaneous, so he instantly knew what he needed to do.

≈   ≈   ≈   ≈

The entrance into the house was neither as quiet or as easy as Hubbard thought it would be. It had been a long time since he'd entered a home like this. He was younger, more fit then than he was now. The left side of his body was completely inside the house, when he lost his grip and smacked his face against the window sill, splitting his lip. He tasted blood.

Once fully inside the house, Hubbard looked around, gaining his bearings. The house was dark, not a light on anywhere, only very little shined in from the outside of the home. As his eyes adjusted to the darkness, he became aware that he was in the kitchen. And that someone was moving toward him.

Hubbard grabbed at the knife, latched to the belt around his waist, however the attack was already too far along for him to defend himself. The bat reflected what light there was inside the house, just enough for Hubbard to see it before it connected with his right arm. The connection had sufficient force to knock his footing loose, and Hubbard fell against the wall. The excruciating pain was momentarily disorienting, and both the pain and the disorientation made it impossible for Hubbard to hold onto the knife, which fell quietly to the carpeted floor.

Thanks to adrenaline, or Hubbard's innate violent tendencies, or his history of participating in physical clashes, he pulled himself together mentally, and immediately strategized how to survive this attack. The use of the bat told Hubbard three things. Whoever was swinging the bat didn't have a gun, or he would have used it. Hubbard, though, did have a gun. Two, in fact. His and Gray's police issue. He didn't want to use either one. The gunshot blast would cause too much alarm in the neighborhood.

Second, from a physical standpoint, the man with the bat didn't think he could physically control Hubbard without a weapon. Hubbard figured that would work in his advantage the longer the altercation lasted. And finally, that another swing was certainly coming his way.

Hubbard dropped to the floor just before the bat connected with the wall above him. Where his head had been. Drywall dust rained down on him, the bat stuck in the drywall. This left his attacker's body exposed. Hubbard wished he had a knife in his hand. He'd jab it straight up into the man's body. Instead, he grabbed the man with his left hand – his right arm almost useless from the attack – by the underwear he was wearing and then kicked the man's knee as hard as he could, knocking him to the ground as well.

This created space for Hubbard to get to his feet. Plus, it disconnected the man from the bat stuck in the wall.

Carson's knee wasn't broken, but it hurt, which made him feel alive. He used the kitchen counter to pull himself to his feet. He grabbed the bacon pan from the stove and rushed at the man, but the man easily moved out of the way of Carson's feeble attack. That was when Carson heard him laugh, which infuriated him. Enraged, he blindly attacked again, connecting the pan to the man's body. The connection and the weight of the pan bent Carson's wrist backward and he lost hold of the pan. Even when the pan fell to the floor, Carson wanted to continue his attack, so he wrapped the man up in what he thought was a nifty wrestling move. He tried to drive the man backward, but the man jerked his knee straight into Carson's midsection, jolting him upward. The air left Carson's lungs immediately and his strength sapped.

Hubbard could tell he'd hurt the homeowner, whose grip weakened after the knee to his chest. So he kneed him again for good measure, then he tossed the man aside. Hubbard was tired of playing games. While the man sucked in air, Hubbard went looking for the knife.

"What's your name?"

Still twisting on the floor, regaining his lung capacity, Carson didn't respond.

Hubbard's eyes had grown fully accustomed to the darkness and he found the knife quickly. He also took a second to lick the blood from his split lip.

"I don't have any money for you. I have an ATM card you can have. I'll give you the code." Carson finally pleaded with his burglar.

"I don't want your money."

"I don't have jewelry either." Carson groaning still.

"I want the girl. Valerie. Where is she?" With the most casual of movement, Hubbard leaned over Carson and plunged the knife into his leg. It was different stabbing someone with his non-dominant hand. Felt new even. Exciting in a way.

The young man never saw it coming. Carson threw his head back in pain and his cries reverberated off the kitchen walls. As Carson writhed in pain, Hubbard, again casually like this was a normal thing for him to do, pulled the knife from Carson's leg.

Taking a good, long look at Valerie's captor, Hubbard was surprised that he looked like a teenager. A pale, thin, and vacant teen. Hubbard squatted next to Carson and spoke calmly, like there were no hard feelings.

"She's here, yes? In one of the bedrooms?"

Carson didn't respond verbally. Maybe he couldn't. The pain was unbearable. And new to him. But his eyes told Hubbard what he needed to know.

"Did you hurt her?"

"No," Carson spat out the answer quickly. He wanted Hubbard to know that. His eyes, though, said yes.

"What's your name?"

The response took longer this time. "Carson."

"Last name," Hubbard demanded.

"Anderson."

Hubbard showed Gray's badge to Carson, like it was his own identification.

"You're a cop?! You can't just stab me in the leg then."

Hubbard thrust his left arm forward and shoved the blade into Carson's stomach. Popped his skin like a balloon. Carson groaned when it happened. He didn't scream out. He didn't flail about on the floor. Just groaned and jerked like he was going to vomit. Then shock set in and he just laid there. Bleeding. In total disbelief that this was happening.

Hubbard stood and walked to the adjoining living room. He peered carefully into the room and saw a long, dark hallway.

"Valerie?" Hubbard called. "Valerie, it's the police. Are you all right?" Hubbard waited but got no response. "We're going to process this man, and then we'll get you out of the room, okay?"

Silence.

"Okay." Finally, a muffled female voice emerged from the darkness down the hallway.

Hubbard, excited about finding her safe, returned to Carson and bent over him. He stepped on the young man's chest and pulled the knife from his abdomen then he stabbed Carson in the neck. Twisted the blade around and around before withdrawing it from the wound and thus releasing a flood of blood.

On his path down the hallway, Hubbard had already forgotten all about Carson Anderson, but he became aware again of his right arm throbbing. He moved the arm. It hurt like hell, but it worked. Nothing broken. Purely a soft tissue wound. It'd bruise, but he shouldn't be too limited from it. He stopped in the only open bedroom doorway, Carson's bedroom. He took off his shirt, wiped his face of blood, cleaned the knife and sheathed it, and then dropped his shirt on Carson's bed. He found a shirt in Carson's dresser and slipped it over his head. He noticed a single key set among a pile of coins on the top of the dresser. Hubbard stacked the pennies in one pile, the nickels in another, then the dimes and quarters in their own respective piles before scooping up the key into his hand.

Hubbard said into the locked bedroom door where Valerie was being held prisoner. "Valerie, are you there?"

Hesitantly, she replied, "Yes."

"I'm going to open the door now." He held the key near the lock.

"Wait!" She yelled in a bit of a panic, which froze Hubbard in his footsteps. A minute later, she called out again. "Now it's all right."

Hubbard pushed the key into the lock. It fit and turned. The door pushed open and Hubbard flicked up the light switch. Again it took a moment for his eyes to adjust, but there she was. Ten years later. All grown up. But, to him, she was the same little girl he met when he traveled with Rev. Hindman. The sight stilled him. He couldn't believe it. He thought he'd never see her again, having acted to coax her into a safe haven forever. But, to know, when she needed him again that he was there for her … that made him the happiest. He would've done the same for any of the girls.

Hubbard noticed her bruised left shoulder. It incensed him, made him happy he killed what's-his-name. "It's okay," he told her. "You're safe now."

"Thank you," she said.

Hubbard showed her Gray's badge, and Valerie, on the bed and wrapped in the bedspread, started crying with an emotional force that startled both of them. He hesitantly moved toward her. She did need him. He sat next to her on the bed and held her until she was all cried out.

"Let's get you home," he said.

She laughed nervously, excitedly. "Yes, please."

She motioned to the leather strap still binding her to the bed frame.

"Right," he said, and he quickly set out freeing her foot.

"There are clothes in the dresser," she told him.

Hubbard found them in the drawer and handed them to her. "I'll give you privacy."

"No!" She looked frightened. "Yes, I mean. Just don't leave."

He understood. She wanted to keep her protector close, so he could keep her safe. "I'll turn away."

"Where is he?" she asked, pulling on her jeans while favoring her hurting shoulder.

"He's been taken." *Straight to hell for hurting you.*

Another relieved feeling came upon her. She slipped on her T-shirt then asked, "Where's everyone else?"

Everyone else? For a split second, he felt offended, but then he realized she thought he was the police and this was them rescuing her. Hubbard figured he had to get her talking if he was to get her out of the house, to keep her from asking more questions. "How did he subdue you, Valerie?"

"Ether."

"Are you dressed? Can you show me?"

"I just need shoes." Valerie hadn't seen them yet, but since her clothes were in drawers, she guessed her shoes would be in the closet. And they were. She slipped them on and then said, "Here." Valerie pointed him to the bathroom sink, led the way to it. "I got free once and dumped them all out."

As he studied the ether bottles, he said, "Good job. I'll need a bottle for evidence." Because of the amount of bottles she dropped into the basin, not all of them fit and some still contained liquid. He snagged one with his right hand. "You ready to see your parents?" he asked, turning back to Valerie.

"Yes!"

"Come on." Hubbard wrapped his supportive left arm around her, and they left the bedroom for the living room where they found the front door.

"There it is," she said. "It was there the whole time."

"What's that?" he asked.

"The door."

≈   ≈   ≈   ≈

Gray was slumped over in his car's front, passenger seat. Hubbard wasn't sure how he'd explain Gray, and Valerie didn't give him time to think of something either. She stopped without warning and Hubbard's arm came off her shoulder since he wasn't expecting her to stop. He turned back, ready to snatch her if she showed resistance.

Valerie looked at the house where they came from and then the neighborhood street. There were no police cars, no media vans, no helicopters. And who was the guy in the car?

This isn't right. "What's going on?"

Hubbard held out his left hand for Valerie to take hold. "God sent me to save you." Instead of taking his hand, Valerie kicked into a run for survival and screamed as loud as she could.

Hubbard lurched forward and swatted at her feet, tripping her. Valerie landed hard and knocked her face against the pavement, dazing her, making her immobile long enough for Hubbard to grab hold. He hurriedly dragged her to Gray's car, opened the back door and pushed her into the backseat. By then, her thoughts had cleared and she began fighting him hard. *How could this be happening twice?*

Despite her able fighting, Hubbard ripped the T-shirt from his body – right arm screaming in pain – and doused it with the ether. As Valerie clamored for the door latch on the other side of the car, he jumped on top of her and held the ether-soaked shirt over her face, struggled against the pain in his right arm until Valerie passed out. He let up the pressure on her and felt drained from the aching and effort. But he couldn't rest. He had to get out of the neighborhood before someone saw him and tried to stop him. He had more to do.

CHAPTER 64

Maybe it was the heat of two to-go coffees he was carrying – one for him, one for Gray – but Parker broke a sweat before he made it from his parking space at the police department to the building's rear entrance. He was dragging this morning, so he figured Gray must've been in worse shape, considering the newspaper articles and the upcoming interview with Dateline. Hence the coffee.

Parker hated leaving Gray last night. Something about the look in Gray's eyes made him think he should stay, but Gray kept pushing him to go home, kept saying he was going home too after he finished typing the day's reports. Parker made him promise. And, how long was he supposed to fight Gray on the issue?

In the long run, though, Parker felt like he should've stayed. He was up half the night worried about his friend anyway. He knew yesterday's newspaper articles wouldn't amount to the pressure Gray would experience today. It was one thing for Gray to have to face the truth in writing, it was a whole other terrible, unthinkable, worst-idea-ever thing for Gray to have to actually *talk* about it. And on camera at that! Boudreaux really was pushing Gray too far.

Once inside the station, the sweat evaporated quickly from his brow and face. He went straight up to the Criminal Investigations office, where his and Gray's cubicles called home. He expected to find Gray there, though he wasn't. Parker checked his watch and saw it was already 7:33 a.m. Gray usually was already there by this time, but no one else in the office had seen him yet. Parker checked the locker room shower and dressing area, but he didn't find Gray there either. Nor in the conference room studying case files. Parker set down the coffees, tired of carrying them. And realizing he wasn't going to find Gray. He called his cell. No response. Worry wrapped Parker like a heavy blanket. Then guilt set in. *I should've stayed with him.*

Parker sat at the conference room table and got hold of his thoughts. While Gray was usually at the department by 7:30 a.m., he often wasn't. So this wasn't outside the norm. *I should just calm down.* If this had been any other morning, he wouldn't be worried. But, it wasn't any other morning.

Parker surveyed the messy table. The pizza box from the night before was still at one end. Their paper plates, napkins and drink debris there too. Case files were spread across the table. A laminated map sat atop one of the piles of folders, showing the radius of the searches they'd completed. He saw Gray's notepad then picked it up, wondering what he'd worked on the night before. The last entries were the full contact information for two people – Carla Jansen, related to the case, and Denise Gains, Gray's ex-wife.

That doesn't bode well for how Gray spent his night.

His fingers bounced across the telephone keypad. After six rings, Denise picked up. Her voice sounded dry, scratchy, and tired.

"Ms. Gains, this is Detective Jeffrey Parker with the Lakeland Police Department."

"Is Becker all right?" she asked immediately, her voice resonating concern.

"Did you hear from Detective Gray last night, ma'am?"

"My God, what's wrong? What's happened?"

"Nothing that I know of," Parker replied. "I'm his partner and … Ma'am, did you hear from Becker last night?"

"He came by very late, woke me up. But, he was only here about 20 minutes."

"Did he say where he was going?" Parker asked hopeful of an answer.

"No. He was upset when he left."

"Forgive me for asking … upset about what?"

She took what felt like a long time to respond. "Life."

Parker sighed then said, "Thank you for the information."

She asked before Parker could hang up, "Detective … can you let me know if he's okay?"

"I'll have him call you when he turns up. Thanks again for the information."

Parker hung up the telephone and sat at the table, thinking about Gray's state of mind if he went to his ex-wife's house, wondering why he hadn't gone home like he said he was going to do. Parker considered Gray's frame of mind and actions. Gray had searched for Denise and Jansen's addresses. He went to see Denise because he couldn't stop thinking about her after she showed up yesterday. Then he'd need to get his mind off Denise.

What would he do? Go to Jansen's house? No, he left the address here at the department. Say he didn't go to Jansen's old address, what would he have done? He'd drive until he could sleep.

Parker flipped through Gray's notebook, finding no other ideas about what Gray may have done last night. He hoped Gray wouldn't stop for a drink, but it was damn possible. Parker slammed his fist against the table, mad at himself. *I should've stayed with him.*

Parker pulled his cell phone from his belt and dialed Gray's cell phone again. This time leaving a voicemail. Then he texted Gray: *Call me.*

The news crew would be arriving soon and setting up, if they weren't here already. Boudreaux would be looking for Gray. *Maybe Gray's just running late?* Parker theorized. *Hopefully.* But he somehow doubted that was the case.

He went to the lobby front desk receptionist. Parker figured he'd see if anyone downstairs had seen Gray. If not, he'd leave strict instructions to be called the moment Gray walks through the doors because Parker had to go looking for him; he couldn't just sit and wait. In the lobby though Parker was sidetracked, seeing a familiar person in the waiting area.

Frank McDonough, who was still nursing a hangover, sounded as groggy as he looked.

"Morning, detective."

"What brings you here so early?" Parker asked.

McDonough propped himself straighter in the seat. "Is Detective Gray here? I need to see him."

Parker checked his watch and then looked at the receptionist, who shook her head. "No, he's not in yet."

McDonough looked devastated.

"What is it?" Parker asked.

"I …" As much as McDonough's head ached, his pride hurt worse. "I need to apologize to him."

McDonough confessed his actions from overnight, getting drunk and how he treated Gray. He was ashamed and embarrassed.

"It happens," Parker said. "I don't want you to worry about it. It was nice of you to come down here." McDonough's update on Gray's activities during the night only made Parker's worry more intense. "I'm going to have someone drive you home."

"I don't need that," McDonough protested.

"You do. It's all right." He patted McDonough on the shoulder. "I'll have Becker call you when he gets in."

Parker made the arrangements with the receptionist to get the man a ride home. Then he rushed up the stairs, returning to his desk.

He dialed Gray's apartment number. No answer. He dialed Gray's cell again. He left another voicemail.

All signs indicated to Parker that Gray visited a bad place last night.

CHAPTER 65

Before sunrise, Hubbard had found a quiet, unassuming motel in west Lakeland. He needed a place where he could think about his next move and not be detected by anyone. How suspicious would it have been to be driving around all morning with two people passed out in the car? Someone surely would have seen them. Plus, he couldn't handle the stench of Gray's vomit any longer.

Before entering the motel office, Hubbard slipped on a T-shirt from Gray's duffel bag stored inside the Accord's trunk. It was well before usual check-in time, but Hubbard slipped the motel manager an extra $40 and, voilà, he had a cottage. Hubbard parked the Accord in front of cottage number six. He opened the door and then unloaded Gray and Valerie, to his right arm's displeasure.

The room smelled of mothballs and insect repellent, which was a better smell than inside the detective's car. The curtains were tattered at the edges, and the bedspread looked older than Hubbard. The carpet was so worn it stood flat, and the padding beneath it had no cushion. There was a time in Hubbard's life that this place would've been a dream home.

When Hubbard laid Valerie onto the bed, dust rose from the spread. He dropped Gray on the floor between the full bed and the wall-unit air conditioner. There was a 27-inch television set in the corner on a small table next to the bathroom entrance. A radio alarm clock rested on the stand next to the bed. Hubbard unloaded the belongings from Gray's car. He used another one of Gray's garments to scoop out the vomit from the car. Then he checked the parking lot one more time for people who might have seen him carrying two limp bodies into the cottage, and when he was sure no one had – it looked like a place where everyone minded their own business – he went into the cottage and locked the door.

Inside, Hubbard eyeballed Valerie. She was breathing fine and still under control of the ether. Gray, however, was waking, so Hubbard retrieved a new bottle of whiskey he'd found at Gray's apartment and straddled the man. He jammed the opening of the bottle into Gray's mouth and tilted the bottle back.

"Drink it," Hubbard ordered.

The liquid poured into Gray's mouth and caused him to swallow mouthful after mouthful, but much of the liquid ended up overflowing onto his shirt and the floor.

Valerie, having pretended to sleep when Hubbard checked her, watched from the bed. Horrified and scared. When Hubbard stopped pouring the liquid down that man's throat, Valerie closed her eyes again. Hubbard pushed Gray over in a drunken heap. He emptied the bottle, pouring it all over Gray's passed out, limp body.

"This is all you got." He threw the empty bottle at Gray, squatted and gripped Gray's face. "I could kill you ... but you have no life to take." Hubbard shoved Gray's head to the ground. Valerie heard it hit with a thud.

As Valerie pretended to remain asleep, Hubbard moved away from the man and focused on her. He repositioned her on the bed and then used a secondary set of Gray's handcuffs to secure her right wrist to the bedpost. Valerie could tell this guy was different than this first guy who'd taken her.

Whoever the first guy was, his issues were sexual. This guy, he had a sense of violence intermixed with pain and anger. She was afraid to fight back.

Hubbard tore the alarm clock out of the electrical outlet and took it into the bathroom with him. He closed the door. Soon the radio came to life. Valerie heard the sound of rushing sink water. She lifted her head and tried as quietly as possible to get Gray's attention, but the attempt was unsuccessful.

Inside the bathroom, Hubbard pulled his and Gray's guns from his jeans pockets, stacked them on the toilet tank's cover. He saw in the mirror that blood splatters still stuck to his face. For a moment he worried about the motel manager having seen them, but he summarily dismissed him, feeling the old guy didn't really care. In a place like this, seeing no evil and hearing no evil was the best policy.

Hubbard's right arm where Carson had struck him looked bad. The reddish coloring was fading to various hues of blue and purple. It seemed to be spreading beyond where the bat made contact too, taking up most of his upper arm. He shrugged his shoulders at the injury and flipped on the faucet. Washed his face while listening to the news. The National Public Radio anchors' manner and tone always helped calm him. And he needed calming today. He was amped up, and he wasn't sure what exactly he was going to do. He hoped the Morning Edition's sporadic reporting about Valerie's case would give him ideas, but so far, it hadn't. In fact, all it had done was made him more upset.

When the anchors discussed the arrival of the third letter and what it meant to the case, Hubbard slammed his fist against the mirror. He hadn't sent any letter, and if the cops were dumb enough to follow that lead, so be it. He had Gray. He had Valerie. She was safe. That's what was important. Her.

But his mind kept veering back to what put her in danger? Who put her in danger? Who allowed her to be in danger's way?

See, I am sending an angel ahead of you to guard you along the way.

When the news ended at 8:30 a.m., he clicked off the radio, knowing what he had to do next.

CHAPTER 66

As Gray came to, he attempted to sit up, progress which was denied by the large air conditioning unit. Gray smacked his head on the corner of the ground unit and fell back to the floor, moaning in discomfort. He hadn't yet realized his hands were still bound. He did, however, realize he was still drunk, his mind still cloudy, and his body still numb. It was an unmistakable awareness. That must have been why hitting his head didn't hurt too much.

His glassy eyes scanned the strange room, and they rested on Valerie – swollen black right eye, blood clotting the shallow scrapes on her cheek and forehead. She lay awake on the bed. Her right hand cuffed to the metal, straight-spindled headboard. But she was smiling, happy to have someone with her, even though she had no idea who he was. She figured he was in the same grim situation, so he probably wasn't a bad guy, which to her meant he was a friend.

"Are you all right?" she quietly asked.

"I'm drunk," he replied too loudly for Valerie's taste.

She shushed him. She'd been faking sleep and didn't want her latest captor to know.

"Help me," she pleaded.

Gray closed his eyes to fall back to sleep.

"No," she objected.

The pills he'd taken to help him sleep and the liquor he drank to forget his pain were still governing him. His neck went limp and his head fell to his left. In his stupor, he dreamed of Gracie coloring in a book while sitting at a small child-sized desk. Then the same images woke him abruptly. They burned his body, and he began sweating.

"Can you hear me?" Valerie pleaded with him. "Please."

She cried, seeing her hopes fade desperately in his drunkenness. The badge the new guy used. The handcuffs she was now wearing on her right arm. She knew this drunken lump of man on the floor must be a cop. She just didn't know who the man in the bathroom was. She hesitated to think him the real Pen Pal.

"Gracie?" Gray's head rolled back and forth against the wall.

Valerie moved closer to the edge of the bed, closer to Gray. "I need your help," she said and dried her eyes with the bedspread. "Come on, please."

Gray lifted his head. His eyes remained closed, as if still asleep. "Gracie?"

Sober up! she wanted to scream. Instead she said, "I need your help to get us out of here. Can you help me?"

Gray fought with all his might, but it felt like something was holding him down. His mind transferred him back eight years ago. Gray saw himself in the front seat of a wrecked vehicle. He couldn't get his seat belt unfastened. The thought of being back in that seat made Gray quickly give up. He grew more tired than he could ever remember being. He let his head fall back and strike the wall again.

Valerie didn't know what to do. She became more and more frantic. She went from one man's captive to another man's, but this time she thought she had someone who could help her. This was her best chance. Two against one. But, *he's in no shape to provide her help.*

"What's your name?" She tried a different approach.

"I'm your daddy."

If he hadn't been drunk, she'd think he was crazy. She actually didn't know how he was functioning at all. She'd watched their captor pour a 750 milliliter bottle of whiskey down this guy's throat.

"I'm your daddy," he whispered.

She had to do something to get him in the game. She didn't like it. "Daddy."

"Gracie!" Gray's head jumped to attention. He eyed Valerie intensely. "You're not Gracie." And his head fell back against the wall again.

Come on! "I am. I'm Gracie." She would be anyone if it would wake him up. "I'm Gracie, and I need your help."

"Help?" Gray said. His eyes were clinched shut. He pictured himself frantically searching the field on that unforgettable night. "I'm trying. I'm so sorry."

She had no idea what he was talking about. "I know. I know. But it's okay."

"It's not okay!" he shot back at her, too loud again.

She shushed him again and watched the bathroom door. She expected it to burst open and their new captor to charge out, but the man stayed in the bathroom. She turned back to Gray who was now leaning against the bed, with his head resting on the edge. Valerie moved close and spoke softly into his ear.

"Make it up to me." She watched Gray blink unresponsively. "You love me, right? I need your help."

A tear dropped off the bridge of Gray's nose.

"Don't be sad. Don't cry." She hated doing this, but she needed Gray's help. "Forget the blame, make up for it now."

Valerie teared up as her words hit home. Gray shook his head again, eyes still clinched shut. "I miss you." Gray sat completely still, as tears streamed from behind his eyelids. In his drunken vision, his mind pointed his eyes up the tree now.

Despite the heartbreak in his voice, Valerie simply didn't have time for his grief.

"I watch you every day," she told him, hating the idea she was playing with this man's pain. "I see you. I protect you."

"Better than I protected you." Up the tree, jammed between a branch and the trunk, Gray saw Gracie's car seat.

"Daddy." She waited for him to respond. She hoped he'd open his eyes and look at her. He didn't. "Daddy, please. Look at me."

Gray slowly turned his head toward her. His watery eyes met hers, and he quickly turned away.

"Look at me. Look in my eyes." She waited as he finally did as he was told. Valerie thought of her own father. "I love you."

Gray began shaking, hyperventilating, and he sealed his eyes closed again.

Valerie inched closer to him. Although still on the bed, she got close enough to gently kiss his cheek. Gray soaked up every slight touch and sensation.

"I need your help," she said and moved across his face to kiss his other cheek.

Gray, again, didn't react when she placed her warm lips on his cheek.

"I promised you I'd never let anything happen to you." Gray leaned his forehead against hers. "I would've liked to have said good bye."

What is it going to take to snap this guy out of it?

Valerie leaned into him again. "Don't let me down again."

Gray's eyes shot open at those words.

The bathroom door swung open.

Valerie was caught.

CHAPTER 67

"What are you doing?" Hubbard demanded to know.

"I was worried about him. You made him drink so much whiskey." She looked back at Gray whose eyes were again closed, sleeping. The last ten minutes had been for nothing.

"He's dead anyway." Hubbard spoke with no emotion toward Gray.

"Why are you doing this?"

Valerie needed to get her new captor talking to find out if he was the real Pen Pal. It was mostly important because she didn't know if this was the third day of her abduction. If it was and he was the Pen Pal, she would be freed today. In death. And that wasn't what she had planned.

"I saved you from that evil man." Hubbard looked insulted she hadn't given him credit for that.

Valerie jerked her right arm in the air. The handcuff clanked against the metal headboard to bring his attention to her confinement. "Forgive me if I don't feel so saved."

"You should thank me."

"Let me go, then I'll thank you."

Hubbard looked away from her. "I can't do that."

Valerie's emotions built inside her. "Why?"

"None of this was supposed to happen!" Hubbard exploded in response, frightening Valerie. "I did all this because of fathers like him." Hubbard pointed at Gray's crumpled body. "Bad things happen to their little girls. Fathers either stop it or they cause it." Hubbard rounded the bed and pulled Gray off the floor.

"What are you going to do to him?" Valerie protested.

Hubbard dragged Gray toward the door, adrenaline killing the pain in his arm.

"Wait. Wait. No, don't hurt him. Leave him alone," she pleaded. If he took the cop away, she'd have no help, no way to get out. "You're the Pen Pal, aren't you?"

Her words stopped Hubbard in his tracks. He just looked at her, surprised at the despair in her voice, the pain on her face.

"Why would you send me those letters? What did I ever do to you? What did any of those girls do to you?" Tears poured down Valerie's face.

Hubbard dropped Gray on the floor. "You really don't remember?" His shoulders slumped, as did his emotions.

"Remember what?"

"We met at an Early Gospel Class?" *She didn't remember.* Valerie's father let her go to the bathroom by herself. More than 500 people present and he let her go to the bathroom alone. Anyone could have walked off with her and no one would have known. It was lucky for her that she happened upon Hubbard, whose children's bible learning class had ended and he was reviewing the workshop receipts. She asked him where the bathroom was. He helped her to find her way there and then back to her father. He protected her better than her father had – *an angel to guard you along the way* – and she had no thanks in her heart, just contempt for his ongoing protection. He sent the letters with no intention of ever coming after any of the girls. He just wanted their fathers to love them more, care for them better.

"At a what?" she asked.

"I protected you with the letters," he said.

Valerie's voice filled with scorn. "Your plan didn't work. You wanted to keep us safe? You wanted to save us? Is that what you wanted? Because Amanda's dead, jackass. She couldn't take the life you subjected her to. She got drugged up and was raped and killed. Way to go." She screamed as loud as she could to get her point across. And maybe someone would hear her.

Hubbard stood frozen. The news about Amanda chilled him to the bone. Was Valerie lying to him? Maybe to get under his skin?

He stepped over Gray's body and walked to the bed. "How do you know?"

"I hired a private investigator to find all the girls. To prove to me you were a piece of shit joke. That this whole fucking idea of yours was lame and stupid, and it didn't do anyone any good." She paused and then pressed him, knowing she'd shaken him. "You failed. You can't protect people. Because shit happens. The world happens." She felt so empowered screaming at him.

He had failed, he knew it now. *Right idea,* he thought. *Wrong audience.* Hubbard had placed the emphasis on the wrong people. He should have never threatened the daughters.

"Give me your father's phone number."

"Why?"

Hubbard hesitated. "I'll tell him where to find you."

Valerie hesitated. "Last time you told us that, you also said I'd be in pieces."

"No pieces. Give me the number," Hubbard ordered. There was something different in his eyes now.

"I don't want to," she said. Her fear of him and his violent presence returned quickly.

"You said some hurtful things to me just now. No one talks to me like that. And you made me want to hurt you, but I don't want to do that. I want you safe. But him ... " Hubbard pointed at Gray's hunched over body. "I don't mind hurting him. So give me your father's number or I'll kill him right now." He pulled the knife from its scabbard. "I'll drag him up on the bed next to you and strangle the breath from his body so you can watch. I'll cut him open and soak you in his blood. I'll take his flesh and feed it to you."

"All right." She didn't have a choice. "All right."

After he wrote her father's cell phone number on his hand, Hubbard opened the door of the room and peered out. No one around. Outside the room on the nearby street, cars passed at high speeds, but he was willing to bet not a single driver cared about the happenings at this shoebox-style cottage motel.

As Hubbard dragged Gray through the door, Gray's eyes popped open and burrowed into Valerie's body. She felt them and looked his way. She was shocked to find him coherent in any way. He pointed with his eyes. She didn't know what he was pointing at. *What is he trying to say?*

Then the room door closed, and she was alone again.

She looked over the edge of the bed where he'd been laying and saw a shiny object on the floor almost six feet from her ... *key to the handcuffs!*

CHAPTER 68

Parker gently pushed the door open, hand on his weapon, concerned to find Gray's apartment unlocked. He had only been there once, about two years ago, and not much had changed. It looked like maybe Gray had gotten a new lawn chair for the living room, but that was about it.

"Becker?" Parker called out before entering.

He stepped in and immediately felt the stuffiness of the apartment. With the door open, the heat from the Florida climate overpowered the air unit. The apartment smelled stale, then further into the apartment, Parker recognized the scent of liquor.

"Shit." Parker took his hand off his weapon.

The bed surprisingly looked slept in. The whole room was in disarray though. Maybe Gray slept here more often than Parker knew. Or, maybe Gray just never made his bed. It looked like he never picked up dirty clothes either. A small wastebasket overflowed with trash. Parker rummaged through it quickly, looking for clues from the night before. The bin had food wrappers, receipts, empty bottles of water, and the like, but no clues.

Parker saw an oval-shaped spot in the carpet. He felt it. Still wet. He smelled his fingers. Whiskey. *Dammit, Becker.*

Parker's cell came to life, ringing and vibrating at the same time. He grabbed at it quickly, hoping Gray was finally calling him back, but he let it go to voicemail when he saw Boudreaux's name on the display. After the ringing stopped and the call went to voicemail, he dialed Gray's cell again.

≈   ≈   ≈   ≈

Hubbard set aside his map and pulled Gray's Accord to the edge of State Road 33, north of Lakeland, where there was nothing for miles. Right where he wanted – out of town and a long walk from anything. He reached into Gray's pocket and retrieved his cell phone, which immediately rang. Hubbard thought he'd pushed the wrong button on the phone, causing an alarm, but he saw on the display that someone named Parker was calling. He pressed the ignore option and then slipped the phone into his own shirt pocket.

Gray's car door squeaked when Hubbard opened it and then again when he closed the door. He rounded the car and opened the passenger front door. He scooped up hands full of sand and tossed it into the floorboard to cover Gray's vomit from the night before. The smell had grown worse and worse, and it made Hubbard despise Gray more.

Hubbard opened the back door where Gray, still cuffed, was sleeping off his drunkenness. Hubbard checked for witnesses before reaching into the car toward Gray.

CHAPTER 69

August 1 – 845 a.m.

He had been awake, he had heard her, and he'd helped. Valerie almost cried she was so excited. So relieved. So close to escaping. The ten minutes she decided to wait to confirm the real Pen Pal had actually left her were excruciating. Each passing minute seemed like a week. She had to be sure, though, that he'd gone. If she'd tried for the key and he came back inside, catching her, then her chances of escape may have been gone forever. However, if she'd waited and he came back in, the odds were – she gambled – that he wouldn't find the key and she'd be able to lie in wait for another opportunity to use the key. So she convinced herself to wait, which may have been the hardest thing she'd ever done.

But, after ten minutes, there was no amount of logic that would override her hopefulness. Valerie turned her back to the door and sat up on the bed, her right wrist still connected to the bedframe via handcuffs. She stretched out her left leg toward the small key as far as she could, but she couldn't reach it. *The cop helped, but he could've left the key closer.*

She scooted on the bed, further from the headboard where the cuffs held on to her wrist. Scooted so far that her arm straightened out and her shoulder strained. She pushed her hip out and then stretched her leg again, used the rubber top of her sneaker to grab the key and pull it back toward her. She repeated that until the key – *her freedom* – sat directly in front of her. She scooted back toward to the headboard, giving her shoulder relief. Reached down with her left arm, her bruised shoulder mildly irritated by the movement, and snatched up the key. Stared at it, sitting in the palm of her hand, for a moment in disbelief.

Her heart raced. She had felt so many emotions since being taken from her car near her home. Hope was the most powerful of them that she'd had during her ordeal. But now, holding the key in her hand, she knew what true hope felt like, knew the true power that hope held in life. *You must believe.*

She fumbled with the key, fitting it into the keyway and turning it. She gasped aloud and again almost cried when the ratchet released and the arm swung open. Valerie couldn't believe it. *Thank you, Gracie's dad.* There was too much going on inside her mind. Too much emotion. Too many thoughts. So many future opportunities just became possible. With this one key. Valerie sat frozen a moment, wondering if this whole thing was real. Then she heard a vehicle outside. Tires rolling over gravel. *Oh no!* She felt fear. Real fear. *I have to get out of here.*

She jumped off the bed and pulled the dingy curtains back from the window to see the lay of the land, to see where she could go to get away. To see if he was coming back. She saw that there were other standalone cottages like the one where she'd been taken and held. Each looked like it had its own curb appeal, each with a front yard, flower bed, and driveway. Three cars were parked outside their respective cottage. An elevated pool structure had been built right in the middle of the compound. No one was using it at the moment. And, last she saw, in the center of the horseshoe thruway, another cottage marked OFFICE.

The vehicle she had heard rolling over gravel came to a stop outside the office. A man got out of the car and went inside. She let go of the curtains. Searched the room. Still trying to figure out her options, now feeling safer since confirmed the Pen Pal hadn't returned. *Phone!*

She'd call 911. She'd call home. *Wait! Dad!* She needed to call her dad. She'd given the Pen Pal her father's private number. The one only she knew about. Not even her mother knew of the phone. *I need to find a phone.*

Valerie scanned the room. *What? No.* She must've missed it in the excitement, like she missed seeing the front door the first time she had a chance to escape. She scanned it again, this time running around the room, physically scouring the room for it. *How can there not be a phone?*

"No." she said, realizing she'd put her father in danger, that she was on the cusp of being free, but he may be on the cusp of something terrible. "No!"

Valerie threw open the cottage door and did the only thing she could think to do. Run! She ran toward the office cottage. But she didn't want to go inside. There was probably a phone in there, but she wasn't sure she trusted other people. No, she wanted the car.

As she neared the car, Valerie could hear the engine still running. *Yes!* Totally elated, she yanked open the car door, hopped in, threw the car in gear and drove off before even closing the car door. She reached the end of the horseshoe and pulled right out into traffic. Cut off other vehicles. She didn't care. She was free and she needed to help her father.

Quickly she got the rusty, old car to 45 MPH, and then the tension from the last few days released. *I'm free! I'm really free!* Valerie began crying, not able to hold it in any longer. She cried and drove. She didn't know for how far or how long, but the release quickly resulted in a feeling of extreme exhaustion. So tired that her tears dried up just as she realized she had no idea where she was.

The road had changed from the cottage motel to an industrial warehouse area to lot-after-lot of mobile homes and mobile home communities. Add to that that she'd never been on this road before or to this part of Lakeland. She was lost, and there was a harrowing feeling in that realization. She knew where the grocery store was located closest to her house, the mall, church, the movies, and that was about it. Anywhere she ever went, she had to search online and learn the directions before taking the car out, like she did before going to the newspaper building, like before meeting William Ford.

How do I get home?

Where can I find a phone?

CHAPTER 70

Hubbard steered Gray's car into a gas station near the Interstate 4 connection in north Lakeland, across the street from an all-night chain restaurant and a motorcycle dealership. After stopping the car, Hubbard kicked open the squeaky door then rounded the car to the pay phone. He thought about using Gray's cell phone to make his call, but decided against it. Too traceable. He fumbled in his pocket for change, and finding the right combination to make a call, he slipped the coins into the slot then dialed the telephone number that Valerie had given him.

"Valerie!" Jack answered after seven rings.

"You wanna see her?"

"Who is this? This is a private line."

"Is that right? Is Valerie only supposed to use it in case of emergencies? I'd say this is an emergency, Jack."

"Are you the one who has her?"

"You mean, am I the Pen Pal?" Hubbard stacked the remaining coins in piles on his palm.

"I don't like that name."

"Neither do I. Now shut up." Hubbard closed his fist, destroying his stacking job. "Say another word and it might as well be good bye." Hubbard waited, and Jack remained silent. "Good. I enjoyed your mea culpa on the news last night, but I didn't believe it. I know what you were doing. You were antagonizing me, Jack, weren't you?"

"Yes."

"It worked." He worked at stacking the coins again.

"I want to see her again."

"How 'bout I trade you for her?"

"What?"

"If you're really sorry about letting her get kidnapped, then let's trade. Save her now by giving yourself up."

"Done. Time and place?"

"No police. No Marie. If you bring or tell either one, no one ever finds Valerie."

"Time and place."

After supplying Valerie's father the rendezvous information, Hubbard hung up the receiver, dropped the coins into his pocket, and then dashed across the parking lot and into the convenience store to grab a snack, a bottled-water, and a car air freshener.

≈   ≈   ≈   ≈

Mike Todd parked his personal vehicle, an F-150 truck, in front of the convenience store. When he'd pulled into the lot, he noticed a car similar to Gray's by the pay phone. He hadn't seen Gray in a couple days, and when he saw the articles in the paper, Mike had grown very concerned about his morning coffee buddy. He actually knew very little about Gray, but the articles filled in many holes. If Gray were at the store, at least Mike could see him and let him know he was being thought of.

However, instead of Gray heading toward the Accord, Mike noticed another man approach the car he thought belonged to Gray. Disappointment spread quickly through him. As Mike pulled on the latch of his truck door, the other man opened the Accord's door. The hinge squealed. Mike froze, looked at the car again, thinking the hinge sound was quite a coincidence. Gray's look-alike Accord moved in reverse and turned. Its tail end pointed toward the highway patrolman. He'd been parking behind Gray on the interstate almost every day for a very long time. He'd memorized his license plate, but hadn't known he had until that moment.

That was Becker Gray's car, but that was not Becker Gray behind the wheel.

CHAPTER 71

He sat on his bed a moment, as thoughts spun in his head. Jack didn't know if he should believe the caller. *How 'bout I trade you for her?* Though, he wanted to believe that he could do something to help his daughter. He wanted that desperately. And what did *trade* mean? *No, I know what it means.* She'd be free, he'd be dead. Which was a preferable outcome to him. But how could he trust the Pen Pal, if that's who really called. And how could Jack trust that Valerie was still alive? *I should've asked for proof of life.*

He navigated the phone's menus and found the number that had just called him. He selected it and pressed the Call button, waiting … No answer. *Dammit.*

Jack knew the phone call wasn't a joke. No one had that cell phone number except Valerie. Not even Marie. So how did the caller get it? Valerie had to have provided it to him. *She has to be alive!*

Jack eased his breathing and looked around the master bedroom. He'd been walking in and out of the room a dozen or more times every day for almost ten years. Everything in the room had grown into the walls to him, had become nonexistent. As he looked around, he'd forgotten that on his dresser there was a photograph of he and Marie at their wedding. Pictures of Valerie as she grew up stretched the length of one wall. A chair that he and Marie had purchased at a garage sale before Valerie was born. Jack hadn't thought of that chair in years. After they purchased it, he sanded it down and repainted it. Marie reupholstered it. That was the chair Marie first sat in to nurse Valerie when they both came home from the hospital. It was where Jack sat and pulled Valerie's first tooth. It's where Jack held Valerie almost all night when the letters arrived ten years ago. *She has to be alive.*

He wished he owned a gun. Never before in his life, even after the letters had been delivered, had he thought he'd ever want to hold a gun with the sole purpose of killing a man. Sweat dampened his hands, as it felt like a fever was breaking out across his body. He realized that principles, like living a non-violent existence, were just fleeting notions, simply situational beliefs, only justification for taking the easy road, just excuses for people to not explore the world around them, for not facing their deepest fears. But now, in this situation, he didn't care that he wanted to betray his principles. He would do anything to keep his daughter safe. Maybe that was his one true principle.

He remembered he had a weapon of sorts. Jack went to his dresser and dug around in his top drawer. Way in the back behind socks, trinkets, and other memorabilia, he found it. A small pocketknife. The blade was only two inches. It wouldn't kill a man, but it might shock or disable a man temporarily, at least long enough for Jack to get the upper hand. He pushed it into his front pocket and then was on his way.

Marie saw him emerge from the hallway that led to the bedrooms. She moved off the living room couch. "I made lunch while you were resting."

"I'm not hungry." He swiped the car keys off the table next to the couch.

"What's going on?" she asked him.

"I have to go out."

"What? Where?"

"Work called."

He eased past her, heading toward the front door and avoiding eye contact.

"Work called?" She put her hands on her hips. "You're going to work? Now? In the middle of all this?"

They'd been together for 24 years. Marie knew something was going on, and she knew Jack was shutting her out. He wasn't a good liar. And he knew that she was on to him already.

"I just need to file a report. There's a deadline I forgot about." He tried anyway.

He was at the front door, gripping the knob, and her words stopped him from leaving.

"You had better not open that damn door without talking to me."

He held in a sigh and turned.

"What have you done?" she asked.

"Nothing, Marie."

"Who was it that really called you?" She raised her voice desperately, emotions taking over.

"Work, I told you."

She stared him down, gave him her best *I don't believe you* look, until he broke eye contact. Marie wasn't getting her way, so she lashed out at him. "You're an idiot, if you think you're leaving here without telling me the truth."

"I can't," he managed to say.

This was hard for him too. Leaving her. Trading himself for his daughter. He expected to be killed. The Pen Pal wanted him now, not Valerie. And Marie wouldn't let him go, if she knew the truth. Or, maybe after all these years, all their fights, all their stresses about finances, about how to raise a child they'd kept a prisoner, how to remain a family through the darkest of times, maybe he didn't want to know if she'd stop him from leaving. Or, maybe he was just telling himself that to make leaving easier.

She spoke calmly again, trying to appeal to any of Jack's sensibilities. "You put out that reward, Jack. Did someone call to convince you they could help as long as you pay them?"

"No."

"That's a fool's errand, Jack." She yelled again, frustrated and angry for not getting the results she wanted. "You want to believe someone can help, but they can't. No one can." Tear drops rose and fell from her eyes. She continued yelling, "Not even you. There's nothing anyone can do about it. She's not coming back."

Shocked by her own words, her breath caught. She slapped her hand across her mouth. Guilt instantly gripped her and squeezed her tight. Marie's emotions soaring here and there had been her way of trying to make Jack talk to her, but her words – *She's not coming back.* They came out of nowhere. A surprise even to her. *How can I feel that way*, the guilt made her ask herself. Truth was, she had felt like that since Valerie had been taken. She didn't want to admit, but she did. The odds of survival weren't in her daughter's favor.

Marie kept her hands over her mouth, as she made her way – ran almost – back to the couch. She sat down on the edge of it, rocking back and forth. She wanted to throw up. To collapse on the floor and cry until she had exhausted herself. She screamed through her hands. The guilt of those words – *She's not coming back* – tore at her insides like a grinder tearing apart a tree stump.

Jack edged his way into the living room and watched his wife cry into her hands. He wanted to be mad at her for what she said, for her not believing. Perhaps if he hadn't just received that call, he would have been mad. But not now. He sidled up to her, sat down. He used his strong arms to pull her close.

"I didn't mean it. I didn't mean it. I didn't mean it." She repeated those four words until she'd almost hyperventilated.

"I know," he'd say after every few repetitions.

She finally fought against him though, pushed away from him. "No!" She stood up, repulsed at herself. "I don't deserve comfort." She cried more. "I did mean it!" she screamed. "I did. I want her back, but I don't think it'll happen." Marie fell to her knees and cried again into her hands.

Jack stayed on the couch, not knowing what to do. He wanted to comfort her. He wanted to tell her that he at times had doubted Valerie's return as well.

"How can you be so calm?" She again was shouting.

Jack stood. This was going nowhere. "Marie." He waited for her to look up at him. "It's okay to have doubts."

"You hate me."

"No." He held out his hand, palm up. Finally, she took it, and he guided her with it to her feet and into his arms. "No, I love you." He kissed the top of her head.

They stayed like that for a while. Neither of them counted the time. Eventually Marie's guilt morphed into embarrassment, she broke the embrace and coiled way from him. She closed herself off to him despite still being vulnerable and needing him. She wanted to give him an ultimatum — *stay or go* — but she was afraid he'd still leave and she didn't want to see him make that decision.

"I have to." He knew she wanted to ask him to stay.

He moved close again and kissed her. Gently on the mouth this time. Then he wiped her tears from her face, while she half-heartedly smiled at him. He smiled back and stared into her eyes. It felt like years since he'd done either of those two things.

"Don't worry," he said.

Then he let her go and walked to the front door.

"Jack?" she called to him.

He stopped, his hand again on the door knob. He didn't turn around this time when he spoke. "She'll come back." *I may not be, but she will.*

CHAPTER 72

Boudreaux jotted down all the information he could from a frantic Marie Hardy. The poor woman had been through enough, without having her husband run off on some wild goose chase. Marie's fear was that Jack was chasing his hope of helping Valerie, but he was doing so foolishly. He'd received a phone call on a private number, she'd told the chief, and then rushed out of the house.

For Boudreaux, Marie's concern seemed justified. Jack Hardy had told the world if anyone could get him alone with Valerie's abductor, he'd pay handsomely. It was entirely possible that a creative criminal found Jack's secret cell phone number and called him, offering Jack exactly what his wishful thoughts had wanted – an offer Jack would have to accept.

At Marie's prompting, Boudreaux turned on the television news. Jack Hardy's departure had been caught on live TV, now in replay. Boudreaux watched the scene play out, listened for a clue in Jack's responses to reporters' questions, but there weren't any.

He leaned back in his chair, feeling overwhelmed at all the things revolving in his atmosphere that he couldn't control – the Hardy's being one of them. Boudreaux very quickly could have two missing person cases within the same family. He called his desk sergeant and placed a BOLO on

Jack Hardy's vehicle, with specific instructions to follow the vehicle and see who Jack was meeting. And then bring them all in for questioning.

As Boudreaux hung up the telephone, he concentrated on his immediate situation. The Dateline crew had arrived a while ago and was almost finished setting up their gear in Boudreaux's office for an in-depth interview about the case. The journalist, Robert Cain, was annoyed. He was supposed to meet with the two lead detectives upon his arrival, but neither detective had been made available, leaving the journalist with only Boudreaux to interview. He sat on the couch in the corner of Boudreaux's office, jotting down notes and questions, feverishly texting and constantly checking his watch. But, more importantly to Boudreaux, it left *him* with Cain. And his plan to draw out the Pen Pal about to blow up in his face.

Boudreaux picked up his telephone again and dialed his secretary, demanding Gray and Parker's presence. She told him she'd try them again, that no one in the building had seen Gray, and that Parker was here but had since left.

Boudreaux grinded his teeth in annoyance then punched in Parker's cell number. He wanted to slam the phone down into its cradle when the call went to voicemail yet again.

Where the hell are Parker and Gray?

≈   ≈   ≈   ≈

Increasing the speed of his F-150 truck, Mike Todd pulled alongside Gray's car. He stayed back about a quarter of a car length, just enough to see inside the car but not close enough to give up his presence. The windows were tinted, which made it more difficult to see the driver, but he mentally noted what he could discern: white male, no distinguishing features, not Becker Gray.

Mike slowed and pulled behind Gray's car. At the next red light, he took off slowly allowing a good deal of space between the two cars, so he could tail it without suspicion. Mike didn't want to jump to unfounded conclusions about the car or the driver. It was possible Gray had a relative or friend in from out of town and that person was just borrowing the car. That would also account for why Gray hadn't been on the interstate the last couple mornings. On the other hand, Gray never struck him as someone who had a lot of friends – he only talked about his partner – and he didn't seem like the borrow-my-car kind of guy either. Yet, Mike conceded, he didn't really know him. Despite that thought process, it still didn't sit well with him.

CHAPTER 73

Breathing in sand finally closed Gray's chest. He pushed off the ground in a fit of convulsions, his lungs searching for clean air. He coughed so much his stomach, back, and head hurt. But was that really from the coughing? From the familiar way his body was reacting, he knew he'd been drinking. So, the pain and discomfort could really be from the drink and dehydration.

Gray moved into a crawling position, which resulted in his stomach turning. The sensation of impending vomiting overwhelmed him quickly. He tried to slow his breathing to control it, but it was no use. His body lurched and heaved until he had nothing left inside his stomach, until there was no strength left in his muscles. That weakness set in swiftly, and he fell over on his side, rolled on his back to recover. For a minute, he enjoyed the clean air finally filtering into his lungs. The oxygen helped Gray's mind fight a black out. Then his mind kicked in again.

Where am I?

He pulled his right arm out from under him and propped himself up. Looked around. The bright sun bounced off the sandy terrain, which made his head hurt worse. He was in the center of a grassless field. Rows of trees lined the area about 20 yards from him, like they were standing

HUMAN AFTER ALL

guard over him. He wished their shadow stretched far enough to cover him.

How did I get here?

Valerie Hardy's face flashed across his mind. He shook away the thought before a couple other brief images jumped through his thoughts. They were all very sketchy and disjointed, but he came to realize that he had been with Valerie the night before. Then another image scorched through his head. Made his stomach turn again.

He was with Gracie too?

How?

Gray struggled to his feet, expecting the movement to induce vomiting. His body's main reaction, though, was imbalance. He swayed back and forth, thinking he'd fall over, but he waited long enough that his equilibrium stabilized.

I gotta get out of here.

Gray checked the pocket where he usually kept his car keys, but it was empty. He checked another, then became panicked, patting his other two pockets. He looked back at the sandlot, but he didn't see them there either. He realized all the usual contents of his pockets were missing. He didn't have his cell phone. Or his wallet. *And if they're gone ... Oh shit.* He grabbed at his Glock, but all he found was an empty holster.

≈ ≈ ≈ ≈

Crunchy grass, leaves, sticks, and wooded debris made the walk to the road painful against Gray's bare feet. As he made his way, he had the shade of the trees, so that helped his hang over, but he still struggled against the affects. Though, once he could hear traffic, his pace picked up, and he dealt with the pain. Breaking through the tree line, he paused. A semi-trailer truck flew by, whirling wind and dirt behind it, which then

- 325 -

rained down on Gray. The dirt pelted his face and the wind pushed him back a step. He leaned against a tree trunk to keep from falling over.

During the hike from the sandlot to the road, Gray tried to piece together the night before. All these random pieces of information floated through his head. Not chronologically, not linearly. Just piecemeal. Flashes of bits and pieces of places, people's faces, and other random things. He remembered going to Denise's house. Gray pushed aside his thoughts about her, the family she started after Gracie, and the things she had said to and about him. *I'll deal with that later.*

A cluster of four cars approached. Gray stepped out of the tree line and thumbed the cars, but none of them stopped. He stepped back under the tree shade. Thought about the night before again. McDonough. He remembered how drunk he was. *That's when I started drinking.* Then his mind shifted immediately to his daughter. A quick shot of guilt flowed through him. Guilt for the night she died and for his drinking again. It was a painful connection for him – drinking and Gracie – but he pushed that aside because he'd been with her last night. How? What had happened? Memories of Gracie's life webbed through his mind. Her laughing repeatedly as a baby at the same dumb face he used to make. Twenty or 30 times in a row before she tired of it. The way she loved eating bananas. He used to let her squeeze them in her fingers then eat the slimy goo. The way she'd call graham crackers damn crackers. Surprising to him, a smile had spread across his face.

He figured the experience of being with her had to be a drunk imagination. A dream perhaps. Then he remembered being home. In his bed. Wanting to sleep so badly. Then he was on the floor. He recalled the yank of his hair, the jerk of his head backward and something being jammed into his mouth.

A pick-up truck came his way. Gray rushed out from the shade, marched out into the road. Instead of thumbing, he began waving his arms, flagging the driver to stop. Begging actually. The truck, filled with day-labor workers who knew little English, pulled to the side of the road.

"La policía," Gray said, once he realized the barrier. He pointed at himself.

The driver laughed at Gray. "Si no está la policía, entonces, ¿dónde están los zapatos?"

Gray knew the word zapatos meant shoes, and he guessed they didn't believe he was police. "Un poco español." He held up his thumb and forefinger, keeping them not far apart. "¿Teléfono?"

"No."

"I need help. SOS."

"Help." The driver said, nodding his head.

"Sí. Por favor." Gray pointed at the driver and made a motion that looked like he was controlling the steering wheel, then pointed at himself then down the road. "To Lakeland."

≈   ≈   ≈   ≈

As Gray rode in the back of the pickup truck, the sun beat down on him, accentuating the aspects of his hangover. That accentuation was why, when he began associating the roads they were driving on with his drunkenness the night before, he thought he was hallucinating. But it wasn't a hallucination. He knew he'd been to this part of town while in the Pen Pal's captivity. But why?

Gray banged on the cab window. "Alto! Alto!" He called to the driver to stop. "Por favor."

The driver pulled into the next parking lot accessible along the road. Gray looked around, willing his mind to recall the night before.

"¿Qué estás haciendo? Qué se necesita para vomitar?"

Gray ignored the man, not knowing what he was asking anyway. Then he saw what he was looking for – a point of reference. A realization, more so, of where he was and why he might've been here with the Pen Pal.

"Rojo." Gray pointed at the red house ahead of them. The one on the corner of Carla Jansen's street. "Por favor."

The truck pulled back into traffic, drove to the red house, and turned onto the residential street.

"Pausado."

Seeing Jansen's old house, Gray banged on the window again. "Alto." The truck stopped with a jerk. Gray lost balance and struck the side of the truck. He hurriedly regained his bearings and hopped off the bumper.

"Gracias. Gracias," he said.

The truck began to pull away.

"No, no, no. Un momento por favor."

The driver looked annoyed and Gray was sure he was regretting helping the gringo, but the driver sighed and threw the truck in PARK.

"Gracias."

Gray hurried to the house, one lot down from where the truck had parked and across the street. The carport was empty. Only old oil stains remained behind. Gray tried the carport door, which was locked. He looked through the closest window, but he didn't see anything through the curtains. So, Gray walked to the front of the house and looked at it, studied it, tried his best to recall the night before. *What the hell?* He knew he'd been here, on this street, but this house wasn't ringing any bells for him. Many images and thoughts had come back to him, but not all of them made sense. And that nonsense made him question some of the recollections. But, this street … he knew he had been here. He turned in the front yard and looked back at the truck. Then a bell went off in his head.

The house behind the truck. A dark blue Nova sat under the carport. He and Parker had known Carla Jansen died long ago, but they couldn't figure out why someone had her license plate. From the distance and his slightly blurry vision, he had the same uncertainty he and Parker had while originally watching the video from the convenience store. The one when Carson Anderson stopped to fill up his car with gas and had used Valerie's credit card. "Could be a T or a 7."

Gray began walking toward the house. Awareness of his shoeless feet returned. Acorns, sticks, and pebbles on the asphalt underfoot sent sudden pains up his legs, but he kept on toward the house, even hurried. As he approached, he saw the smashed right, rear quarter panel, which fit his and Parker's blitz attack theory explaining how Anderson kidnapped Valerie.

"I was here," he told himself. He remembered sitting in his car, staring at the house. Then a wave of memory returned. He remembered vomiting in the front passenger seat of his car and then kicking his shoes and socks from his feet. He recalled watching the Pen Pal walk toward the house.

And returning from it with Valerie.

"Oh no."

He jumped the steps to the front door, which he found unlocked. Gray pushed it open, announcing himself as police.

"Is anyone here? Hello," he called out, receiving no response.

He saw the men in the truck, stupefied at his behavior, but he ignored them. One of the guys slid out of the truck and stood next to it, watching Gray. He imagined they were discussing leaving Gray and getting away from whatever he was doing. But they hadn't left yet. Gray held up his forefinger, asking them for another minute. Then he stepped into the house.

Television and stand on his left, recliner, couch, and coffee table to his right. Straight ahead of him through a doorway, he saw a dining table. He called out again, but no one responded. He stepped further into the house and saw a hallway to his right. He decided to forego the hallway search. He didn't like the close quarters walk without his weapon, so he ventured into the kitchen instead. As he approached the doorframe, a refrigerator blocked his view of the rest of the kitchen, but he saw the open window. He saw what looked like blood on the window ledge.

Using the protruding refrigerator as cover, he poked his head into the kitchen, where he saw more blood, pooled on the floor. And the body of Carson Anderson. His first thought was to check for signs of life, but a second of realization passed, and Gray knew there was no life left in him.

Gray left the kitchen and hurried down the hall. He pushed open the bathroom door, then poked his head into Carson's bedroom, where his eyes landed on a discarded, bloody shirt. Gray stepped back into the hallway and pushed open the other bedroom door. Leather binds attached to the footboard. The bed cover had been torn off and now sat in a pile on the floor.

"She was here." His recollection was right. He was relieved at that thought.

Where is she now? He remembered leaving his handcuff key for her. *And where is the Pen Pal?*

Gray rushed through the house, trying to remember what he'd touched, so he could include it in his report. He found a phone in the living room, where he punched in Parker's cell phone number.

CHAPTER 74

Boudreaux might as well have been waiting for Parker at the front doors of the police station.

"Conference room now!" he called from the staircase, reversing his stride and heading back upstairs.

Parker rushed to the lobby front desk and asked if Gray had shown yet. The Public Safety Aid answered from behind a thick wall of bulletproof glass that she hadn't seen him. Parker checked his watch. Gray was later to work than he'd ever been. *He's gone. The publicity was just too much for him.*

"Parker." Boudreaux's strong voice echoed off the high ceiling and tiled floor.

Parker looked at the stairs to the second floor and thought of what was awaiting him. Boudreaux would explode. Not to mention the mess Gray's disappearing act could make of Valerie's case. *Why would Gray do this?* Parker knew Gray could be self-centered, but this was too much.

His legs carried him slowly up the stairs toward the conference room. Parker needed more time to think of what to tell Boudreaux about Gray and of what to do next, but the stairs went by too quickly. All he had was the truth. And the truth was no good.

Parker saw Boudreaux and the news camera crew down the hall near the conference room. They were waiting expectantly.

"Chief," Parker said, "I need to make a quick phone call."

Boudreaux pulled open the door to the conference room. "Later." He pointed into the room, nonverbally commanding Parker.

"I really should do it now." Parker had no one to call. He just wanted to buy more time. In front of the news crew, Parker knew Boudreaux wouldn't cause a scene. He thought his chances were pretty good that Boudreaux would let him make the phone call.

"Come inside," Boudreaux said, trying to control his temper. "You can call from in here." Boudreaux said to the news crew, "We'll be right out."

Parker hung his head, giving up, knowing he wouldn't cause a scene in front of the news crew either, and he trudged down the hall and entered the room.

"Where have you been?" Boudreaux said as soon as he closed the door. "You have a cell phone for a reason, and, damn it, when I call you, you better answer it."

Parker checked his phone, like he didn't know Boudreaux had called him.

"Don't act like it's the phone's fault," Boudreaux knew. "The TV crew's been here for hours, and I got nothing for them. Where's Gray? Nobody fucking knows."

Before Parker could answer, Boudreaux continued.

"But that's not even my biggest concern." Boudreaux sat down behind the table. His mood seemed to change and so did his demeanor and tone, both seeming to say, *Things just got worse.* "Marie Hardy called not too long ago. Seems as though Jack got a call on a secret cell phone and then took off without a word."

"What?" Parker was happy to talk about anything except Gray. Even this. "Why wouldn't he tell us he had a phone?" Parker sat down across from Boudreaux as possible scenarios played across his brain. "And since no one knew about the cell phone," Parker hypothesized, "I bet no one knows the number."

"Can't even get a dump on it. Marie Hardy's searching the house for a copy of the bill. If Jack's smart, she won't find it."

Parker was lost. "Why would he have a phone no one knew about?"

Boudreaux thought of his own family, what he'd do for his daughter and son in such a circumstance. "For Valerie. A number only she'd know."

Parker understood. "So if she was in an emergency, she could call it. Wait!" Parker jumped out of his chair. "Her phone." He rushed out the door.

Parker and Boudreaux, the news crew in tow, made their way through the building to Maddy James' office and the small onsite crime lab. Her desk looked like organized chaos, tired, and worn, much like she did even though it was morning. Her hair a bit of a mess, pulled up in a makeshift bun, and her eyes puffy from too many hours worked and not enough sleeping. Maddy nursed a hot cup of coffee as she watched the men enter the lab. She was happy to see Parker, but with each additional person who entered behind him, she grew more unexcited. With both cameramen, Boudreaux, Parker, and her staff inside her lab, it suddenly felt very cramped. And the light from the cameras was too much for her eyes.

"Where's Valerie Hardy's cell phone?"

"No good morning?" she shot back, grumpily. Her tone devoid of flirtatiousness. "Just get me the phone?"

"I need the phone, Mad?" Parker's voice was stern.

"Hold this." Maddy handed Parker her coffee before squeezing by the chief and the cameramen to get to the other side of the room. She reached into the Hardy evidence box and retrieved the phone stored in a plastic bag.

"Here." She tossed Parker gloves to put on. He handed the coffee mug back to her and then pulled on the gloves. "And now here." She handed him the phone.

He pressed the power button but received no response from the device. "It's dead."

Maddy moved quickly. "I have the same phone. Hold on," she said, edge still in her voice. She rummaged through her purse, finding her on-the-go cord.

When it booted, Parker pressed the menu options on the phone and pulled up the contact list. There were two numbers under her father's name. One listed as DAD and the other as DAD 911. Both contacts sat below a contact named D K in the contact list.

Parker wrote down the DAD 911 number on a piece of paper from Maddy's desk and then handed it to Boudreaux.

"I'll get this to IT," Boudreaux said, heading for the door. "See if we can't track it."

The news crew hesitated.

"Go with him," Parker said. He watched them go and then turned back to Maddy. Her grumpiness had seemed to change. She was friendly again. He saw flirtatiousness in her eyes again.

"What? Now you're going to be nice to me?"

"I didn't like all those people in here. You're good, just not all of them. And I don't think the chief has ever been down here."

"I'm going to use your phone," Parker said to Maddy.

He moved to her desk and quickly dialed the number associated with D K in her contact list, thinking possibly D K was David Kilborn's number. He was a private investigator whose number they had found in Valerie's phone log that they'd received from the phone company. Gray had left a message for Kilborn, but as far as Parker knew, Kilborn hadn't returned the call.

"David Kilborn Investigations," a receptionist picked up the call.

Parker cleared his throat, caught off guard, half expecting the number to be wrong or disconnected, and said, "This is Detective Jeffrey Parker with the Lakeland Police Department in Florida. I need to speak to David Kilborn please. It's urgent."

"He's not in the office right now. May I take a message, detective?"

"No, we already left him a voicemail, and he hasn't called back yet. I told you, this is an emergency. I need to talk to him right now."

"Please hold." She sounded annoyed, like every caller said that to her.

Parker waited. Then he heard ringing in the phone. Three rings and a man picked up. "Detective, this is David Kilborn."

"Finally."

"I know. I'm sorry. I did get a message from a detective in Lakeland, I just haven't had a chance to call back."

Parker sat on the edge of Maddy's desk. "Your name came up in a case we're investigating, and I need to ask you a couple questions."

"Happens all the time. Go ahead."

"Valerie Hardy," Parker said, thinking that would spark Kilborn to kick into an explanation, but Kilborn stayed quiet, waiting on a question. "Do you know her?"

Hesitation was present in Kilborn's voice. "She was a client. What's this about?"

"You don't know what's happened to her?"

"I guess not."

"It's all over the news. We're getting tips from Oregon. You're in California, right? The news has reached the west coast. How do you not know?"

"I don't watch the news. Not in my business. I see enough shitty stuff. So, what happened to her, detective?"

"What was the nature of your relationship?" Parker asked.

"I told you, she was a client. I'm not telling you anything else unless you tell me what happened to her and what you want from me."

It was Parker's turn to hesitate. Usually when interviewing someone, Parker would think through the questioning beforehand. He hadn't had that luxury this time, and the conversation wasn't going as he would've liked it. "She's missing."

Kilborn kept his reaction silent. Parker let the silence hang. Maddy moved close to Parker, who put the call on speaker so she could hear too.

"David?" Parker finally asked.

"What do you know about Valerie, detective? Or better yet, do you know about the letters Valerie received from the Pen Pal?"

"I do."

"What do you know about the other four girls?"

Parker didn't like that Kilborn had taken control of the conversation, but the private investigator was finally talking, which Parker took as a good sign. "We know Amanda Richards died in a club in L.A."

"And the other three?"

"Last report, not much."

Silence again on the line from Kilborn.

"Why do you ask?" Parker tried to bring Kilborn back into the conversation.

"Valerie Hardy hired me to find the other girls. To make sure they were all safe, so that's what I did. I didn't ask her why, but I assumed she wanted to go public with her story."

"She did," Parker said. "And it got her kidnapped."

Nothing from Kilborn again.

Maddy grabbed Parker's arm, moving against him. She mouthed, "The other girls?"

Parker nodded. "David, the other girls. Were they safe?"

"One's in Mexico, working at a restaurant near the cruise ship ports. One's in Wyoming, going to school. And the other's in New York City. None of them are unscarred by the whole thing. Tiesha Knight, in New York, is the worst of the three. Spooked so bad she rarely leaves the apartment she shares with her father. The other two are ... functional."

Maddy's sigh was sad. She leaned against Parker, using his body warmth for solace.

"How did you two communicate with each other?"

"Chat rooms online. Burner phones. I'd keep a phone for a couple weeks, and then toss it. Get another one. We did that three, maybe four times. I do that if a client seems to prefer privacy."

"Would you mind sending us whatever information you've been able to gather? It would really help the investigation."

"Do you have any leads?"

"We do. I think we're close." He lied. Parker wasn't going to give any more details away. "And this information you provided helps. Thanks." Parker gave Kilborn the contact information he needed to send the files and then ended the call.

Parker stayed still for a minute, thinking about the call, processing what it meant. "I need to go," he finally said.

"Sure." Maddy stood on her own, releasing Parker from her grip. "What did that call do for the case?"

Parker handed Valerie's cell phone back to Maddy, so she could return it to the evidence box. "It just confirmed Valerie's frame of mind. She was determined to put herself out there." He tugged off the rubber gloves and trashed them. "Maybe in a way she was trying to help the other girls too. If she could prove he wasn't out there anymore, maybe she could help them heal their scars too."

Parker's cell vibrated in his pocket. He pulled it out, not recognizing the number, but he used the call as another reason to say good bye to Maddy James.

"This is Detective Parker," he said into the phone as he waved to her and threw open the lab door.

"Parker … it's Gray."

Parker stopped walking. "Where the hell have you been? Boudreaux's going nuts, looking for you. Hell, I've been looking for you all morning, too. I went to your apartment." He whispered, "There's whiskey all over the floor in your bedroom."

Gray cut off his partner. "I'm at Carson Anderson's real home."

"What are you doing there?"

"I need you to come pick me up. And I need shoes. And a whole lot of water."

Parker's head spun. "Hold on." Parker moved quickly down the hall, checking doors along the way. Some were locked, others led to occupied rooms. He finally went into the bathroom at the end of the hall. He made sure he was the only one in it and then locked the door. "I need you to tell me what's going on. Shoes, water, you need a ride? What the hell, Becker?"

"There's no time," Gray said.

"There's time," Parker commanded, his voice bouncing back at him. "What is going on?"

"We were right. The Pen Pal didn't take Valerie. It looks very much like Carson Anderson did."

"So you decided to go see him?" His question was saturated in frustration, irritation, and sarcasm.

"Just shut up a minute. You want the story or to ask me questions?"

"Why are you at Carson Anderson's house, Gray? And what are you about to do?"

"Last night," Gray ignored Parker, "the Pen Pal took me from my home, and I led him here. To Anderson. Who he killed. And now Valerie's gone. He has her." Gray breathed between each sentence like he had been exercising. "But he doesn't."

"You're inside the house, aren't you?"

"I am."

"You've confirmed Anderson's death?"

"I did."

"What happened after he killed Anderson and … you're saying he took Valerie? How'd you get away?"

Gray thought about his time with Valerie, the key he had left her, the things the Pen Pal had said to him about having no life to take. And it all meant something. "Listen, he's going after Jack Hardy. I think he left Valerie behind. She really wasn't his focus. It was the girls' fathers all along."

Parker considered that. "Marie Hardy called not long ago saying Jack took off. He left the house without notice. We have a BOLO on his car."

"Put one on my car too. I think the Pen Pal has it."

"He took your car and your shoes?"

"And my phone." For the first time in the conversation, Gray's voice contained excitement, as a realization settled in. "Get a trace on my cell phone. That's where we'll find Jack Hardy."

"Then I'll come get you."

"Bring me a Glock too."

"Jesus, Becker."

"Just come get me. There's shoes in my locker. And I seriously need some water."

CHAPTER 75

The road sign indicating the mileage to reach Tampa told Valerie she was traveling in the wrong direction. At the next break in traffic, she cut the wheel hard and whipped the car around. The turn radius was wide, and the tires spit up grass and dust as she went off road. Worried about her father, she pressed on the gas and quickly caught up to the slower traffic on the two-lane road. She passed when she could despite the double-yellow center lines while looking for a place to stop and phone home.

There were many businesses along the road. The kind where a small office sat in front of a huge warehouse. She thought about stopping, but there was always a reason not to. Outside one of the offices, Valerie saw a man step out of his truck. He left the car door open. And he stood there, like he was waiting on something – something like Valerie to stop so he could take her.

Valerie wasn't raised to trust other people. Her parents had taught her to be safe, to stay away from people she didn't know. Those people she didn't know could be the people who want to hurt her. And now she truly believed them. Danger indeed crept beyond every corner.

She thought of how she wasn't afraid of William Ford and Michael Edwards. Or of David Kilborn – not that she met him face to face. Why had she trusted them? She'd spent time online with them, getting to know them. Maybe that was it. They turned out to be trustworthy. *Well, maybe not Edwards totally.* Surely not all people were bad. *But how do you know which ones are or aren't?*

A retail plaza appeared on her left, anchored by a clothing store. She recognized the store name, but not the location. She remembered going to that store brand other times with her mother. All the sales people were wonderfully friendly and helpful, and, as such, she figured she'd be allowed to use their phone.

Valerie cut across oncoming traffic and zoomed through the intersection, braking hard and pulling into the parking lot. There were no parking spaces close to the entrance, so she steered the stolen car down one of the parking rows. The closest parking space was halfway down the row. Pedestrians sauntered about the lot. She watched a mother walking her with toddler along the front of the plaza. Valerie noticed the woman change hands with her child, moving the boy from her left to her right, away from the man who appeared to be loitering nearby. She didn't take that as a good sign, and she sped away from the plaza and careened back into traffic. Again not knowing where she was.

She kept thinking of her father and the possibility of him being in the Pen Pal's hands. Who knows what would happen to him. She blamed herself. She kept thinking she should've given the Pen Pal a wrong number. *It was stupid to give him the right number!* He left after she gave it to him. He didn't even check it to make sure it was the right one. *He knew it would be.* It dawned on her that her mother and father probably had the same type of feelings and thoughts after Valerie had been kidnapped – worry, blame, doubts, fear – and it made her mad that she'd put them through that, that she'd caused all of this.

Her foot, while she blamed herself, pushed heavy on the gas, and after nearly colliding with a car pulling into traffic, she realized she recognized where she was. And she knew how to get home. This time, on purpose, her foot pushed the pedal down.

≈   ≈   ≈   ≈

Her hands shook with overwhelming emotions, as Valerie turned the wheel and steered the car onto the street where her home was located. The houses she'd driven by and ignored thousands of times, today, seemed new to her, like she was seeing their vivid details for the first time. But she quickly shook that off, noticing what was new about the houses – yard signs in each of the yards. SAVE VALERIE, one read. BRING VALERIE HOME, another. And a third, VALERIE STRONG. Big yellow ribbons adorned the trees in the yards, or the mailboxes, or on the front doors. Valerie cried again, unable to control herself, despite being tired of crying. Her neighbors were supporting her and her family. Her neighbors. People she paid no mind to as she drove by their homes. She'd met a few, mostly just saying hello or waving when she drove by. But, here they were, wanting Valerie to come home. She'd been so wrapped up in her own world, in her own worries, that other people didn't matter to her. She always thought her world was small – her, her mom, and her dad. That was it. But there was more in her world than she knew. Strangers were there for her. She smiled. *I'm home.*

Valerie stopped the car, seeing what was ahead of her. Her tears dried up. She put the car in PARK and absentmindedly left the car running as she stepped out of it. Dozens of news vans lined the long residential street. Most were concentrated right in front of her house. Like when she'd stormed out of her house before being abducted. Only there were more vans now. Many more. And many more reporters too. The road ahead looked blocked off. She thought about knocking on the front door with the big yellow Valerie ribbon and asking to use their phone. But she decided against it. This was her home, and nothing was going to keep her from it ever again.

She nervously stepped away from the car and began walking down the street toward her house. With each step closer to home, she felt stronger. She felt like tears were forever behind her. Like her battle was over. Her posture straightened, confidence high, and strength returned.

As she approached, a few reporters noticed her walking toward them. She could tell they weren't sure who she was yet, but the realization was coming. And when it came, the crowd would come at her. Lights, camera, action. She looked a wreck, but she didn't really care. All she wanted was to see her mother and father. To hold them. To apologize. To be protected again. Nothing else mattered.

The realization spread through the crowd of reporters. *Is that her? That's Valerie. She's back!* Then the crowd assembled, organized, and they rushed toward her, surprise and jubilation on their faces. But the crowd didn't mob her, like she thought they would. They blocked the road, just by sheer mass. Cameras rolled. No one said anything, but they had their microphones and tape recorders at the ready. It was almost like they were sizing her up before pouncing and feeding on her. Most surprising of all to Valerie, they started clapping. And cheering. Then a gap opened through the middle of them.

"Valerie, how did you escape?"

"Where is the Pen Pal?"

"Where were you?"

"What are the cuts on your face from?"

"How do you feel?"

Questions were directed at her from the crowd, but the clapping and cheering continued. It warmed her heart. People cared. She had no idea.

"Thank you," she said, knowing no one could hear her.

Then she started walking toward the gap that had spread throughout the middle of the group. Her pace quickened as she entered the tunnel. More questions came at her, but she couldn't hear them. She felt numb. The faces of the people covering her story flashed by her. Smiles and tears of their own. She emerged from the opening in a run and rounded her direction toward her home's front door. But she stopped again. Frozen. All of this was on live television, and her mother must've been watching. Marie stood on the front step, waiting, like she'd been there the whole time that Valerie had been gone, expecting her to come back at any moment.

Valerie felt the crowd gather behind them, quiet now, watching. But she ignored the feeling.

She and her mother rushed toward each other and embraced. Tighter than they ever had. Marie Hardy remembered the first time she'd ever held Valerie, right after her daughter was born. This was better than that moment. And Valerie felt so loved, so at home, so protected, so thankful. For her parents. For everyone who supported her. Valerie and Marie both laughed, overcome with joy. In fact, so full of joy, it was as if sadness didn't exist.

"Where's dad?" Valerie asked into her mother's ear. When Marie didn't respond, Valerie pulled away, seeing in her mother's eyes that the Pen Pal had already gotten to her father.

"I don't know. He left."

It was like chaos broke out in Valerie's mind. Broken thoughts swirled, disconnected from logic. Emotions soared. She felt dizzy with fear and panic. Then guilt. She had to do something.

"Where is he?" she shouted to the reporters.

Marie held onto her arm, like a leash.

"You saw him leave. Where'd he go?"

Valerie broke free of her mother's grip.

"Valerie, no," Marie said.

Valerie ignored her and rushed to the crowd of reporters. "Who knows where my father went? Come on," she said when no one answered. "Somebody has to know!"

CHAPTER 76

Jack Hardy parked along Ariana Street, just a few parking spaces from an elementary school. He dusted off memories from when he and Marie delivered Valerie to kindergarten in Idaho for the first time. She was immaculately dressed, perfectly groomed, new lunch box in hand, and an anxious smile on her face. Jack and Marie thought their daughter would be frightened to go to school for the first time, leaving mommy and daddy behind, thought there'd be some type of separation anxiety. There wasn't. Not Jack's little brave one. She was always too brave, and that was what had gotten them into this mess.

He hated himself for thinking it again, but as he pulled himself from his car, he wished he'd let Valerie convince him to have a gun in the house. If he'd purchased one, he'd have had it with him now. He'd shoot this guy right in the head ... right after he found out where he had Valerie locked away.

Jack moved away from the car slowly, hesitantly. He stepped onto the curb and scanned Dobbins Park. Mothers watched their children as they played on plastic fortresses. Fathers and neighborhood kids played basketball, a woman walking her dog made her way around the quarter mile walking track, children pushed other children on swings, and a teenage boy flew a kite in a huge field behind the park. Two birthday parties were underway at two different pavilions. Jack could smell the hamburgers being grilled. But he saw no kidnapper, no evil monster.

Jack fingered his small knife in his right front pocket, opened it, got it ready to use. He powered on the cell phone in his left front pocket and thought of feeling his way across the keypad and dialing 911 then just leaving it on. But he didn't. He was afraid if he got caught, the guy would get away and kill Valerie.

He exhaled one of his remaining breaths of hope. *Who am I kidding?* Chances were good that Valerie was already dead. He hated the thought, and it made his eyes water, but he couldn't help thinking that.

Where is this asshole?

Ten minutes passed before Jack realized there was one man all by himself. He stood beside a huge camphor tree at the northwest corner of the park, right near a metal arch displaying the park's name. The man was casually playing with coins in his hands. Jack fought to control his emotions. Anger soared through his veins, igniting every muscle with adrenaline.

In case this wasn't the Pen Pal, Jack – as nonchalantly as he could – made his way to the corner of the park. Because if the Pen Pal saw him speaking with this guy, he would think Jack hadn't listened to directions? And Valerie would be as good as dead. But, he had to approach the man, had to know if it was him.

The man looked as carefree as any other person at the park, like he was enjoying himself. There was nothing suspicious about him. His eyes weren't checking the park for police. His attire wasn't disheveled. He was wearing jeans and a T-shirt. He wasn't nervous, wasn't agitated, wasn't in a hurry, as Jack had imagined the Pen Pal would be. This couldn't be the Pen Pal. He looked too normal. Too casual.

"Jack," the man called to him like they were friends, slipping the coins into his pocket.

Jack's heart jumped inside his chest. He felt the blood rush out of his face. He was surprised his legs still worked as they carried him toward the man.

"I met you here in public, like you asked. Now we need to go," Hubbard said.

"I'm not going anywhere with you." Jack's defiance even surprised himself.

"Then Valerie dies." With that, Hubbard walked past Jack toward the parking area along Ariana Street.

"Wait," Jack called to him.

Hubbard stopped and turned. Took a deep breath and exhaled before speaking. "All you had to do was keep Valerie safe."

"I did."

"The current situation dictates a different conclusion."

"For ten years, I kept her safe from you."

"No," Hubbard said. "For ten years, I made you care for her."

"You don't make any sense." Jack rubbed his face, like he was scrubbing off his confusion. "How did you target her? Why her?"

Hubbard shrugged one shoulder. "God led her to me."

Jack exploded with anger and grabbed Hubbard by the shirt, ramming him against the nearest camphor tree. "God didn't do this! You did!"

"People are watching."

Jack's anger pushed the blood back into his face. He wanted to take the man's head and slam it into the tree trunk.

"A father's main job in raising a child is to keep it safe."

"You have some sort of father issues?"

"No."

It shocked Jack how relaxed Hubbard was.

"I have Jack Hardy issues. I warned you, and you failed to comply. I used you as an example to the world. And you failed. You didn't protect her."

"You're trying to teach the world a lesson?"

Hubbard peeled Jack's hands from his shirt. "Yes. Children are precious, Jack. You needed to learn it. So did the world."

"The world didn't learn shit from you. And parents? All you taught me was fear."

"Fear that resulted in you taking better care of her."

"What the fuck is wrong with you?"

Hubbard smiled, unhurt by the question. "I'm giving you one last chance, Jack. It's the ultimate test. Will you trade your life to save your daughter's?"

"Prove to me she's alive."

Hubbard shook his head. "Trust, Jack."

Jack's hesitation ended the conversation. "Good bye, Jack." Hubbard walked away from him.

"I'll trade!" Jack exclaimed.

"Deal's off. She's dead," Hubbard replied without turning back to Jack.

"Bullshit." Jack rushed to catch up to him.

Hubbard opened the passenger door of Gray's Accord and held his arm out inviting Jack inside the vehicle.

≈   ≈   ≈   ≈

Parked at a residence along the west side of the park, not 100 yards from the gate where the man driving Gray's car met another man. Mike Todd watched the puzzling interaction. He wasn't sure what was going on, who the guy in Gray's car was, or who he was meeting. Or why the meeting was confrontational.

He dialed Gray's cell number again. The ringing of the number blasted through the truck's speakers via Bluetooth. No answer. Then voicemail picked up. Mike hit the END button. *The plate!* Then he called in to his dispatch, identified himself and his badge number, then maneuvered through the protocol to run a plate number.

"Florida, A-G-P-4-7-1."

Dispatch came back after a minute of silence. "Plate is issued to Jackson Lane Hardy." And the woman at dispatch read off the address.

Oh, shit. "Thanks," Mike said, ending the call. "Jack Hardy." How is this little rendezvous connected to the case Gray was working? Why was Jack Hardy meeting a man who was driving Gray's car? Mike began doubting himself. The situation was too odd to make sense out of. *No.* He pushed his doubt aside. *Something isn't right.*

He dialed the Lakeland Police Department number. When the Public Safety Aid answered the phone, he identified himself and asked to be connected to Detective Becker Gray in Criminal Investigation.

"I'm sorry," the aid said. "Detective Gray isn't in."

"I don't remember his first name," Mike explained, "but there's a Detective Parker. He works with Detective Gray a lot."

"Right, we have a Detective Parker," she told him. "But he's not in either."

"What about their CO?"

He was put on hold for a moment before the receptionist returned. "He's unavailable. Would you like to leave a message?"

"Then how about his CO? Jesus Christ, get me someone! I need to talk to somebody now!"

≈   ≈   ≈   ≈

Hubbard walked around the Accord and slid into the driver's seat. He winked at Jack Hardy, like everything would be all right. Gray's cell rang from his pocket again. Hubbard pulled it out, checked the number. It was the same one that had been calling repeatedly over the last 40 minutes. Hubbard pressed the ignore button and turned the car on. He reversed out of the parking space and then drove toward Harden Boulevard. At the stop sign at Lincoln Avenue, Hubbard checked his rearview mirror to see if the F-150 was still following him.

And it was.

CHAPTER 77

The truckload of migrant workers had surprisingly stayed until Gray dismissed them. After he reached Parker by phone and knew he was getting support, he thanked the men and sent them on their way. Then he waited, staying outside the house to not contaminate the crime scene any more than he already had.

Sitting on the step of Carson Anderson's front door, his thoughts returned to the night before. He replayed everything he could remember, struggling against dehydration and a headache to dislodge a nugget of information about the Pen Pal. Had he said his name while they were together? Did he say anything else that may help? What were his physical attributes? What was he wearing? The pieces of the night just didn't fit together for Gray, and he wanted to punch the nearby wall in frustration. And he probably would have, if he hadn't seen Parker's police cruiser turn onto the residential street. He stood to meet Parker by the curb but hesitated when he saw that Parker's cruiser was only the beginning of the caravan. Three patrol cars followed. Two crime scene vans. Coroner. And apparently they'd picked up a couple extra cars in tow – probably reporters.

Instead of hurrying to the curb, Gray walked slowly, knowing the more people Parker brought with him, the longer it would take for them to get out of there. Parker anchored his vehicle the farthest away from

Anderson's house, leaving the rest the cars to occupy the space directly in front of the crime scene. As those peers emerged from their vehicles, embarrassment washed over Gray like the flu. He knew he looked a wreck, shoeless, worn, and as dry as the desert. He blamed himself, unsure what he thought was going to happen when Parker showed up. What, they were going to get in his car and speed away, leaving the crime scene unprotected?

Gray stood front and center on display like a billboard as the crew headed toward the house. He saw the looks they gave him. He saw the quick glances down at his bare feet.

"He's in the kitchen." He tried to ignore their faces. "Straight through the living room."

"You first on scene?" one of the patrolmen asked.

Gray ignored the patrolman, who'd approached him. He turned to Maddy James' crew. "Listen, there's blood on the window sill in the dining room. And a bloody shirt in the bedroom on the right."

"Detective?" the patrolman asked again.

Gray ignored him again. "And the bedroom at the end of the hall ... on the left. That's where Valerie Hardy was held captive."

"Detective Gray?"

Parker's voice answered for Gray. "Why don't you build a perimeter? Keep those reporters out of here." He was still walking toward the house, calling out from the road.

"I need to get a report."

"I know you do." Parker finally stepped onto the property. "You will. Now go on."

The patrolman stuffed his notebook back in his pocket and went to meet the other two officers to build the perimeter Parker had asked for.

"Usually," Parker said, finally reaching Gray, "it's the other way around. Us asking them for first report." He held up a pair of running shoes and a bottle of water. "Which one you want first?"

Gray snatched the bottle of water and tore off the plastic cap. Rim against lips, he tilted his head back and drank almost the whole bottle in one chug. Only about a quarter of bottle remained when he dropped his head and took a huge breath, like he'd been under water too long. "Thanks."

"Sure." Parker pointed with his head for the two of them to walk away from the others. Gray followed Parker, who stopped when he felt like they were far enough away from the others and could speak privately. "Now what the fuck happened last night?"

Gray shook his head. "I've been trying to piece the whole thing together."

"Just tell me what you got so far."

Gray finished off the bottle of water. "The Pen Pal came for Valerie. I'm guessing he saw it on the news and came to rescue her. He figured out where I live. Caught me by surprise inside my apartment. And he shoved a bottle of whiskey down my throat." Gray left out a few details leading up to this interaction. "He wanted to know where Valerie was. I told him Carla Jansen's address just to give him something, not knowing Carson Anderson lived a couple houses down."

"Wait a minute. When did you see McDonough and your ex?"

How the hell did he know that? "Before. That doesn't matter." Gray quickly kept going with the story, as the crew moved around Carson's yard, back and forth to the vans.

Parker's cell rang, but he ignored it.

"I made him bring me with him. To show him the way. But really to stay with him. Even though I was drunk, I didn't want to lose him. I don't remember much, but he came here. And we left with Valerie."

"She was all right? Went with him willingly."

Gray shrugged his shoulders. "I guess. I don't know. I mean, he had my wallet. My badge."

"He pretended to be a cop to win her trust."

Gray shrugged his shoulders again.

"Where'd you go after you left here."

Gray's posture slumped. "I don't remember."

One of the crime scene techs closed the van passenger door. Took keys from his pocket and then locked the door. *Keys!*

"Keys!" Gray grabbed Parker's arm. "I left Valerie my handcuff key." Then it came back to him. "We were in a bedroom. She was cuffed. I left her my key. If she got it, she could be free now."

Parker smiled, handed the shoes to his partner. "She is."

Gray took the shoes and asked, "She is? Valerie?"

"It was just on the news. Chief called me on my way here. She got free and found a car and drove home." Parker patted Gray on his shoulder. "You did it."

Gray laughed awkwardly, not because he was proud of anything he did to help Valerie, but because he had a weird sense of parental relief that came from Valerie having acted as the proxy between him and his daughter.

Parker's cell rang again. This time he pulled it out of his pocket to check the screen. "Put your shoes on. Let me see who this is. They've been calling me over and over."

Gray loosened the laces and dropped his shoes on the ground, as Parker moved away to speak on the phone. It was so weird for Gray to have a connection with Valerie, when he hardly recalled the time with her. Yet the time left a sense of calm and ease over him. And her safety meant the world to him.

"No," Parker said approaching Gray. "Stay on the line. Here." He gave the phone to Gray and yanked the radio off his belt. "Let's go." Parker rushed off toward the cruiser, almost screaming into the radio.

Confused, Gray saw a call was still connected on Parker's phone. "Hello?"

"Becker? Jesus, where have you been?"

"Mike?"

Parker shouted from the cruiser. "Come on!"

Gray pushed his heel into the shoe, now both feet securely inside the sneakers, and he took to a run toward the vehicle. "What's going on?" he asked into the phone?

"I'm following your car right now. Jack Hardy and some other guy are off to somewhere."

"Oh, shit," Gray said, tossing the water bottle on the ground and increasing his pace. "Don't lose them." Almost flustered, Gray nearly dropping the phone when he jumped into the cruiser next to Parker. "Go!"

Parker turned the car around quickly, tires screeching as he did so.

"Where are you?" Gray shouted over the accelerating engine and the air conditioner.

"We were heading south on Harden from Ariana." Essentially, six streets run parallel to one another crossing Lakeland in a north-south direction. Harden Boulevard was one of them. "Turned onto Edgewood. Crossed Florida and still going. Hold on." In the east-west direction, Edgewood was able to dump a driver off at four of the main north-south roadways.

Gray switched the phone to speaker and lowered the blasting cold air to the lowest setting. He and Parker waited for Mike Todd to start speaking again. Meanwhile, Parker headed south.

"All right," Mike said. "We just crossed Cleveland Heights. Still east on Edgewood. Where are you guys?"

Parker said, "I'll take 98 south." He hit the lights and siren on the cruiser. He raised the radio and called in Mike Todd's position.

"Mike, is Jack Hardy still alive?" Gray asked.

"As far as I can tell," Mike said. "Who's the guy driving your car?"

"You see the news about the Pen Pal?"

"You're kidding?"

"Have you been made yet?"

"No. I'm keeping a safe distance."

"Good, don't lose my car. I think he aims to kill Jack Hardy."

"Copy that. If I need to run him off the road, let me know, and I'll do it."

Parker held the radio away from his face. "We have Polk County Sherriff's coming from the Bartow direction and our guys coming from all over. Don't run him off the road. Let's come at him as a united front."

"Ten-four," Mike said. "We are nearing New Jersey. I'm running the yellow light, but I'm still on them."

Parker radioed in the update to command, who was coordinating the efforts of all the agencies and personnel involved. At New Jersey, they'd already crossed two of the main north-south roads. That only left Lakeland Highlands Boulevard and Highway 98, where Edgewood ended. Lakeland Highlands stretched the length of about half the city as well as into the unincorporated area, and 98 ran hundreds of miles south and north of Lakeland. As Gray listened to Parker and the others on the radio, he agreed that 98 was the road the Pen Pal was likely steering toward.

"All right, Mike," he said. "We are going to start barricading the route, so keep us updated. We have teams setting up blocks on Highlands." The main reason Hubbard would want to turn southbound onto Lakeland Highlands would be to jump on the Polk Parkway, a toll road that cut across the county, making it easier for residents in the south of Lakeland to reach the interstate.

"What about the parkway?" Mike asked. "You got an onramp ahead there."

"Your boys are setting up those blocks," Parker said, referring to the Florida Highway Patrol. "Plus, sheriff is going to block south on 98 and we got north. We'll split the off shoots with the deputies. I think we'll have him locked in."

CHAPTER 78

The truck was still behind Hubbard. Two cars back. It had moved closer as the traffic lights on Edgewood became more frequent. Whoever was following him hadn't wanted to lose him and, Hubbard suspected, he didn't know he'd been made. But who was following him? And when had he picked up the tail?

"Jack," Hubbard said.

"What?" Jack's voice emitted weakly, like he'd given up, like he had no fight left in him, and like Hubbard had already won. *Which I have.* It's one of the things Hubbard found most appalling in a father.

"What were my instructions to you when we spoke on the phone earlier?"

"Fuck off. I'm not playing any more games. Just tell me where Valerie is and then get on with it."

Maybe it wasn't Jack who brought a tail with him. Then who? Hubbard checked Gray's cell phone. He'd let the phone go to voicemail 17 times, but the calls had stopped about ten minutes ago. Most of the calls came from the same number.

As Hubbard steered past the intersection of Lakeland Highlands, the road curved in a wide S-turn where it changed from two lanes to four. Hubbard saw the Highway 98 intersection ahead, down the straightaway road. It seemed like the perfect place to make his move and lose his tail. Hubbard laid down gas pedal and weaved between the cars ahead of him, keeping an eye on the truck, which was now forced to blow his cover.

Jack Hardy gripped the door, feeling the car lurch forward. "What are you doing?"

Hubbard watched the rearview mirror. "Just getting to where we're going."

Jack noticed where Hubbard was looking and turned around in his seat. "Is someone back there?" He scanned the vehicles traveling behind them. A truck moved from between two cars and emerged as the closest vehicle behind theirs. "I didn't tell anyone!"

Hubbard grunted.

Jack felt fright, knowing if the Pen Pal thought he'd brought help, that he and Valerie were both as good as dead. But instead of panicking, he tried something else. "What's your name?"

"Oh, Jack, like that matters."

"It does to me."

"It shouldn't." Hubbard slowed for the upcoming intersection, where the roadway widened to include a left and right turn lane. He checked behind him. The truck was still coming, although maintaining a safe distance. He timed punching the gas for when the turn lanes had emptied and before the north-south traffic took off. The car lurched again and zipped into and through the intersection unscathed – he checked the truck, which had to stop at the traffic light – and unfollowed. He pressed the gas pedal down further to create more space.

"He's going for it!" Mike shouted into his truck's Bluetooth-enabled communication system. He pressed on the gas, like he'd follow. "He went!" But, then Mike hit the brakes, thinking better of gunning it through the intersection. "Goddammit." His tires squealed and the smoke and stench of burnt rubber cradled the vehicle.

"Did you lose him?" Gray asked, his voice coming through the truck's speakers. "Don't tell me you lost him, Mike."

"Hang on."

Mike inched the truck out of the eastbound lane, crossing into oncoming traffic. The further the nose of the truck moved into westbound traffic, the more horns blared.

"What are you doing?"

"Hold on," Mike said.

Now fully in the westbound lane, Mike blared his horn and picked up the pace. He kept on his horn, and as quickly and cautiously as possible, he too finally made his way through the busy intersection.

"Mike, where are you?" Parker's voice came across the speakers. His voice more muffled than Gray's voice, since he was further away from the cell phone.

"Just turned north on 98." He pushed the gas harder.

"We just established a blockade ahead. Near the Grove Park shopping center."

That was only about mile ahead of Mike.

"Traffic should start to back up."

"It'll force him to make a move," Gray added.

"I can't see him," Mike said.

"You saw him turn left though, right?" Gray asked.

"Yes."

Mike looked over the top of the cars in front of him, as he came to stop in traffic.

"What about the side roads? You've got some that head clear over to Combee and others that cut back to New Jersey."

"We have personnel standing by in those locations," Parker said.

$\approx$ $\approx$ $\approx$ $\approx$

Gray and Parker, heading south on 98, could see the traffic backing up. That was a good sign. The blockade was indeed in place, as they'd been told it was. The Grove Park shopping plaza edged closer on their right. They were closing in on the Pen Pal, tightening the noose. But with all the stoppage, their progress was stalled. Gray pointed at the median in the middle of the road, so Parker steered over the concrete separator and drove through the center of the road, making his way toward the blockage via turn lanes. He cut the siren but kept the lights.

"Tell me this: what do you know about this guy?" Mike asked.

"Not much, Mike."

"So you don't know for sure what forcing him into a corner will do?"

"You mean, what will his reaction be?"

"Right."

Gray and Parker thought about it.

"That silence doesn't sound good."

"Why do you ask?" Gray asked.

"Because I think I see the car. He's stuck in traffic."

"You know what?" Gray said, "I have an idea."

Gray leaned toward Parker, who was trying to navigate between all the traffic. Horns blew, people were flipping him the bird, and calling out to him. Obscenities, he was sure.

"How do you merge a call?"

"That button. With the two lines coming together. With the arrow," Parker said. "What are you doing?"

"He has my phone." Gray hit the button Parker had described.

"You're just going to call him?"

"Why not?"

Gray dialed the number. When the phone began ringing, the MERGE button lit up again. Gray pressed it.

≈　　≈　　≈　　≈

"Well, it does matter," Jack Hardy protested. "You've terrorized my family for years, whether you meant to or not, and I want to know your damn name."

Hubbard struck the steering wheel with his fist. "What is with this traffic?"

Jack's lack of understanding of the situation frustrated Hubbard. The inclusion of "*whether you meant to or not*" proved it. "If you would honestly recognize that you are at fault here, then I'd tell you my fucking name, Jack." He hit the steering wheel again. "Why isn't traffic moving?!"

Hubbard felt the phone vibrate before he heard it ring. He snatched it up from the cup holder in the center console. He saw PARKER was calling.

"Becker, you made it back to civilization, I see. How's your head?"

"I'm fine, thanks," Gray said.

Hubbard pushed the speaker button. "Hang overs. They're a bitch, wouldn't you say?"

"I've had a few bottles of water. And I'm running on adrenaline right now, so, like I said, I'm fine."

The traffic. Hubbard realized Gray and the police were causing the traffic jam. He outstretched his neck, trying to see over or around the cars in front of him. He couldn't though. Gray's Accord wasn't positioned correctly.

"Well, that's a shame. I was hoping you'd feel the aftermath of drinking so much last night. You were quite drunk when I found you. I supposed I underestimated your tolerance."

Hubbard checked his rearview again. He saw that the truck was back there. A couple cars behind.

"I'm full of surprises today. Speaking of which, Valerie escaped. She's home safe."

Jack Hardy caught his breath. He perked up in his seat and excitement welled inside. His fight returned. Jack pushed his hand into his front pocket.

"As she should be, Becker. Forever and always," Hubbard replied, condemning Jack once again.

"What about you?"

"Safety?" Hubbard looked all around him, trying to figure out what to do next. "It's elusive sometimes." To Hubbard's right, there was a row of cars stuck in the same traffic he was. Beyond that row, he saw railroad tracks and one of those climate controlled storage facilities. To his left was more congested traffic and then a well-tended cemetery. The grounds stretched farther back than he could see. "But it usually appears when you need it."

"Or it turns out it's false hope."

"Is that what you called to tell me, Becker."

Traffic moved again. About half a car length.

"No," Gray said. "I called to tell you the walls are closing in."

A sheriff's helicopter buzzed by. Hubbard watched it turn in the air and head back his way.

"Walls are as trapping as time, detective, and both only trap the simple minded."

"And you're no simpleton, right?"

The car directly behind Hubbard in the jammed traffic pulled a U-turn, cutting off traffic moving in the other direction. It hurried away from the traffic in the opposite direction. Hubbard thought of doing the same thing.

Gray continued, "I guess it does take quite a special mind to terrorize 8-year-old girls and their loving families."

The traffic behind Hubbard moved forward, including the truck that had been tailing him since he met Jack.

Jack Hardy came to life. "Not anymore!"

He yanked the small pocket knife from his pocket and attacked Hubbard. Stabbing him with the two-inch blade. All defensive wounds, but enough that Hubbard was slow to react to the pain and shock of the attack. But, Hubbard was more of an animal than Jack. He took two quick hits to the chest from Jack's knife simply to smash Jack's head against the door window. The first hit dazed Jack. By the fourth, he was nearly unconscious and fully incapacitated.

"Jack!" Gray called through the speaker phone. "Jack, are you there? Mike, go!"

Hubbard realized the man in the truck was Mike, and he'd been ordered to come to the rescue. So Hubbard kicked open Gray's squeaky car door and stepped out of the car, his own gun in his hand. He turned toward the truck and ran. The truck door cracked open, and before Mike could thrust his weapon toward Hubbard, bullets exploded into the truck's windshield, through the door and window, and ultimately through the bones and meat of Mike Todd.

"Mike! Mike?" Gray's voice could be heard through the truck's sound system.

Around Hubbard, people dispersed from their cars. Horns blared, engines idled, but mostly screams and running footsteps surrounded Hubbard. But all of that was white noise for him. Hubbard might as well have been alone. He watched blood drip from inside the truck cab to the asphalt. Satisfied, then he turned, walked back to Gray's Accord. He reached inside and found Gray's Glock under the driver's seat.

"Mike? Are you there? All units. All units. Shots fired. 10-24. Officer down."

Hubbard scanned north then south. Police lights were still quite far away. Police either on foot or motorcycles were headed his way, he was sure. Patrol cars wouldn't get through the mess of traffic and people scattering. He had a minute.

"Becker." Hubbard turned off the speaker and put the phone to his ear.

"You sonofabitch."

"You judge me," Hubbard said, standing outside Gray' car, "but I have purpose. You have nothing."

"I'm coming for you, Hubbard." His breathing gave away that he was running.

"That was a ridiculous retort. You're a pathetic, mundane stereotype, Becker. Worse, you don't even know it."

"I'm going to take your purpose and jam down your throat."

Hubbard laughed into the phone. The police lights were closer, which meant the officers he was sure were coming on foot were closer too. "As fun as this is, Becker, I need to get going."

"You won't get far."

"Maybe."

Hubbard raised Gray's Glock and fired three rounds into the car at Jack Hardy, without looking, without bending into the car and locking eyes with the man he so loathed.

Gray called out from the phone, "What did you do?"

"I kept my promise to Jack Hardy."

Hubbard dropped Gray's cell and took off in a run toward the cemetery.

CHAPTER 79

"Thank you again, Sharon and Phil," Valerie said to the news crew who had volunteered to lower their microwave mast and drive her wherever she wanted to go. Phil, the cameraman, had a police scanner and knew they were tracking Valerie's father. And that's where she wanted to be.

She rode in a swivel desk chair, mounted to the floor so it wouldn't roll around in the back of the news van. Valerie sat, facing forward, watching out the windshield. To her left from floor to ceiling a wall of console equipment had been constructed, including a laptop for editing, video screens, and a protruding microphone for voiceover work. On the desk, a handheld controller for the mast had been attached by Velcro to hold it in place.

"We're happy to help," Sharon, the on-air reporter, said. She was in the front passenger seat, turned sideways so she could talk to Valerie.

"You're sure they're up ahead?" Valerie asked, looking at Phil, who was driving the van. She was worried about reaching the scene – and her father – in time. Valerie didn't know what "in time" meant – or she didn't want to think about it – but she wanted to beat it, whatever it was.

"This is where they're talking about." He tapped the police scanner attached to the dashboard of the van.

"Valerie," Sharon said, "here." The reporter handed Valerie a protein bar from her purse. "When's the last time you've eaten?"

"I'm not sure." She figured her stomach was too twisted to eat, but she accepted the snack and then she accepted a bottle of water. "Thanks."

Valerie tore the wrapper open and took a bite of the bar. It was a tasty combination of salty and sweet. And she was hungrier than she thought.

"And thanks," Valerie said with her mouth half full, "for not asking me any questions about this whole thing."

"It's okay. I want to." Sharon smiled, fighting her urge to pressure Valerie into an interview. "But you need help today. Maybe another day we talk."

Valerie smiled, grateful. She chugged down the water.

"Hold on, Sharon," Phil said.

Sharon seethed. Phil picked the wrong time to interrupt their conversation. She was working on getting Valerie to commit to a future interview. This assistance for Valerie wasn't complete altruism.

"What is it?" She grinded her teeth to keep from barking at him

He increased the police scanner's volume. The conversation taking place included codes and locations that Valerie had never before heard. She heard 10-93 associated with Sylvester, 98, Lowry, Richmond, Commerce Point, Fredricksburg. A lot of 10-20s and 10-23s. 11-54s. 11-24. It sounded like normal conversation to the people on the scanner. But it was when the reports of 10-32, 417, 10-71, and 10-00 that Phil stopped the conversation and cranked the volume.

"Yeah, what is it?" Valerie asked.

Phil stopped the van, traffic halted in gridlock. "They have the roads ahead blocked off. I don't know if we can get closer in the van, but

... " His voice trailed off, concerned how the news may impact Valerie. He knew Sharon wanted a story. He wanted it too, but Valerie and her family needed to be safe more than they needed a story.

"But what?" Valerie and Sharon asked at the same time.

"There's shots fired up there. An officer is down."

"Oh my God, Phil, are you sure?" Sharon asked, her seething instantly gone. She thought of the next story.

Valerie wondered about the gun fire. Was her dad involved somehow? Was Gracie's father there? *I caused this.*

"That's what they're saying," Phil responded.

"We need to get up there," Sharon said.

"I don't know how unless we walk it."

"How far is it from here?" Valerie asked.

"Almost a mile, I think," Phil said.

Valerie pushed open the van door and jumped out, ignoring both Sharon and Phil's protest. Her feet pumped into a running pace. She wasn't fast or especially fit and her baggy jeans slowed her down, but she was going to find where the shooting had occurred. And she was going to find her father. *In time.* She ran down the middle of the two rows of parked cars, hoping no one would open their doors as she ran by. Then she heard a motorcycle engine. Coming from behind.

She turned and stumbled a bit as she slowed down. Even at full pace, she was not going to make it to the scene quickly. She needed another plan. And maybe this was it.

She flagged down the motor bike, traveling between the rows of cars like she was. It was a huge beast of a Harley-Davidson bike, and the rider couldn't have been more stereotypical looking of a Hell's Angel gang member if he had tried. He was someone she'd normally not approach, but everything she ever feared was almost a mile up the road, not where she was standing.

"Can you help me get past the police blocks. I think my dad's up there in trouble."

He recognized her from the news coverage, but he didn't say so.

"Get on," was all he said.

She did. Valerie slipped onto the seat and held on tight. He walked the bike between two parked cars and then kicked it into gear, finding the first curb cut and rode onto the sidewalk. He sped up. The Grove Park shopping plaza past quickly on their right. They hopped the curb coming off the sidewalk and blew through the blockade, which was no longer letting anyone through. The police there seemed more interested in talking to one another and holding their radios close to their ears than in stopping the motorcycle from breaking through. One of the cops ran after the bike for about ten paces, but the others stayed and listened to their radios.

The ride was loud and bumpy but fast. "Thank you." She hopped off the back of the bike.

"No need." He blew off her thanks and heeled his kickstand. "I'll be right here, if you need another ride."

Valerie smiled. *Some people are nice.*

"Go on," he urged.

Valerie turned toward the street. People were out of their cars and gathering down the road. Police on motorcycles were arriving. Police with K-9s were jogging down the street. A sheriff's helicopter hovered overhead. Sirens were sounding in all directions. But she saw no other activity. Where had the shooting taken place? What was happening?

She spun in a circle, looking for something. She didn't know what? She expected her father and the Pen Pal to just be here, waiting on her, out in the open. But then, looking in the cemetery, she saw Gracie's father. He was running alongside a larger man. Four patrol officers were spreading out, looking for something. Or someone.

Valerie burst into a run again, following the man who'd left the handcuff key for her, the man who had helped her escape. Her adrenaline pumped so hard, she didn't feel any fatigue. She didn't feel her heart pumping fast. Didn't feel heated. Nothing. Her mind focused solely on finding her father.

CHAPTER 80

"Hey, come here," Parker shouted at the groundskeeper near the mausoleum.

He'd been tending to the shrubs and grass surrounding the marble building, but he had stopped to watch the commotion. He had heard the gunshots and the associated screams, horns, and other noises, the helicopter overhead, so he had climbed up and into the bed of his utility vehicle to see over the cemetery wall. That's where he was when Gray and Parker saw him.

By the time the keeper got off the bed of the vehicle, using his rake as a walking stick, Gray and Parker had made their way to him.

"Police," Gray announced to him, pointing at Parker's badge since he still didn't have his own. "You see a man run through here?"

"What's going on out there?" But he didn't get an answer, so he kept talking. "Yeah, there were a bunch of people in and out of here," the guy said. "I think they were coming in and hiding from whatever was going on. Those were gunshots a few minutes ago, right? Like, a bunch of them?"

Again no confirmation from the police men.

"A lot of them came in that way." The keeper pointed to the property's exterior wall, running along the busy highway. The wall ran in sections of 20 feet. Then the red brick wall would have an eight-foot break before another 20-foot section. In those eight-foot breaks, trees rose up and cast warm morning shadows over the people buried there.

"Where'd they go?" Gray asked.

"All around. Most of them left though. There's probably some still hanging about."

"I want you to show us, but we're looking for a white male who probably looked like he was running to get away, not to hide." Parker said, holding his radio to his ear, having turned down the volume so no civilians – or the Pen Pal – would overhear the communication.

"Oh, boy. So you think whoever was doing that shooting ran in here to get away?" He looked panicked. "I don't know. I don't remember noticing that. There were some people hanging around the backside of this." He pointed at the mausoleum. "And a couple ran that way." He pointed toward the back of the property.

Parker used the radio to tell the other officers who were gridding their way through the cemetery what the groundskeeper had said.

"Show us the backside here," Gray said.

"Of course." He dropped the rake and led the detectives around the side of the mausoleum.

CHAPTER 81

That was all Valerie needed. To see the guy with the rake point. But, she wondered where he was taking Gracie's father. But, then, she didn't care. Valerie, still in an adrenalized sprint, headed straight for the groundskeeper's utility vehicle. It wasn't until she hopped into the rigid front seat that she realized she was breathing hard. Valerie had to take a moment to figure out how to crank the engine, and the adrenaline faded as her thoughts kicked in. Her lungs ached and her legs throbbed from running. Her hands shook with nerves and fear. She became aware again of stiffness and slight soreness in her left shoulder. She tried to ignore all of it.

Turning behind her, Valerie checked for Gracie's father. She didn't want to be seen by him. She knew he'd try to stop her. *But, he wouldn't.* Luckily not seeing him emerge from the corner of the building, she scanned the property ahead of her. Green grass, marble headstones, statues, and perfectly manicured gardens had been meticulously planned throughout the property. She had never been to a cemetery before, she remembered. Her grandparents had all passed when she was too young to recall. Neither of her parents had siblings, which meant there was no one in their lives to die. *Except for us.* Her thoughts returned to her father.

Valerie caught her breath and then saw the Pen Pal run from behind a statue of Jesus Christ praying. Instantly her anger kicked in, and the feeling of being out of breath and that of physical soreness dissipated. *Where's my dad?* She found the ignition and turned the key, threw the gear in place, and floored the gas pedal.

The muffler system must've been broken because the vehicle's engine screamed out that it was in use. She turned around in the seat and saw Gracie's father and the other two men with him, in a jog, round the corner of the mausoleum. She also saw police with K-9's entering the property through the entrance gates.

When Gray and Parker saw Valerie pulling away in the tractor car, they sprinted toward her. She thought she heard Gracie's father yell something, but she ignored whatever it was. Valerie directed the vehicle toward the back of the grounds where she'd seen the Pen Pal making a mad dash for escape.

Behind her, she saw police on motorcycles entering the grounds. They'd catch up to her quickly. Gracie's father and the large guy were still running after her. Valerie still had time to get to the Pen Pal first. But how much time? The police were closing in.

When Valerie faced forward again, she didn't see the Pen Pal running any longer. She had a general idea where he was headed, so that's where Valerie continued steering the vehicle, only turning the wheel to avoid large headstones. Otherwise, she drove straight across the grounds. The police on motorcycles stayed on the paved paths, maintaining more respect for the grounds than she was.

The Pen Pal quickly came into view again. At the very back of the property. Near a hill, which was about six feet higher than the rest of the grounds. It ran along the whole backside of the property. He ran up the hill, turned and surveyed the scene behind him. Cops running toward him from the left. Police dogs let off their leashes and bearing down on him. Motorcycles snaking their way through the grounds. Helicopter overhead.

And Valerie leading the pack in a tractor. He locked eyes with Valerie, who willed the vehicle faster. He smiled, turning her stomach. Then he disappeared, instantly like he jumped into a hole in the ground.

Valerie beat everyone to the hill. She hopped out of the vehicle and ran up the hill, seeing that the Pen Pal hadn't escaped through a hole in the ground. He had just jumped down the back side of the hill, which was higher than six feet on the backside. Down the hill and to her right, there was a long shed. The kind in the back of her next door neighbor's yard. But longer. About 40 feet long, she figured it measured. The door, looking more like a garage door than the kind her neighbor had, was open. A radio played from inside. It was the groundskeeper's work area.

Had the Pen Pal gone inside? Or, had he kept running into the neighborhood beyond the property line.

The police dogs blew past her, frightening her. She hadn't noticed they were in full sprint and not attached to their human counterparts. Checking behind her again, police were coming in from every direction. *I want him.* She didn't know where the Pen Pal had gone, but she figured the dogs did. She hurried down the hill chasing them and wondering the whole way where her father was.

CHAPTER 82

Gray and Parker and the motorcycle officers arrived at the bottom of the hill at the same time. The detectives ran past them though. The officers, leaving their helmets on, hurried off their bikes then rushed up the hill after Gray and Parker in support. The K-9 officers were closing in and so were the patrol officers who had fanned out across the property in search of the Pen Pal.

Parker turned up the volume on the radio again, so he could hear the communication while running. He did so in time to hear the officer in the helicopter tell them he'd lost the runners in the trees. After a flat field, separating the cemetery from neighborhoods, several large groups of tall oaks aided in the separation. The officer radioed that he saw them and the dogs go in but not come out. Gray, Parker, and the others continued forward, following the sounds of the dogs barking.

More communication blared across the radios. It sounded like echoes throughout the group of officers, as they had turned up the volume as well. The echoes confirmed that finger prints had been recovered from Carson Anderson's home. They had been run through the various crime databases where a match was found. Samuel James Hubbard. Priors included aggravated assault and burglary. The voice on the radio ran through the physical description, which Gray confirmed to Parker with a nod.

The group of officers found the dogs jumping and scratching at a cement wall, surrounding a condominium community. The K-9 officers leashed the dogs and led them around the wall to the community entrance so the dogs could pursue further. Gray and Parker, as well as some of the other officers pulled themselves over the wall and continued the chase. The remaining officers followed the K-9 personnel and would catch up on the inside.

The community ran in a circle. The one-story structures contained two condominium units. There were also three-story buildings spread throughout the community. The structures ran along both sides of the street. The officers spread out again, Gray and Parker staying together and the others teaming up. No one was to go alone. Hubbard had shot two men and he had to be ready to shoot more. Gray and Parker had their weapons in hand, Gray holding a loaner from Parker since Hubbard had his.

They knew, from the dogs, that Hubbard – and probably Valerie – had made their way into the neighborhood. But with so many residences, there was little chance they'd easily find them. They needed help.

Parker turned the volume down on his radio again and called in their position. More patrol cars were en route and should arrive in less than a minute. They decided to wait, but they heard a woman's cry to their left. At least they thought it was to their left. The voice could be bouncing off concrete walls and coming from anywhere. Nonetheless, Gray and Parker headed to their left anyway.

CHAPTER 83

Valerie, without pause, followed the Pen Pal right through the condominium's front door. She had to find out where her father was. Behind her, Valerie left the front door open, which she hoped would be a sign to Gracie's father and the other police to look inside.

The home smelled like broccoli or Brussels sprouts or some other food that she didn't like to eat. The smell reminded her that it was about lunch time. She heard low whimpering coming from somewhere ahead of her. She swallowed hard, nerves and fright setting in.

The living room directly in front of her. A panoramic painting of the beach ran along the living room wall opposite the front door. In the back right corner of the living room, she saw the entrances to two bedrooms. On the wall adjacent to the bedroom door hung a full length mirror. The sunshine bounced off of it, making her look like a ghostly creature entering the home.

To her left was a dining room with a kitchen situated behind it. A family sat at the dining table along with the Pen Pal, looking like they were having a meal together.

"Valerie." Hubbard greeted her.

"What are you doing?" she asked through heavy breathing from running.

"Having lunch with this family."

Dad, mom, and a daughter sat at the table. Everyone looked petrified. Hubbard sat at the end of the table, where he could see the entrance. Mom had her back to Valerie. Dad and daughter sat across from each other. They both watched Valerie, begging with their eyes for help. Valerie noticed the mom holding her child's hand, keeping her calm. Or maybe it was the other way around. She also noticed all the forks, spoons, and knives are stacked in front of Hubbard.

"My work, Valerie, was meant to encourage fathers to provide proper care to their children. Something must've gone wrong with it because this man comes home for lunch and leaves the front door unlocked. I walked right in." Hubbard glared at the dad. "I'm so tired of seeing men like him ruin children's lives."

"You know what went wrong? You're a lunatic."

His demeanor changed, and when he turned back to Valerie, he seemed relaxed. "No need for name calling." He feigned offense, but it looked more like he was laughing.

"Where's my father?" she asked, ignoring Hubbard, sure whatever emotion he was expressing wasn't genuine.

"Jack. Jack. Jack." He looked at the father sitting next to him. "You'd like him. He's like you. He takes his daughter's safety for granted. It took me to save her and to keep her protected from the world's evil. And look at what a strong woman I turned her into. Look at the fire in her eyes. She can do anything now. Look at her. I did that."

She was tired of hearing the Pen Pal's drivel. His convoluted sense of reality.

"No, you're wrong. You didn't do that. My father did. He protected me from people like you."

She saw her words digging into Hubbard's mind making him genuinely angry, and she liked the way it made her feel.

"He's the one who made me strong. It's his fire you see in my eyes, not yours. It's him!"

She noticed him balling his fists in rage.

"He made me strong enough to stand here and look you in the eye."

She decided to push him further, see if he'd break and just tell her where her father is.

"He gave me the tools to realize you're a lowly piece of shit. A delusional, self-absorbed psychopath. He made me not afraid of you."

Hubbard jumped up, unable to listen anymore. "You don't know me!" He slammed his fist against the table, snatched a fork from the table and drove its prongs into the man's hand.

The father screamed out in pain, falling out of his chair. The daughter cried out.

Valerie ignored Hubbard's actions. "I know enough about you."

"All I wanted was to help you!"

Valerie grabbed the mother and pulled her away from the table. The chair she was in fell over. "Go," Valerie commanded, kicking the dining chair out of the way.

Hubbard saw what Valerie was doing and grabbed the daughter's arm, keeping her at the table.

"Let her go," the mother cried out.

"Just go," Valerie said, pushing the woman behind her, using herself as a shield.

"If she leaves, I'll kill this one," Hubbard snarled. He pulled the girl close to his body. She kicked and screamed.

"No!" the parents yelled simultaneously.

"She's only four," the mother added.

Valerie stepped to the table, and pushed the mother again. "Go."

"Go," her husband told her, so she did. Reluctantly.

She walked slowly, looking at her husband and daughter, like it may be the last time she'd see them alive. As she made it to the entrance, she took one last look, then rushed outside the house, screaming for help.

Valerie said, "You'd rather kill him."

Hubbard looked at the father. Pathetic. On the floor, holding his injured hand. Blood seeping onto his clothes and the carpet. *Why didn't the pull the forks out and attack me?* Pathetic is right.

He looked back at Valerie. "Like I did Jack?"

Valerie screamed unintelligibly, somehow knowing that would be the Pen Pal's response. But somehow not expecting it either. Or her reaction. She grabbed the table and used it to charge toward Hubbard. The plates of food rattled and the glasses of drink spilled. And Hubbard backed up quickly to avoid the table running him over.

Gray and Parker charged into the home, weapons pointed straight in front of them, announcing their presence. But, Valerie didn't stop her advance toward Hubbard, who now took out his weapon – Gray's Glock. That escalated the situation. The father got to his feet and moved away from all of them. He stood in the middle of the living room, begging them to save his daughter.

Gray and Parker spread out, making it impossible for Hubbard, if he shot, to hit both of them. All they had to do was control Valerie, who by now had trapped Hubbard in the kitchen with the dining table, which blocked the walkway.

Valerie didn't act like she knew Gray and Parker were there to help. She just wanted the Pen Pal. To put her hands on him. But the table now blocked her path. So, she stopped to think about what to do next. Go over the table? Over the counter? Pull the table away. Then she saw his weapon, but she wasn't afraid. And, she realized the Pen Pal was not focusing on her any longer.

"Put the gun down," Gray ordered.

Hubbard laughed. "I'm not doing that."

"What's the play here, Hubbard?" Parker asked. "You're not getting out of here like this."

"You're a big fellow," Hubbard said to Parker, not allowing Parker or Gray to control the situation.

Hubbard lifted the Glock to the girl's head.

"Stop him," the father pleaded to Gray and Parker.

"You should've done that!" Hubbard shouted at the man. "Not rely on other people to protect her."

"Oh my God, shut up!" Valerie shouted, grabbing the child's plastic drink cup from the table and launching it at the Pen Pal. It sailed by his head and struck the cabinets behind him.

"Valerie!" Gray shouted. "Back off."

"Shoot him."

"No, my daughter is there," the father protested.

"He won't hurt the girl," she said.

Gray said, needing to stop Valerie's antagonizing, "Hubbard, we have about thirty cops surrounding this place. SWAT sharp shooters are set up and have you in their sights through that kitchen window there. It's time to stop."

"You learned my name, Becker. Good work."

Valerie looked at Gray with tears in her eyes, sorrow taking over for the anger inside of her. "Enough! He killed my father. He killed him." Then the anger returned. "Now you kill him!"

Parker said, "No, he didn't."

The news surprised even Hubbard.

"He shot him," Gray said. "And he's hurt really bad. But, he's not dead."

"That's a shame," Hubbard said. "He so deserved it."

Valerie ignored Hubbard's provocation. "Are you sure?"

Gray said, "I am. He's on his way to the hospital now."

"You can join him," Parker said. "The officers outside will take you there now. You just have to go outside."

"No. She stays," Hubbard demanded.

"And then what, Hubbard?" Gray shouted at him.

"No," Valerie said. "You've stolen enough of my time."

"No, you stay!" Hubbard commanded.

All the studying Valerie had performed in the last few years came flooding back into her mind. All the research and hypothesizing rushed through her head. *I know him.* Valerie turned to Gray and said, "He won't kill the girl. So just shoot him."

"I gave you purpose, Becker. I saved you, Valerie."

"No, you didn't." Valerie turned her back to Hubbard. "You didn't accomplish what you thought you did. You're a fool." She knew this would hurt him the most. "And I don't care about you anymore, and I'm sure as shit not afraid of you anymore." She turned to Gray. "You shoot him and you kill him." She headed for the door.

"Valerie! Valerie!" Hubbard called to her. "Fine. I'll give up the child, but you have to stay."

Valerie halted her exit. She turned and studied him. She believed him.

"Please stay," the dad said to her.

If she stayed, he'd give up the girl. Then what? He'd traded Valerie for her father. *Dad.* She smiled, again realizing she knew the Pen Pal. Knowing that he was only trying to stop her from going to him.

"No."

Her response made Gray nervous for what Hubbard may do next. He stepped to his right for a better angle at Hubbard, if he needed to shoot in order to save the girl.

"I won't stay."

"Please," the father begged.

"I'll hand this precious girl over to you."

"No. I'm going to leave and go to the hospital to see my father. I'm going to hug him and thank him for every sacrifice he ever made for me. For protecting me."

"Then I'll kill her," he told Valerie.

"No, you won't. After I leave, you'll put the gun down and you'll give up that girl. You won't let the cops kill you because your crusade would die too. And you can't have that." She stepped closer, but Gray waved her off advancing. "But I hope they do kill you."

"You only think you know me," Hubbard said.

But she ignored him and walked out the front door into the sunshine.

"Well, that was rude," Hubbard said. "You try to help someone, and this is how you're treated."

"Put the gun down, Samuel," Parker said.

"She did pretty well, you know. Most of what she said was true. But, there's still one father I can teach."

"Put the gun down!" Gray shouted.

Hubbard locked eyes with the girl's father. "You will take better care of her from now on, won't you?"

"Yes. Yes. I will. Let her go. Please."

"I know you will."

Hubbard, lowered the gun from the girl's head and turned his wrist and extended his arm. He opened his fingers. The weapon now rested gently in his palm. Then he slowly lowered his arm and allowed the Glock to slide off and come to a stop on the kitchen counter separating the kitchen from the living room.

Gray held his weapon on Hubbard. Parker moved quickly to the counter and swiped up the gun. He jammed it in his belt. As he moved to the table blocking the kitchen walkway, he was going to pull it away and go into the kitchen. But he stopped. He and Gray saw Hubbard smile.

"You need to remember," Hubbard said to the father.

Neither Gray nor Parker knew what Hubbard was going to do, but something was definitely about to happen.

"Hubbard, don't move," Gray said, stepping closer in case he had to shoot. He wanted to make sure there was less distance between them to fire. It would make his accuracy better.

In a hurried motion, Parker yanked on the table, moving it out of the walkway. He rushed around it to get to Hubbard and the girl.

Hubbard locked eyes with the girl's father, ignoring Parker's movement and Gray's commands. He knew he was caught, but he still wanted to teach this father a lesson. He lifted the girl's arm toward his face. He smiled madly, then simply snatched the girl's pinky finger with his teeth and bit as hard as he could. The girl erupted in pain, and she fought to pull away from the him. The father screamed at him in horror. Gray wanted to shoot, stepping even closer, but he couldn't because the girl was moving too much. But, Parker got to him quickly. He stomped on Hubbard's knee, shattering the connection between his femur and tibia.

Hubbard collapsed to the ground, grunting in his own pain. He dropped the four-year-old girl onto the kitchen tile. Gray rushed to the counter and kept his gun trained on Hubbard. Now free of the girl, Gray could shoot if necessary. He wanted to. *Give me a reason to hurt you.*

Parker cradled the girl and stepped on Hubbard's neck to keep him subdued.

The house quickly filled with more police officers, who rushed past the father, Gray, and Parker to get their hands on Hubbard. They ignored his pain, tossed him on his stomach, and zip-tied his hands and legs together, like a wild animal.

The father took his daughter from Parker and cradled her. Four paramedics entered once the scene was secure. Three converged on the girl and the fourth examined the fork damage to the father's hand.

Since Hubbard was subdued, the personnel in the kitchen thinned out. Gray holstered his loaner weapon and walked around the counter and met Parker in the kitchen. They stood over Hubbard.

"Don't do anything, Becker," Parker warned.

Gray ignored his partner and squatted down over Hubbard, who was still laughing. The girl's blood smeared on his face. Gray wanted to say something, he wanted to hurt Hubbard. He wanted to break every rib in his chest. He wished he had been the one to crush his knee. All the things Hubbard had said to Gray during their time together festered under his skin. Gray had purpose. He had been a good father. He was not nothing. He wasn't pathetic.

"I'm going to enjoy watching you age behind bars." That was the best he could come up with, and it didn't feel good at all. Not the way causing Hubbard physical pain would have. But it would have to do.

Then Hubbard laughed again and spit the girl's pinky from his mouth. He laughed harder.

Reason enough.

Gray swung his fist like a hammer on the jaw's temporomandibular joint. Right next to Hubbard's ear, immediately dislocating the Pen Pal's jaw. Parker yanked Gray away from Hubbard, who rolled on the floor, feeling new pain.

"Jesus, Gray."

The paramedics ignored what was happening. So did the father. So did the other officers milling about. In fact, they actually moved and stood in the door to keep anyone else from entering.

"All right," Gray said. "Let me go."

Parker held onto Gray another moment until Gray's muscles relaxed, and then he let go of his partner.

Gray took a deep breath and stepped closer to Hubbard, who had rolled over again. He faced Gray.

"Becker ... " Parker warned.

"I'm just checking to make sure he's okay."

Parker looked around and noticed no one was coming to Hubbard's aid. When he looked back, Gray had squatted down next to Hubbard again. Hubbard tried to talk but couldn't. Gray smiled this time. Hitting him had felt good. Then he reached toward Hubbard. *So will this.*

"Becker ... " Parker reached out for Gray's shoulder, but he was too slow.

Gray grabbed Hubbard's jaw and wiggled it. Slowly at first, then with more pressure and violence. Hubbard shouted again, the pain excruciating.

"Dammit, Becker."

Parker pulled Gray off the ground, stood him up. Moved between his partner and Hubbard.

"I was confirming his jaw was broken."

"I see that."

"For the report."

Gray held up his hands in the air, telling his partner he was done. He inched around Parker and headed for the front door, savoring Hubbard's groans of pain.

EPILOGUE

Gray drove a police cruiser, since his personal car was still being processed for the case against Samuel Hubbard. It had been three days, and he still didn't know when the Honda Accord would be released. He'd hardly been home since Hubbard had abducted him. Only once a day for a change of clothes and then a second trip yesterday when he let in the cleaners to shampoo the carpets in his bedroom. Really, Gray had been shacked up in the cruiser. Parker had offered the extra room at his house, but Gray turned it down. The way Hubbard abducted him, in the state that he was in at that time, and the things Hubbard had said to him shamed Gray. At least that's what he thought, so he didn't want to stay with Parker, he didn't want to go back to the place where he'd been abducted, he just didn't want to face any of it yet. But the time would come.

Two nights ago Gray had purchased a cheap pair of sunglasses at a convenient store in West Palm Beach, where he ended up watching the sun come up before driving back to Lakeland. They still sat oddly on his face, not sure he'd aligned the nose pieces correctly. He couldn't remember the last time he'd worn sunglasses. They weren't really his thing. He thought people looked like jerks when they wore them. *Pompous assholes is more like it.* But, in consideration of purchasing them, Gray thought they would prevent people from recognizing him. The news stories about the case had multiplied in the media since Hubbard had been captured, and Gray's face was in more places than he liked. Maybe, too, he had hoped the glasses would make him appear more aloof, so people wouldn't approach him.

His duffle bag, sans the usual bottle of whiskey, road in the back seat. Gray pulled it between the driver and passenger seat and set it on his lap. From a side compartment, he pulled a pen, a checkbook, and an envelope, then tossed the bag again into the back seat. Gray peeled the checkbook cover back and scribbled on the first check in the book. In a loose and hurried handwriting, he made the check out to Denise Gains in the amount of $4,000. He signed his name and wrote *FOR DIVORCE COSTS* in the Memo line. He slipped the check into the envelope and wrote her name on the outside.

He remembered stopping by her house the night he'd gotten drunk. She said awful things to him. *Well, truthful things.* But he wasn't writing her a check because of any guilt. It was worse than that.

Gray pulled himself from the car and walked to her front door. He licked the envelope flap, wetting the glue, and sealed it.

He wrote the check because Hubbard's message about parenthood weighed heavily on him. And he kept thinking about Denise. She was a good person. And she'd been a good parent to Gracie. He surmised she was probably a good parent to her son too. Reality shouldn't be that money could stand in the way of her continuing to be a good mother. Gray hated that Hubbard had found a way into his head.

He slipped the envelope in between the door and the rubber seal. Gray pushed it in as far as it would go, so it wouldn't blow away or get wet if a quick Florida rain shower passed through. He thought about knocking – Denise's car was there in the driveway – but Gray decided against it.

$$\approx \qquad \approx \qquad \approx \qquad \approx$$

He pushed the car door open again and peeled himself from the front seat. As Gray rounded the cruiser, his lungs noted the air in the hospital's parking garage was thick with car exhaust and humidity. He lifted the latch of the passenger front door and tugged the door open to retrieve a thermos and two disposable cups. He hoofed it through the garage, sunglasses still perched upon his nose – *like an ass.* He kept his face pointed at the ground so as not to be recognized. And it worked. No one stopped him to talk.

He rode the elevator to the third floor of the hospital and made his way to Mike Todd's room. He slipped past the nurse's station. The nurses were in the middle of shift change and paid little attention to Gray. Or, he considered, they recognized him – even wearing sunglasses – and just let him go through to Mike's room.

The room was still dark. The curtains hadn't been parted yet. A small light above the bed was dimly working. But, to Gray, seeing someone he liked under even that dim light made it seem like a spotlight. Mike Todd had been shot four times by Samuel Hubbard. Twice in the left arm, once in the right chest, and then once in the lower abdomen. He'd had two surgeries so far to save his life.

He set the thermos of hot, black coffee from the local coffee shop on Mike's table, and he placed the two cups next to it. Mike, when he woke up today – if he woke today – would know that Gray had been there.

Gray sat in the visitor's chair next to the bed for a few minutes, watching Mike breathe. He thought about their near-daily conversations, which almost always started with a discussion about Gray's car door.

"You ever getting that fixed?"

"Probably not."

"All it would take is some WD-40."

Gray smiled, liking the consistency and simplicity of whatever their relationship was. He hated the result of it though – Mike, lying there before him, filled with bullet holes.

The day nurse entered. "Oh, I'm sorry to interrupt, detective. I should've known you'd be in here."

"No problem. How is he today?"

She hung a new bag of clear liquid on the rack attached to Mike's bed. "He had a stable night."

"Good." Gray stood.

"You don't have to on account of me coming in," she said.

"It's fine. I need to get going. If he wakes today, will you tell him I came by?"

"Of course," she said.

He pointed at the coffee. "And that I left that for him."

"I will," she smiled.

"Thanks."

"See you tomorrow morning, detective?"

Gray smiled affirmatively and then pulled the door open and left.

In the hallway, he saw Valerie Hardy coming his way. She too was bringing morning refreshments to the hospital. Coffee and bags of food from a fast food restaurant. She wore a pair of sunglasses too. Gray was embarrassed because he froze, seeing her, instantly unsure of himself. But that faded slightly when she smiled brightly upon seeing him.

"How's your dad?" he asked.

Jack Hardy had been shot by Hubbard twice. One bullet left a large hole in his chest where the bullet had lodged against bone, and the other grazed Jack's temple. The man was amazingly lucky that more damage hadn't come to him. Reports had been that Hubbard fired blindly into the car. More than two shots.

"The doctor said he'll be fine." She shrugged her shoulders. "Eventually."

"Better eventually than never," he said, knowing it sounded awful. But the situation was weird and uncomfortable.

"I guess you're right."

They stood there, looking at each other, with nothing to say. Yet, the air was heavy because they did have a lot to say to one another. Well, Gray, at least, did. Valerie having pretended to be his daughter, the opportunity to say good bye – he couldn't put into words what that meant. He didn't know what it meant.

"Hubbard admitted to sending the letters," he said instead. "He told us he met each of you girls at, like, a revival church event. Detectives have spoken to all the parents, including your mom. Only one vaguely recalls the event."

"My mom told me. So random."

Gray smiled at her. "How are you?"

Valerie either didn't know how to respond, didn't know the answer, or refused to say it out loud. "How are you?" she countered.

"That hotel room … " He tried.

"I know," she said, cutting him off.

Gray breathed it in deeply, let it out slowly, relieved she had let him off the hook and he didn't have to complete that sentence.

"Come by and see us when my dad's awake?"

"I'll be here tomorrow morning. I'll come by."

≈   ≈   ≈   ≈

"Becker, it's been a while. I must admit I was surprised to see your name in my appointment book."

"And I admit I was surprised to make the appointment," Gray replied as he looked around the department psychologist's office. Nothing had changed in it since the last time he'd been there. The office still conveyed a warmth that was probably meant to make it easy for people to open up and tell Frances Vandenhill everything. Gray had not been normal people. He hadn't told her anything.

Vandenhill was a small-framed, 45-year-old, bookish woman. Her glasses were too big for her face, her hair was ten years out of fashion, and her style was not of trendy magazines. To Gray, it was her voice that made her so successful. Soothing and understanding, it was.

She turned the page of her spiraled notebook and wrote Gray's name at the top. "I reviewed your file this morning." Vandenhill sat, relaxed in her comfy leather chair, waiting for him. After a few minutes of silence, she said, "You made the appointment."

There was a nervous coldness in his chest, a tightness. A heart attack right at that moment wasn't a bad alternative to talking about himself. This is how their sessions had always gone. Sitting together. In silence. Until the timer bell rang. Then he'd leave. This time, though. He planned on it going differently. Though not easily. He stayed silent, building courage.

Vandenhill had read the articles about Gray in the newspaper, while following the Valerie Hardy case. She had worried about all the exposure and focus on Gray in the media. She knew he had secrets he'd wanted to keep – from himself and the world – but she had no idea what they were until the reports came out. Vandenhill never would have thought the result would be anything near a positive outcome for Gray's well-being. Yet, there he was sitting in her office of his own volition.

"Would you like me to start?" She wanted to help him along, feeling an uncomfortable eagerness.

He sighed, relieved. "Yes, please.

"Are you still having trouble sleeping?"

"Depends what you call trouble." He wrung his fingers together. Legs shook nervously. "Pretty much," he admitted.

"How's the relationship with your parents and brother?"

"Still my fault. You probably saw the newspaper articles," Gray offered, preferring not to run through the normal questions she used to get him talking.

Now she was getting somewhere, she thought. "I followed the case."

"It was an interesting few days."

"Interesting how?"

"It was hard."

"Hard how?"

He froze, trying to figure out how to articulate the thought.

"Did you drink? To get through the pressure."

"I – " Gray lowered his head. Leaned back on the couch and looked about the room again. He noticed the soft coloring, sweet fragrance of candles burning on her desk – lavender, he thought – the dim lighting, and the soothing security of Vandenhill's warmth.

"I had a daughter and a wife a long time ago."

About the Author

Chris Wendel is a Florida native and author of five titles, which span his love of fiction and his experience as a small business owner. When not writing, Chris enjoys music, cooking, traveling, and soccer. He lives in Florida with his family.

His full bio is available at www.cwendel.com.

Want to know what happens next?

Visit http://www.cwendel.com/ and join his reader list for information on the next installments of the Becker Gray stories and for exclusive, free content.

And then turn the page for a sneak peek at the next Gray story …

CHAPTER 1

"Do you cut yourself?"

"Not physically."

Becker Gray stared at the ashtray on Karen Vandenhill's office desk. It looked like 40 marbles melted into a drooping bowl-like structure. He wondered where it had come from. Did she have a child who made it for her at summer camp? And why an ashtray? Not many people smoked anymore. Did she?

Gray realized then that he knew nothing about his department-appointed therapist. He'd been seeing her for almost five months straight, and he couldn't think of anything specific he knew about her. In a city like Lakeland, Florida, Gray should know two out of five people just for growing up there and never even leaving for college. Add on his law enforcement background and he should know three or four out of five people. So, he thought it was odd that he didn't know anything about Karen Vandenhill before therapy. Then again, he wasn't all that surprised either.

"Then how?" she asked.

Gray didn't respond. Instead, he waited her out. Eventually she'd make a note on her pad of paper, realizing he was done talking, and move on. While ignoring her question, he scolded himself for not paying attention. He hated these sessions, even though he initiated them this stretch of time. He tried to keep the conversation at surface level, but every now and then she'd catch him not paying attention and he'd answer honestly. And then he'd find himself in a conversation he didn't want to have, like this one.

But she didn't write in her pad though.

"Becker, have you made any new friends?"

"Where did that come from?"

Gray shifted in his seat, almost leaning away from her and her questions. It was the first time during this session that he'd adjusted his sitting position. Vandenhill made a note of that on her pad.

"I've been thinking about it lately for you." She leaned forward, countering his retreat. "You seem to enjoy your friendship with your partner, but I was thinking maybe you meet someone who isn't connected to your work life."

"Why would I do that?"

Vandenhill smiled, happy – and surprised – that Gray was entertaining the idea. She responded, "Friendship enhances the human experience."

"I don't think so."

"You don't think friendships make peoples' lives better?"

"Not that," Gray said, moving in his seat again, narrowly closing his posture. "I don't think I'll be making any new friends."

Vandenhill noted his response, then asked, "Why?"

"I'm good." He dismissed the notion.

"The holidays are coming up. Friends are very important this time of year."

"Is that why you asked if I was a cutter? You think I'll kill myself this holiday season?"

"Since you brought it up ... "

Gray chuckled at her. "You're serious?" He said, when she didn't move on to a new topic, "That's not for me."

"I don't think it is." She clicked her pen twice. She did that sometimes. It marked the end of a conversation, when she wanted to change the topic. "What are you doing for the holidays?"

"Nothing. On duty, I suppose."

"You won't see your parents? Or your brother?"

"My schedule doesn't really allow for that." Gray thought these questions were ridiculous. What did it matter if he saw his parents? Why did she care anyway?

"What about Detective Parker?" She leaned against the back of her chair again.

"I don't know what his plans are."

"I mean, will you spend time with him?"

Gray shrugged his shoulders. Then he remembered something, and he hoped sharing it would get her off his back. Within a few more questions. *There are always more questions.* "The mayor invited me to a Christmas party."

"The mayor?"

"I'm a big deal since the Pen Pal case." A smirk slid across his face, faux bragging. Right before he kicked off these sessions again with Vandenhill, he solved a case that thrust him into the national spotlight.

She laughed. He had a smart wit, when he let his guard down. But, she didn't want to encourage him. "Well, are you going to attend?"

"Sure."

It was a noncommittal response.

"I think you should."

Gray nodded, accepting her statement as an opinion and not a suggestion.

WHISPERING OF ECHOES (*An Excerpt*)

Wanting to use the rare moment of flowing communication with Gray, she moved on to the next subject, clicking her pen. "Have you picked out a vacation spot yet?"

"You've covered a lot of ground here, doc." He scooted to the front of the chair cushion, like he was positioning himself to leave.

"How's that?" Vandenhill smiled, knowing the answer, and twirled the pen between her fingers.

"You've gone from me cutting myself to my family and now to my vacation. The cutting thing was new, but the rest we talk about all the time."

She tapped the pen against her pad. "The friendship topic was new too."

"I guess it was."

They both knew he was delaying the response. He waited for her to move on, and she waited for him to answer.

Finally, "Well?"

"Well what?" he asked.

His wit had lost whatever amusement it possessed earlier in the conversation.

"No." Agitation clearly in his tone. "I haven't done any of the homework you assigned." He stood to leave.

She stood too, clicking her pen. "Think more about it. I don't want to make it mandatory."

93069140R00226

Made in the USA
Columbia, SC
08 April 2018